CHARLES H. CROSS

was born in Sheffield and spent his early years without much direction. With a misspent youth playing video games and tabletop RPGs he somehow fell into a career as an Engineer. After a brief sojourn in Barnsley, Charles and wife Jo moved to a quiet village in Nottinghamshire. Here, they hope to turn their love of writing into a full-time career. The Man-Butcher Prize is Charles' first published novel and he hopes to release many more.

ACKNOWLEDGMENTS

There are many people who have helped me along my writing journey and those that follow are key amongst them.

Thank you to Will Mullens for being my first ever beta reader. Thank you also to Thea Marler, Penny Greenwood, and Abigail Burrow for being my most thorough critics.

Without Cakamura Design to create stellar cover art and Azgaar who built an excellent map making tool, my book wouldn't be anywhere near as polished as it has become.

THE MAN~BUTCHER PRIZE

CHARLES X. CROSS

www.charlesxcross.com

This paperback edition 2020

Copyright © Charles X. Cross 2020

A catalogue record of this book is available
from the British Library
ISBN: 978-1-8380101-1-9

The right of Charles X. Cross to be
identified as the Author of the Work has
been asserted in accordance with the
Copyright, Designs and Patents Act 1988

Printed and bound by Ingram Spark

For Jo, without whom this wouldn't
have been possible.

Also by Charles X. Cross:

Crooked Empires: Vol 2 *coming soon*

Crooked Empires: Blood and Crystal
(An ongoing podcast available via
www.charlesxcross.com
and popular podcast providers)

PART 1

1681

Despite the countless revellers, William located his patron in record time; it wasn't difficult to spot her two-foot red wig studded with strawberries and a meringue fascinator. Even amongst the motley collection of masked gentry in their finest and most outlandish, she was unmissable. In contrast, William had opted for the more sober shades of his profession – plain brown and black linens to more easily cling to the shadows.

Sheltered in a conveniently placed arbour, close as lovers, she pressed him against her excessive hooped skirts, whispering with murderous intent.

'That's him.' The patron, who William only knew as *The Daughter*, held out a slender finger, her excitement barely restrained. Strange, given that he would be killing a man in less than half an hour, and even more unusual because he could only assume the target was her own father. 'The one with the pig mask.'

William peered into the courtyard, spying between fronds and trailing flowers that gathered around the arbour. The target was portly, and though his long tailed suit was of the highest grade, it pinched tight around his midriff. William wondered whether the suit was his own; if it had been borrowed it would explain the ill-fitting nature and prove the man not as wealthy as he projected. It was often the way of a contract killing; the target owed money.

'In the judge's wig?' William asked his patron just as the man drifted behind a stem of blooming honeysuckle that obscured line of sight.

'*Pig mask over a pig face,*' was her only muttered response.

William didn't think he was supposed to have caught that last part so kept his attention firmly on the target. He shifted his position, found the target's wig and mask in the crowd, and tried to memorise every detail of sculpted pig. Everyone at the party was similarly disguised, and he didn't want to make some amateurish blunder by killing the wrong man. The whole 'masque' was a bit of fun on the nobles' part, but also aided more underhanded dealings, and William was sure he wasn't the only one attending who would be breaking the law that night.

The target handed over a pair of tickets to a red jacketed guard, straightened his wig, and led his lady-guest through the large double doors. Even though his face was concealed by a porcelain mask, the rest of his attire was conspicuous enough to make him easily identifiable. The man was a renowned judge, and the wig he sported was the same one worn each day in court. Perhaps the gown draped over his evening wear was also judicial garb, but William didn't know enough about such things to be sure. He stifled a grin; this job would catapult him through the ranks without breaking a sweat.

'Here.' The Daughter delved her hand into a velvet pouch to retrieve a fine lady's wig, and a mask that may have been intended for a child from the size of it. 'It's all I could find at short notice.'

'When you insisted on supplying the items required…' William halted the admonition of his patron; her piercing green eyes hardened through the holes in her plain white mask. She was paying him an awful lot of money after all, and only those with the loftiest stations in the empire had leverage enough to take out a completely anonymous contract. It was best not to upset her.

'I do love a challenge.' He grinned confidently, donning the small mask. The rounded edges, that were supposed to reach his ears, pinched the skin at either side of his eyes. 'And the weapon?'

William's hand instinctively patted his hip where his flintlock usually rested. He felt naked without it, but it was safely stored in a guild outpost. He wouldn't be without it for long; once paid he would retrieve it.

'Don't worry about that, it's all sorted.' One of her wide green eyes winked jovially. She tossed the wig over his head and pulled the powdered grey ringlets tight around the mask. 'There, you can barely even tell. It just looks like you have a freakishly small head; the people here are far too highborn to even mention it.'

The Daughter discarded the velvet pouch between two pronounced tree roots, linked his arm, and led him out of the arbour into the courtyard proper. They weaved deftly between the boisterous crowds of party goers, those too irrelevant to be invited inside such a prestigious event. The tug at William's arm reminded him just how keen this woman was to be getting on with the sombre deed. Perhaps this job paid so highly because it had been rejected by more esteemed members of The Assassins' Guild, and he was the only one foolish enough to take it. He pushed negative thoughts away, they had no place in a killing.

'What mask does your partner wear?' William tried to quell his nerves with details; they had been over the plan twice already. The Daughter would get him past the guards and a potential pat-down, and then her associate would provide a tool with which to kill the target; a knife, garrotte or other such subtle weapon. If William got the target alone, he could strangle him, though it was far from his preferred method of working.

'Don't worry about my partner, he knows the plan even better than you do, I'd say. Remember, he'll call you Francisco Asino, and once he gives you the weapon, look for me.' She indicated her tall red wig. 'I'll stay close to the target so you can find him easily. Then, it's *all* you.'

'Right…' William didn't see the point in stating the obvious; pale and blonde, he didn't look like he was from Conejo. At least he was familiar enough with the accent to approximate it should anyone talk to him.

They reached the building of austere white stone and imposing columns, halting at the end of a long red carpet that stretched from the open doors like a forked tongue. William could see inside to the light, warmth, and wine, and wished he could attend something like this, just once, without having to spoil everything with a spot of murder.

'Francisco Asino and guest,' The Daughter announced to the guard on the left, who unlike his companion, was wielding a clipboard and quill rather than sword and shield.

'Mr Asino.' He ran his finger down the parchment and nodded. 'Welcome.'

William eyed the doormen for a moment longer, to ensure neither wore a firearm of any sort. Given their prevalence in the guild, William rarely saw security without one, but Fairshore was a long way from most of the contracted murder, and nobles did love their traditions. Polished breastplates, heavy conical helmets, and soft-soled shoes encumbered with huge rosettes were hardly suitable for serious guardsmen. The escape would be much easier; it was a blessing these men had been so archaically outfitted.

'Thank you very much, gentlemen.' William made his best attempt at imitating a Conejan accent, and bowed with a flourish so wild that his grey wig nearly slipped off. Though he had picked up a few accents from more worldly assassins and mentors, hearing it now he could tell Conejan was definitely one of his weakest.

The foyer was enormous, with high frescoed ceilings and two sweeping staircases leading to a viewing balcony above. Though the room was amongst the largest William had ever seen, it was made compact with the quantity of guests, waiters, and servants of every discipline. Two men barked laughter with the confidence only provided by extreme wealth, and a few women in frilly dresses tittered along obediently.

'This way.' The Daughter led him into another room like a mother leading a toddler. He would not have endured such treatment in normal circumstances, but mingling with the upper echelons was new to him. He resolved to trust her guidance, for the time being.

A multi-use auditorium spread out, sloping downwards to a wide stage. He had seen set-ups like it in various cities, rooms that could be used for a tea dance in the afternoon and dog fights in the evening. But, like the foyer, it was grander in scale than William could have imagined, and populated with even more outrageous costumes. A few guests sat talking in warmly lit alcoves of silk drapes and velvet cushions, but most watched the stage, where the host was bestowing awards on his fellow nobles.

The Daughter stopped for a time as if watching the acceptance speech being enthusiastically orated by the winner of the "Most Modest" award. William tried his best to look as if he was paying attention, while subtly searching for his target through the restrictive eye-holes in his undersized mask.

'There he is.' The Daughter indicated the target in a huddle of chatting nobles. 'I'll join their conversation, you mingle a little; my partner knows we're here. Your weapon will be ready any minute, Francisco.'

With that, she unhooked herself from his arm and slithered away through the press. Out of his depth, alone in unfamiliar territory, William had been led every step of the way by his giddy patron. Instinct told him something wasn't quite right. More reasonably, he assumed it was because he was used to taking charge. An assassination contract was often no more detailed than a name, and in some cases, a preferred method of despatch. The patron never assisted like this, but clearly The Daughter wanted a piece of the action. For the amount she was paying him, he shouldn't complain. Besides, his good reputation would be almost guaranteed after tonight.

He sidled to the edge of the room, taking a glass of wine from a passing waiter's tray; he drained it to settle his nerves. Even at the periphery, he was jostled by puffed sleeves and sharp elbows. He would have to wait for the judge to visit the restroom, there wouldn't be anywhere else quiet enough to get the job done in secret.

'Francisco Asino!' a jubilant man bellowed above the general grumble of the crowd.

William stopped still. He had envisioned a quiet whisper in the ear, not to be announced to the entire party. Worse, it had been a summons from the host, prancing about on the stage.

'Mr Asino, come and collect your award!'

William took a step, then faltered; there couldn't be another Francisco Asino here, could there? The fox-masked host was staring right at him, pointing a gaudy staff of office so everyone assembled turned to watch.

'Ladies and gentlemen, Mr Asino, has been voted…' The man stood aside as his glamorous assistant wheeled a small tea trolley onto the stage. 'The most likely to make the headlines!'

A wooden crate sat on top of the trolley, which looked conspicuously like something an arms dealer would use to ship their wares. William swallowed as the crowd parted, and he resumed his march, his feet feeling heavier with each step. He almost stumbled as he ascended to the stage.

'We have a very special prize for you,' the fox-host continued. 'We know you'll be leaving the country very shortly, so we didn't want to weigh your baggage down with another trophy. Instead, we opted for something useful. Something you can use at this very party.'

William reached the side of the fox-host and thanked him in his pathetic Conejan impersonation. His fingers trembled over the box, rough planks clearly stamped with import marks. All eyes focused on him.

'Make it count,' the fox-host whispered, gleeful as his patron, and slipped into the curtained wings.

William cursed under his breath. Stuck on the spot, feeling entirely set up, there was only one thing he could do. He curled his fingers under the lid and levered the coarse wood open on squealing hinges.

The Daughter had taken on board his request for a garrotte or knife, but had put her own spin on things. What lay before him, nestled in straw, was a kind of double crossbow. The weapon was fine enough, almost as finely decorated as his pistol, but far from the subtle instrument of death he had requested. Two knife-tipped bolts protruded above the stirrup, linked together by a thin wire.

He looked up at the crowd. Only a few were turned away from him, his target amongst them, deep in humorous conversation. The Daughter was in the circle with the target, the main focus amongst their laughing huddle. She had swapped wigs with someone and was playing some kind of strange noble's parlour game – a good distraction should William raise the crossbow. The judge's focus was certainly held by whatever she was doing, so maybe her presence on the job wasn't such a bad thing after all.

William's fingers flexed over the crossbow. While it was the polar opposite of how he'd wanted this job to pan out, it wasn't entirely a loss. There were lots of lunatics in the guild who garnered quite the positive reputation by publicly despatching their targets, and it *was* a fallow year after all. It was tradition to go a little over the top in a fallow year. He'd heard a mad bomber had blown up an entire bridge to take out a single target a few months back, and ever since then, her name was on the lips of everyone in the guild.

Perhaps this was just the thing he needed; a very public success to secure his name in the minds of any who sought a killer's services.

He took up the crossbow and aimed it just below the judge's wig – so the garrotte would slice off his head in a shower of fame-bringing gore – and pulled the trigger.

It had been a long time since William visited Valiance. It was a fine city then, a beautiful white stone backdrop for dark memories. In subsequent years it had greyed, stained by smog that clung to the damp air. Burgeoning industry had established itself and become bloated, spilling the city out in slums across once green fields.

He reached the outskirts by early evening and rode hard to get past the poorest districts before dark. The horse he'd stolen didn't seem to enjoy the change in surroundings, braying at the merest twitch. It was an old thing, accustomed to farm life, well away from thundering carriages and coal smoke. William wasn't overly enamoured with the city either, but beggars couldn't be choosers.

Once in the relative safety of the lamplight, he eased on the reins, slowing the horse to a trot to save its labouring lungs. He didn't stop; there were eyes watching under worn hat-brims, and guild enemies everywhere. It was even possible a guild ally would confront him, given his recent history. He set a hand on his pistol for comfort, and so anyone watching knew he meant business.

The smell of smoke built as he passed through a new industrial district. Though he was familiar with the city, it had changed a lot, and there was no trace of the park he had expected to use as a landmark. He crossed a bridge spanning a stagnant pool and took the wider of two forking avenues. He didn't recognize any of it. He considered stopping to ask someone for directions but the state of the townhouses made him reconsider. Such a disparity of wealth in a place made folk uneasy, too eager to raise their status, and all the more ready to con or steal.

The sky bled an icy drizzle, matching William's sour mood with its poor outlook. He pulled a blanket from his pack and wrapped it around his shoulders, cursing his lack of suitable travelling gear. The loose knit wool didn't provide much warmth and the cream tones were marred with faint blood flakes that even the most fervently scratching fingernail couldn't free from the weave. He might have been more prepared, but had left Fairshore in a hurry and had made few excursions into civilisation since. The cities he'd braved were none too welcoming, but he hoped, despite initial appearances, Valiance would be different.

He made his way down another thoroughfare with a more affluent feel to it. The houses were larger and brighter, not their original white, but they had been cleaned recently. A constable smoking a pipe nodded to him from a stationary carriage, perhaps it was a warning, but William took it as a greeting and returned a nod in kind. It did cross his mind whether the price on his head had raised any since last he'd checked, but imagined the wider world might be starting to forget about "The Masquerade Killer". If only that were true in guild circles.

Reasoning that his chances of being identified were fairly low, he finally decided to ask for directions. While the constable was part of an organization dedicated to eradicating assassins, he was also the most trustworthy looking fellow William had seen within the bounds of the city. He pulled on the reins, stopping himself beside the carriage.

'Good evening.' He nodded a second time and turned his head so the lamplight wouldn't fully catch his face. 'I've been away a long time, this place isn't quite how I remember... you wouldn't direct me to Tarrow, would you?'

Tarrow had been one of the seedier boroughs last time William had visited, he didn't like to think what kind of state it might be in now, given the trajectory of Valiance as a whole.

'Tarrow?' The constable mused, stroking the oil from his moustache. 'If you're looking for a good time or place to stay, Barton would be a better bet, and it's not half as far.'

'I have friends in Tarrow.' William wondered if the location of the guild outpost remained secret or if it had become more of an *open secret*. He didn't want the constable to determine him a guilder, let alone identify him.

'Tarrow, eh?' The constable sucked on his pipe, he had a hand cupped over the bowl to stop a targeted raindrop from extinguishing it. He mused for a moment and studied the half of William's face he could see. 'Head down here a ways, to the statue of the Twin Fates…'

William shifted in the saddle, turning himself a shade.

'Lovely little square that, just on the edge of Barton.' The constable rested the pipe in the corner of his mouth, the bit clicking against his teeth. 'Then, if you still want to go to Tarrow, take a left and keep going until you feel like turning back.'

'Thank you.' William dipped his head, and without wasting a further second where he might be recognised, kicked his heels into the horse's flanks. In a moment, he was away down the street, wind and sleet biting at him.

Though the stop had been short, the old mare had caught a second wind, and he made good progress to the square. True to the constable's word, it was the nicest place William had seen so far in the city, though given his route through the factories and slums that wasn't too difficult.

The statue of two intertwined torch bearers was surrounded by a wide expanse of cobbles, bordered by high end traders and numerous eateries that were still open at the late hour. His gaze found a couple in a window, sharing a sweet dessert in the warm candlelight. He lamented his destination by comparison.

A shiver came under his blanket, now sodden and transferring the cold to him all the quicker. He spurred the horse again and made for Tarrow. As soon as the pooling light from the square faded behind him, the road began to narrow and wind. Street lamps became sparser, but dyed horn lanterns – that hung beside doors – kept the cobbles visible under a scarlet hue. Surroundings became more familiar to him as he neared the "old town", and once he was fairly certain where he was, he turned off down a crooked lane for the outpost.

The smell of smoke here was more medicinal than industrial, and the heavily cambered road collected channels of grease-swirled water around blocked drains. Washing lines that crossed the murky sky seemed to drag the leaning terraces inwards with the weight of sodden smalls and forgotten linens.

William slowed his horse to a trot to navigate the narrow way and avoid the residents, all the time aware that they might be more than they seemed. A hunched old woman – in a blanket similar to his own – with a heavily obscured face could just as easily be a guild spotter. A homeless urchin, crouched under an overhanging roof, might be more than just a cutpurse. This was guild territory, all bets were off, save for those that were rigged.

He slipped off the back of his horse and led it to the side of the road when he finally saw the outpost. He'd be in the dry and warm soon, with a mug of ale, at the side of a roaring fire. The reins were tossed over an iron railing set into the wall and knotted. He left the blanket over the horse, but took his pack, lest any thieves seek what was left of his silver.

The outpost was from any estimation just another house. Dead flowers wilted from lilting window boxes, grey render cracked from rough cut stone, and broken windows had been covered with linen drapes. He stepped into the sheltered doorway and thumped on the wood. Curls of red paint came away with his palm. The brass knob twisted and the door creaked open to a sliver of shadow.

'Name?' The voice was older but William recognised the man inside as the same he had known before.

'William of Fairshore.' He set a hand on the wood, ready to be allowed inside.

'We're not open to visitors.' The door edged closed.

'It's William…' He stuck his boot in the gap and yelped as it was crimped tight. He couldn't pull it back out. 'Come on, let me in. You know me.'

'I do, yes.' The shadow inside shifted and the door pressed tighter onto William's foot. 'You're William of Fairshore, The Masquerade Killer, that's right, isn't it?'

'Yes, but…' William twisted his foot to try and retrieve it, but the door pressed ever tighter. He set a hand on his pistol.

'I wouldn't do that if I was you.' A hammer clunked behind the peeling wood, a deeper noise than would be made by any little flintlock. William raised his hands, and removed his weight from the door. 'Good. Now, we're not open to visitors, so please… leave.'

'Would you please just tell Marilyn I'm here?' William tried.

The pressure was released from his foot. Instinctively, he pulled it to safety. The door slammed in his face.

'Please!'

There was no response.

He turned with a sigh; the rain had worsened. He stepped into the street and took a long look each way, the constable's advice echoing in his ears. Maybe he should have stayed in Barton after all. He could still go back, but the thought of spending his last few coins on one night's accommodation needled at him.

Frigid rain poured down his face, pulling locks of pale hair into his eyes. He trudged back through the gutter to his trembling horse. Perhaps it was best to put the city behind him and try again elsewhere. He patted the old mare's flank and felt the hot air from its nostril on his cheek.

'William.' A hushed voice startled him from a nearby alleyway. His hand moved for his pistol, but when he saw who greeted him, his arm fell limp. Huddled tightly in a cloak, illuminated by soft light spilling from an outpost side-entrance, was the person he had come to see.

'Marilyn!' He beamed, feeling the millstone lifted from him. 'I knew you'd help.'

He splashed through the gutter to the alleyway and clutched her by the shoulders, taking her in. Time hadn't been kind, grey wisped through faded russet, lines had become trenches about her features, but her eyes still had the same vivid glee. He embraced her, relieved to have someone on his side after all that had happened.

'I'm so glad you're here,' he continued. 'I thought they'd turned me away.'

'William, I…' She eased out of his grip. 'I thought you'd come here, I'm glad you came, I wanted to see you, but… I can't help you.'

'What do you mean?' As the millstone resettled around his shoulders, it felt all the heavier for its brief absence.

'You've been blacklisted,' she hissed through clenched teeth. The whites of her eyes showed as she cast about in search of spotters.

'Blacklisted?' William felt sucking dread in the pit of his stomach. 'Why? I killed one man. That pales in comparison – most guilders do far worse.'

'It's not that you killed the wrong man, accidents happen, but damn it William did you kill the *wrong man*. The Mayor of Fairshore? That's rotten luck from The Old Gods.' She patted her heart – some religious pageantry. 'Nobody will deal with you now, your failure went too public. The guild wants to distance itself from you; preserve its image. So I can't let you in, and I can't offer you any work. If I do-'

'What am I supposed to do?' he interrupted. 'Give it all up? Become a farm hand? I don't bloody think so. I can shoot better than most you have holed up in that little outpost of yours. I made *one* mistake.'

She pursed her lips; this was something he wasn't going to like. 'I can only tell you what I told Ojo…'

'You want me to throw my life away?'

'Ojo won.' Her eyes cast downwards.

'That didn't end too well for him, did it? And I'm not him; he was a different breed – made for it. I'll catch a bullet after ten minutes, it's just my luck. Like you say, an old god's curse. I'm not going to throw my life away like that. There must be another way, just give me a chance. One job.'

'I can't.' She pulled a crumpled piece of paper from the folds of her cloak. 'Take this, they have a sponsorship scheme now. You can enter with no risk; the sponsor stakes their life on your behalf. Then, if you prove yourself, you might get whitelisted again.'

'You said it yourself, nobody wants to deal with me.' Though he protested, he took the flier, flattening its creases in his hands. 'Who in their right mind is going to pledge their life for me?'

'Use your imagination; kidnap someone, bribe someone, I don't know.' There was a thump from inside as someone came near to change a barrel. 'I have to go. I can't be seen with you. Good luck.'

William blinked as Marilyn left him alone in the rain; she didn't turn back. The latch clicked as the door closed. Distantly, a constable's whistle could be heard. Though Tarrow was one of the more criminal boroughs in a particularly felonious city, he couldn't help but think the call to arms was related to him.

He looked down at the flier, somehow not so surprised by Marilyn's suggestion. If he was honest with himself, the idea had been flirting in the dark pits of his mind for a few weeks. With the revelation of the sponsorship scheme, it seemed his decision was made. He would be competing for the Man-Butcher Prize.

1672

Hand in hand, William trotted beside his father, oblivious to the reason they deviated on their route home. His mother was a few steps ahead, enjoying the cool salt-breeze, her heart-shaped face turned up to meet it. She had pale hair, like his own, and eyes that belonged to the grey northern seas. Her excitement was infectious, and though the streets were quiet, William anticipated their walk would end at a fair or firework display.

As a family, they paused on the bridge spanning the river that fed the Fairshore estuary; three large wooden arches that rested on stone plinths far below. William was lifted and sat on the carved rail, his father's strong grip holding him as safe as could be. They had done this a few times before, but only ever in the day to watch the ships. At night, despite the lack of embarking clippers, it was even more impressive. Moonlight and stars danced across the waves like vast schools of glittering fish, and the sea seemed to stretch endlessly.

This was contentment: a word William would learn as he aged, but at seven years old, simply a feeling.

He leant forwards, trusting his father to hold him as he studied the plinths below. Something floated beneath the arches; pale and intriguing. Perhaps a lost sail or errant albatross. Fairshore was a safe haven, far removed from wars and the ever-expanding frontier, but such details did little to restrain a young boy's imagination. He craned closer, fascinated that he might just identify a corpse, jettisoned contraband, or even the raft of a pirate fleeing the hilltop gaol.

Then the bridge was above him, and he was falling, turning over and over in the air. His father's seemingly unbreakable grip was gone before he had even noticed it slacken. Water hit him like stone, frigid, and permeating every extremity with pain. The shock made him gasp water, and his arms flailed aimlessly. Up was merely a concept in the black of the undertow. Offering him little recourse, the current swirled around his tiny body and snatched it away from all that had been familiar.

There was little explanation for his survival, other than the gods having willed it, or the age-old adage about "stranger things happening at sea". Many years later, William would suppose that once he'd bobbed out of the estuary, it *had* happened at sea, so fell into a category of oddities that could easily be dismissed. Now, however, he hadn't the capacity for such existential reflections, he was just a little boy trying to survive.

When the water finally released him, and the first of his wits started to return, William found himself in a slick mass of roiling fish. Coarse rope burned into his cheek, compounded by his entire upturned weight and over fifty shimmerfin flopping on top of him. The ocean spanned beneath and far out to the horizon, lit by an early morning sun. Disoriented by the lurching upward motion, and the close brush with death, he found himself unable to call for help. The winch shuddered to a halt, suspending him and the netted fish high above the ocean. The shoreline was absent, and he realised, so too were his mother and father.

The arm holding the net swung over the deck of a large wooden ship. A few men below pulled aside red painted grates, opening a dark pit. By degrees, the haul was lowered between the grates, and down into the hull. William stayed still and quiet, even until the knot at the bottom of the net had been loosed. He fell into a heap of swiping fins and breathless gills.

'Gut and scale them,' a well-to-do voice called from above deck as the grates were slid back into place, leaving only small squares of winking sun. 'We have two days before we reach Bleek's Bay, and we're half a tonne off quota!'

The ship's hold was large but divided by hanging linens, streaked with grime and guts. Shackles hung from the ceiling on rusted chains, swaying and jangling against the movement of the ship. The whole space was dim, illuminated only by candles flickering in yellowed horn lanterns. Seawater, fish blood, and unwashed flesh dampened everything, allowing shadows to well all the deeper.

Shimmerfin flopped on the boards, their wet tails adding to a jumble of noise – the low drone of workers and the thump of butcher's knives on wood. William rubbed his salt-stung eyes, still floundering under the weight of fish.

A blood-stained drape was kicked aside, permitting a man access to the fresh catch. His cheeks were hollow, and his ribs prominent of his sallow chest, painted with gore. He seemed to be a slave with a singular task: gutting fish. The mere sight of him screwed William's eyes tight with fear. Chains dragging at the man's wrists and ankles rattled painfully close as he cudgelled and collected an armful of fish, but he was gone almost as soon as he arrived.

William stayed still until he was sure the man had left, and was about to dig himself out of the heap, when another fish-gutter flapped through the linen, even more horrifying than the first. With lopsided shoulders and a crater in his head – which took up the space of one eye and almost the entirety of where his brain might have been – he barely looked alive at all. He moaned, mouth slack, as his gaze rolled over the fish. Somehow, though this man was far more horrific than the first, William couldn't bring himself to look away.

'Gut and shale,' the crater-headed man slurred the top-deck command. 'Gut and sale. Gut and…'

His one wandering eye fell on the boy, and he squealed with excitement. Hunched over, he lumbered forwards and snatched for pale ankles. William tried to scramble over the mountain of slippery fish, but the harder he struggled, the faster the shimmerfin gave under his weight. He screamed loud and shrill as he was dangled over the fresh catch. The halfwit clamped crooked fingers over his mouth, and gurgled a wordless reprimand.

'Shut up, Lamebrain!' another slave yelled from behind a bloodstained drape.

William was carried into the halfwit's workspace; a gut-soiled table, rack of knives, and buckets of prepared fish enclosed on three sides by drapes. A hole that might once have been for a cannon let in the early light, viscera trailing from the sill. With a thump, William was set on the table. The slick stump of a fish head smeared across his cheek.

He wrestled against the filthy hand around his mouth, and lashed out with juvenile fists, but the half-headed slave was too strong for him. Without difficulty, his hands and feet were bound with ropes borrowed from rigging, and his mouth was stuffed with a scrap of canvas.

'Gut and scale.' Lamebrain broke into a gleeful smile at his perfect pronunciation. Nodding to himself, he repeated it while he retrieved his scaling knife.

William thrust his calls for help into the gag and kicked his bound limbs with all his strength. A knife sullied with fish-scales and slimy residue was pressed against his forearm. The blade scraped upwards, whipping his body like a rankled viper-eel.

'Lamebrain!' another slave huffed. 'If I've told you once, I've told you a hundred times! Cudgel them before you kill them. It keeps the meat good.'

Footsteps approached, and the halfwit paused, bearing his meagre collection of rotted teeth.

The filthy curtain was thrust aside and the other slave stepped into Lamebrain's workspace. When he saw William, his eyes bulged so far from his skull they were in danger of dropping out. He rushed to Lamebrain, and although William had been scared of him before, in that moment he took him for his saviour. As the man's face turned dour and his eyes darkened a shade, that hope was quickly doused. Perhaps he feared what might happen to a pair of slaves caught with a bloodied knife and an injured boy, and decided it was best to be rid of any evidence.

'You're causing him pain.' The slave grasped Lamebrain's wrist and pulled the knife out from beneath the flap of skin. 'He'll be too frightened to cudgel now, his juices will be all aboil. The best thing to do…'

The slave turned to the rack, retrieved a cleaver and raised it over William's throat. 'Is to give him a quick and painless death.'

William writhed and yelled and kicked, but was powerless to protect himself. There was a piercing scream and the emaciated slave staggered backwards, the handle of Lamebrain's scaling knife protruding from between his ribs.

'My fith! My scraps. My fiss,' Lamebrain hissed and pulled another knife from the rack, this one larger and brutally sharp. He leapt for the starved slave.

William rolled off the table and thumped to the boards below, wriggling like a worm through an earth of entrails.

There was an almighty clap and a ball of hot lead seared a path through draping curtains. Blood sprayed from Lamebrain's fist. Two of his fingers and the large blade dropped to the floor, the aforementioned tip sticking in the sodden wood beside William's head. While the halfwit stumbled back, screaming and cradling his hand, the other slave raised his arms into the air – wincing against the pain in his side, and struggling to breathe.

Paralysed with terror, William lay still.

Boots approached, and from the purposeful rhythm they struck, anyone in hearing could tell they were polished. A flintlock poked through the gap in the curtains first – silver barrelled and etched with wild flowers – then moved to peel them aside for the first mate that followed. He was a tall man, but slender, and had a pale face aside from the brown blotch of a mole on his left cheek. Black wiry hairs bristled from it, as full up with indignation as their liveried owner.

'What's going on? You're here to gut fish, not each other.' The first-mate trained his pistol on the starved slave, planting his polished footwear firmly amongst the discarded offal. His eyes followed the slave's guilt-ridden gaze to William, huddled on the floor.

'The boy,' the slave uttered softly. 'This dolt tried to gut him.'

'Came in wivv da fisss.'

'Is that so?' The first mate pulled aside the frogging of his jacket and slid the flintlock into a leather holster – affixed with a silver belt buckle. 'Then, do you know what we have here?'

The first mate knelt beside William and brushed the hair from his eyes.

'A stowaway?' the emaciated slave suggested.

'A mermaid.' The first mate smiled and flicked his tongue across his lips. There was a slight twitch in his eye, which might have been a wink given more jovial circumstances. With a grunt, he pushed himself back to his feet, pulling the large knife from its groove in the floor as he did so. 'Do you know what a mermaid is, boys?'

Lamebrain kept his mouth shut, softly whimpering for his lost fingers. The other slave shook his head.

'An ocean beast. It lures ships to the rocks by appearing as whatever is most desirable.' The first mate pointed to William with the tip of his knife. 'This one appeared to you as a little boy. What do you think that says about the state of your mind, eh?'

'It was Lamebrain who found him.' The gaunt slave tried to deflect the first mate's attention.

'Don't point to him; he couldn't conjure a thought if he had two weeks preparation time.' The first mate lunged, adding the second knife to the growing collection in the slave's ribs. His other hand clamped around the gasping mouth to prevent any noise, releasing only when all fight had been bled from his victim. He let the slave crumple.

'Lamebrain.' The first mate pulled his tailored jacket straight and stepped over the body. 'You did a good job finding the beast. You'll get extra rations, I'll see to that. Now get back to your tasks, and on the double, you've got this sorry sop's fish to do as well now.'

Lamebrain hurried from the space, dragging his chains in his wake. If his missing fingers still troubled him, the distant and shambling giggle did well to disguise it.

'Come on then.' The first mate gathered William tenderly in his arms. 'Don't you fret about those fools, they won't hurt you now.'

This was the calmest William had felt since he tumbled from the bridge, huddled close to the man's chest for warmth and comfort. Now that he was safe, he was certain to be taken back home and reunited with worried parents. Every step towards the sunshine above strengthened his belief. As they made the deck, he smiled weakly; safe.

'What's going on down there?' It was the well-to-do voice from before, the one who had barked commands from the top deck. Perhaps the captain.

William didn't wriggle in his saviour's grip. His small hand fiddled with an embossed silver button, distracted by the flash it made in the sun.

'Nothing much, Captain,' the first mate replied nonchalantly. 'The slaves found a stowaway, they were fighting over him, might have actually eaten the poor bugger if I hadn't found out. I'm going to get him back to my cabin, get him cleaned up. Once his arm's better he might be some use on board; or in the galley.'

'Yes, yes, get him cleaned up, good plan,' the captain echoed.

The first mate's steps were softer now that they had been dampened with fish innards. His breathing was comforting, though slightly elevated, and his hand stroked William's head to calm him. He crossed the vast deck, then down a set of stairs, through a tight corridor, and into his modest cabin.

William was set gently onto a narrow bed. His mother would have scolded him for making such a mess on clean sheets, but his saviour seemed not to notice. He said nothing.

The first mate closed the door, then paced the cabin to retrieve a bottle from a dark wooden cabinet. William assumed it gin, from its oily nature and the pained wince as the first mate took a healthy sniff. A glass-bellied lamp was lit and placed on the cot-side table.

A little frantically, the first mate threw his soiled jacket off, leaving it in a heap on the floor. He almost lost his balance as he removed his boots. His hand trembled as it ran through his messy dark hair.

'I can't believe they managed to dredge you up.' The first mate took another lungful of the acrid liquor. 'I thought creatures like you to be more elusive than that.'

William didn't understand the man enough to follow what he was talking about, but did know that the atmosphere had soured. There was something unwholesome about this man, something untrustworthy. He shuffled towards the headboard to increase the distance between them.

'To think, a mermaid on our very own ship.' The first mate rolled up the sleeve of his shirt to show a tattoo of a fish-tailed woman sat atop a rock. 'I was told all about your sort as a child, I never dreamed you'd be real. It's just a shame that slave chose *this* as your current visage.'

The bottle sloshed as it was set beside the bed. It had a few symbols painted on the side that suggested the contents to be something a little more medicinal than plain old gin. It made sense, as the first mate had done nothing but smell the foul brew and his eyes had gone wide and unfocused.

He looped a hand around his silver belt buckle.

'Let's see if we can make a woman of you yet.'

The first thing heard by the crew was the man's cry as the lantern smashed against the side of his head; the second was the protracted shriek as oil spilled across his flesh, spreading its flame. Shortly after, a flintlock clapped.

The men came running, but it was already too late. The blaze had spread from the mattress to the floor, the walls and the drapes. The first mate lay unconscious at the edge of the blaze, while the boy stumbled and coughed through the cabin door. There seemed to be more fuel than just lantern oil, but smoke hung heavy and black, and nobody had time to investigate. One sailor braved the fumes to haul the first mate from within and cloak the flames with his jacket.

'What happened, boy?' Another crewmen shook William violently, but he didn't have the right words to reply. He was heaved up in the man's arms and carried to the deck.

As soon as the firefight had started, it was abandoned. The flames spread relentlessly, consuming anything and everything in their expansion. Calls for the lifeboats came from all around. Men fought each other, any companionship temporarily forgotten in the panic. Smoke poured from the lower windows and cannon ports, choking the salt wind.

William was tossed on a rowboat, joining three crewmen, the captain, and the smouldering body of the first mate, somehow, still alive.

'Give Bennet and the boy the last of it.' The captain turned away from the offered flask, chivalrous to the last. 'They need it more than I.'

Obediently, the sailor, too honourable, dehydrated, or stupid to realise he was nailing his own coffin, gave the last of the water to William. In a few greedy gulps, it was almost empty.

'Leave a little for the first mate.' The sailor tried to retrieve it, but William tipped his head back. By the time the sailor had snatched the canteen away, the last drop had been supped. 'Damn it boy, can't you listen?'

'Oh leave him.' The captain waved his crewman back lazily, his eyes slow to focus. 'Can't you see there's something not right with him? He hasn't spoken since we found him. I don't think Bennet will mind all that much; dying of thirst before he wakes will be a more comfortable passing. Gods know why the rest of us have to suffer.'

The captain lolled against the edge of the boat and looked up at the night sky. He began to mutter about the North Star, and how he could have gotten them home if they hadn't lost the other rowboats and one oar in "that damned storm". He had reloaded the first mate's flintlock and held it close for when all hope evaporated, perhaps to spare his own suffering, or at least give the child a quick death. It was forgotten in his exhaustion, and before long, he succumbed to sleep.

One by one, the others followed their captain, leaving William awake, hungry, and alone. Surrounded by the becalmed inky sea, and the cloudless black sky pierced with stars, there was nothing to suggest where the land lay. A slim crescent moon reclined against the night, watching the boy in the little boat with languid curiosity.

For a while, William tried to paddle with the solitary oar. The haft was too thick for him to properly grip, but in both hands he gained enough purchase to heave backwards, the way he had seen the sailors do. The oar scudded out of the water, almost overbalancing him. With the second pull, he kept the haft high and drew it towards his chin. Star-brushed ripples pushed away as the little boat began to move; maybe a hand span, maybe a stride. The distance was hard to gauge.

By the fifth stroke, he glanced up to find the moon on his other side, impassive. He had only managed to turn the boat a half circle. His arms trembled, strained by the weight of saltwater and the futility of his efforts. He let the oar go and it slipped free of the crooked rest. There was nothing to do but watch as it bobbed away over the ocean swell, until its slightly darker shape was lost.

A weak groan rattled from the first mate. Still alive. William huddled away from him and into the crook of the captain's armpit for shelter. At least he had been kind, even if it was too little and too late.

'Thompson, Captain,' the first mate wheezed, somehow regaining his consciousness after such a protracted time. 'The boy, Thompson, he's a beast… from the depths.'

William took the flintlock from the captain's chest. He had never held one before, but he had seen his father use one to smash empty bottles from twenty paces. Pistols were dangerous. They could rob a man of his life with the pull of a trigger. He held it in both hands, arms still shaking.

'He's come to sink us all…' The first mate's eye rolled in its socket, spinning over the grotesque wire-sprouting mole. That side of his face was practically beautiful compared to the other; his flesh had melted like wax, seamlessly blending his weeping eye with red flesh that faltered at the whittled exposure of charred wooden teeth. He fought to prop himself upright, then saw the unconscious crew and the little boy toting a flintlock.

In later years, William had often thought that was the exact moment he should have put the poor deranged sod from his misery. But young William was still coming to terms with the darkness of the world, and had not yet been inducted as a murderer.

'Don't shoot…' The first mate fell back into his state of unconsciousness, and at some point between that, and the passing of a merchant vessel, died.

1682

William still hadn't found his sponsor. In Garland, he hadn't spent too much time looking, too concerned with distancing himself from his crimes. In Lex, he had started his search, but it seemed that there weren't many willing. Given his soured reputation, anyone he asked thought becoming his sponsor was tantamount to suicide. He had garnered a few cracked ribs and a black eye for merely proposing the idea. Things had been different in Galmany, he even managed to convince a man to join him. Unfortunately, that man's self-destructive tendencies couldn't wait, and William found him face down in a dawdling river one bright and breezy morning.

Once in Grod, with his injuries long healed, his tactics changed. Asking didn't work; anyone foolish enough to accept had already been snapped up by more punctual assassins. Abduction became the more viable option. The balance of plotting and travel, however, was harder to keep than anticipated. Finding a man well suited to sponsorship, whilst also trying to get to the competition in time, proved difficult. It didn't help that his funds were perilously low, that all but one bullet had been spent, and that his old mare had yielded to its many years and died. When kidnapping, it was better to be cautious than caught and lynched.

He tramped to a halt, exhausted from the relentless travel. His back was stiff; he pressed fists into the base of his spine to quell the ache. It felt as though he had walked almost fifteen miles since the last coach had impolitely dropped him at the side of the road – the driver had been too well armed to challenge. Since then, a few more travellers had passed, but a stranger headed to Blackbile was not a welcomed passenger. Some politely declined, others whipped their reins and fled, most sneered at his lack of coin, but all of them had denied him one way or another.

A horse whinnied some way back down the road and he turned to look. Squinting against a persistent late-summer sun, he tried to gauge the likelihood of begging a lift on the shabby looking farm cart. Probably no greater than any of his previous attempts, but no worse either. As it was still a considerable distance away, he opted to rest on the grass verge and wait.

Sitting down was a task in itself, and once the weight of his pack was transferred from his feet to his arse, he couldn't help but breathe a sigh of relief. He shuffled the straps from his shoulders and reclined onto his belongings, wishing they were anything other than lumpen and hard. Though it was a considerable improvement to trudging.

He swilled a mouthful of stale water and spat to clear the residual grit and road dust. As he stretched out his legs, the soles of his feet began to ache. It was a wonder that the true pain of travel never started until one attempted a rest. He choked down another measure from his flask and idly rubbed at his feet through worn boot leather. If he was turned down again, he didn't know what he would do. Languish on the verge until he was scraped up and mulched for fertiliser, perhaps.

As the steady rumble of the cart approached, William dragged himself up off the floor, feeling all the heavier for his rest. He moved into the roadway. That way, if the driver wasn't of a mind to stop, he would have to swerve into the verge and risk a rut damaging his wheel. The old farmer could choose to run William down of course, but it was quicker to fire a flintlock than encourage a lazy horse to gallop – especially with the weight of a laden cart behind it.

'Hello there!' William set his pack at his feet and waved amicably. 'Any chance of a ride?'

Fortunately for the farmer driving the shabby cart, he chose to stop. Even at a few yards his smell of sweat and manure carried strongly. Looking William up and down, he drawled, 'where are you headed then?'

'I'm going to…' William hesitated. The truth would ensure a long walk; he chose to lie. 'I'm due in Starakow.'

His heat-hazed geographical recollections told him the arm-pit town of Starakow was a day or so beyond Blackbile, and considerably safer.

'Are you now?' The farmer plucked a strand of barley from the wide pocket of his filthy dungarees and popped the stalk in the corner of his mouth. 'Well, I can only take you so far, and I'm not one for giving free rides, especially not at a time like this. You'd be taking up the seat of one of my customers.'

In the back of the tumble down cart was a collection of the seediest sort William had ever seen: a portly woman covered in boils, a wall-eyed boy with wide cheekbones and upturned pig-nose, and a tall slender man, crumpled up like a swatted spider to keep from touching any of his fellow passengers. He could hear one more grumbling in the back, but they were obscured by the others.

'I'm transporting spectators and contestants alike up to Blackbile,' said the farmer, chewing like a cow on cud. 'And that don't come without a modicum of risk to myself, so I'm forced to charge. It's a fair sum mind.'

William blinked dumbly, worried for a moment that his fatigue had gotten the better of him. Another cursory glance over the passengers reaffirmed the farmer's destination.

'That's a relief.' He grinned. 'In truth, that's where I'm headed.'

'Great news.' The farmer wrung his hands greedily and pulled a coin purse from between his thighs. 'That'll be five silver bits, and I expect any firearms aboard to be unloaded and blades sheathed. Save for mine that is.'

'Ah, well… I don't actually have any money.' The prospect of walking the remaining miles to Blackbile was a poor one, so William was getting a little desperate.

'Never mind.' The farmer readied himself to whip the horse's rear end. 'Those scrawny legs could do with a little exercise.'

'Hang on.' William reached into his bag, his fingers deftly dodging a collection of worthless knickknacks and keepsakes before finally wrapping around the hilt of his flintlock – he had stowed it there in the hopes of looking innocent, but it seemed that hadn't worked out. He planted his feet and whipped the pistol up, training it on the farmer's tanned pate.

The hammer clicked back under a practiced thumb. He twisted his grip slightly so the sun winked off flowers engraved in the silver flintlock, asserting, 'you'll take me where I want to go.'

'Well I never…' The farmer plucked the spittle soaked barley from his mouth and flicked it to the road. 'If you had such a fine item for trade, why didn't you just out-with-it to begin with?'

The farmer was about as ruffled by the pistol as he would have been by a turnip. He delved a hand into his dungaree pocket.

'Stop that.' William shook his flintlock. Highway-robbery style bluffing only worked if the victim was afraid, and he was ever-so loathed to spend his last bullet on a farmer. 'I don't want to kill you, but if I have to, I will. I need this ride. My feet are sore, my water's running low, and I ran out of food miles ago. I'm desperate, and you know how desperate-men can be.'

'Steady on now.' More cautiously, the farmer withdrew his hand from his pocket.

William tensed, ready to shoot if he saw the hilt of a firearm. Instead, what came out was a well-worn monocle.

The farmer raised it to his eye and peered through. 'That is one fine weapon you've got there, son. Trade it to me, and it'll pay for your passage.'

'We're past that now,' William snarled. He was impressed by the farmer's level head, and supposed that was down to tilling land in guild territory. He wondered if the man would make a good sponsor. 'I'm threatening your life; take me to Blackbile or lose it.'

'Oh, I don't think so.' The farmer reclined in his seat and turned to the passengers huddled in the back of his cart. 'What do you lot think? Is he bargaining or threatening?'

'Whatever it is, it's done.' A terse northerner at the far side of the cart stood up. The top of his head was barely visible behind the portly woman. 'Excuse me, miss.'

The woman shuffled her bulk across the bench-seat almost flattening the pig-faced boy, who cringed into the folds of the spidery man's jacket.

The northern man was a diminutive three feet tall, but no less intimidating. His face was crooked, and one large tooth protruded from a split in his lip. The hair atop his head had been tonsured, and while the centre was sprouting stubble, the edges hung lank and greasy. He rolled his shoulders to adjust a long brown coat and clambered onto his seat for a better vantage. Though his hair suggested devotion to a religious order, the sizable blunderbuss in his hands ruled out that possibility.

William weighed the odds; a mad dwarf with a gun as big as he was, easily surpassed an eighteen year-old blonde stripling with a flowery pistol.

'Let's kill him and be done with it,' the little man snarled, flecks of spittle flying from the cleft in his lip. 'I don't have time to wait around.'

'My argument isn't with you.' William kept his flintlock trained on the driver. He had been too slow to react to the little man's announcement, stunned by how awkward it was. 'I just need a ride.'

'Why bother us at all?' the spidery man shuddered the words out, cringing against the unclean presence of the young boy and wringing his hands nervously. 'Leave us be.'

'Right, that's it!' The little man fumbled in his coat for shot and powder. 'Let me load this thing and I'll have his head off.'

'Stop.' William balked, swerving to aim at the little man. 'I'll only give you this one chance.'

A gun-hammer clicked, and the sound chilled him to the core. In the driver's seat, the farmer had taken the opportunity to draw and cock his own pistol. Now William had two enemies and still only the one bullet.

'You should have pulled the trigger when you had the chance, boy. Now, lower it,' the farmer insisted.

William kept his pistol up. The little man continued to calmly load his blunderbuss.

'I said lower it!'

William sighed, defeated; he couldn't take the both of them. For a killer, he really was too lenient sometimes. One of the more renowned assassins might have had them all dead in seconds and been off on the horse before they hit the ground. He just had to learn to commit to a killing, not dance around the thing like a politician around truth.

'Toss me the gun, boy. It's a fine piece and I'll keep it for the trouble you've caused us,' the farmer spat. 'Then kneel down. I have to be hard-line about these things, what with going to Blackbile. If the guilders think I'm going soft, they'll string me up before dawn.'

A spume of fire and lead shot sprayed from the small man's blunderbuss, and the farmer's head was turned to the consistency of jam. Not the cheap stuff, but mid-tier cottage-style with whole strawberries in the aspic. It showered over William; wet, warm, and with the pervading odour of turning bacon. The portly woman screamed and rolled over the side of the cart. Thankfully, she landed with a kink in her neck, so the shrieking ended abruptly.

'He does go on, doesn't he?' The little man planted a boot on the farmer's drooping corpse and shunted him to the floor. 'Couldn't let one of the livestock take out a fellow guilder, even one as lowly as you, M.K.'

M.K. was a decidedly worse nickname than the full title in the tabloids. Given the circumstances, William decided not to press the issue.

'You'll have to drive us though.' The small man shivered as he took a seat. 'I'm terribly afeared of horses. They let *flies* crawl on their eyelids.'

That thought had never really occurred to William, but he supposed everyone had their weaknesses.

'Hurry up, we'll miss the opening festivities at this rate.' The short man tapped the driver's seat impatiently. 'Plus, I've a fat whore with my name on her; branded her myself.'

William set his belongings in the rear of the cart, catching sight of a wriggling cocoon of canvas and rope. Its shape and muffled cries suggested it contained a person even smaller than the assassin.

'My sponsor.' The little man patted the cocoon happily, and set his blunderbuss across his lap.

William felt a pang of jealousy, and wondered if he should kill the little assassin and take the sponsor for his own; he decided not. His reputation couldn't take the hit should news spread that he was a backstabber as well as a failure. He could offer to buy the sponsor, but some members of the guild could be a little changeable, so it was best to keep interactions to a minimum. There was always a good chance a snap decision would see the little man trying to take his head, something the murder of the farmer had proven he was entirely capable of.

William slid his baggage under one of the bench seats near the spindly man – who seemed quite pleased the portly woman had alighted and left so much room for him to spread out – then moved for the driver's perch. He had to step over the farmer's corpse, so made sure to pocket the coin purse and tuck the additional pistol beneath his belt as recompense for being spattered with brain-jam.

'Onward!' the little man roared.

Taking the reins, William was glad that among various methods of killing, he had acquired a few other skills. Princely among them – at least at this moment in time – was the ability to drive a cart and tend a horse. It reassured him that the blunderbuss wasn't immediately reloaded. So long as he stayed useful, he hoped to avoid another stand-off.

Although Blackbile was hailed by some in The Vitulan Empire as a pit of crime and depravity, William found the place surprisingly welcoming. There had been a little trepidation that his place on the blacklist would deny him entry, but that was only foolishness on his part. While anyone listed was denied work, it was actively encouraged for them to compete. He imagined the guild saw it as an easy way of purging unwanted members, but – should he do well – it was also beneficial for all parties to restore his right to contract. He passed a cursory check at the outskirts without issue.

At a pedestrian choked junction, he steered the cart to the side of a shabby general store – pocked with evidence of woodworm and gunfire. With the proximity of the competition, every road to the centre would be equally burdened and continuing with the cart would prove difficult. The morbid tourists came to view the ensuing mayhem of the contest, in spite of the risk. More sensible residents were in the streets too, readying themselves to vacate to Starakow for the duration. It was a well-known fact that, on average, six times more spectators died than entrants. Given that, and a purposeful lack of analysis, William favoured his odds.

'Thanks for the ride M.K.' The little man hauled the bound midget over his shoulder and hopped from the cart. 'I'll see you at the opening ceremony!'

'Yes. Thank you kindly,' the spindly man added with more than a hint of sarcasm. The loose skin on the backs of his hands rolled around as he massaged them together. He seemed to consider saying more while he fiddled with a white ring on his finger, but decided against it and unfolded himself from the seat. As he moved from the cart to the floor he didn't lose an inch in height and would have actually gained a little had his back not been as stooped. 'Come boy, and stop touching me!'

The piggy child gave a thankful and snotty grin to William, then trotted after his lanky companion, holding up a hand to be led by, undaunted by the rebuttal.

William sighed. Although he had never managed to drop his guard for the thought of a blunderbuss turning him to paste, he had enjoyed the idle chatter shared on the road. Having been on his own so long, he had forgotten what it was like to share a journey, and now that his companions had dispersed, that lonesome weight was hanging on him again. He was compelled to call out for them – maybe they could walk together to the square – but all had disappeared into the crowd.

He stepped down from his perch and took stock of the place. While he had heard many tales of Blackbile in his years amongst guild-folk, he had never actually made the Sinner's Pilgrimage before.

There was a horrible, overriding stench to the place, earthy yet sulphurous. The result of a natural spring and active volcanic pits that converged some way up the mountainside. By the time the waters reached the town, they had coagulated into a vast grime-choked river that looked more like roiling earth than a torrent of water. There wasn't much guessing as to why it had been dubbed the Landslide; killers could often be the antithesis of creatives.

In addition to its distinctive scent, the river was also uniquely suited to the needs of the townsfolk. The murky torrent was the ideal place to lose a body, or dispose of one's faeces, and could have been the main reason Blackbile's founders chose to settle where they did. William, however, didn't feel that the river's benefits outweighed the significant downside. To him, the pervading odour was more than a little distracting, and being unaccustomed could prove a significant disadvantage in the competition.

As the sun disappeared behind the craggy volcano, the temperature plummeted. Thick ash-flakes began to fall from the sky like snow. Women in mud streaked dresses popped parasols in the crowd, ungainly affairs of smirched leather, quite unlike the painted silk and paper counterparts of Fairshore.

Cold, and gaining his own covering of ash, William was reminded of the thick coat in his pack. He had stolen it after Valiance but had not much cause to wear it since. Dragging his feet from the sucking mud, he wobbled around the side of the cart. If he hadn't been so preoccupied with the thought of the upcoming event, he probably wouldn't have been surprised that all his belongings had been stolen. Given that the opening ceremony was only three hours away, he was actually quite startled. He cursed and kicked the cartwheel. There was nothing much of value, but it was all he had to call home.

It was a small comfort to have a pair of flintlocks on his belt and more coins than he had started the day with. There was more solace in thinking on the light-fingered thief going through his pack to only find a coat, an eight-year-old tournament flier, a fist full of completed contracts, and a bottle of what looked like blood. Then his imagination strayed too far, and he pictured the thief tossing the collected affects into a hearth to feed his ire.

He sulked for a good minute before buoying himself enough to peer into his coin purse. Eighteen silver pieces; not bad. He could buy himself a week in the grottiest tavern and still have spare for a little ammunition. Plus, if rumours were true, participants got cheaper rates than commoners.

Loosening his belt a notch, he delved his hand into his undergarments to store the farmer's coin purse with his own. There would be countless pickpockets here, children and adults alike. He couldn't trust anyone, not even the lamest half-rotted leper, or the most pious man in the chapel on the hill. He kept his eye on the upturned cross on the black spire; it looked to be pretty central, a good landmark to keep his bearings in the muddle of crooked houses and intertwining streets.

He set off, preferring to walk, rather than battle his way through the traffic with the cart. He would be fighting here soon enough and it would do him good to learn the streets. It occurred to him that he could have sold the horse and cart for another silver piece or two, but by then he had reached the end of the street, and both had been stolen already.

'Excuse me.' A stranger pushed out of the crowd; a young Scoldish lad with mud smirched clothes and wire frame glasses.

William's instinct told him something was wrong. The lad may have seen him counting his coins, and though he looked harmless, could be part of a gang. His hand found the flintlock on his belt and rested there, ready. As he subtly scanned his surroundings, he found a few people dotted amongst the shifting flow of the street, watching him in stoic silence. One of the group worried him in particular, a large woman who might have been seven feet tall if the mess of knotted hair was included. He wondered if her bulk might protect her from a bullet – specially designed arms had to be used against giant beasts on the southern continent, and this woman was the closest thing to a rhinoceros William had ever seen. She was a guilder, no debate about that.

'Are you William of Fairshore?' the lad asked, a slim smile spreading across his face.

William's instinct shifted. A mugger seemed less likely, but an assassin tasked with eliminating any embarrassments to the guild; that was possible. In fact, something had been whispering at the back of his mind for a few months now, that he might find himself on the receiving end of a contract. As of yet, no attempt had been made on his life, and this lad didn't seem like much of a threat – despite the watching rhinoceros. He had no weapon, and looked even greener than William. Like many of the tourists here, he could just be a fan. Deciding to remain cautious, William kept his hand on the flintlock, and replied, 'yes.'

'Oh, good! I've got something for you then.'

If the initial approach had set William on edge, the way the Scoldish lad replied – with a slight widening of his smile and cheeky twang to his words – nudged him over the brink. His grip tightened around the pistol's handle and his thumb tensed on the hammer. If there were any sudden movements now, somebody would be losing their life.

'Here.' The lad took off his glasses and casually tossed them to William. They bounced off his chest and fell into the muck by his feet. 'Wear these, you might shoot straight next time!'

The gaggle of collected onlookers burst into raucous laughter, none more-so than the girthy brute. William sneered and made a comment about how the jibe hadn't been that funny, but it was lost under the needling merriment.

As the flow in the street was beginning to falter, and a more organised crowd was forming about William and the cackling Scolds, he opted to curtail his humiliation, and stomped off towards the chapel. A few more insults were called in his wake, but thankfully the brutish guilder – and probable ring-leader of the group – was swamped by adoring fans. He did take some satisfaction that he crushed the delicate eye-glasses under his heel as he turned. They wouldn't be laughing when he won the prize.

The sludgy roads led him towards what he hoped was the centre of town. There were sign posts, but each one was either vandalised or had been positioned to direct people down the dingiest alleyways. He didn't want to ask for directions; that wasn't done in Blackbile unless you wanted to wake up without a few of your organs. He was sure that sooner or later, he would spot a more genial guilder to point him in the right direction. Until then, he had to hope that the flow of the crowd would lead him to the town square in time for the ceremony.

He bullied his way out of the mud and onto a wooden boardwalk that hemmed the road, finding himself amongst a group of tourists he presumed would be heading the right way. They were discussing the upcoming events, the best kills from previous years, and who their favourite winners had been. By their excitement and furtive glances about the street, William could tell they were on the lookout for guilders to swarm for autographs or perhaps slip them a note requesting their services. None of them seemed to recognise him, or maybe they did and just didn't care.

1672

William sat silently in the galley of his new-found ship, peeling the skins from potatoes collected in a bucket. He had been aboard the merchant vessel for almost a month now. From what he had gleaned from conversations between the adults, they were headed for the Silken Coast; somewhere he had heard of, but had no idea how far away from home it was.

He slipped a knife through a skinless potato and tossed it in halves into the cook's waiting pot. His chores helped to keep his mind off the loneliness and sickness for home. While he was kept busy, he was also well fed and treated kindly by the merchant's journeyman-apprentice – whose position aboard the vessel was only eclipsed by the captain.

In a way, he preferred it here. There was no school, and he wasn't caned for poor comprehension. Yet, deep inside, he still felt that lonesome pull for his mother's happy face and the comfort of his father's leading hand.

'How's the stew coming?' The journeyman hammered down the steep ladder-like steps into the galley. Too tall for below decks, the young man straightened as best he could, leaning over William like a well-meaning older brother. 'This'll be your last chance to impress. We make port tomorrow.'

William responded by tossing another finished potato into the cooking pot. The initial shock of near-death three times over had waned, and the flap of skin on his forearm had healed to a red-pink smear, but he still couldn't bring himself to speak.

Though the journeyman had often been heard barking orders or reprimands at the sailors, he had been endlessly affable with William. He smiled widely, rolled up his coat sleeves, and sat on the nearest bench. Like many on the ship, he seemed to think William was simple, and even despite that, didn't treat him like a beast of burden.

'I wanted to come and speak to you before we reached port.' The journeyman pulled a short dagger from his belt and started to peel a potato. 'After our stop in the Silken Coast, we're headed back to Thego. There's a strict border there and they monitor all of the imports quite closely. Anyway, the long and short of it is, I've spoken to the captain and he says we can't take you with us.'

William dug a black eye from a tuber, then sliced the white flesh in half to add it to the others.

'The Silken Coast isn't exactly the nicest place in the world, but there is law there. You'll be safe; looked after.' The journeyman fidgeted uncomfortably. 'I understand your position, I was there myself once…'

The journeyman faltered at William's continued lack of acknowledgement, as if it was all a waste of energy, and the time at sea had starved the boy's brain.

'I'm meeting with one of my master's contacts to deliver an artefact. I'll see if I can trade you to him as an apprentice. You'll be free to earn your own wage then, like me, and perhaps one day you might become a master. Become your own man again.' The merchant tossed his peeled potato into the pot and started on a carrot. 'It's not a bad life, I promise you that.'

'Mr Basar?' A bell tinkled overhead as the journeyman opened the door of a dingy pawn shop. He had a long, leather-bound package strapped to his back, and though he seemed to be suffering under the weight of it, he allowed William inside first.

Echoing the cramped and cluttered city outside, the shop was overstocked and poorly arranged. In contrast, the place was eerily cold – where the sun had bathed the streets with relentless heat – and so dark one might think it was dusk. The only light eked from a few guttering candles and the grimy glass pane in the door.

'Mr Basar, are you here?' the journeyman repeated and unravelled a sand-beaten scarf from around his face.

'I'm here.' A hunched old man, leaning heavily on an ivory topped cane, shuffled from the back room through a bright cascade of hanging beads. 'And who might you be? I was expecting to be dealing with Mr Goodrich in person.'

'I'm his apprentice,' the journeyman replied. 'My master deemed the pair of you even; given the delivery of this.'

He moved to the counter – a long lacquered table with an inset glass display. With considerable effort he hitched the rope off his shoulder, took the weight of the package in both hands, and set it carefully on the wooden top. 'He won't be dealing with you again.'

'I see.' The old man flexed his slender fingers over the bindings, then deftly loosed them. Leather and wool padding parted to reveal a stone sword, etched with runes, perhaps prised from the hands of a weathered statue. Some relic of a pillaged civilisation. Like the beads behind, the old man's eyes glittered in the dim light. 'He really has outdone himself. It's truly a shame we won't be doing any more business again in future.'

The pawnbroker struggled the sword into both arms, his face a picture of pure exertion, and his back crooked under the weight. As he turned, there was a foul popping sound from one of his joints, but nothing gave way. Without a free hand for his cane, his progress to the back room was painfully slow. The animosity shared between him and the journeyman was made obvious even to young William, when help was neither offered nor requested. Moments later, he returned more thoughtfully, with his hands tucked deep in the pockets of his sun-bleached smoking jacket, as if the whole thing hadn't been a showcase of an old man's shortcomings. An errant strand of lint stuck to his forehead betrayed he had quickly mopped his brow.

The journeyman puffed his chest out to look more important– or to lord his youth and status over the old trader – and nudged William closer to the counter.

'I have a deal for you; should you be willing to listen. *This boy.* I found him amongst a lifeboat of dead slavers. I'd take him for my apprentice, but being only a journeyman myself, am prohibited. Thus, I need to offload him. He doesn't speak – think he might have been through some trauma or had the sense stoved from him – but that sort of thing can make them very loyal. Especially given his age.'

William tried not to listen. Though the merchant had made him swab the deck, haul pails, and peel potatoes, he had fed and watered him well. The man had even persisted in speaking to him, despite never getting a response. As such, William had come to admire him as more of an older brother than anything else, and hearing the merchant discuss him as a commodity sent shivers across his skin.

'So what you're telling me is, you haven't paid for him, and you haven't got any papers of ownership.' The pawnbroker leaned over the counter to look down at the boy more closely.

William averted his gaze, suddenly more interested in the shrunken heads, washing boards, and blunted training swords than the wart-nosed shopkeeper.

'That means my buying of him won't be without a peppering of risk on my part.' Mr Basar shook his head apprehensively. 'What if his parents come looking? I'll be tossed in the dungeons and labelled a nonce for keeping a fair thing like that about these parts.'

'You can see why I'm not that keen on keeping hold of him,' the merchant chuckled. For an accredited journeyman, he really was a terrible negotiator.

A wide smile spread across the wizened face of the pawnbroker. 'I'll tell you what: give me something in trade, and I'll take the brat off your hands.'

'You want *me* to pay *you*?' the journeyman scoffed. 'I'm not stupid. I know your ties. Even with his illegitimacy, you'll be able to fetch a semi-decent price or get some convincing papers.'

'What ties do you refer to exactly? Or are you just taking a punt, given that I own a back alley pawn shop?' The broker slid a leather bound ledger from a shelf of crystal globes, shells, and lead shot.

The journeyman said nothing.

'A punt then. Young man, I admire your tenacity. Very well, I'll deal with you, but I do run a reputable business, at least in the eyes of the taxers. You'll have to trade me something so I can give you a little coin, or the books won't balance.'

'This is the only thing I have of any value,' the journeyman grumbled and untucked the silver barrelled flintlock from under his belt. He set it on the counter and slid it over to the broker with a flourish. 'Be careful, it's loaded, I've been using it instead of my standard Gill Brothers'. It looks a little better, and perhaps performs a little better.'

A shiver passed over William. The last time he'd seen that gun, he'd pointed it at the burnt wreck that had once been a man named Bennet. The etched flowers did little to disguise the true purpose of the thing.

'I like it; a custom. Made by the younger Gill I'd wager.' The broker turned it over in his hands and set it on the shelf behind him. 'I have one of the elder Gill's myself.'

He pulled a twin barrelled flintlock from inside his jacket and added, 'the barrels are pinched to slow the bullet and silence the shot. It allows me to do my business however I please; with little fear of governmental intervention.'

Two gouts of smoke thrust from the flintlock and the journeyman's throat split. He toppled backwards and slumped against the door. The bell trilled a little, but nobody heard it, because – contrary to the pawnbroker's claim – the gun clapped as loud as any other.

William dashed to the fallen man, ignoring the ringing in his ears. Horrified, he watched the life pump from the journeyman's gullet.

'The older Gill was somewhat of a charlatan, I think you'll agree,' the pawnbroker sneered. 'I'm glad you've brought me an example of his brother's work; the younger Gill was always the master. Oh, and don't worry about me and the boy, I pay my protection rights, so I highly doubt there'll be any guards rushing this way.'

The journeyman let out one last gurgle.

However briefly William had known this man, he still felt sorrow over his death. He had been kind, and that had been something to treasure of late.

'Maybe now your master will deign to speak with the likes of me,' the broker said to the journeyman as if he hadn't already perished. He took a draft of the smoke curling from the mouths of his pistol and turned his glower to William.

'Well boy, you owe your allegiance to me now.' He lifted the counter top on a squealing hinge and crept closer, sinking low to speak in a way he might have thought was more welcoming. His spine and knees clicked like the priming of his flintlock.

William clutched himself into the corner wishing for home and for all of this to be over.

'Do a good job and I won't sell you into the sex trade, understand?'

William nodded slowly.

'How are you at digging boy?' The broker snatched at his skinny arms, testing the strength of childish muscles. 'What about carving meat? We need to get rid of your previous owner, or the both of us will be for the long drop. What do you say? Will you help an old man?'

1682

Nestled rather conspicuously between tumbledown shacks, was a luxurious guild-owned hotel. Painted blood red with white supports and window frames, it stood out vibrantly against the greys and browns of the ash-choked streets. If William's last three jobs had gone well, he might have opted to stay in such a place, but it was most certainly not amongst his current options.

As he neared the hotel, the flow of tourists slowed. He could see that a large crowd had formed to watch the opulent doors – set back from the road at the top of red carpeted stairs – and were in danger of clogging the entire street. While he was interested in what might have drawn so much attention, he didn't want to be late for the ceremony, so pushed his way forwards between gawping commoners.

'It's him!' one of the podgy spectators screamed, drawing the attention of nearly everyone in the vicinity.

For a brief moment, William thought he had been recognised, even through the mud, blood, and ash. He gritted his teeth, swallowed a curse, and turned to greet whoever might have spotted him. Then he saw the hotel doors had been opened wide by liveried bellhops, and a very familiar man stepped from within.

The prize champion of seventy-six, Ojo Azul, seemed to glide through the hotel doors, and took each step down to the boardwalk as though he were a king greeting his subjects.

William stopped, mouth slackening. Ojo had been dead for years; a legend murdered for the glory of besting a prize-winner. Though so many claimed to have been the one to do it, finding the true culprit had been impossible. William had believed the stories in principle. Nobody had seen the man in nearly a decade; but there he was, very much alive – a little older, silver stripes cutting through oiled black hair – no mistaking him.

'Azul! Azul!' William called and waved his arms in the air, but his attempts were smothered in the adulations of the crowd. 'Ojo, it's me; William!'

He charged into the throng, weaving between sweaty bodies, bony angles, and unknown fleshy pouches. Nails clawed at his skin to prevent his progress, but he was stronger and more resilient than his slight frame would suggest. Each body in the gaggle was circumvented by either force, dexterity, or a swift jab of his elbow, and soon he was at the forefront of the press.

Ojo was facing the other way, distracted by his adoring fans. A few gave him gifts, which he passed on to a clutch of guardsmen who had followed him into the street. Others wanted his signature as proof of having met him. Some slipped him papers scrawled with the details of potential hit jobs. They might have been intended for the winner of this year's competition, but it wasn't every day the opportunity arose to employ a living legend to despatch one's enemies.

'Ojo, it's William.' His voice was drowned in the crowd. He tried to get closer, to reach out and touch him on the shoulder.

A bodyguard rapped the back of his hand with a gauntleted fist and grumbled something under the crowd's furore that might have been "keep your distance", or something less polite.

'I'm an old friend,' William mouthed overtly in the hopes that he might relay his message despite the growing cheers in the gathering.

The guard didn't seem to buy it, instead resting his hand on his sword.

A horse drawn carriage thrust its way into the horde and Ojo Azul began to make his way towards it.

'Ojo!' William shouted one last time.

He didn't know if he had been heard, or whether chance had favoured him, but as Ojo stopped to greet a few fans he spotted William. His eyes were still as sky-bright as ever, offset against the terracotta tones of his skin. He stepped forwards and held out his hand to shake. William took it with gusto, spouting a garbled memoir about everything that happened since they'd last met, and interrupting himself with how good it was to finally see the old killer again. It didn't matter that most of it, if not all, was lost under the thrum of the growing crowd; William was too excited to stop himself. He had been alone for too long.

Ojo released his grip, reached into the pocket of his black silk jacket – embroidered with silver snakes on the lapels – and pulled out a card. A palm was held out to an assistant and quickly filled with an ink-charged fountain pen. The whole display looked well-rehearsed, but everything always had with Ojo. He scratched a message on the card and handed it to William, then gathered his guards around him and swept away.

Bewildered and exuberant, William couldn't take his eyes off the old assassin until he had been whisked into his carriage and disappeared down the road. In the rush of emotion he had paid little attention to the card clutched in his hands, and when he looked down, was stunned by the elegance of it. Thick, bleached-white card; expensive. The ink was so rich and black it could only be imported from the Amaris Isles.

> *For my favourite fanatic.*
> *I invoke the gods' blessing.*
> *Ojo Azul*

William's smile faltered, he had expected an invitation to dinner – or at least a drink – and had been left with platitudes.

The flow of tourists resumed towards the square. As the crowd shifted, he noticed a few people cradling similar cards. At first he thought nothing of it, but when he heard one greasy teen boasting about the worth of a prize winner's signature, the realisation hit him like a rifle butt to the face. Ojo had taken him as a fan. He crumpled the card and stuffed it into his pocket.

The bitterly familiar swell of loneliness filled his chest. How did Ojo not recognise him? It didn't make sense. He thought about it as he walked, trying to explain away the hurt at being snubbed. Eventually, he reached the conclusion that, in the eight years since Ojo last saw him, he had changed an awful lot. Puberty had stretched him out and peppered his chin with sparse stubble. He would barely resemble his nine year old self, so Ojo hadn't rejected him on purpose. He could still remake the connection, they just needed time to speak, without the noise of the crowd.

The press eased a little as the roadway opened into a grand square. Although William had never been there, he knew from paintings that the layout was reminiscent of the senate courtyard in Vitale. Yet here in Blackbile, the buildings were crooked and constructed nearly exclusively from grey knotted wood. The town hall was the most notable exception, a huge edifice of red-brick and volcanic rock topped with a large dome.

High wooden bleachers had been erected, festooned with ribbons and crowded with spectators eager to see the opening ceremony. At the far end of the square, at the foot of the steps to the imposing hall, was a stage and lectern. Officials were bustling about making last minute preparations. He squinted to make out the prize committee, and although he was too far away, imagined he could see the wild hair of the mayor and the sweeping robe of the Amarian Swordmistress.

He forced his way through the press, avoiding hawkers of cat meat and hot cider, squeezing around voluminous skirts, torch bearers, and all kinds of folk. Finally, he halted at the edge of a threadbare carpet. The centre of the square had been reserved for guild members only, hemmed in by frayed velvet ropes. Queasy, anxious, and brimming with excitement, William took his first step towards victory. As his foot came down, he pictured himself winning the prize, and could almost hear the crowd chanting his name already.

'Not so fast there.' One of two guardsmen – who William had initially taken for loitering guilders – held a palm out to stop him. 'Only guild members beyond this point.'

William looked the pair up and down, gauging whether they posed much of a threat. There was a chance they were confidence tricksters or thieves, but their uniforms looked shabby enough to be genuine. Real guards then, but whether they intended a shake-down was not yet determined. Their muskets were hanging casually enough on straps, but the shiny bayonets, and the board, parchment, and brass-nibbed pen intimated business was meant.

'I am a guild member?' William tried, just as surprised as he was relieved that neither of the men seemed to recognise him. While he was by no means as famous as some of the guilders here, he was as infamous as any of them.

Hoping to forgo announcing his name to the pair – lest he subject himself to a similar ribbing to the one administered by the young Scoldish lad – he pulled up his sleeve to show his assassin's brand. Pink and slightly glossy, the fan of half-moons was as distinct as the day it had been seared into his flesh, though thankfully not so painful.

'Well, I'll be.' The taller one pushed the brim of his cap up. 'You really don't look the sort lad, but I suppose that works to your advantage.'

'Just need your name for the register,' the short guardsman added.

'It's…' William sighed, letting the pause drag a little too long between words, 'William of Fairshore.'

The little guard scratched the name down on his parchment.

'In you go then, and enjoy the competition.' The taller guard stepped aside.

'Is that it?' William pursed his lips, half expecting a delayed punchline from the guardsmen.

'You have a nice day now.'

Pleasantly surprised, William stepped into the cordoned-off area. While the press nearer the stage was even tighter than in the bleachers, at the rear of the carpet there was some space to manoeuvre. He craned his neck to look for a good route to the front. He wanted to see the ceremony and prize committee more than he'd realised, and was actually quite excited about the prospect of entering the competition. The reality of what would happen should he lose had been conveniently pushed far into the dark recesses of his mind.

'You're not letting him in are you?' A brutish guilder stood at the back of the crowd had noticed William's exchange with the guardsmen, and once he'd been allowed entry, wasted no time in objecting. 'Blackbile's no place for you, *William of Fairshore!*'

'You're not here to kill the mayor are you?' teased the brute's unfortunately-identical twin sister. 'Heard that's all you're good for.'

The big brute let out a chuckle and didn't stop when William set a hand on his flintlock, instead adding, 'watch what you're doing with that thing, you might have somebody's eye out.'

'No fighting, please.' The taller guardsman set a hand on William's shoulder. 'Violence is prohibited until the competition starts.'

'You won't be laughing when your brains are scattered across this carpet, or when I win the damned prize.' William shook off the guard's grip and stepped towards the brute. He pulled the pistol from his belt.

'Leave him be…' Another assassin had arrived at the edge of the carpet and was giving her details to the note-taking guard. 'He's just here to enjoy the ceremony, watch the prize being won, why do you have to belittle him like that? It's Genevieve Cholmondeley… Col-mon-de-lay.'

She supervised the correct spelling of her name on the guardsman's papers, then with a single hand – gloved to the elbow in finest kid-skin – pulled aside a loose lock of auburn that spilled from her fashionable bun. Behind it, only very small, just under her ear, was a tattoo of the guild's mark.

'You two toddle along now.' Genevieve waved off the two brutes, who were more than happy to oblige given her sinister reputation.

William, despite feeling even more embarrassed by her supposed rescue of him than he had been by the initial jibes, felt compelled to thank her, as he had also heard of her exploits. 'You really didn't need to…'

'I did.' She drew alongside William. 'I hate it when cats toy with mice.'

She stood taller him, maybe six feet in height and toned, despite appearing almost as slender. She wore a near-black corseted dress, with matching lace-edged skirts pinned up and the sleeves removed to allow better movement. She didn't have any visible weaponry, but it didn't ease William at all. Genevieve was known to be an excellent sniper – perhaps even better than the first Man-Butcher – and when she wasn't sequestered away with a rifle, a companion was; ready to blow the head off anyone who dared challenge her.

Against his better judgement he opted to pursue the conversation a little longer. Perhaps because he was still pining for a little companionship or because underneath the assassin's cold demeanour she really was quite attractive.

'What you said about me, that I'm here to watch, it's not true.' He grinned, unsure if he was intending to impress, or simply salve the embarrassment of earlier. *'Actually,* I am entering the competition.'

'Oh dear…'

Whatever William had expected her reaction to be, the withering look and sudden disinterest was not it.

'Fear not, anyway,' she added absently, studying the crowds. 'I won't be wasting a bullet on you.'

'You might not get the chance,' William scoffed, his confidence somehow bolstered from being thought so low. He could shoot better than most, he knew that, and if everyone thought he was the sum of his most public and embarrassing failure that might just give him the edge to win.

Genevieve's sour grimace twitched into a subtle smile – the first he had seen from her. She stopped studying the crowd, looked at him, and said, 'you surprise me. Most daren't talk to me, let alone *talk back.'*

For one dreadful moment William thought he might be about to lose the contents of his skull, but Genevieve coiled a hand around his arm. 'Let's get a good spot, I'd like to see a little clearer.'

The contact sent a shiver down his spine. Not because she was dangerous, although she certainly was, but because she was the first woman who had spoken to him in a long time who hadn't tried to illicit a payment. He swallowed an abundance of saliva, and suddenly she was leading him through the crowd.

It was interesting to see so many guilders in one place, and to get a measure of what kind of competition he would have for the prize. There were hundreds of assassins: gunslingers like William, furtive garrotte users, riflemen, and brick-house bruisers. But there was also a whole raft of oddities. From bombers with spark-powder grenades, flame belchers, and eastern rocketry, to the most insane who thought they might simply battle their way to the top with a whip or sharpened chair leg. These were people that could only exist in the guild, where logic was shunned in favour of foolish brilliance and bloody spectacle.

Amongst them, William couldn't relax, but felt he had the energy for anything. Although many a guilder had been pushed into such a grim profession by the darkest of histories, positivity and excitement spread through the crowd like fire across oil.

'Have you been to Blackbile much?' William asked as Genevieve skirted them around a group of robed cultists.

'No more than necessary, I'm not over enamoured with the smell. Though, I do come every two years to watch the prize being won. I was actually here for the first. That *was* a blood bath, put me off ever entering.' She cast a glance his way. 'Obviously things are different now. Everything changes when you have a child.'

The initial excitement William had felt when he heard Genevieve had been at the very first competition was hampered somewhat by the news that she was a mother. The line of questioning he was about to pursue about Lord Beechworth and Terrowin the Man-Butcher was curtailed before he could utter a syllable. He instead reconsidered his position, the short lived romance that had been tickling at the back of his mind faltered. This woman had a child, she might even have a husband, and what would he think of William linking her arm and hanging on her every word.

He idly studied the rooftops for any winking sniper lenses, of course there were many, employed to put an end to any violence that might occur in the build up to the competition. Strangely, there were none on the town hall roof.

'Have you been before?' she questioned.

'No, I always wanted to. Ever since Ojo won; but I always too busy working.' He would have continued, but the situation that saw him here was entirely too depressing to keep dredging up.

'Oh yes, Ojo, I was surprised to hear that he'd actually been alive all these years. I bet that was hard to keep a secret.'

William nodded but didn't say anything. It was better for her to believe that he had known all along, rather than tell her the truth. He still couldn't quite comprehend it himself, that his closest ally and mentor had completely abandoned him.

'This looks as good a place as any.' Genevieve unhooked herself from William's arm and stopped behind a wheelchair-bound cripple and an elderly woman bent near double to rest on her cane. From here the pair had a good view of the stage, not too far away, and not too near that the crowd began to smother. The fact that they needn't crane over the decrepit guilders in front of them was merely a bonus.

While William watched the committee gather on the stage, Genevieve picked specks of ash from her gloves. Upon assessing that they were as pristine as could be, she asked, 'why are you entering anyway? It's one thing to come and watch, it's another entirely to compete. Especially when your chances of winning are as slight as a threadsnake.'

William reconsidered going into the detail of his downfall: how work had dried up, how he was desperate to prove that he wasn't a failure – he needn't bother.

'M.K!' A familiar accent picked itself out above the hubbub of the crowd. William turned with a sigh. Somehow, somewhy, the little assassin from the farm cart had found him in the crowd.

'You found your way then?' The little man stomped up, making room for himself between William and Genevieve. Although he barely reached her waist, he was able to give the female assassin a full appraisal.

'Name's Aler Goldin. Goldie to my friends.' He tongued the cleft in his lip and cocked one eyebrow. It was inappropriate but also disarmingly pathetic. 'What a pleasure it is to meet you.'

'Likewise.' Genevieve patted him on the head as she would a child, causing him to balk in utter confusion. It wasn't that he didn't realise she had no interest in him, but that he couldn't fathom as to why. Too much time around ladies of the night often inflated a man's ego like a pig's bladder.

'Not much of a spot you've got here. I can't see bugger all.' Goldin pulled on the cripple's chair and tried to get his foot up on the rear wheel to boost his height. 'Is there anyone on the stage yet?'

'What the devil do you think you're...?' The cripple flailed his arm behind his head to try and alight the intruder, but the movement in the chair only caused it to overbalance further. Goldin, opting to save his own skin, hopped off the chair rather than set down a foot to steady it, and landed comfortably on two feet just as the cripple's chair fell flat onto the mud-soaked carpet.

'You imbecile!' The cripple lashed out with the larger of two shrivelled arms. The hand only sported three fingers, covered in warts, and looked more like a chicken's foot than any human appendage William had seen.

'It's diseased.' Goldin recoiled, nestling his shoulder at the back of William's leg so that he wasn't the first in line should the cripple's claw-like nails be tainted with sickness.

'I'll see you burn for this.' The cripple spat foam, his bulbous head purpling with rage.

Genevieve sank to a low crouch and took one of the handles of the wheelchair. With ease, she lifted the crippled man upright. He was still flustered, but calmed down drastically under Genevieve's sombre gaze. Whether it was because of her striking appearance, or because he knew who she was, it was hard to tell.

'Thank you, miss. Really, you didn't need to.' He took on an apologetic tone, clasping her hand in his chicken-claws.

'Oh, I did.' Genevieve shot a look at William, reminding him that she didn't like it "when cats toyed with mice", but this time added, 'any upstanding assassin would do the same.'

William pursed his lips, taking the dart of unspoken scorn. Though he hadn't actually partaken in the toppling of the cripple, he hadn't stepped in to help for fears similar to those Goldin had espoused. He thought he might have helped had he been the one wearing kid-skin gloves, but a point he wouldn't dare vocalise was moot.

'It eases my shrivelled heart to know that not everyone in our organisation is a self-centred dolt,' the cripple sneered in Goldin's direction.

'You're too kind.' Genevieve smiled. It seemed a little forced to William and he couldn't help but think that she was deceiving the cripple somehow.

'I'm Genevieve.' She offered her hand and the cripple shook it enthusiastically. William wondered if making friends before the competition began was a scheme on the markswoman's part and if he had been caught up in a similar ruse. Now that he thought about it, he was less inclined to shoot her than he would have been before they'd met.

'Genevieve Cholmondeley? I've heard much of your achievements in guild meetings, I'm so glad you've decided to enter. I know it's a little defeatist on my part, but I actually have money on you to win.' The cripple smiled wide and warm, though half of his teeth were missing or somehow misshapen like half-burned candles. 'I'm Dr Barber.'

'You're Dr Barber?' William blurted, suddenly very interested in the man he had dismissed as some plague ridden cripple. 'Why aren't you on the stage?'

'Well, I took a step back from organising things this year. I thought, why not have some fun myself?' The doctor shrugged affably. 'I have too many doppelgangers cluttering up my surgery as it is.'

William ignored the words he didn't understand, too preoccupied and star struck to think of anything other than a hundred questions. 'So, is it true you can bring people back from the dead?'

'Well, it isn't as simple as that.' The doctor cringed as if the rumours of his prowess weren't exactly true. 'There is a certain kind of mountainside orchid that makes quite potent smelling salts and I have been known to work miracles with a scalpel.'

'Yes, but didn't you bring back Man-Butcher Karin?' William's thoughts suddenly pivoted. 'Did you bring back Ojo Azul?'

'Please, the details of my experiments are private – but no I didn't.'

'But you did bring back Man-Butcher Karin?' William pressed, looking around at his new found companions in awe. Somehow, neither Genevieve nor Goldin looked all that impressed with the shrivelled little doctor.

'Please be quiet, I'm trying to watch.' The old woman – who was accompanying the doctor – leered at William.

He looked to the stage just as a man – dressed in the finest silk suit he had ever seen – arrived among the collected committee members. William knew him to be both the richest and most skilled assassin the world had ever known. Lord Beechworth was not only imperial nobility, he was also a founding member of the guild, and the first ever Man-Butcher. Thankfully, William's squeal of delight was covered by the rising cheer of the crowd. Moments later, before William had the chance to collect himself, the mayor appeared at the lectern.

The mayor was just as William had imagined from reading about him. A suit reminiscent of the Garlish style, streaked with dust and ash. Two tufts of black and grey hair that remained resolute on a bald pate. Heavy golden chains of office and robe around his shoulders that made him out as an imperial senator. He wasn't as imposing as the other assassins on the stage, but what he lacked in killing prowess, he made up for in enthusiasm.

'Ladies, gentlemen, elses, and otherwises,' the mayor boomed over the din of the crowd. 'Welcome! To our eighth bi-annual competition, the Man-Butcher Prize!'

In an instant, everything in the bounds of the velvet ropes erupted into raucous celebration. A few pistols clapped bullets to the sky. William was jostled by an over eager neighbour and Dr Barber's chair was almost toppled again. This time, Goldin helped to steady him, which surprised and impressed William in equal measure.

'This year we fight to show our strength,' the mayor continued. 'We fight to show our tenacity, and our adaptability. And much like my old friend Terrowin the Man-Butcher, we fight to show that we are fearless.'

The crowd roused into a furore of appreciation. Somebody amidst the assassins let off an iron flute of gunpowder and coloured streamers launched across the sky. The mayor left his lectern and began to pace from one side of the stage to the other.

'Now, I'm sure most of you are aware, but some of you may not be, so it bears repeating.' The mayor took on a slightly more official tone. 'We on the prize committee have been considering this for many years now.'

The mayor strode past the committee members – now sat in two neatly organised rows of chairs. William tried to pick out the ones he had heard of. He had seen Lord Beechworth already, and the Amarian Swordmistress was obvious from her unusual makeup and fine brocaded silk dress. The others were more difficult to determine from their appearances and looked more akin to money lenders than once-famous killers.

'Every two years this competition is held, and while enjoyable, we lose too many of our best members.' The mayor paused at the edge of the stage. 'So, in an effort to encourage the return of previous champions, and entice more cautious blood, we have tweaked the rules – just a little.'

William pursed his lips.

'Every entrant is to have a sponsor. Someone who is willing, or not so willing, to stake their life for the entrant. Each of you will protect your sponsor and eliminate those of others.' The mayor was building the drama in his voice a now. 'If your sponsor is killed, don't worry, you may still compete for the prize by staking your own life. But, and this is the important bit, you will be allowed to bow out with your honour and life intact should your sponsor perish. Enabling the continuation of fruitful business, and another attempt for the title in future events.'

William gritted his teeth, his lack of sponsor pulling at him now more than ever.

'Now, these new rules do have their detractors, I will be the first to admit. But don't forget, twice the bodies in the competition means twice the carnage, twice the bloodshed, twice the heartbreak, and twice the excitement.' The mayor's voice was back to the almighty boom it had begun with. 'Now get going, signups are open for the rest of the coming week, if you don't have a sponsor, find one sharpish.'

The dome atop the roof of the town hall erupted in a ball of flame; bricks, smoke, and mortar shot out in all directions. The audience screamed and the assassins readied themselves for battle. Some dove to avoid cascading shrapnel. Then a green hue swelled from the detritus. A spume of red and purple and yellow shot into the air with a wicked screech. Lights popped against the clouds and smoke burst in the most vibrant hues. The initial trepidation was washed away with relief and delight as the onlooker's realised the coloured explosions had been planned.

Too concerned with the narrowing window to find his sponsor, William failed to get caught up in the excitement.

'Together, the entrant and their sponsor,' the mayor roared with wicked glee as the fireworks filled the smog choked sky, 'will rip, tear, blast, buck, and bludgeon their way to victory. The Man-Butcher Prize awaits!'

1673

The memory of the journeyman's disposal had been seared into William's brain and revisited a hundred times over. But like a well-trodden path, the memory gradually eroded until it was unrecognisable. After five months with the pawnbroker, cutting up the journeyman's body had stopped crying him to sleep, turning to a mundanity not worth thinking about.

Winter solstice had been and gone without celebration, or even mention, though on that particular night the broker had changed into more formal attire before leaving. William had been left alone in the cellar with his list of chores and a weighted chain dragging at his ankle.

He barely had any time to sleep. During the day he was let off his chain to help in tending the shop. Sweeping floors, wiping counters, and not looking customers directly in the eye were his three main duties. In the evening, he would be returned to the cellar and his weight, to itemise stock and see to any other menial tasks. He had made bread one day, and cut the sores off the old man's feet another.

One afternoon, after he had finished polishing a collection of antique spoons, he found that the door dividing the stock room and the shopfront had been locked. On his knees, he pressed one eye to the keyhole, rewarded with a direct view of the back of the counter. He squirmed, turning this way and that, and at best was granted a glimpse of the pawnbroker's faded smoking jacket.

There were voices coming from the shopfront, and to his surprise he recognised them both: the broker, and the captain of the journeyman apprentice's ship. William hadn't spent much time with anyone aboard except the cook and the young merchant, but the captain's voice had carried into the darkest part of the hold. Uncommonly deep, a bellowed command always poised on the end of a sentence.

'Perry disembarked and was sighted in the district. Give me the truth of it, Basar,' the captain growled, rapping his hand on the glass counter top.

'That may be, captain, but he never arrived.' The broker's voice had a timbre that William had never heard before; sorrowful and apologetic. 'I would love to have told you otherwise, but I waited all night. To be honest, I thought I was waiting for Mr Goodrich himself. Indeed, I couldn't imagine a street thug accosting such an imposing gentleman, so just assumed the artefact hadn't been located yet. His apprentice on the other hand, so *naïve*... I suspect he was easy pickings.'

'Street thugs?' The captain sounded doubtful. It didn't suit him.

'Oh, yes.'

William could practically hear the broker's sick glee breaking through his melancholic warble.

'The place is rife with crime, contrary to what you might have heard, and half the constabulary is owned by organised gangs. Even a man such as myself has protection rates to pay.'

The captain mused for a moment, forestalled. A man used to obedience and honesty in his crew, thwarted by such a lowly creature. 'Well, please, if you hear anything, get in touch.'

'Good day to you.' It was almost possible to hear Basar wringing his hands.

William screwed up his fist and struck the door. He was surprised at the sheer noise of it against the dusty silence of the back room. Then his second hand joined the drumming. Over and over he thumped the wood, desperate for help.

'What's that?' the captain asserted, making himself louder and bigger over the crooked broker.

'Just my dog. It's a big brute.' The broker kicked the door. 'Quiet in there, or I'll bury you in the yard.'

William pounded on the door again, more ferocious and rapid than before.

'That doesn't sound like any dog I've heard.' The captain primed his flintlock. 'I think you should open that door.'

'I wouldn't want it to bite you.' The broker's excuse was weak and everyone knew it.

The counter top squealed as it was lifted and thumped heavily aside. There was a tussle as the captain shoved his way past the old broker; keys rattled in the lock. A gun poked through the gap first, on the off chance the broker had been truthful about the dog.

William stepped back, tears blurring his pale eyes as he stared up at the captain through the swaying curtain of glass beads. He was as brilliant up close as he had been from the far end of the deck. All perfectly organised frogging and gleaming buttons. His hair even maintained a perfect coiffeur having been stowed under his hat all day.

'Is that you, boy?' He looked down at William, confused for a moment, before he realised what his presence here meant; that the journeyman *had* arrived and the broker was lying.

There was a loud clap of gunpowder and blood erupted from the captain's chest. He toppled much like the journeyman had, only this time, onto William. The dead mass pinned him to the floor. He tried to wriggle free, but the captain was too heavy.

With a click the broker locked the main shop door, then calmly turned the sign to "closed" and lowered the blinds. His flintlock was reloaded in the gloom and then his wizened face peered over William.

'I'd normally kill a slave for something like that.' The broker chewed on something unknown in his mouth, in that way that a lot of old men seem to do. 'I still might, but I need a cup of tea first.'

Basar stepped over William into the back room, then disappeared up the staircase.

Unable to move, paralysed from the weight of the dead man and malnourishment, William was trapped. Blood pumped over him until it turned cold and coagulated on his clothes. Fatigue and shock dragged him into sleep, and only then was he taken to the cellar. The broker disposed of the captain alone.

William tried to flee many times after that, but the cellar was deep under the earth and the stairs were steep and slippery. He hadn't the strength to heave the iron ball strapped to his leg any further than the second step. The only person who ever heard his cries for help was the broker one night, having returned to fetch his hat. Ten lashings with the buckle end of a belt promptly stopped any further attempts to escape.

Disobedience had been driven out of William. Even when he saw the calendar, and realised it was his birthday, it didn't encourage him to free himself from the perpetual servitude. He tended the shop silently; planned to bide his time until evening. Then he would rush through his chores to give himself a few hours of rest, and savour his scraps as if they were the finest red velvet cake.

It was almost as if the broker could sense he wanted to keep his head down. He sniped at him over every little thing: a triangle of unswept dust in the crook of a doorframe, an ornament displayed at an angle on the shelf. It was the coin deposited into the wrong compartment of the lockbox that almost bought him another flogging, a punishment William was determined to avoid.

In the late afternoon, the broker made his way groaning and creaking up the stairs to the storerooms above the shop. William had never been allowed up there. So he continued with his work, pricing worthless knick-knacks that were sold as foreign treasure.

By and by, it occurred to William that he was alone; that he was unchained. Such restraints were impractical in the shopfront and unnecessary when the broker's gun was always in reach.

He stepped around a tall display cabinet to stow a wand from Marjore with a pot of other such useless sticks. Wood rattled against the clay pot. Light glimmered from the polished handles. William looked up. Just a few feet away, flanked by grim faced statues and tasselled scarves, was the front door. Unlocked. Three feet of bare wooden boards stretched between his feet and the door. Beyond was the street, and freedom.

Terror clutched him. Terror that he would be out in the world, terror that he would be caught before he got there. For one aching moment, William's heart was silent as he listened to the stillness in the shop. There was nothing, not even the shuffling of the broker's heel or the tap of his cane. William hoped the old man had simply died, perhaps that a vein had burst or that he had spontaneously combusted. Maybe even fallen and broken his... not his neck; that was too quick. Perhaps his ribs, so he could slowly asphyxiate – aware of his inevitable death.

Something shifted upstairs; a box lid. Not dead then, just quiet.

He turned his chin towards the imposing door. It seemed larger than before, more than just dry wood and a thin pane of glass. The blind was up, like an open eyelid. Through it, he could see the beating sun – somehow powerless in the dingy shop – and the faceless blur of people passing by atop high carriages. He could become one of them, unseen and unknown. Or he could run straight into a fresh hell; into the clutches of a more ruthless slaver. He might board a ship and be reunited with his family, but he wasn't so sure that was possible anymore.

His shoulders squared to the door. In his gut he felt this was the right thing to do. Once open, the bell would trill and the broker would know he had fled into the streets. His foot shuffled forwards, a few toes closer to a new life.

There was a scrape of soft leather on wood as the broker returned to the stairs.

The bell swung on its pendulum, knocked by a rare customer. A man stepped inside, stooping his head, even though the lintel was a generous six feet in height. Coffee-rich flesh, glossy black hair oiled and trimmed just so; a man from the south, cased in road-dusted clothes from the north. He let the door swing closed behind him, ringing the bell again. Every movement was precise, fluid yet unhurried, like a prowling cat. A huge and intelligent beast that did not belong in the civilised world.

As the man turned his azure glower upon him, William knew what the spectre of death truly looked like. He didn't balk under scrutiny – strengthened by his time away from coddling parents. This man's arrival had cost him his one chance at freedom. The moment drew between the pair in frigid silence, until finally the southerner dipped his head in passive greeting.

'Mr Basar?' The man called out, shifting his sights to the backroom door. He moved for the counter and William retreated behind it to his stool and the labelling of produce – shrivelled by the weight of his failed escape.

'Won't be a minute,' the broker replied, reaching the foot of the stairs. With a few grunts of exertion he made it through the backroom to the shop, hauling a roll of hessian tied with twine. The hanging beads clattered as he entered. 'Help me, boy.'

William leapt off his stool and took one end of the bundle, lifting it over his head to the countertop.

'I trust you're Mr Azul, you certainly look Conejan.' The broker pulled the frayed end of a string to loosen the first of three knots. 'Here about the artefact?'

'I am, yes.' The blue-eyed man shot another cold glance towards William, forcing him back to his stool in the corner. 'When I heard such a humble place as this had come across something so *unique*, I had to see it for myself. Tell me, how did you get your hands on it?'

'I have a somewhat famous merchant adventurer wrapped around my little finger.' The broker used a yellow stained nail to pull the last of the twine from the wrappings. 'I could tell you who, but you wouldn't believe me.'

The foreign customer smirked, and the broker unravelled the contents from the bundle. Inside was the etched stone sword, the slaver's silver flintlock, a belt buckle, and collection of buttons.

'Forgive me.' The broker swept all of the journeyman's effects to one side. 'I obtained all these things together, haven't had time to sort through everything yet.'

'No matter.' The blue-eyed man leant closer to better look at the carved sword. 'May I touch it?'

'You may, but just bear in mind, if anything's broken you have to pay for the pieces.' The broker made an attempt to accompany his weak humour with a warm smile, but his natural demeanour made it obviously disingenuous.

The customer took up the carving by the hilt as if it was a real sword and not some delicate antique. He even swung it a few times as if it had ever been intended for combat.

'It's not as heavy as it looks.' He jostled it loosely between his forefinger and thumb to get a better feel for it, before setting it back on the counter. The broker rubbed the base of his spine in disagreement. 'How much?'

'Why don't you make me an offer?' Though the broker managed to abstain from his habitual hand ringing, the prospect of receiving vast quantities of gold seemed to set him on edge. His hands flirted together, fingers caressing varicose veins through loose skin.

'I'm not in the business of haggling.' The Conejan turned to look at some of the other items in the shop as if he had completely lost interest in the carved sword. 'Tell me what you want for it, and if I can afford it I'll buy it. If not, I won't.'

The broker clearly didn't like this.

'One-fifty.' A high bid. 'That's gold pieces, not imperial grana mind.'

Mr Azul mulled it over as he strolled the shop, looking across the array of weaponry for sale. After a minute, he picked up what looked like a tapered staff with a notch in each end. Swords, umbrellas, and ivory headed canes rattled around as he removed it from the crowded display barrel.

'Do you have the string for this?' He turned to face the broker.

'I do somewhere.' The broker slid the sword across the counter to the huddle of effects in front of William. He lifted the hinged top and moved to a display in front of the smoky glassed window.

'Throw it in with the sword and you've got yourself a deal.'

William was surprised by the offer. From his time in the shop, he had learned the value of things; in comparison to the sword, even the umbrellas, the bow was practically worthless. For a hundred and fifty gold pieces, the broker would twine a bowstring from his own gizzards – or more likely William's – if it saw the deal done.

Basar pulled the contents out of a pot on the display shelf and scattered them out. A few military badges and some pearlescent beads tumbled to the floor. A bundle of something fibrous was still wedged in the bottom. He reached in with two long, gnarled fingers.

'I knew I had one around here somewhere,' he said triumphantly, stretching out the string and pulling any knots free. 'It's not the finest there is, but it'll see you good.'

The broker coiled the string back up neatly and passed it to Mr Azul, who instantly unfurled it again. It was pulled taut twice to test its strength, producing two tones like that of a dull sitar.

'This should do nicely.'

The broker bobbed his head, and shuffled towards the opening in the counter, eager to confirm the sale in his ledger.

'Holden Goodrich sends a message.' Mr Azul whirled on the heel of his polished black shoe. 'No matter your intentions in the dispatching of his associates, the last deal between the pair of you has been had.'

The warning came just early enough that Basar knew his fate before the bowstring was slipped around his neck and the panic of near-death set in. William had seen it coming, but didn't move to help. He watched as the broker tried to claw the string free with frantic fingers, though it had already pulled too tightly into his flesh. With two flicks of each wrist, Azul wrapped the string more securely around his fists. Basar's legs lost strength and the pair lowered to the floor. He kicked for a time and just as his life was about to slip from his body, the string was released.

Leaving the broker wheezing and drooling on the boards, Mr Azul stood easily and straightened his coat. With feline calm, he approached the counter.

'I'm taking this back for my employer.' He began to rebind the sword in hessian. 'He wanted you to know that he could have you killed at any moment. Compared to him, you have few friends, little coin. Do not dare even mention his name again. It will not take much effort on my part to find you, the guild has eyes everywhere.'

The broker gasped and choked phlegm.

'If I were you, I'd thank the New Fates that Mr Goodrich has a reputation to preserve.' Azul knotted the last bit of frayed string around his sword and bow.

With one hand massaging his throat, Basar subtly reached for his flintlock. The hammer was caught on his belt. He fidgeted and rolled onto his side, fumbling to undo the buckle.

'Oh, it's too late for that Mr Basar.' Azul tightened the second string on the bundle calmly. 'Your boy has different plans for you than my employer.'

The broker's blood-shot eyes drifted to William, who stood atop his stool wielding the silver barrelled flintlock – taken from the journeyman's discarded effects. Basar fought with his belt, whooping panicked breaths, heaving to free his flintlock. The belt slipped a little, trouser fabric tore, and the pistol pulled free.

Azul padded across the room and planted the silver tip of his boot in the broker's ribs. The pistol fired wide, shattering a glass cabinet and splitting a shrunken head. Black sand spilled from the fissure. Not satisfied with a simple rebuke, Azul crushed the broker's jaw under his heel. A collection of Basar's teeth dribbled from broken lips as he recoiled into a whimpering ball.

'Go on then, boy.' Mr Azul knelt over the broker and grabbed a fist of his shirt to prop him up. 'Finish the job.'

William's hand began to tremble, his finger too weak to flex.

'What's your name boy? Mine is Ojo. Tell me, what does this man feed you?'

William was too tense to form words.

'Is it vegetables?'

He nodded.

'What about a little piece of meat; every now and then?'

Another nod.

'Those things you eat, even the plants, they're all living things. You took away their lives, so you could continue your own. It's a simple fact of the world: life feeds on death.' Ojo stood and took a few steps away from the bleeding broker. 'And right now, to continue with your life, you need to take it from this man. He won't continue to feed you once I leave. I daresay he'll reload that gun and shoot you with it.'

William recalled the journeyman, and the captain. Hot and cold blood, unmarked graves. He would not be buried with those men.

'Life feeds on death,' Ojo repeated his mantra.

William squeezed the trigger. The pistol clapped and bucked in his weak hands. A ball of steaming lead careened across the room and punctured the broker's chest. He screamed a spray of blood; another slack tooth slipped free of its sinew.

'Not the best shot I've seen,' Ojo commented. 'Looks like you've punctured his lung. He might survive for a few hours, but no physician in the Silken Coast will have the skills he needs. Death within the next twenty four is inevitable.'

William lowered the flintlock, still quivering, but unable to divert his gaze from the painting of pure dread across the face of the broker. All the pain Basar had put him through was at an end.

'I imagine it's only a matter of time before somebody comes to investigate.' Ojo picked up the hessian bundle and cast a quick glance William's way. 'You should leave.'

William's triumph was short lived. Ojo was right, the heavily bribed town guard would eventually pay a call on the pawnshop, and there was no telling what they'd do to a murderous slave like William. Once more, his chance at freedom was snatched away. Yet through the tumult of exhilaration and panic, one thought rang clear; meeting the Conejan assassin was a chance at a different kind of life all together.

William's mind was made up. No-one told Mr Azul what to do and he wanted to be just the same. He cleared his throat, feeling a crackling pain in his gullet as he worked dormant muscles. He fixed the assassin with glassy eyes and shuddered out his cry for help, 'take me with you?'

'It's not an easy life being a killer.' Ojo turned to go, but even as he did so, a change of heart became evident in his expression. 'But you've obviously got a talent for it, and I could make use of an apprentice.'

PART 2

1671

Mr Ruth wasn't an imposing man. His sallow cheeks, weak chin, and pallid complexion made him appear sickly and pathetic. Vesta would have felt sorry for him, would have taken him for a vagrant, had he not worn the most expensive attire and inspired the most primal fear in her. It wasn't from any might or threats on his part, but the lack thereof. His eyes were like deep wells; dark and cold. So once the deal between him and her father was done, it was a relief to see the back of him.

She had almost completely forgotten him, when a letter – bearing none of the marks of the postal service – arrived in early spring. She was eating brunch with her father when the butler brought in the morning's deliveries. They had been talking about her schooling, and while she took a moment to drink some freshly pressed orange, her father leafed through the envelopes. As the first few beads of sweat began to coalesce on his brow and his cheeks lost their usual rosy lustre, Vesta knew Ruth would return.

'Jane,' Vesta's father called for the help. He knew all their maids by the same name, and somehow they could always tell which one he meant. 'Take Vesta to her rooms.'

The left hand maid bobbed a curtsy from her position near the sideboard. Vesta didn't want to go with her, she wanted to know what was happening and somehow help her father, but his stern expression and refusal to meet her gaze brooked no room for protest. Obediently, she pressed a kiss to his cheek, mentally damning him for folding the letter away as she approached, and allowed herself to be led upstairs.

When her chamber door clicked shut behind her, Vesta attended her dolls as would be expected, arranging their dresses and braiding their fine hair, all the while listening to the house and the street below. It wasn't long until the shrill and insistent doorbell echoed down the landing. She set down Zabal, a culturally insensitive doll her mother gifted before she was taken by the illness.

The small china cup in front of the tanned native figure was filled with imaginary tea, and Vesta kissed its forehead before preparing to leave. She popped the buttons on her white day dress and petticoats, and wriggled out of them. Then, dropping to her belly in lace frilled bloomers and chemise, she crawled beneath her enormous bed to retrieve a pair of her brother's trousers – pilfered and stashed for an occasion such as this. Coupled with her faun spencer, Vesta felt quite dashing in the black trousers, even if the crotch was stuffed with her voluminous bloomers.

She moved to the door, conscious that if she was caught disobeying her father, she might feel his birch switch across her legs. He had disciplined her brother that way many times, but until now she had never been so wilful. She eased the cut-crystal door handle clockwise. The mechanism gave easily, oiled meticulously by one of the Janes. The door opened a crack, scuffing against the lush carpet. She had never much noticed before, but now she was trying to be silent, the sound seemed to carry as clearly as the front bell.

Sliding through the narrow gap, she guided the door back into the frame even more slowly than she'd opened it. She could hear a maid now, three rooms down, wafting the wrinkles from bed sheets and folding them with lavender.

Vesta crept away from the door; off the bare floorboards and onto the eastern carpet that ran the length of the hallway, hoping it would dampen her footsteps. Jane was too busy in her task to notice her hurrying by.

As the corridor opened to the upper landing of the entrance hall, she risked a peek over the wooden handrail. Below the grand

chandelier – stocked with beeswax candles ready for evening – her
father and the butler were discussing in hushed tones. Her father had
the look of a man heading to the gallows. She had seen that once.
Not the hanging of course, that would have been lewd for a refined
young lady, but she had caught sight of a man being led to the square.
From her distance on the first floor, she could see her father had the
same dogged look. She slinked away from her vantage, lest she be
caught spying, and listened to their exchange.

'He awaits you in the study, sir.'

'Yes. Good. Thankyou.' There was a tremble in her father's voice.

'Shall I return with a little tipple, sir?'

'Please.'

The pair parted, and once Vesta heard them leave the hall, she
hurried to the staircase and padded down. She hadn't really
considered where she was going from here; she couldn't likely get
into the study without being seen. Hearing a noise from upstairs she
was compelled forwards. She dashed across the lacquered floor and
skidded to a trio of sofas that had been arranged to form a square
with the carved hearth. She ducked and waited for someone to shout
out; nobody did.

If she could find a way through the kitchens, she could sequester
herself into one of the seldom used service doors that were the
fashion when the place was built. They were designed to conceal the
help, but also allow them to hear when they were being called; she
couldn't think of a better place to eavesdrop.

The butler emerged from the kitchen pushing a trolley topped
with a pristine white cloth, ornate cut glasses, and a matching
decanter. As the door swung shut behind him, she noted the clatter
of pans – the cook had arrived early. Sneaking through the kitchen
wasn't as good an idea as she had thought.

The butler made slow progress while she reconsidered her plan.
She didn't worry about him spotting her; he was old, hard of hearing,
and near blind. A second idea started to form, a little more risky
perhaps, but certainly more direct. Underneath the cloth on the
butler's trolley, there was a shelf of just the right dimensions to
successfully contain a person of Vesta's size. If she could make a

distraction and slither under the cover, that would be the best way into the study. It was decided.

There was little to hand. The small reception table – usually hosting a folded paper or forgotten pamphlet – was frustratingly empty. The pot plants had been removed by the scullery Jane that very morning to be re-potted. The house cat – that she might have riled up and sent the butler's way – was sleeping soundly in a sunbeam at the far side of the room. She cursed under her breath. The man may not have the best eyesight, but she couldn't risk leaving the safety between the sofas, and there was little time remaining.

She looked to the hearth. It was one of the few fires in the house that seldom went out; an insistence of her departed mother. Vesta hoped to toss a poker or ash-brush across the room, but all the implements had been removed for polishing. She damned the god of spring and its edict for cleanliness. The only thing to hand was a small bit of stick that had fallen from the grate. It was maybe two inches round and six long, smouldering a little at one end; a few taps against the hearth-side took care of that. She held it by the uncharred end and weighed it in her hand. Not that heavy; she could toss it without causing too much damage.

The butler had nearly shuffled all the way to the study door; she had to act quickly. Without putting too much thought into it, she hurled the stick in the direction of the front entrance. It landed on the highly lacquered boards with a thump and skimmed to a tall window, slipping under the folds of a heavy curtain. The butler jumped and winced at a twinge in his back, turned towards the door with a scowl, and directed his ear for the sound. He left the trolley to investigate, approaching the likewise disgruntled cat.

Vesta smirked and scuttled for the trolley. The butler had moved all the way to the front door and was peering out to the gardens, grumbling. She lifted one side of the cloth, grateful the shelf was empty, and bundled herself underneath. With a few deft flicks she settled the cloth back into position.

The butler muttered something about stupid children, dismissing the noise as a pebble on the window, or a game of knock-and-run. Aside from Vesta and her brother, he was of the opinion that all children, especially those of the working classes, should be sent to the work houses. Many times he had advocated to Vesta's father that anyone without the intelligence to enjoy an Arabella Flatt operetta should be sterilised, as if an artist could in any way make that happen.

Aged hands clamped onto the trolley and began to push. The difference in weight was considerable, but the wheels, like all moving parts in the house, were well cared for; and the butler seemed to presume that the increased effort required was the result of his recently twisted back. Vesta clamped her hand over her mouth to keep from giggling, the excitement of her infiltration momentarily outweighing the worry for her father.

The cart stopped suddenly. She tensed herself ready for the cloth to be pulled aside. Then the butler knocked on the study door.

'Refreshments for you sir,' he called out in an exceptionally posh accent that was not at all his own.

'Bring them in,' Vesta's father replied through thick mahogany.

The door swung open and Vesta was pushed inside. She closed her eyes and tried to feel the motion to determine where exactly in the study she was being pushed to. A slight right turn behind the armchair, another small swerve to the right; that must have been to avoid the globe.

The trolley slowed before colliding with something hollow and wooden. The drinks cabinet, she was fairly certain. It was empty; any liquor had been moved to the kitchens after her father realised he had a problem with drink. Not that it caused him to consume any less. If anything, it meant that if he wanted a drink, no matter where he was in the house, all he had to do was trill a service bell.

'Thank you so much Leighton.' Her father moved towards the trolley, his leg brushed the draping cloth, almost making contact with Vesta's shoulder. 'Leave us, please. I'll pour.'

'As you wish, sir.' Leighton's shoes shuffled away. The door closed.

'Would you like one?' Vesta's father removed the stopper from the decanter and started to glug the contents into one of the glasses.

'No, thank you.' Mr Ruth had a nasal aspect to his voice that matched his sickly visage. Vesta knew it to be him, even without seeing him. 'But by all means, you help yourself – now, where was I?

'My wife. She goes away, right?' Leather creaked as he made himself comfortable in one of the wing-backed chairs. 'And for once I can do what I want, have a drunken evening with my colleagues. Anyway, I kiss this whore. That's all, just a kiss.'

Vesta heard her father swallow. He poured another dram.

'And I don't know how, but my wife finds out. Comes straight home. You've never seen anything like it; all my things were in the street. But in my house, she's the boss. Now my wings are clipped, I have to accept that; no more nights out. I've stopped drinking altogether – my own decision – so I don't get myself into trouble again.'

'I'm sorry,' Vesta's father interrupted. 'Why exactly are you here? I finished the painting for your associate; is he not happy with it?'

'Of course he is, he loves it.' The carpet shushed Ruth's feet as he stood up. 'My associate, he's a good man for the most part, but like my wife, he's also jealous and over-protective. He wants his portrait to be the only one in our community; unique. So when he heard you've been speaking with some of our *business rivals*, well, he was not very happy at all.'

Vesta couldn't resist anymore, she had to see what was happening. Gently, she lifted the cloth and peered through a gap in the folds. Her father was stood on the other side of the sofa, she could just see his upper half.

'I haven't committed to paint anything yet.'

'Sometimes, a kiss is as bad as a fuck.' There was a clicking sound; she could only see Ruth's back – the tailored jacket and patter of dandruff on the shoulders.

She saw her father's eyes widen. Then the visitor lunged at him, and dragged him out of view. Expensive fabrics tore, men grunted and struggled. Laboured breath whistled through flared nostrils. Her father staggered onto the sofa, but Ruth was atop him in an instant. A knife flashed in his hand. They wrestled, but Ruth had a wiry strength, and soon had her father's hand pinned to the back rest. The blade pressed to his knuckles.

'And sometimes wings must be clipped,' Mr Ruth hissed through a feral grin.

Her father could only look away; at that moment, his gaze met Vesta's.

The knife pressed down, and sharp steel bit deep into flesh and bone. He buried his face into the leather cushion to spare Vesta his anguish; the blood curdling cries betrayed his intentions.

Petrified, tears breaching the dams of her eyelids, she could never have imagined something so horrendous could happen, but as her mother had always said "misery multiplies". A shout came from the hall, muffled at first, but as the call was repeated, Vesta began to make it out.

'Fire!' The butler burst into the study, and paused as his rheumy eyes made sense of the blood. 'What's going on here?'

'Thank you once again for your most excellent painting.' Mr Ruth pushed to his feet, cleaned his knife with a handkerchief produced from his pocket, and made for the door. His footsteps were steady and relaxed as he weaved around the butler and headed out past the glowing blaze.

Vesta's father propped himself up, crimson drool trailed from his lip; in the struggle he had bitten his tongue. He held up his hand and studied it, his face a picture of confusion and shock. Though his thumb and little finger were intact, his first two fingers were gone, and his ring finger – adorned with both his and his late wife's wedding bands – was only held on by a sinew. In a daze, he attempted to straighten it, but only managed to twist off the anchoring spindle of skin. It fell into his cupped palm; he pocketed it.

Vesta emerged from her hiding place and shouted for her father to move. The glow from the hall was brighter by the second and the acrid smell was becoming too hard to bear. He was too numbed to obey. She called to the butler, but he had succumbed to a fit of coughing. Smoke was billowing under the lintel.

With her father delirious, she knew there was only one cure. Her hand clenched and she swung with all her might. Father grunted; the sliver of tongue, that had only been partially severed moments before, slipped from cherry stained lips. She recoiled, caught in indecision, too horrified to know what to do. The fumes caught in her throat.

'Sir?' one of the footmen called from the doorway. He had a torn cloth over his mouth and smoke blackened skin. 'Sir, we need to get out of here.'

It was impossible to tell whether it was the build-up of smoke in her lungs or the relief that somebody had come to help, but Vesta became very dizzy. As she staggered, her father, numbly aware of the danger, reached out to stop her collapsing. His hand grasped without fingers.

Her head cracked against the trolley.

1682

Although the last of the opening ceremony's fireworks had finished and all members of the committee had adjourned inside the town hall, many of the spectators remained in the square. The tourists had turned to food and alcohol, making the periphery a hotbed of noise, music, fighting, and vomiting. While some of the guilders had opted to join the merriment, many stayed within the bounds of the red carpet, mingling with old friends and allies.

Goldin, Genevieve, Dr Barber and the old woman had formed into a little group; each discussing their plans for passing the time over the coming week, and what exactly they would do if they won the prize. William was there too, but he hadn't been paying all that much attention and had lost the flow of the conversation. Instead, he was plotting and panicking in equal measure; concerned for his lack of a sponsor.

Caring little that he was interrupting the old woman mid-sentence, he turned to Genevieve and blurted, 'have you got a sponsor?'

She nodded with a smirk, gauging that *he didn't* with a wicked swiftness; it didn't help his mood.

'What about you?' he asked Dr Barber.

'Oh yes.' The cripple bobbed his head.

'And you?' William snapped the old woman, who was still annoyed about being interrupted. He couldn't believe that he was comparing himself to the decrepit old hag; the thought that even she might have a sponsor where he did not was unbearable.

'No,' she replied, perking his hopes a little. 'I'm Lord Beechworth's sponsor, he's my grandson. I'm ever so pleased he's including me in all this…'

William turned away, ignoring her. His gaze passed across Goldin; he knew the little assassin had a sponsor already – someone he'd kidnapped. He continued in search of anyone in a similar position, sans-sponsor at such a late stage. Finding a tall dopey-looking guilder, he pressed for an answer, 'have you got a sponsor?'

The man's great boulder of a head swung idly in his direction, his eyes bloodshot, high on ether or some spark powder concoction. He looked about as dangerous as he was intoxicated, and though William already regretted speaking to him, he asked again.

'Do you have a sponsor?' He spoke slowly, hoping the response would be positive – that there was some kind of sponsor raffle or market where he might easily acquire one. 'Are you getting a sponsor here? In the town?'

'Come on, lad, we can sort this out,' Goldin tried to interject.

We? We can sort this out?' He scowled down at the little man. 'You're part of the reason I'm in this mess, I could have taken that farmer if you hadn't blown his head off.'

'Me?' The sluggish ape prodded himself in the chest, belatedly acknowledging the question. The finger made a sturdy thump against his barrel chest. William ignored him, his attention solely on Goldin.

'I don't bloody think so.' The little man stomped his feet. 'That farmer would have had your head off if I hadn't intervened. You should be thanking me!'

'Thanking you?' William grabbed a fist of his own shirt and shook the brain-blotched fabric, adding sarcastically, 'Oh yes, thank you very much.'

The big ape of a guilder set one gargantuan hand on William's shoulder, the rough skin catching on his crumpled collar. 'I'll take you as a sponsor.'

'Hang on, you can't do that, I'm a guilder.'

The large hand started to drag William backwards, he reached for his pistol on instinct, then stopped; violence was prohibited before the competition began. He didn't want to save himself only to be taken out by a rooftop sniper. As he staggered backwards, he tried to twist out of the guilder's grip. Underfoot, filthy water and slick mud had bled up through the carpet; he lost his footing.

There was a distant crack. William slapped to the floor. The intoxicated guilder followed moments later with a ground shuddering thump. Breath and blood wheezed out of his neck, burst open by a precise shot. William watched as all the rooftop scopes winked in his direction. He cringed in anticipation of a second bullet. No more came.

He opened his eyes, just in time to catch those of other guilders rolling at his pitiful display.

'Have you calmed down now?' Goldin offered him a hand up. He took it, but the little man could only aid him to his knees; he had to stand under his own steam. 'Do you want my help then? I know Blackbile a damn sight better than most, and that definitely includes you.'

'Sorry about that, and… yes, please.' He patted himself down to little effect. A spatter of blood had been added to the myriad stains on his shirt and the seat of his trousers had been saturated with mud and wet. He looked down at the big guilder that had attacked him, blood was still trickling from his yawning neck. William considered his fate; their positions could have been so easily switched.

'So, the way I see it.' Goldin set his hands on his hips, as unperturbed by the disturbance and death as the rest of the guilders seemed to be. 'You can either kidnap someone, pay someone, or convince some idiot that you're actually going to win this thing. You definitely don't want anybody too willing.'

'Yes…' William was still distracted, though grateful for the assistance. He noticed that their other companions had taken their leave during the commotion – a smart decision. 'Do you know where Genevieve went?'

'What does it matter to you?' Goldin shook his head. 'It's better off that you keep your distance from her, a boy your age.'

He had a distant look in his eyes for a moment, then snapped his fingers.

'I tell you what. I've got an idea for how we can get this all sorted out.' He set off quickly through the press. William could only follow, elbowing people aside to keep up with the little man – far better suited to slinking through crowds. He sent a superstitious prayer skyward that his new found companion would prove an asset rather than a burden.

'You'll thank me for this!' Goldin strode under the velvet rope, William ducked after.

The consistency of the mud had evolved from a thin layer of brown liquid on reasonably solid ground, to a churned paste that seemed almost a foot deep in places. A cross-eyed tourist staggered across William's path, carelessly huffing ether, it was mere seconds before he was face down in the muck – the expensive contents of the glass vial disappearing into an ashy puddle.

A couple of people stopped Goldin to ask for his autograph – impressive as he passed most people at the height of their hip, so didn't get noticed by many. William caught up and stood idly while the assassin finished exchanging compliments with his adoring fans.

'Excuse me.' A Vitulan woman, maybe six years William's elder – with glossy chestnut hair tied in a halo of plaits around her head – tapped on his shoulder. She was pretty, but not enough to erase the lingering thoughts of Genevieve in the back of William's mind. 'Are you an assassin?'

'I…' William faltered, wondering if this was another ploy to embarrass him. 'I am, yes.'

'Thank goodness.' She tucked a wisp of hair behind her ear. 'I was hoping to get a job done, ideally before the event starts; I didn't recognise you, so hoped you might be cheap.'

William let out a long breath through his nose. On balance, this was probably one of the better things he could have hoped for. She wasn't trying to embarrass or mock him, but as a blacklisted assassin he was forbidden from taking contracts. 'I'm sorry, but I'm a little up against it right now, a bit too busy to be taking on jobs.'

'I understand.' She bit her lip and tucked her hands into the pockets stitched to the front of her green linen dress. 'However, if you change your mind, I'm staying at The Brazen Bull. I'm willing to part with fifty silvers if that's anything to you.'

The price was insulting, even to William. Granted, it was more money than he had to his name currently, but killing a man was killing a man, and that demanded bright gold. He liked to think that even if he was allowed to contract, he would still turn her down.

'I'll think about it.' He waved a hand in token thanks and watched as she walked away; he didn't imagine anybody else would be accepting her offer. He turned to find his diminutive guide.

Goldin's fans had left and it seemed that the little man had been watching William's exchange. Something about the way he stood there appraising him with a wry smile implied he had an opinion.

'I just don't have the time.' William scowled.

'Of course you don't.' Goldin didn't sound sarcastic, but William couldn't be entirely sure that his agreement was genuine. 'You don't need that money anyway do you? Fifty silver, that's nothing.'

William became aware of the pouch of coins in his trousers; a pouch so small that it could easily be stowed there and forgotten about. That fifty silver might just tip the odds in his favour when it came to finding a sponsor and – if he could work out the logistics of it – he might even be able to make the target his sponsor.

'I'm not allowed,' he admitted.

'Aren't you?' Goldin shrugged. 'I thought that was for guild contracts. It looked to me that she was approaching *you* and not *the guild*. Which, in my humble opinion, is none of their business.'

William pursed his lips and mulled for a moment, before muttering, 'maybe I'll pay her a visit then.'

'I think that's for the best,' Goldin agreed. 'But she won't be back at The Bull while nightfall. Why don't we examine our options first? There's a place not too far from here where you just might find a sponsor daft enough to be bought with fifty silvers. I'll lead the way.'

'Here we are!' Goldin proclaimed, stepping onto the boardwalk. 'This place'll solve *all* your problems.'

William stopped in the middle of the street, not even bothering to hide his disappointment. He had assumed they were headed to some guild sponsored den of iniquity, or one of the many independent iniquity-dens located about the town. This place looked more like a twee cake shop William might have frequented in Fairshore. Indeed the entire shop front had been painted in pink and white, festooned with window boxes and baskets of artificial flowers; though – given that it still sat in the middle of Blackbile – the walls had been dulled somewhat by dirt and ash. Painted on a sign above the door in exquisite joined-up writing was the name of the establishment: Melting Moments.

'Come on then, time's wasting.' Goldin was positively aglow with excitement.

'I suppose a cup of tea and slice of red-velvet might do me some good.' William sighed, following the little man. 'But straight after, I need to figure out how I'm going to get myself a sponsor.'

'*This* is where you'll get your sponsor.' Goldin turned the channelled brass doorknob – it had been scraped of all its gilding by some opportunistic thief. The heavy door opened to the bouncy melody of a tack piano and the murmur of drunken merriment. They passed into what could only be described as a saloon, filled with the type of men who hadn't the integrity to join something even as morally bankrupt as The Assassins' Guild. Tobacco smoke and the tang of gunpowder hung in a rich cloud that overwhelmed the senses. William finally understood; an independent den of iniquity.

Every hard faced thief, crook, and murderer looked with a sneer to the new arrivals; more pointedly at William. The only ones who didn't were a half-dozen unconscious drunks and the workforce of remarkably stout whores, who were far too busy soliciting their wares.

A shot thumped into the wooden ceiling, spat from a comically-small pistol concealed in one man's sleeve. A clutch of wall-eyed, one-eyed, and toothless patrons cackled and celebrated the minor flinch it had garnered from William. A quick glance up at the peppering of similarly sized holes advised scaring newcomers was a popular pastime.

Goldin continued to the bar. William followed, keeping his wits about him for any further threats. On second glance, at least three of the men he'd taken for unconscious louts were actually dead, pocked with bloody holes. The upstairs hand rail was smashed in more places than it was intact, and somehow, a corpse had ended up on top of the makeshift cartwheel chandelier. The body couldn't be long dead, as the chandelier was still swaying; drawing a figure of eight in blood on the floor.

William wondered if it was wise to have followed Goldin into such hostile territory, especially when the two flintlocks he owned only had the one paper cartridge each. Palpable aggression churned in the smoke haze; he didn't want to be here and the thugs knew it.

'Afternoon, Grim,' Goldin greeted a huge man sat at a table with a yellowing corpse. They each had a flagon of ale, though Grim seemed to be making more progress on his. 'Thinking of running for the prize this year?'

'Thinking about it.' The big man downed dregs and tossed his empty flagon. 'If I can get myself a sponsor.'

Goldin paused and sucked on his protruding tooth thoughtfully. 'What would you say to becoming a sponsor? This fine young lad's a guilder, and he's here looking for a willing volunteer. I like you, so I'll let you have first refusal.'

'Very kind of you.' Grim broke off from talking to Goldin to take up the flagon sat before his festering companion, softly muttering, 'you don't mind me borrowing this, do you?'

He blew the foam off the ale. 'I'll take you up on that offer.'

William was conflicted. After all his failed attempts on the journey here, it had taken Goldin all of five minutes to secure him a sponsor. He wasn't sure whether that was a sad indictment on his own skills or the foolhardy nature of the Blackbile residents. The thought of teaming up with a man whose only companion was a mouldering cadaver didn't fill him to the brim with confidence either.

'I refuse,' Grim snorted.

The instant deflation on William's face encouraged the most outrageous guffaw from the spluttering brute. Ale sloshed on the floor.

'Thanks for that Goldin. First refusal's always best, you get to see the hope drain out.' The big man wiped foam from his chin. 'If it were so easy I'd have a sponsor myself wouldn't I? I've been around and asked, nobody's willing. I'm sure you'll get plenty more refusals before the night is out, I can't imagine you inspire much confidence. You're better off spectating.'

William grimaced. 'Thanks for the advice.'

'Cheer up, boy.' Grim tossed a silver coin. 'Have a drink on me. Lift your spirits a little. You never know, they might be a bit more gullible now they've had some ale.'

William caught the coin. It was nice of the big man to pay for his first drink, but it also meant that he couldn't just turn around and leave the place, which was what he wanted to do. He reluctantly followed Goldin to the bar, wondering exactly what kind of assassin the little man was to be known in a place like this.

'Afternoon, Goldie. Not seen you for a while.' The woman behind the bar winked at William. She was perhaps twice his age, not entirely bad looking, but it was hard to tell under the thick layer of make-up. 'Who's your little friend?'

Though a corset pinched at her waist, she was almost as wide as Grim. She leant forwards on the bar, displaying her plentiful bust.

'This is William.' Goldin clapped him on the back.

'Nice to meet you.' She offered him a lace gloved hand to kiss; he only shook it. Thankfully, she didn't look too put out. 'What'll it be then, boys?'

'The usual, if you please.' The little man clambered up the cross beams on the legs of a high stool and perched at the bar.

She smiled pleasantly, her painted beauty spot lifting on full cheeks. A red sherry was poured into a fluted glass with gold edges; she passed it to Goldin with much eye-fluttering. By way of payment, the little man kissed a silver piece and set it safely in her cleavage.

'And you *William?*' Her lips caressed the syllables of his name, her tongue tasted it like a syrup and pecan slice. Unlike Goldin, who was practically laying across the bar in sultry satisfaction, William wasn't so overpowered by a whore's marketing techniques.

'Whiskey and- Just whiskey, please.' He would have preferred the drink with a touch of orange, but adding anything to hard liquor was considered territory for women. While he could get away with it in some of the finer establishments of the empire, he imagined old prejudices would prevail in a dive like this. The last thing he wanted was to look weak in front of the tavern cutthroats, especially after his earlier flinch.

She poured him a healthy glug and he sat beside Goldin.

'So what brings you to our fine establishment?'

'Well, this lad's looking for a sponsor, and I...' Goldin looked over his shoulder. 'Is Gertrude here?'

'Gertrude? Gertrude?' The barmaid pondered theatrically. 'She goes by Goldie now, having your name on her was putting a few of her clients off. She's in with one of them now. I'm sure once she's finished she'll come and find you.'

'Ah well, that should give us plenty of time to ask-about then.' Goldin swallowed his sherry.

'If it's a sponsor you're looking for, I'd try those two.' The barmaid pointed to two men reclining in a shaded nook. 'They're the only ones Grim didn't ask.'

'Lambs,' Goldin grumbled at the sight of them.

William couldn't imagine the type this pair of men might be if even Goldin didn't like the look of them. To him they looked fairly reasonable: plain linens, trimmed hair, stoic expressions. The only thing he could infer from their quiet drink in the corner was that they might be a little boring, which he supposed – given Goldin's eccentric associates – might be exactly the reason the little man took against them.

'Well, we have to start somewhere.' Goldin grimaced, slapped his thighs, and wriggled off his stool.

'What do you mean by "Lambs"?' William asked in a hushed voice.

'It's some cult,' Goldin replied in a stage whisper, so that William and half the drunken patrons could hear him easily. 'They're all a little unhinged from what I've gathered, probably best if I do the talking.'

They crossed the room together, coming to a stop across the table from the potential sponsors. The two cultists eyed them blankly, saying nothing. William waited for Goldin to introduce them like he said he would, but something had the little man distracted. One of the cultists slurped the head of his beer, the other cracked his knuckles. They didn't scare William – the garish woolly cloaks thrown over the backs of their chairs would be enough to make anyone look soft – but the stretching silence was irksome. He opted to speak first.

'A pleasure to meet you-'

'Goldie!' a woman screeched from the top of the stairs, enlightening William as to what exactly had distracted his little companion in the first place. 'What are you doing here?'

The whole building seemed to shake as she rumbled down the stairs. She was perhaps the biggest of all the whores William had seen to date, which was impressive considering the collection of plump women plying their wares in Melting Moments. She bounded to Goldin and scooped him up in her arms, nearly suffocating him in a cleavage so expansive even the whalebone stays protested.

'Gertrude!' Came the muffled shout from Goldin. As he was released, white powder blotched his face. 'It's good to see you again.'

'Why don't we go upstairs?' She set him back on the floor. Goldin looked at William, silently begging for permission to indulge in such a sumptuous treat.

'You can handle yourself, can't you lad?' The little man was already leaving.

'I'll be alright.' He waved Goldin off confidently, then turned to the two cultists, who were already looking distinctly less impressed than they had been when he first arrived. 'Afternoon, gentlemen.'

He indicated to the vacant seat at their table. 'May I sit here? I have a little business proposition for you.'

The one who had cracked his knuckles nodded slowly.

'William, William!' Goldin shouted from the top of the staircase. Somehow, in the time it had taken to walk from the table to the upstairs balcony, he had found a bottle of sherry and waved it to get William's attention. 'Look at this!'

He lifted the frilly dress of the portly whore beside him, exposing two vast and pasty buttocks that looked remarkably like sacks of grain. In the centre of the left hand cheek, comparatively small given the size of the canvas it had been singed onto, was Goldin's name and the crude drawing of a smiling face.

'What do you think of that then?' The little man beamed triumphantly over the clientele.

William's expression was more akin to a grimace than any kind of smile. While he was impressed with his companion's enthusiasm, he was equally aware that the cultists were not. He watched with pursed lips as Goldin slapped the whore's rump and proceeded to chase her giggling into one of the many bed chambers. Laughter faded and the cultist's corner seemed to draw particularly quiet. William turned hesitantly to the men he would have as sponsor.

'So, about the competition…'

1673

Vesta watched her father paint; saw his brush quiver, noticed flecks of wrong-colour spattering the bucolic scene. It was, in part, down to his missing fingers, but was also influenced by his building dependence. Alcohol had become a necessity. It wasn't a daily tipple, it wasn't even a want. The broken old man needed the acrid liquid to function.

The current canvas was his last. There had been three, but one had been skewered with a fist, and the other had been tossed out the window. The latter had narrowly missed an old man before shattering on the cobbles. In Vesta's occasional dark moments, she wished that the old man had been struck and possibly killed. Her father would have been taken away to a prison or work camp, and the majority of her problems would have been solved. Instead, she was trapped here, her father dependant on her, and she on her brother. She wasn't sure it was possible to live in a waking hell, but it certainly felt like a damning purgatory.

Her father was struggling with a particularly awkward spear of evergreen foliage, weighed with glistening snow. He was trying his best to ignore the devastation his trembling hands were wreaking to the surrounding foliage, but the irritation was swelling in him. A few attempts prior, Vesta had considered the landscape rather good, but it wasn't perfect; her father had pressed on, making the thing ever worse with his efforts.

As he glanced about, making sure she wasn't observing his failure from across the room, Vesta looked down at her book. She had been trying to read it all day in an effort to saturate her mind in history – to forget the world and lose herself in the woes of others for just a little while. But the words on the page failed to grab her. Father's ineptitude was as distracting as it was frustrating. Though she made a concerted effort to read, she might have gone over the same sentence ten times. There was little point in it.

She pushed herself up from the little table, rocking it on its mismatched legs. Her feet were bare against the coarse boards and barely made a sound as she crossed the room that served as their kitchen, scullery, dining room, lounge, study, and bathroom. The latter service was at least concealed behind a set of faded screens. In the opposite corner, a large pail of well water was hidden under a console table, while a more manageable jug rested on the badly varnished top.

Back in Vitale, one of the Janes would have brought her fruit cordials and tea. Now, her brother would draw the first bucket of water in the morning to wash before work, and she would haul the rest as was required throughout the day. Father never touched it, opting – from what she could tell – to subsist entirely on spirits.

Careful not to waste a drop, she poured a measure into an earthenware mug. The thought of dashing the contents into her father's face provided a little quiet levity, of course she would never do it. As she set the jug back on the table she found herself wishing, not for the first time, that tonight would be the last she would have to put him to bed. Surely the tremors would worsen soon. If only they would just take him.

She swallowed that dark hope with a mouthful of cool water, and paced to the window. Her brother would be home soon and she liked to watch for him.

Their two rooms were situated in perhaps the tallest building she had ever entered; the street was some five floors below her. It would have been quite impressive had the "affordable housing" been anything but a towering brick and soot slum of desperation, crime, and violence.

Two years would be adequate penance. Two years and she would be allowed to leave. It was a comforting thought, though she doubted she would abandon her father even then.

For a few minutes she watched the small comings and goings in the muddied streets far below. Unlike the more civilised parts of town, when the collection of faeces was reserved for the dead of night, the soil cart often came through at noon. One such eye-and-nostril sore was parked directly below. She opened the window, thankfully high enough to avoid the worst of the stench, and peered over the sill.

Two strapping lads were hauling human waste in great casks from the moat that collected around the building. A benefit of living on the top floor, she supposed; one hadn't to worry about defecation from above while attending to one's own business. Halfway down the building a window opened and a rump was set on the sill. Some people saved their waste in urns to toss down at the soil collectors for a cheap laugh. Others – like this gentleman – preferred to do the job right.

Vesta chuckled at the disgusted cries from the soil men as they were spattered with wet and warm waste. It was cruel to laugh, but it was one of the only things that made her feel like she hadn't the worst lot. There was nothing better for one's self esteem than dampening someone else's.

Across the street, she noticed the familiar figure of her brother, prominent over the malnourished locals. Though he was named after a Gael saint, Aiden couldn't look more of a Vitulan senator; slim, with short hair, a straight back, and rich olive skin. He would have joined the military if it hadn't been for the house burning down and might have carried them to an even loftier station.

It wasn't worth thinking about now, that avenue was well and truly closed. Once their father lost himself to drink, it was clear Aiden couldn't leave them. His wages were the only reason they still lived; he paid for the two poor rooms in the slum, and kept them fed, watered, and – in father's case – plied with alcohol.

He walked with another man, sharing an intense conversation. That was certainly unusual. She had never seen any work colleagues, and couldn't possibly expect any of their old friends to come calling considering their vast reduction. The pair walked until they were almost level with the entrance of the building, then ducked into an alleyway. They talked for a few more minutes, then traded two small packages.

Vesta's stomach somersaulted. She wasn't a fool, and knew they could only hold one thing: opiate paste. She shut the window. Bile rose in her throat; not brought on by the stench of faeces, but the realisation that they were no longer above the fetid locals. Their long fall from grace had finally landed them square in the pits of society. She wanted to cry. For the mother and father she used to have. For the brother who could have lived a good and honourable life. She didn't like to admit it, but most of all, she mourned their loss of wealth. Life ahead had turned from one of comfort and luxury, to one of hunger and strife.

She returned to her chair and her book.

Opening the dusty tome to her previous page, she was confronted by the envelope she had used for a mark. Neatly folded, addressed in the finest script with Vitale postal marks stamped in red ink, was an invitation to Adelaide Bennet's Finishing School. She had been offered the placement in light of her familial tragedies, and while she had initially ignored the offer, the reality of life should she refuse was becoming painfully apparent.

She turned the expensive paper over in her fingers, careful not to upset the particular folds. She reconsidered the offer. Her brother would have one less mouth to feed, and maybe once graduated she would be more capable of paying him back in kind. If educated, there was a slim hope she could endure a convenient marriage, which was certainly better than slum life.

'Evening.' Aiden tramped through the door – Vesta had been daydreaming on school far longer than she realised. His shoulders were sloped, his eyes dull and lacking their usual life; not quite the picture she had convinced herself from a distance. Perhaps her appraisal of him was only a projection of her dour mood.

He set a full bottle of liquor beside their father, and hesitated. It was the convenient pause she required to hide her letter.

'I haven't managed to get us anything to eat.' He sounded guilty, but forced a smile as he met her gaze.

'I'm out tonight; working.' He sat next to her. 'I'll bring extra food in the morning; there's a nice baker in the market. I might barter something good, we could celebrate with a cinnamon roll... or something like that.'

He never was a very good liar; even if Vesta hadn't seen his illicit transaction, she would have known something was wrong anyway –

at least, she liked to think she would. She smiled softly, said nothing to the contrary, and squeezed his fingers affectionately.

'I've got a new job helping out the soil men near the harbour. I'll be working through the night from now on.' His smile faltered and he worried his bottom lip.

Vesta nodded her head, and wondered if she really had the guts to leave him to bear the burden of their father alone.

'Anyway, I just came up to give father his drink.' He stood and tussled her hair, adding, 'sorry; sorry for all of this.'

After months of consideration, Vesta finally tore up the invitation to the boarding school. She watched each scrap burn in the parlour hearth, glad she had come to terms with their very different life.

By degrees, their fortunes had improved from the absolutely hellish slum, to a tolerably sinister abode with a veneer of middle class aspiration. Her brother's drug dealing – and other night time work she didn't concern herself with – had enabled them to rent a modest terraced house on the fringes of the industrial district.

Set back two paces from the road, behind a low brick wall and rusted iron railing, the front door opened into a narrow hallway. It allowed access to a small sitting room, a slightly larger kitchen with space for a rectangular table, and – up a narrow staircase – two bedrooms with a modest window over the street. Vesta and Aiden shared the one room, but his nocturnal employment meant they used it on different schedules. The latrine was at the end of a small courtyard and only shared with one other household.

Though their new home was not exactly what she would call comfortable, she reminded herself that all things could be possible in time. Her place was with her family, and her brother's work was a necessary evil to keep them from the gutter.

On reflection, one of the most heartening improvements, had been the adjustment in her father's mood. There was less pressure on him to paint for their keep, so he made a hobby of it, shrugging off his mistakes and keeping his temper well under control. He was still addicted to the alcohol, but managed it in a more gentlemanly fashion. Most afternoons, he left the house in his good suit to drink in a tavern with new found friends. It didn't matter that they were also alcoholics of varying degrees of functionality.

When they moved away from the slum, Vesta packed up her school books for good. In the first weeks, as they were still unable to employ a maid, she had dusted and scrubbed every inch of the house. She'd painted walls, and stained the woodwork, waxed the floors, and even persuaded her brother to hang new paper in the sitting room.

As time passed, she fell into a routine, and though actively seeking gainful employment, she couldn't seem to shake the bad influence from her brother. Twice a week she would go to the market to keep their larder full, and if she didn't come back with at least one item that hadn't been paid for, she wasn't happy. Though she didn't intend to continue stealing bread and buttons from street-traders, it was an excellent training ground for her sleight of hand and distraction techniques. Crime could really pay dividends, a truth her brother had opened her eyes to.

As the last of the boarding school invitation fizzled away to ash, Vesta withdrew to the kitchen.

Today, she had managed to steal a bag of sugar from a stall and half a pound of dried fruits from an old lady's sack. She would bake a cake for the family. Not something she had ever done before, but it couldn't be too difficult, and she had pilfered a cook book for just this occasion.

'Vesta.' It was her father. He emerged from his studio-come-bedroom, dressed and ready to go out. 'I'm going to the Harp and Flute for a few hours. If you're asleep when I get back, I'll try to be quiet.'

'Love you, father.' She was creaming the butter and sugar. 'Don't be too late.'

Though she already knew he wouldn't be back any time before dark. It would at least give her the opportunity to finish the cake intended for their family meal the following day, provided she hid it well enough from his drunken hunger. In a high cupboard would be best. Before she retired to bed, she would leave out a heel of bread and piece of cheese to sate him.

The rest of the afternoon was spent baking and reading. Just as the sun started to turn orange in the sky, she pulled the cake from the stove, and set it on the counter to cool. Her brother woke as it went dark, and she hurried into the larder to retrieve the stew prepared the evening before. She would warm it through and serve it with buttered bread.

As Vesta returned to the kitchen, her brother was looming over the steaming cake.

'It's hot,' she warned him deliberately too late. His scalded fingers pulled away sharply and he stuffed them in his mouth to quell the ache. She smiled with superiority. 'I told you.'

He shrugged and moved to the other side of the kitchen, then garbled something unintelligible around his fingers.

'What?' She hefted the pot onto the stove top.

'Is that cake for our visitor?' he asked again, removing his fingers from his mouth and clamping them under his armpit.

'Visitor?' Her eyebrows furrowed.

'I thought I told you this morning.' He returned not-so-subtly to the cake. This time, he was armed with a knife to extract himself a slice that would cool a little quicker. 'I've been doing quite well of late. My boss's boss is paying a visit before I head out tonight. This cake and a pot of tea should do nicely. Might be better if you save the stew until after he's gone. We don't want the place stinking.'

Vesta fixed him with her best withering look, but he didn't seem to care, he was entirely wrapped up in the incredibly important task of blowing the curls of steam from his cake slice. She sighed, and hefted the pot back into her arms, this time swaddled in a small towel to keep it from burning her.

She definitely wouldn't be putting up with any of this once she got a job. They would all have to pitch in with the house work; she couldn't be expected to do everything.

With the stew successfully stored, she collected another pan and sprig of lemon leaves to make a fresh tea to go with the cake.

There was a knock at the door.

'Hurry up. Get the tea on.' Aiden tried to neaten his bed hair then pulled a leaf off the sprig to chew the stench of his breath away. 'I need to make a good impression.'

'Go and get the door,' she said dismissively.

She set the pan on the stove and filled it from a pail of water, then tossed in what remained of the sprig. To think, she used to have a host of servants to make tea, and at least twenty flavours to pick from.

Her brother moved into the little hallway and opened the front door with a click. He traded a few muffled greetings with his superior, but it was hard for Vesta to make out. She imagined Aiden might be divesting the man of his hat and coat, and hurried a wooden spoon around the pot, trying to brew the tea a little quicker.

'Please, call me Eldridge.' The visitor's voice came a little clearer as they neared the kitchen. It had a certain nasal familiarity to it; a shiver ran the full length of Vesta's spine. Without even turning around, she knew who it was. 'It's a pleasure to finally meet you, Aiden.'

'Please, come in.' Footsteps padded on the rug and the hallway door closed. Vesta kept stirring the tea. Then her brother said exactly what she had hoped he wouldn't. 'This is my sister, Vesta.'

She turned hesitantly and her eyes fell on the face she had last seen when her father lost his fingers.

'A pleasure to meet you.' The nasal crook approached her with his hand outstretched. Her eyes darted to the kitchen knife her brother had sliced the cake with. It was good, sharp steel; and it would be oh-so-easy to plunge it into his gut. But there was something about the curl at the edge of Eldridge Ruth's lips and the warmth in his eyes; he didn't recognise her.

'Likewise.' She bobbed a little curtsy, forgoing the handshake. 'I've made lemon tea and fruit cake; I *do* hope it's to your liking.'

'Oh, that sounds wonderful; and such delightful manners. A rarity in ladies of your tender age.' He beamed in the presence of her educated and refined acknowledgement. 'Your brother and I need to talk a little business; I do hope you can forgive our brief meeting?'

'Yes, of course.' Vesta racked her mind for any poison she could put in his tea at short notice, obviously she had nothing, unless he had an allergy to staveroot. It wasn't worth it just to unsettle his stomach. So, she had to play the obedient servant and sister, then when she had the chance, stove his head in. 'I'll serve tea directly.'

1682

The two cultists stared silently.

'So…' William sipped his whiskey, letting the fiery liquor trickle over his tongue before swallowing. 'I'm an assassin, not here for either of you mind. I'm in town to run for the Man-Butcher Prize. The only problem is: I don't have a sponsor yet.'

The two men shared a look, conferring in an unspoken code. William really hoped that they weren't weighing up whether or not to shoot him. If one bullet was fired in anger in a place like this, he could see the whole saloon erupting into a furious brawl.

'I was wondering…' He twiddled his thumbs. 'If either of you two gentlemen wanted the honour, or knew anyone who would be willing to become my sponsor?'

The mute conversation came to a head. The right-hand man broke their silence, asking calmly, 'how long have you been a guilder?'

He had high cheekbones, which somehow made him look like he was the superior of the two, and a little scar just beneath his left eye. He kept a blank expression at all times, and when he moved for his drink William couldn't help but notice the muscles beneath his thin shirt. There was certainly more to this cult than singing and flagellating.

'Since I was eight,' he said proudly, tugging his sleeve up to show the well-worn guild brand. 'Trained by Ojo Azul himself.'

The cultist's face softened as much as his angular cheekbones would allow.

'What do you go by? Might we have heard of you?' the second cultist questioned. Stout, with a tightly curled beard, he seemed to have taken his title of Lamb to heart. 'Do you have a proven track record? We wouldn't want to back a beginner.'

William's smile faltered. He was experienced, but his success rate of late wasn't exactly glowing. This was where it all fell apart.

'My name's William. I don't need a flashy alias, I just let the quality of my work speak for itself.' He leant forwards on his elbows. 'You remember the Masquerade Killer; that high profile botch-job in Fairshore? The one where the mayor was killed by mistake.'

The cultists nodded. It had been plastered across most of the imperial gutter-press tabloids, coinciding beautifully with an otherwise slow news week.

'I was the one who killed him.' William pulled his thumb across his throat. 'I'd have done it even without the Fairshore revenge purse; can't have an assassin bringing our kind into such disrepute. Don't let my appearance fool you, I'll take out anyone. Other assassins; men, women, it doesn't bother me. Mark my words, I'm going to win the prize this year.'

William was glad he had mastered the art of bullshitting years ago. The words tripped off his tongue far more glibly than the shameful truth.

'Well. You do sound confident at least.' The high-cheekboned cultist had a little smile across his face now. William couldn't believe that they might actually take him up on his offer. 'You're painting yourself as quite the hitman; you can't be entirely perfect, surely?'

'No, obviously.' William racked his mind for a believable untruth. 'I'd have to say, I have the tendency to work too hard. I spend all my time moving from job to job and never really leave any time for myself. In a way, I'm just *too* dedicated.'

Even William could tell that was too much.

'It must be a lonely life, being an assassin.' The stout one finished the last dregs of his beer, his otherwise stoic features now maudlin.

'Tell me, are you a religious man?' Cheekbones asked, scraping his small scar with a fingernail.

'I never really looked into it.'

'We can help you with a sponsor.' Cheekbones reclined and flicked whatever dead skin he had managed to collect under his nail. 'But we have conditions; are you interested to hear them?'

'Yes,' William answered a little too enthusiastically.

'A few of our members are in the running for the prize already, our leader is keen to raise our profile, you see? And a win for our cause would do nicely.' He ran his finger across the table top, underlining his plans. 'All our assassins and sponsors can work together, there's nothing in the rules against it. When our men are the only ones left, the sponsors will gladly give their lives for the Cause, *and we will have our winner.*'

He drew out that last part, savouring it.

'It would only increase our chances if we had a pairing with a proven guilder. We have more than enough members willing to act as sponsor for a fellow Lamb. What do you say?'

William bit his lip. He'd pretended to be a choir boy for a job once, even attended a lecture on The New Gods to get close to a target. But he had never joined a cult before.

'What exactly does it entail?'

'There's a simple initiation ceremony.' Cheekbones had become positively friendly now. 'And you'll need to pay a tithe of sixty one silvers; then you'll be a fully-fledged Sacrificial Lamb.'

'Now, I know what you're thinking,' the stout cultist interrupted before William could speak. 'Being a Sacrificial Lamb does not mean that you're going to be sacrificed. Check any dictionary, sacrificial just means relating to sacrifice. You won't be killed necessarily, you're just as likely to be the one doing the killing. Does that make sense?'

'I suppose so.' William was still focused on the tithe he couldn't afford. It was a sure fire way to get not only a sponsor, but a bit of illicit cooperation. Several teams working as one had a far better chance to succeed. Then he only had to kill the other sponsors, who would be more than willing to take an early death, and he would be named Man-Butcher.

'We'd be happy to have you as part of the team.' Cheekbones offered a hand to shake. 'How about it?'

'Count me in.' William took the cultist's hand to seal the deal. 'I'll just need to get the tithe together.'

'Excellent.' The stout cultist stood and fixed William with a friendly grin. 'Another drink, *brother?*'

'Oh, yes please.' William rubbed his hands together. The oppressive atmosphere in the saloon had gone, and everything seemed to be turning for the best. It was good to be a part of a family again.

'We'll have the ceremony in two days, you can bring the tithe with you then.' Cheekbones was slightly more officious than his counterpart, though allowed himself the thinnest slice of a proud grin. 'You've seen that impressive chapel on the hill? That's ours. You'll be baptized there. I pray you look forward to it; it's a once in a lifetime opportunity.'

William patted his hands merrily on the flanks of his trousers. He didn't need Goldin or anybody else to guide him. He was an experienced killer and had easily negotiated the perfect deal on his first attempt. Now all he had to do was accrue the funds. That woman's low-priced hit job should do it. Fifty silver she'd said, and two days would be ample time to kill off any idiot she might have cause to tangle with.

Blackbile was an entirely different place at dusk. The ash that hung in the air during the day had settled to form a barrier over the churned mud, making it easier to get from place to place. Street lamps burned with an inviting orange hue, though the carnival atmosphere of the impending competition was subdued. Many of the tourists had retired to their accommodation for fear of increased crime rates through the night. Others were collected in and around the numerous taverns that seemed to appear in every fifth building. As such, the boardwalks had become impassable, so William had to trudge in the road.

He walked with his hands in his pockets to keep the chill wind at bay. He was headed to The Brazen Bull, a tavern on the outskirts of town, where he hoped to secure a private contract, and maybe cheap accommodation for the week. Goldin had opted to remain at Melting Moments, a place William wasn't too keen on returning to, so they had said their goodbyes for the time being.

A carriage thundered past at an alarming pace, making minimal effort to avoid him. Mud flecked his trousers and a lantern hanging from the siding clipped his arm. He spat a curse at the painful shock of it, and reached for his pistol. Taking his aim on the whorled decal on the back of the carriage, he assessed it to be owned by a fellow guilder. Black and gold filigree patterns adorned it in a tasteless show of wealth and the smell of incense trailed in its wake. It stung his nostrils with its potency, even from such a brief passing.

He had hoped to fire a shot into the cab, but it was against guild rules to kill another assassin before the competition. He could at least take out the driver to inconvenience the guilder – and it had been the driver's own carelessness that had clipped him. By the time he had reasoned himself into taking a shot, the cart was too far away; pulling the trigger would only waste what little ammunition he had. He cursed again and kicked a clod of mud.

Thanks to the theft of his paltry belongings as he'd entered the town, he only had the two shots loaded in his pistols. Though he would only need one, it was best to save them both for his upcoming job. Especially considering his current run of luck. He tucked the pistol beneath his belt and continued for the tavern.

As he walked a little further, he became aware of the cold wind on his arm. Blood came away with his fingers when he touched the affected area. He cursed the inconsiderate coachman and stomped to the side of the road. The edge of town was quieter than the centre, but there were still too many people passing for him to sit on the boardwalk.

In between two shops was an alleyway lit with small lanterns; a freshly painted sign indicated the presence of a taproom therein. Two people came out that hadn't been roughed up or robbed, so he felt safe enough to enter.

Coming out of the other side, he found himself in a cobbled square. Squashed behind the shops was an edifice of wood and plaster spanning several floors. It looked to be undergoing some kind of renovation with bamboo scaffolding strapped to two of its three visible sides. He could see people upstairs through the open walls, drinking and laughing. Tourists by the look of them. It was one of the many venues where people would come to watch the carnage from a relatively safe vantage. Tonight it was just serving as a tavern.

Inside, he could at least get himself a drink and clean up his arm before continuing to The Brazen Bull. He didn't want a possible patron to see him bleed, it spoiled the illusion that he was somehow better than a mere civilian. It might even cause her to lower her offered price.

A rifle toting guard eyed William's pistols and grunted permission to enter, perhaps recognising him as a guilder. Within, a vast collection of mismatched chairs were occupied by lively tourists and deathly locals. Passing by one such catatonic reprobate, William slipped a dark jacket from the rear of his chair. Once he had stemmed the steady trickle of blood, he could easily hide it under a thick woollen sleeve.

Finding no bar on the ground floor, he continued up a crooked staircase. Lanterns with stained velum panels – that cast colourful streaks up the cracked walls – cluttered every hook and nail in the first floor tap-room. The space was crowded, but the queue for the bar was mercifully short; most had already lost themselves to an ale or ether haze. He ordered a dram of whiskey and a shot of clear spirit, the latter was for his arm to prevent any rot catching in the wound. The former was for courage, should the cut oblige a stitch or two. He continued upstairs, in search of a quiet corner.

The top floor was open, lacking any roof and the majority of its original walls; balconies constructed on the bamboo scaffolding expanded the space. A few tourists leant on the fencing, too busy enjoying the dour vista to pay William any mind.

He found a quiet spot with a decent view of the chapel and sat with his legs over the edge. Under the clear light of the moon, he could see that his newly acquired jacket was not as dark or assassin-like as he had first thought, but a rather jaunty blue. Not at all adhesive when it came to sticking to the shadows.

He peeled up the sleeve of his shirt. The wound was shallow and had almost stopped bleeding. It wouldn't need stitching, but in a place as filthy as this – and a wearing a shirt so tarnished with old viscera – it wouldn't do to be careless. He dipped his fingers in the clear spirit and rubbed them over the long cut. When he was satisfied the wound wouldn't sour, he drank the dregs and started on his whiskey.

There was a low rumble under the earth and the scaffolding shook against the side of the crumbled fort. A spume of ash belched from the mouth of the volcano. It would still be some time before the dark cloud and sulphurous stench fell upon the town, and it would probably make for another gloomy day tomorrow. For now at least, the air was clear and breathable.

He sipped his whiskey and traced the roads. The main thoroughfares would be easy to memorise, there were only a few that spanned the whole length of the town. The maze of back alleys was another story. Amongst the crooked spires, lean-tos, and high vaulted slate roofs, it was impossible to tell where one road blended into another. They were the key to this whole competition; being able to dissolve into the side streets and reappear wherever could pay dividends for anyone capable.

He became aware of a presence at his back. An ill-advised tourist with no sense of personal space, or another guilder ready to pester him. Either way, it deserved the withering sigh he let out as he turned.

'Fancy seeing you here.' The presence behind closed the gap and sat beside him. 'I thought you'd be busy with your *preparations.*'

It was the woman with the assassination contract. She cupped her mug of beer in both hands and looked out across the town. William opened his mouth to speak, but couldn't for a moment, too conscious of his bloodied arm. He saw her glance at it, perhaps even noticed her assessment of him change. This was exactly what he didn't want to happen, but it would look too strange if he threw on his jacket now. The damage had been done.

'This is part of it.' His eyes followed the length of a middling sized road. 'I have to plan; know the layout I'll be fighting in.'

He found a road that led directly to the market from the main square. That might be a good way to head once the competition started. The route was easy enough to remember and he could keep his ammunition stock filled from the marketeers' stores. He changed his mind; it was too obvious, he wouldn't want to be amongst the main thrust of competitors. It would be too easy to get accosted from behind.

'I see.' She sipped her beer. 'So, sitting up here with a stiff drink is just one of the perks of the job?'

'Exactly.'

'I'm Vesta.' She smiled, causing a little wrinkle on her nose.

'William,' he replied with similar enthusiasm. Despite seeking a contract for someone's life, she was still the most innocent person he had spoken to in days, and that was nice. He actually found himself relaxing a little more in her company than when he had sat alone.

'I asked a couple of other people if they'd be willing to take my job. I hope you don't mind. You did refuse after all.' She pursed her lips and pulled her dark green cloak tighter. 'They were all about as interested as you. Still, there's plenty more guilders to ask; unless you've reconsidered?'

'I've thought about it.' He kicked his legs idly to keep the wind from taking their warmth. 'My day's preparations for the prize have gone better than expected, so I might have some time to spare for a job; I'd need paying upfront.'

'Do you presume me that stupid?' She adjusted the plait that skirted the side of her head and squinted against the breeze. 'I'm not giving up my silver for a job that hasn't been completed. Not in a place like this. For all I know, you'll take it and that'll be the last I ever see of you.'

'I'm not normally this honest with a client.' William looked across at her; she was still focused towards the upper edge of town. 'But I need that money for something important.'

'Well, you'd better take the job and kill the target before then, because I'm not parting with a bronze bit until the deed is done.' Her dark eyes were stern and cold despite being glassy from the harsh wind.

William downed the last of his drink.

'Fine. Tell me about your target.' He gave in. She had the lion's share of the bargaining power in this situation. In a town full of guilders, anyone intending to take out a contract was definitely in a buyer's market. Still, he had to play a little hard to get. 'If the job's worth my while, we can come back to terms.'

One of her cupped hands released from her mug and extended towards the town. 'Do you see that building there?'

William followed the path her finger made, to a spot on the hill where only one building stood prominent. His heart, which had once been buoyed by the fortuitous meeting, sank like a corpse weighed with stone. He uttered its name, 'The Chapel of the Lambs.'

'Yes.' Vesta's finger curled back. 'There's a man in there, I don't know the name he goes by, but he should be easy enough to find. He is the leader of this Flock, and his face is scalded.'

William's mind began to run through the possible outcomes for the predicament in which he found himself. If he was better at remaining unseen, there might have been the possibility he could have killed the scalded man and still joined the Lambs. But as it was, he couldn't rely on himself to get the job done in secret, and he couldn't just take the money and forget about the job; she was too wise for that. Perhaps if he told the Lambs about Vesta's bounty on their leader, they might waive the joining fee, should he kill her instead.

His options all seemed so against the principals of the guild, but he had already been blacklisted, and this job was his own. Their rules of conduct no longer applied to him. He could just as easily surrender her to the cult and reap all the rewards. There was one major sticking point; his conscience tugged at him ever so harshly for even considering it. And more reasonably, he wouldn't likely earn his way onto the whitelist with forbidden tactics. If he was doing this, he had to stand by his patron, and do it right.

'Well,' he started speaking before he had fully straightened everything out in his head, 'I can take the job, but you'll need to trust me, and I need the silver first.'

Vesta shook her head and started to stand.

'Wait.' William put his hand on her shoulder. 'Just listen to what I have to say; I'm not out to con you.'

'Two minutes.'

'The best way into that chapel is through the front door.' He pulled his legs up from the cold abyss and crossed them beneath him as he shuffled around to face her. 'If I can pay their tithe and become a member, I will have every opportunity to kill this scalded man. But I need the money to do that. Your money. Upfront.'

'What's in it for you then?' She seemed somewhat interested in the prospect now. 'You want to spend your fee and come out at the end with nothing?'

'Well…' William wondered exactly how much truth to let slip. 'I've heard the Lambs are going to work together in the competition; if I'm part of their ranks, my chances increase significantly. I'll make the assassination look like an accident, nobody will be any the wiser, and I get the support I need.'

'Do you have much experience with that?' she probed, doubtfully.

'I like to think improvisation is one of my strong points.' A little honesty wouldn't do any harm. 'And, given your pitiful fee, I'm the only person you can afford.'

'You can have your tithe.' She offered her hand to shake. 'But I'm going with you. I need to see this job done right.'

William had been stung by this before. The only reason his last job had gone so shamelessly awry was because he had allowed The Daughter so much control. Then again, as he was Vesta's only option, she was his.

He grasped her hand and shook.

1674

'Is there somewhere more private?' Mr Ruth indicated to the hallway door.

'We can talk here. My sister has a good idea of what I do.' Aiden sat on a padded chair at the kitchen table, allowing the visitor to sit on the recently polished settle.

'Excellent.' Ruth rubbed his hands together and sat. 'I've heard a great deal about you, young man. Your work ethic is beyond comparison.'

'I have my sister to keep, and our father. We've lost so much, and I'm hoping, one day, we can reclaim it. So we all put in our fair share of hard work.'

'Never a better word said.'

Every time he spoke, Ruth's nasal tone tensed Vesta's muscles. She spilled a little as she filled the plain but serviceable teapot. Soon, she thought; she just had to get behind him with a knife or paperweight. Something that would finish the job before her brother had time to react.

'You're a military boy aren't you?'

'I would have been.' The regret was thick in Aiden's voice. 'I went through most of the basic training, but had to leave to attend my family duties. That earned me a dishonourable discharge, so there's no going back.'

'Yes. That must sting; but don't fret. The skills you acquired, even in the brief stint you had in training, will pay off in your new line of work.' Ruth's friendly tone was disarming; he had never been anything but hostile before.

Vesta's last memory of him kept repeating in her head; the tormented scream from her father pushed through the upholstery, Ruth's gritted teeth as he pressed on the back of the blade.

'I hope so.' Aiden nodded sagely.

Vesta loaded a tray with two cake slices and neat second-hand china teacups, with the pot in pride-of-place. She approached the talking men and set the tray on the table. As she had seen the Janes do, she poured two measures of lemon tea with delicacy, taking care to poise her index finger just-so on the pot lid. Manners dictated that the guest was always given the more generous portion, and once she had served them both, she retreated with the empty tray to the stove side. Granted, she was somewhat regretful that she hadn't just tossed the steaming beverage in the man's face.

'Delicious,' Mr Ruth called over with his mouth full of cake.

Vesta thanked him as genuinely as she could manage. Now they were distracted eating she might have a better chance to slip behind the unwanted visitor unawares. Walking across the kitchen with a knife was too obvious and there wasn't a sensible route that saw her pass behind the man.

Perhaps if she went up to her father's room then out the front door, could use the guise of fetching his empty bottles for the rubbish bin outside, then smash one over Ruth's head and stick the shards in his throat.

'I've been in discussions with my associate, and he wants to grow the business. Thus, we need more people like yourself.' Ruth swilled down the cake he had been mincing with a gulp of lemon tea. 'Many people are reluctant to join an organisation like our own. In order to truly expand, we must shift ourselves into a better light in the eyes of the public.

'Part of that will come from bright young men, like yourself.' He took another large bite of his cake, disregarding the supplied fork. He had almost completely finished it, despite talking the entire time. Another facet to his disgusting character. 'I want you off the night work, for something more… public facing.'

'What do I need to do?' Aiden set his plate to the side, his cake untouched. It was unlike him, but when faced with a potential promotion, and such a blatant display of gluttony by his superior, Vesta couldn't say she blamed him.

'Recruiting. Inspiring the youth. Making yourself a beacon in the community. It's a lot cleaner work than your current role, and you'll be remunerated handsomely.' Ruth slid his empty plate underneath

Aiden's. 'Plus a charge account at Monsieur le Classe, so you'll look the part. It's one step closer back to that life you've been craving.'

Vesta was itching to move for her father's bedroom, to set her plan into motion, but her greed was stopping her. Everything Mr Ruth was saying was music to her ears; better hours for her brother, more money. It might even entail a new wardrobe for herself. She longed for a return to the way things were even more than her brother did.

'This all sounds… incredible.' Aiden's eyes shimmered with hope for the first time in recent memory.

Vesta heard the unmistakable scuff of boots on the door mat, then the front door slammed. There was a knock against the wall as the coat rack was nearly toppled; footsteps shuffled across the little hallway. Her father had come home early. A sudden glut of dread swelled in her stomach. She wanted to dash across the room and bar the door, to stop him stumbling in and coming face to face with the man who had taken so much.

'I'm back for more coin.' Father pushed through the door from the hallway, his drunken eye-line downwards.

The door shut behind him as he noticed the familiar shape at the table.

'Eldridge?' He clutched his severed hand tight in the other. It was possible to see the fight-or-flight instincts in his terrified face for a moment. His son was mere feet from the man who had taken everything from them, and Ruth could have any number of men outside. 'What's going on here?'

'Oh, this is a turn up!' Mr Ruth seemed quite amused by the cruel twist of events. He delved one hand into his pocket and grabbed hold of something, but did not retrieve it just yet. 'What a small world we live in. How have you been? Still dallying with your paints?'

Vesta's father stood as still as a hare in the path of a rumbling cartwheel.

'Don't worry, I'm not here to finish the job.' Ruth leered. 'Sit, have a piece of cake; your pretty daughter is quite the baker.'

'Do you two know each other?' Aiden scowled.

'We go back a long way.' Ruth pulled his hand from inside his pocket to reveal a small ivory handled flick-knife. He pressed the inset button to expose the blade, still entirely casual about the whole affair. 'Your father displeased my associate, maybe two years ago? I showed him the error of his ways.'

Aiden's fists clenched, the fiery look in his eyes mirroring Vesta's own murderous intent.

'Settle down, boy. You don't want to do anything rash. If you harm me, you'll end up far worse, and your family will surely go hungry without you to provide for them.' Ruth was punctuating every third word with a little wave of his knife, just to remind everybody exactly who was in control. 'But I would say that this chance meeting is quite fortuitous.'

He paused as if someone might ask him why, but the family were suffocated by their own distemper. He continued nonetheless.

'My job offer still stands, regardless. We cannot choose our family, after all. Though, I only want the most loyal people working for me as we move forward, and it just so happens that the perfect test for your loyalty has dropped square into our laps.' He raised his knife hand to his ear and cupped his fingers. 'I know what you want to say: "how fortunate". Well, I agree.'

The silence was so absolute, not even the long case clock in the hall remarked on the passing seconds.

'Your father's indiscretion caused him a debt of five fingers; I only took three. As I'm a generous man, I'll waive any interest he might have accrued. But he still owes me a little finger and thumb.' Eldridge flicked the knife around in his hand so that the hilt was facing outwards and offered it to Aiden. 'If you would be kind enough to collect them for me, you may consider it a happy start to your new career. Decline and… I'd rather not elaborate in such polite company.'

Aiden eyed the knife. Then reached out, hand quivering, and took it. For a moment he was consumed in his own head. Across the space, Vesta willed him to turn the blade on Ruth, to plunge it again and again into his chest, and rid them of his foul presence, once and for all.

'Do it.' Vesta's father was subdued, seeming somehow completely sober for the first time in years. A tear spilled down his cheek. 'We need the money, my painting… I can't do it anymore, you both need this.'

He placed his mutilated hand on the table.

'No!' Vesta shrieked, taking up the kitchen knife and dashing for the devil before her.

Her feet pounded across the floorboards, the knife raised high, but her wrist was caught perfectly in Ruth's waiting palm. His fingers clamped tightly, and a sharp twist spilled the blade from her grip. Pain lanced through her arm and elbow; another jerk span her on the balls of her feet and pinioned her to the end of the table, just inches from her father's hand.

'Do it,' her father reiterated. 'It's the waiting that's killing me.'

Aiden set the knife across his father's thumb. The blade was too short to span the gap between the remaining digits, each cut would need to be done separately.

'No! Stop!' Vesta kicked out, howling, failing against Ruth's wiry might. 'Please, don't!'

'Do it!' her father roared over her.

The knife pushed down through skin and tendon, channelling between bones to carve a slice in the table beneath.

Another year had brought them to a grander home on a respectable street in a rising bourgeois neighbourhood. Vesta ate well, attended the theatre on occasion, and managed a trio of servants. Her hands were even beginning to soften after their years of domestic service. In her lowest moments, it was everything she had wished for and more. But it wasn't perfect; her brother's demeanour had chilled, and her father had become a recluse. Any pleasure drawn from the four course dinners, ruches of bombazine in her skirts, and each cup of expensive foreign tea, was soured by the criminal truth.

Vesta returned to private study in her indolence, under the close watch of her brother's two underlings. One was a dunce, as tall and broad as their opulent front door. The other was more learned, but insufferable with it. A prodigy compared to his cohorts, but in any world other than his own, nothing particularly unique. He aspired for Aiden's rank, that was blatantly obvious, and Vesta worried he might think it wise to kill for it. She kept her eye as closely on him as he did on her.

'Have you finished your schooling yet?' The pompous underling was watching her today. Her brother had ordered it, he was terribly afraid that she might do something to jeopardise his position, and with good cause.

Now that she had what she wanted, she had little to do but reminisce and regret. She couldn't come to terms with her brother's allegiance to Mr Ruth. That man had taken everything, and in giving it back, had bought each and every one of them. She was just another of Ruth's tools, used to keep her brother in line – keep him loyal. Though it would surely undo her, if she had the chance, she wouldn't hesitate to stick a rusty skewer in his chest.

'It's nearly sun down,' the underling remarked.

'I'm not done yet.' She tended to reply only when spoken to nowadays. She hadn't the inclination to engage any of these thugs in conversation.

'Well, read faster. I want my supper before seven. You know I get terrors in the night if I eat too late.' He ran his fingers through his receding red hair. He could only be about twenty five but looked closer to forty.

Vesta nodded as if his suffering wasn't further motivation for dragging her feet.

'It's easier to read without your lips flapping,' she sneered over her history texts. She enjoyed the mental stimulation, but did worry that her strict education was intended to make her a better commodity to sell off. That was the sort of scheme she could see Ruth forming, another test that her brother would be desperate to pass. All the more reason to put a stop to all this.

The underling scoffed at her insolence and returned to preening his nails with a paring knife that he seemed to carry everywhere.

Without further interruption, the chapter was finished quickly. History had always been her best subject, and in selecting the volume regarding the not-so-ancient founding of The Assassins' Guild, she had hoped to understand how such criminal organisations functioned. Unfortunately for her, the details were sparse. From what she could tell, the guild was a fairly ramshackle affair at the best of times. Nothing like Ruth's regimented gang.

Now she just wanted to see Mr Ruth dead in one of the myriad ways detailed in the book. Bled out on meat hooks, half his head blown open, or simultaneously boiled and drowned in a volcanic river.

'Finished?' The pompous gang-man flicked his last sliver of fingernail onto the library rug.

She snapped the book closed, pushed her chair away from the desk – scraping the assuredly expensive flooring – and made for the door without a word.

The underling stowed his knife and hurried after. Once out in the hall he ushered her towards the kitchens where they would be eating; her brother was using the dining room for some meeting with his larcenous betters.

Her eyes caught Ruth's as they passed in the hall; as ever, she displayed her contempt openly. He and her brother were drinking an aperitif with seven other men, including one whom she had seen in the painting that had cost her father the digits of one hand. *Ruth's associate*, she remembered that much. He was certainly the one in charge, the root cause of all her woes, but not the perpetrator. Her hatred of Ruth burned brighter.

'Take the New Pantheon,' the shortest and portliest of the men spoke like a boiled egg was lodged in his gullet. 'People can be compelled to do the most amazing things when there's a higher power at stake.'

'And, if we give them something to hope for, new recruits will flock to us like never before,' Aiden added to the conversation.

'It would take a miracle for this pivot in our organisation to be a success,' The Associate contemplated, swilling wine in a large glass. He inhaled the aroma casually, everyone waited for him to continue. 'So why don't we orchestrate one?'

Vesta was marshalled into the kitchens and the door was closed behind her. The cook inside was making the last preparations for the dinner party's first course. Despite being service staff he kept a cleaver nearby at all times. Vesta supposed it saved her brother money to have one man fill two jobs.

'What have *we* got?' the pompous underling whined.

'You'll have to sort yourselves out. I'm on my own tonight. I've got these to serve, and the mains to finish *and* glasses to keep filled...' The cook's rambling turned into a low grumble.

The underling had Vesta sit at the counter where the servants ate and went into the larder. There was a little clattering and shuffling before he shouted. 'Can we have the left over soup you're serving?'

'Fine.' The cook took up three precariously balanced bowls, having sprinkled an artful swirl of oil and herbs on the top, and headed to the dining room.

The underling returned with the remaining soup in a small pan and set it on the formidable brass and blacked stove. Then cheerily, he set about cutting up bread and slices of meat. Vesta didn't help.

'I prefer the thick stuff, but a bit of this fancy broth is nice every once in a while.' He gave the pan a stir then sprinkled entirely too much salt into the already fully prepared and seasoned soup. 'Do you like soup?'

Vesta ignored him, not even feigning deafness; they all knew she hated it here. This place was comfortable, but it didn't make it any less of a prison.

'Thank you so much for this.' The cook burst back in through the door with Mr Ruth in his wake.

'It's the least I can do.' Ruth eyed Vesta with derision. 'I'll take these through; you just concentrate on the pig.'

Ruth picked up two of the soup bowls still waiting to be taken to the dining room and left through the hall. Selections of perfectly good trays were stored in the dresser, but of course such a practicality did not occur to a man like Eldridge, so accustomed to being waited upon. Vesta noted the cook's harassed demeanour, the distraction of her minder, and felt the stirrings of opportunity.

'Would you help?' The cook set his hand on the underling's shoulder. 'I've half a pig on the spit out back, needs bringing in.'

The underling sighed and clapped the bread crumbs from his hands before following the cook out to the yard. The second the door closed behind them, Vesta's focus settled on the two remaining bowls. Despite his utter depravity, Mr Ruth was very fond of manners, and wouldn't serve himself before anyone else. Which meant that one of the appetisers was his own; ripe for doctoring.

The cook had exotic herbs that needed to be boiled for hours before losing their potency. It was the fashion of late to eat the most dangerous and outlandish fayre; she suspected it was an effort on the ruling classes part to emulate the daring guilders they pretended not to admire. Just a sprig as garnish might be enough to lame Ruth, she didn't imagine his constitution was particularly strong. However, to ensure success, she would have to poison both remaining portions, and the other would certainly be for her brother as host. She couldn't do that to him.

The sound of water hissing to steam pulled her from deliberation. The soup on the hearth was boiling over. A smile peeled her lips upwards; the mere thought of Eldridge Ruth writhing in agony was almost enough to make her burst out laughing. She hopped from her chair and hurried to the stove. With a square of layered linen wrapped around the pot's handle, she hefted it in both hands; the beef-scented broth slopped and sizzled on the stove top.

Positioned at the hall door, she took care not to spill any scalding liquid. Scared for what might happen, but determined that she would avenge her loss of freedom, she readied herself. Footsteps approached on the other side of the wood.

The door opened and Ruth stepped across the threshold. He had only the time to see Vesta's malicious expression before his eyes, face, and chest were doused in the blistering liquid. The scream that came was enough for two men, high and loud, guttural and filled with dread. Just as agony washed through him, satisfaction swelled in Vesta, but it was only short lived.

As the man crumpled to the floor, she became acutely aware of how badly she had spoiled any chance of a normal life. If the men could catch her, they would kill her without second thought. She had to get out; now.

1682

For the third day in a row, ash hung heavy in the air and the sun was blotted from the sky. It was cold, miserable, but solemnly beautiful. The whole town was swathed in a sinister twilight mist that framed the buildings as shadowy monoliths, as opposed to rundown dens.

William shivered, and though he had managed to scrape together enough change for a coarse new shirt, and had washed his trousers of grey matter and flecks of skull, he was still dirty with soot. The dust clung to him, making limbs heavy with a crust across his skin.

He ached from sleeping on the floor of Vesta's rented room – an economical move he would have rather avoided – and was altogether displeased about her insistence on trailing him until the target was dead. He had tried and failed to convince her to leave him to his work countless times already, and rather frustratingly she refused to see sense. Like any simmering disagreement the arguments would build and wane, sometimes finishing in an almighty row, but more often than not they petered to a period of sullen silence. He just couldn't accept their difference of opinion. So, on route to the chapel for his initiation, he decided to dredge it up again.

'You're only going to slow me down...' He wondered whether one talking point would be enough, and added, 'or get yourself killed.'

'I doubt it,' Vesta replied with a stern confidence; she was battle hardened to their little rows by now. 'I've looked after myself for the last eight years. I know exactly what we're walking into; I can handle it.'

Her tone was steadfast, though William detected a little hastening of her breath. It could have been the steep elevation to the chapel, but she seemed fit enough, perhaps even more so than him. There was a fear in her, which bred doubt, and that could be used to keep her distant from the killing.

While the district around the town hall had been approximately flat, the closer one got to the high chapel, the more precipitous the districts became. Townhouses and shops crowded busy roads, connected via wandering stone stairways and steep little paths cut into bare rock. More than once, William's shoes slipped on the cobbles and drifts of ash, and he was forced to adjust his course. Folk that bustled from the shops seemed more accustomed to the slick cambered streets, and gave no leeway for a foreigner in smooth soles; he started to lag Vesta.

Her purposeful stride was unwavering and the further she drew ahead of him, the more it seemed like their little disagreement had been decided in her favour. Placing his feet purposely in the grooves between cobbles to give him a little more traction, he hurried to keep pace with the rhythm struck by her lengthy legs. As he trotted close, somehow managing to keep his footing while dodging a group of awe stricken death-tourists, he cleared his throat and resumed their debate.

'It takes more than a blade or a bullet to kill a man.' He was trying his best to discourage her enough to turn back, but not enough for her to call the job off all together. She had the coin for both of their initiations, and he still needed her to pay up. 'You have to be able to live with yourself after. I've seen people like you fall to pieces over less than murder.'

'You don't need to worry about me.' She seemed a little more distant now, as if deep in a memory. 'I've killed before.'

An uncomfortable silence slung between them. While he doubted her claim, she did have a certain confidence about her. Not to mention the courage to enter Blackbile unaccompanied. Yet, Vesta was far from the cold hearted sort of woman that typified the guild. He could see her trepidation, even if she refused to admit or project it. Her eyes darted to every shadow when she thought his attention had lapsed, and ever-so-occasionally she worried her bottom lip. The confidence and fear seemed to be in constant battle, and though the fear was losing, William started to wonder exactly what his patron was expecting for them upon arrival at the chapel.

'How do *you* deal with it, anyway?' she asked as they ascended onto a sort of plateau, allowing them a little respite from the relentless climb. 'The guilt?'

'Guilt?' William scoffed. 'I don't have any, I kill to keep going. The same way that you eat meat to not starve, I kill to avoid destitution; life feeds on death.'

He paraphrased what he could remember of Ojo's mantra. Though he had believed in it for so long, he had never actually aired it before. It didn't sound quite as poetic as when the legendary assassin had espoused it, but he could still feel the sentiment ringing true, even if he couldn't vocalise it.

'I suppose.' She didn't sound convinced. 'But it is possible to survive without meat, the monks do it; and you don't have to kill to survive – you could farm, tend a shop – you do it because…'

'Do you want me to kill the scalded man or not?' He interrupted her altogether too-competent sounding argument before the entire foundation of his being was shaken any further. 'You're the one that wants a man dead.'

'I'm not happy about it.' She scowled. 'It's just something that needs to be done, and it would be wrong if I wasn't there.'

Their discussion faltered, and they continued to the chapel in a pall of oppressive quiet. The town too was subdued, the merriment from the opening ceremony had all but died off, and the festivities associated with the firing of the starting pistol had yet to begin. At only two hours past dawn, many of the tourists that insisted on revelling week-through were in bed or otherwise unconscious, making it feel like any number of other tedious Wellensdays.

The chapel loomed overhead, its stone made black by endless soot and ash from the mountain; it looked far more ominous up close. The throbbing light from sconces inside swelled in the crimson stained glass and the spire held a similarly coloured flag on the end of an upturned cross. William noted a high balcony that would provide quite the vantage once the competition started.

A crowd of people outside held banners and chanted something distantly. Presumably part of the initiation. The whole image sought to impress, but under the circumstances of infiltration, it was quite unsettling.

'You told them you would be coming with an extra recruit, so if you arrive alone they might suspect something,' Vesta said out of nowhere, reassuring herself to stay the course.

'True.' He was becoming a little more grateful for her at his side now. Two against a cult was infinitely more agreeable than one.

As they drew closer, it became apparent that the people with the banners were not part of the ceremony at all. They were shouting and chanting things not entirely flattering about the presence of the cult in their borough. Signs sported painted messages like "we will not pay the tithe" and "extortion is not salvation".

William and Vesta shared a worried glance; this group had entirely encircled the steps to the chapel entrance.

'How do we get through?' Vesta asked as if William had experience in passing through an angry mob. He stopped twenty feet behind the crowd, lacking in answers for the time being.

'We won't pay, we won't pay!' The crowd became unified in their chant as cult members spilled from the chapel doors. They were dressed in robes of ceremony; silken gowns of pure white with flowing red scarves around their necks and sheep hide mantles about their shoulders. Most of them held orbs and sceptres of gold and glass, others carried woven baskets.

'Heathens!' a cultist roared at the mob. William recognised the high cheek-boned cultist from the brothel. 'Hell-bound masses, do you not seek redemption from your inherent sin?'

'Crook!' one of the women in the crowd called out and was echoed with a rally of cheers.

'There is only one way into the heavens,' Cheekbones continued with all the charm and gravitas a preacher to a real god might have. 'Selflessness! We Lambs sacrifice ourselves to this higher cause for your benefit, and we offer you your own chance at redemption. Give generously your wealth to the betterment of your community through a tithe to us. Save your very souls by letting go of your greed once and for all.'

The crowd answered with a volley of root vegetables, bottles, and horse dung. It seemed they were not convinced by the promised salvation of the Lambs. Nor was William, but he needed them in the competition.

'You are misguided by the devils amongst you.' An over ripe tomato hit the wall behind Cheekbones with an explosive squelch. 'They must be expunged so that the meek amongst you may be free to contribute your tithes.'

Cheekbones took his sceptre in two hands and twisted each end sharply. A spark shot from the head as if a flint and steel had been struck internally, then gunpowder ignited in a fizz of crackling embers. He fished a glass orb from the basket of a fellow cultist, and used his burning sceptre to light its trailing wick.

'Accept salvation!' Cheekbones shouted as he tossed the orb into the crowd. Bodies scrabbled over one another to get away from the arcing ball, women and children screamed in the press. Glass smashed on the cobbled streets, then the powdered mix inside kindled. Pure white light erupted in the crowd, so bright it singed the retinas: spark powder.

The protestors began to flee; other cultists ignited their charging rods and tossed glass grenades.

William snatched Vesta roughly about the middle, and hurtled for the cover of a garden wall. Ash plumed around them, spiny plants snagged their clothes. He pulled his shirt over his nose and mouth, and instructed her to do the same. This was not exactly the kind of reception he'd expected; religious folk were more civilised, even the zealots usually.

'Let the fires cleanse you!'

Bombs popped like fireworks in the crowd, and soon more than half of the protestors were floored, cradling their faces, or unconscious on the ground. William was sure that at least a few were dead.

When the cultists stopped throwing their orbs and twisted their charging rods to extinguish them, the uninjured townsfolk started to re-emerge. They crept from doorways, alleyways, and from behind abandoned carts to drag away their friends and family members. William was a little wiser, and understood the rudiments of spark powder, so waited until the last wisp of smoke had been carried away on the breeze. Then, seizing the opportunity of the ceasefire, he jumped up, and pulled Vesta to her feet.

'One day you will thank us for the amputation of your rebellious limb,' Cheekbones shouted authoritatively over the writhing bodies and crying children. 'The only way to salvation is through God, and the only way to God is through us.'

He tossed his ignition rod into a basket, and took the moment to bless the townsfolk with a muttered prayer and flamboyant hand gestures. Recognition pulled over his otherwise impassive face when he spotted William marching a very circuitous route through the carnage.

'William, welcome!' He widened his arms like a magnanimous saint.

'Hello.' William failed to match the cultist's enthusiasm. He felt Vesta wriggle her hand free, like a child determined to prove she was all grown up.

'I'm so sorry about that little display.' Cheekbones wrapped his arm about William's shoulders. 'Terrible business, but that's the problem when you set up in a town like this. They're all too used to the ways of the devil, so won't accept a fair tithing lying down. But they're not far from breaking point now; they'll see the light, one way or another.'

William nodded, now entirely comfortable with his decision to side with Vesta against the cult.

They were led inside, to a nave about as welcoming as implied by the building's foreboding exterior. The walls were white and the whole room was aglow with the light from a thousand tallow candles. The Lambs that had been with Cheekbones remained outside, but there were far more in here, stood in regimented groups, chanting scripture in a guttural tone. William and Vesta followed the cultist between two columns of pews left vacant – should any of the locals feel inspired to join – and up a staircase that spanned the entire width of the chapel.

At the top of the steps was a large font, sunken into the floor, and filled with a putrid red liquid. It was unmistakable to anyone with a nose as slowly fermenting blood; a skin had congealed, and a few flies dawdled about its surface. William hoped it was lamb's blood, at least that would be thematically appropriate, but the cultists' display outside suggested they weren't quite so predictable. He could deduce – perhaps because of his own sour luck – that he would need to submerge himself in it before the day was done.

On the other side of the font was a pipe organ that lined the wall with brass tubes, and not far above it, a balcony from which a sermon could be given. Unlike many of the other faiths he had come across, there would be no hope for a peaceful inauguration. In such a fire and brimstone place as Blackbile, the Sacrificial Lambs were exactly what he should have expected.

'Are you ready to join the Flock?' Cheekbones took his place between the pair and the font. 'William? And you miss?'

'Jane.' She nodded, even managed a weak smile.

'Place the tithe in my palm and remove your clothes.'

Vesta didn't hesitate. She offered two coin purses and pulled off her clothes as readily as any back alley bawd. William was more tentative, but had to convince the cult of his sincerity. Making a concerted effort not to look at Vesta, he surrendered his shirt, feeling the cold air against his bare skin. As he lowered his trousers, his two pistols clattered loudly against the floor.

'And the hair tie.'

Vesta was more reluctant to unbind her hair than she had been in removing her clothes. Softly, she loosed the leather band holding her plaits and ran fingers through her hair to remove the knots.

'Do those of you here today, swear to give your lives for the betterment of the Cause?' The pair shared a nervous glance, then echoed him with a yes. 'Will you hold the tenets of the Lambs close to your hearts? Selflessness, purity, obedience, and a swift and stern hand for those who seek to do wrong to members of our good religion?'

'I do,' they lied in unison.

'Then give yourselves up to the font. Wash yourselves in Lambs' blood to cleanse your souls of sin.' Cheekbones lead a small procession of cultists and incense bearers to the far side of the font, then pulled a ceremonial blade from beneath his robes.

William took the first step into the still-warm font. It was thick, far more resistant than water; the very feel of it rose gooseflesh across his body. Vesta followed, now the more hesitant of the two.

Cheekbones plunged the tip of his knife into the scar beneath his eye and jerked it, letting blood flow freely over the back of his hand and drool into the font.

As William took another step forward, submerging his genitals in the liquid, he confirmed in his mind that the entirety of the font's contents had been sourced from cultists in sacrifice. Suddenly aware that the men and women who lined the edges of the room had moved inwards and were now surrounding the pool, William struggled to keep his disgust hidden. Each member pricked their skin in one place or another and added their essence to the mixture.

'Surrender yourselves to our kinship,' Cheekbones instructed with a shudder, pushing the knife ever so slightly deeper into his own face.

William pursed his lips as tight as was humanly possible and sank to his knees. If there were gods, they certainly weren't watching as the warm liquid enveloped him, filling his ears and nostrils with its taste. Making his skin feel dirty and impure. He held himself under for as long as he could stomach then resurfaced. He spat to clear his lips of the coppery liquid, and smeared it away from his eyes.

Vesta was similarly coated in the blood; her dark eyes gleaming in contrast, and hair plastered to her scalp. William found his eyes pulling to the side of her head. There was a small channel – hard to decipher clearly – that she had previously hidden with delicately arranged plaits. It might not have even been noticeable if her hair was dry. When she looked at him, he averted his eyes to save her from self-consciousness, but she was too distracted to notice; sick from the ordeal they had been through.

'Let's see these new recruits.' A new voice echoed through the chamber.

William swept his lank, bloodied hair back over his head as the congregation parted for an imposing man. He wore black robes, red trimming his cuffs and collar. His over cloak was covered in fur rather than wool, fine and straight and grey. His face was painted with fresh blood to make it vibrant, but molten looking on one side from an old burn. Where the scar trailed down onto his neck and the blood-paint finished, it was a deathly pale.

Perhaps the gods existed, and perhaps they had truly been watching. As perfectly as a scene from an Arabella Flatt operetta, the villain of the piece had made himself known and now stood mere feet away. With a face as burnt and miserable as his, the scalded man could only be the cult leader; William's target.

'Emerge from the font, my new brother and sister.' The scalded man walked regally to where their belongings lay in piles on the floor. William began to ascend the steps out of the font, Vesta padding behind. The air was cold and greasy against their blood stained bodies; everything not conducive towards a naked inspection. The scalded man's eyes traced their bodies from feet upwards. He muttered something about fine specimens before speaking more publicly to the congregation.

'These Lambs have spilled their blood for you, and so too will you spill yours for others. We here are one large family, and we give ourselves to the Cause fully.'

'I am your brother and you are mine.' The scalded man embraced William bodily, pressing every contour together in a slimy tangle. 'I am greatly pleased that you will be competing as a Lamb in the upcoming days, it will be an honour.'

'Thank you.' William grimaced, pleased to be released.

He could almost touch his flintlock with his toe from where he was standing. If he was quick he might be able to get off a shot and escape before the blood-letting cultists lit any more bombs; but he was getting ahead of himself. This man's overbearing presence was driving him to hurry; he couldn't. He had to take the target unawares, make it look like an accident, just as they had planned lest he lose the cultist's assistance in the competition.

'I am your brother.' Red-face moved on to Vesta. From her muscular legs and flat stomach, over her breasts to her face, he assessed her. She took it in her stride, but shied a little when his gaze rested on the curious wave in her hair. It still clung to the small divot in her skull. He drew her more carefully into his arms, and kissed her cheek, adding, 'and you are my sister.'

1674

Mr Ruth's eyes foamed with beef-flavoured pus. His skin blistered and popped, and even the inside of his mouth and throat had been routed by the scalding liquid. He screeched and gurgled; his hands trembled around his head, too afraid to make contact with the fleshy ruins.

The joy of revenge was horrifyingly absent. Though Vesta had hit her intended target, the fatty broth had sprayed the wall, the door, and doused the young man that had followed in his employers' wake. Equally scalded down one side of his face and blinded in one eye, was her brother. Cowering against the doorframe, his one remaining eye looked at her wide and betrayed, weeping as freely as the other.

'I'm sorry,' she choked.

Behind her, the underling and cook had returned with the half-pig on a long pole and were wrestling to set it down. Ahead, past her brother and Ruth, the gang leaders came to assess the commotion.

Aiden shook his head in sorrowful disbelief, his mouth trailed drool; his fingers trembled from shock. On one side, his lips were stuck together and he cringed with the pain of parting them. She would never forget that momentary image of true remorse on his face, but as the gang leaders drew close, he became harder, more stoic, and swallowed down the pain. His gaze became flinty, filled with hatred for Vesta, for the position she had put him in.

His half-mouth spat two words, 'kill her.'

Vesta's whole life tumbled to ashes around her. The last thread tying her to this family had been severed. Regret suffocated her; she should have tried harder to find work, she should have dissuaded him from joining the gang in the first place.

A thousand retrospective thoughts would not change the situation. Everything had been spoiled so thoroughly.

She hitched her skirts and ran for her life.

1682

'Vesta, it is *so* nice to see you again.' The red-faced cult leader ran his finger down her narrow jawline, peeling away a dried slick of Lambs' blood.

'Don't touch me!' She slapped his hand away.

'I had presumed you'd starved in some ditch years ago, or been lost to the imperial brothels. But now you are my sister twice; once by birth, and second by the will of God,' he continued with a smile. The burnt side of his mouth rucked back to reveal entirely too many teeth.

She spat blood tinged saliva in his face.

'Mind your manners.' He mopped himself clean with a linen square proffered by one of his devout cultists, taking away a patch of daubed-on blood to reveal the pallid scar of a face beneath. 'It would be wise to make the most of our reunion, as it can only be brief. My deacons have advised me that your sacrifice for the Cause has been moved forward. To just before lunch.'

'So you're going to kill me, just like you did Father?' Her fists clenched tight.

William was desperate to extricate himself from this situation. There were nearly thirty cultists surrounding them, each armed with at least a small knife. By comparison, all he had was two single shot pistols, the indignity of nudity, and a hot-headed employer that wasn't paying nearly enough. He wondered if it was still possible to convince them he had no knowledge of Vesta or her intention to kill their leader; probably not.

'Is that what you think? That *I* killed father?' The red faced man scoffed. 'After what you did, I had no choice; The Associate saw my family as a weakness. Try to see things through my *eye*, then maybe you will come to hold yourself accountable. Just as I do.'

'This is all *your* fault!' Vesta petulantly shoved her brother. Cracks echoed all around as the cultists sparked their ignition rods. 'Don't put me at the centre of all this.'

'What was I supposed to do? I wasn't even home when the fire started, but you were, weren't you?' He snatched her by the hair and pulled her close; words spitting venom across her cheek. 'I've long suspected it was you who sparked the flame. You've done nothing but try to tear apart everything I've ever worked for. Everything I did…'

'Everything you did was for yourself!' she screeched, savagely punctuating every word with a jabbing finger to his chest. 'You're as selfish as me and then some. It's no wonder you've built your empire on the backs of the dim and destitute.'

The cult leader's patience withered. He thrust Vesta backwards. She staggered a pace, then her bloodied foot slipped on a flag-stone, and she tumbled down the steps.

William lurched for his clothes, picked up one of his pistols and barged a few cultists aside. He rocked upright, and trained his sights on the red faced man. The best he could hope for now was a swift and painless exit. It didn't really matter if Vesta survived, but if she did, he would have to give her a stern talking to.

'That's enough!' he roared, waving the flintlock to make sure everyone in the chapel had seen it. 'Vesta, are you alright?'

'Nothing broken,' she groaned and tried to prop herself up; the sparking end of a charge rod brandished towards her eyes sent her cowering back to the floor.

'What exactly are you going to do? Shoot me?' The red faced man chuckled. 'Do you have a death wish?'

'I fancy my chances, one trained assassin against a rabble of lunatics.' William rolled his shoulders and eyed the grenade-toting cultists one by one.

'What about the guild?' The red faced man ambled to William's pile of gear and picked up the other flintlock, the silver one; his favourite. 'They will come down on you like a lump hammer on a heretic's skull.'

'And why is that?' William hesitated; he couldn't afford to be disqualified, and he certainly wasn't going to let himself be killed before he'd repaired his reputation.

'It's against the rules to kill an entrant in the days leading up to the prize – you know that – and it just so happens that I have the honour of competing.' Red-face levelled his pistol at Vesta, and the cultists closed ranks, menacing with their charge rods and glass grenades. 'You'd be hanged, drawn and quartered; and that's just to start.'

That changed things. Though William was blacklisted, he was still a member of the guild, and still bound by their rules. He couldn't kill his target, but he could still escape.

'I'm entering too,' William blurted. 'So you can't kill me either.'

Red-face contemplated a moment, then directed one of his underlings with a hand signal. William heard footsteps to his back and tensed, ready for a fight.

'Go on then.' Red-face casually waved him off, just as one of the large chapel doors was pulled open. 'It's been nice meeting you, I absolve you of your oath. Now go.'

Silently William pulled his clothes on over blood soaked skin, hoping that it wouldn't stain. He couldn't afford another new shirt. Pushing his luck just a little, he asked, 'can I have my pistol back?'

Red-face blinked, incredulous, the barrel still levelled at Vesta. 'I'm using it.'

It was a wrench to leave the gun that had started it all; he would have to come back later for it. Then they'd be sorry. As he turned to leave, he was met with the cowering, blood-soaked, and entirely pathetic Vesta. He owed her nothing, but he couldn't harden his heart to her plight. His shoulders sagged. He had already decided to do something stupid.

Without putting too much thought into it, he planted his feet, about turned, and dashed for Red-face. Both pistols fired. One bullet struck a cultist, and the other smashed a grenade. It popped, flaring with white light. William closed his eyes, and though he tried to stop himself, collided with the cult leader. He fell backwards, landing on hands and knees, but stopped himself tumbling down the stairs. There was a secondary burst, alarmed shrieks, more glass shattered;

the flash was blinding even behind his lids. He heard Red-face call out for help; he sounded hurt, perhaps caught in the second blast.

Quickly recovering from his daze in a surge of adrenaline, William found he had lost his second flintlock in the tumble. He pulled up his shirt, already catching the scent of spark powder in the air, and covered his mouth with the blood sopped fabric. When he could finally see enough through streaming eyes, his ears still throbbing with a high-pitched whine, he scrambled for the first weapon he could make out; a sparking charge rod.

He angled himself in Vesta's direction and scrambled down the steps towards her, ready to crack the head of the cultist pinning her down. When he got close enough, he realised the man was already dead; half his head had been blown off by a stray bullet, adding its contents to the pool around Vesta. He offered her a hand, she grasped it and he hauled her up, thrusting her towards the still open doorway. He followed, shielding his eyes from the painful light of the dreary sun.

They emerged into the square, the cries from the cultists overwhelmed by the reaction of the townsfolk ahead. Naked, and half naked, covered in blood, one wielding a lit charge rod, they must have looked a terrifying sight to the downtrodden locals.

William led the way, darting left, out of sight of any cultists who might have been quick enough to grab a firearm, and avoiding the centre of the glass and gore strewn square. Vesta kept pace, despite a wince in her stride from her tumble, and actually passed him before turning down a narrow alleyway. There, out of sight, she slowed a little, but kept moving. The pair were both breathless now, tired from the sudden shock and exertion, but unable to stop. He tossed the heavy charge rod to the gutter and she stole a forgotten blanket from a washing line, as marred by ash as it would be by blood.

Turning another corner, Vesta wrapped herself and pressed her back to the wall. Still gulping mouthfuls of air, she asked, 'did you get him?'

'Get who?' William wheezed, bending double, his hands rested on his thighs. He looked back; nobody was following them. Yet.

'My brother, I heard him shout, did you get him?' She spat into the gutter and wiped her face, sweat was carrying the old blood into her mouth and eyes.

'I don't think so, no.'

'We have to go back, while they're still in disarray, we can get him.' Vesta, pushed off the wall. 'Come on.'

'No.' William blocked the way back. 'Look at yourself.'

Huddled tightly in the filthy blanket, arms folded, hands pressed in the opposite pits for warmth, she was still shivering. Her eyes were streaming and sore from the filth and the flash and the constant weeping. She had no weapon, not even a pair of shoes. William wasn't much better, yes he had managed to dress, but he was similarly defenceless, and he had caught more of the flaring light. For the time being, his vision was blemished with a fat streak of colour.

'We can't go back, it's done! They'll be ready if we do, and, I can't do it. We missed our one chance, and… You heard your brother, it's against guild rules-'

'You're an assassin!' Vesta wanted to stomp or punch the wall, or punch William – he could see that clearly enough – but she didn't let her frustration turn to violence; because in that moment, she was as delicate as spun sugar. She shook her arms and cried in exasperation, before continuing, 'just break the damned rules! You're an outlaw aren't you? You still have to do it, you have a debt to pay, a debt to me. You signed a contract.'

'And you compromised that contract! I warned you not to come along,' William bit. 'You spoiled it all. Didn't you think it would be pertinent to tell me the target was your brother?'

She tried to force past him but couldn't; raised her fist, and for a moment he thought she might strike him across the face. He would have let it happen too. He had let her down as much as he had himself: ruined her contract, lost the support of the Lambs, and stomped his reputation even further into the muck.

She did hit him, but not in the face, and by the time her fist collided with his chest, the force and will was gone from it. She fell onto him, clutching him in an awkward embrace, the arm that had struck him crumpled up between them. She sobbed onto his shoulder.

He stood there for a moment, then put his arms around her and patted her back. While he had been starting to believe this argument might be the most explosive yet, it had petered away all the quicker from their exhaustion. He hadn't the energy to disagree anymore. Since he had said his goodbyes to Goldin, Vesta had been his only companion, and he couldn't waste any more energy at loggerheads.

'You can only hope someone kills him in the competition, and if he somehow wins, or drops out, then you can put out another contract.' He stroked the back of her head, the hair was lank with half dried blood; clots came away with his fingers.

'I still have a contract with you, you have to kill him.' She wasn't shouting anymore. It sounded more like begging, and with sobs punctuating the words, it made it all the more compelling.

'I can't...' Pursuing this red faced cultist was a fool's errand; he had far too much backing.

'I already paid you, you took it; you have to do the job. You're entering the competition anyway. You can kill him then.' She pushed away, still holding him at arm's length, and fixed him with blood-rimmed bloodshot eyes. Little lines of clear skin trailed down where tears had washed away the dirt.

'Now I'm out of the cult I don't have a sponsor. I can't enter.' He wondered exactly how he might get one now, time was certainly running out and this little expedition had only seen him worse off in every way possible. He didn't like to admit it, but without a decent weapon, he didn't think anyone would be mad or wild enough to join him. 'I might have to try again next time.'

'I'll do it.' Vesta's eyes twinkled, though that might have been from the tears.

'What?'

'I'll be your sponsor if you kill my brother like you promised.'

A few days prior, this would have answered all of his problems, but she wasn't thinking clearly. To press this madness would surely see her dead.

But, if William was more truthful with himself, should he fail to get back on the whitelist, he had no strong skillset to find gainful employment, and lacked any connections to keep him hidden from revenge purses. He had nothing but the clothes he stood in, and if he didn't enter the contest this year, he was done for anyway.

Vesta held him firm, waiting for an answer, stoic as a guild doorman. She had the same desperate hope as him, and was determined to a fault.

'Do you know what being a sponsor means?'

'Yes I know what it means!' She snapped, holding his gaze with an intensity he couldn't refuse. Even if he did, she'd just find another way to kill her brother.

'Well…' Unable to find an argument she'd listen to, he relented. 'Alright then.'

'Thank you, Will.' She threw her arms around him. 'We'll get him together.'

William couldn't say he was happy to have Vesta as a sponsor, but he couldn't turn her away, not when she was offering exactly what he sought. At least he would have an ally at his side. Perhaps his luck would turn for the better.

'We need to go, before the Lambs come looking.'

PART 3

1667

Terrowin reclined. Sat in the high backed chair with his feet on the desk and the curtains flapping ominously behind him, he looked pretty damn good. He chuckled at the thought of the mayor returning and near shitting himself from the sight of a strange assassin in his office, then chuckled again at the thought of the mayor actually shitting himself. He cut his laughter short; the scene wouldn't be nearly so surprising if the mayor heard him giggling from down the hall. He pursed his lips, sat still in his most nonchalantly intimidating pose, and waited.

Where in the seven hells was the mayor anyway?

He pondered for a moment as to whether it was seven or nine hells. He could remember his mother exclaiming "hell's bells" every time he was mischievous as a child – killing a rodent with gun powder, or poisoning that postmaster – and the circus folk had always woken at seven bells. Were there seven hell bells? It didn't really matter.

He shuffled on his arse, losing interest in his trail of thought, and remembered exactly how bored he was. He hated waiting at the best of times, and self-imposed waiting was the worst. The compulsion to just give up his little stunt and go marching into the mayor's latrine was becoming overpowering.

'Not long now,' he told himself.

When the mayor returned – news sheet under his arm, steaming earthenware mug in hand – and the heart in his chest threatened to burst its bounds, Terrowin's sheer delight would be worth all the waiting.

Idly, he opened a desk drawer and found a modest stack of gold coins. Ordering them in his palm so that the profiles of the emperor went from young to old was mildly distracting. He rolled one over his knuckles like his mother used to do, and flicked another in the air. The thought of the mayor's eyes bulging from their sockets and dangling on those fleshy cords sent another shiver of joy through him. He wondered if they would clack back and forth like the metal balls in one of the mayor's desktop trinkets.

The curtains gave a tremendous flap. That would have been a good time for the mayor to return, but he didn't. Bloody hell was it getting cold. Heavy ash floated in and trailed over the expensive upholstery. At least it dragged away Terrowin's acquired stink of sweat, whorehouse grime, and liquor.

An oil lamp on the desk offset the sparse sunlight from the window, and would allow the victim of his impromptu visit to take in his bloodshot eyes and scar-patched stubble. Terrowin actually preferred the way his lank hair threatened to fall out of its greasy sweep; it made him look half-feral. He used to stain it black with oils, but after an incident that left a bald streak across the left side of his scalp, he had let it return to a natural russet.

He flicked one of the gold coins across the room at a bookcase. Not for any reason really, just because rolling them over his knuckles was becoming as tiresome as the waiting. It ricocheted off a carafe with a pleasant *ping*. The mayor seemed to be even less of a reader than Terrowin, as the bookcase had naught in the way of books, and was instead stocked with the most pristinely arranged liquor collection.

He flicked another coin, aiming for a bottle next to the carafe that he identified as being particularly expensive. He missed. Taking aim more seriously, he tried again. This time, the coin rattled between two bottles on the lower shelf. He wouldn't be replacing his pistol with a roll of pennies any time soon. He wondered if he could smash one of the bottles with a hard enough flick; there was little in life more entertaining than the pointless destruction of wealth.

He set his feet on the floor, and flicked a coin as hard as he could. It shot off at an angle and collided with a delicate porcelain globe, smashing a perfect slot and clattering inside. While he was disappointed with his aim, that globe did look to have been considerably diminished in value. His mouth spread to a crooked grin.

'What do you think you're doing?' The mayor was stood in the doorway. He didn't have today's news sheet under his arm, but he did have a steaming mug. Sadly, he didn't drop it. Neither did he clutch his chest, or pop out his eyes. He only raised his thick eyebrows a few degrees, but that was enough. By the gods they were lustrous; an impressive feat for a man only a few years beyond adolescence. Terrowin felt a pang of envy.

'Well if it isn't the prodigal disappointment.' Terrowin exuded calm, his Scoldish brogue softened by years of travel. Granted he was irritated that his grand entrance hadn't gone quite as expected, but he could still pull things around.

'Prodigal what?' The mayor's bright eyes darted to the flintlock on the desk, reflecting the dreary sun perfectly off engraved flowers in the silver – Terrowin had spent a good minute lining it up.

'Prodigal disappointment, as in someone who's not nearly prodigal enough, didn't you hear me the first time?' He rolled a coin over the back of his knuckles. 'Or are you as tediously economical with your senses as you are guild coffers?'

'What do you want here?' The mayor seemed surprisingly composed, not at all like the wheedling sycophant Terrowin expected.

'I fancied a sit down.' Terrowin bounced on the seat. 'And I thought: why not choose the best chair in town?'

He tossed the coins onto the glossy walnut desk top; one landed on its edge and rolled drunkenly away. The mayor's gaze followed it, and by the time it clapped on the floorboards, Terrowin was armed with the flintlock, cocked and ready. The barrel wiggled in the way that everyone knew meant "hands up".

'You've come to kill me?' The mayor set his steaming mug atop a small table, and raised his hands. 'Might I ask who paid you?'

'Oh, nobody's paying me.' Terrowin put his feet back up on the desk and reclined into the chair. 'I just needed something to do on this miserable Tarnsday morning.'

'Well, would you mind taking your feet down from my father's desk?' The mayor's arms looked to be getting tired already, too used to pushing pencils instead of fighting. To think, his father was the creator of the guild; it defied belief. Sadly, the great man had up and died while Terrowin was on route from Scold, and all that remained was his heir, the portly clerk.

'I'm quite comfortable, thank you very much. A wee bit peckish, mind. Have you got anything good? I'm sick of stale bread and I've heard you trumped-up richlings love a foreign delicacy.'

'I could have the staff knock something up for you.' The mayor allowed one of his tired arms to rest on the doorframe.

'Any funny business, or those green eyeball things on sticks for that matter, and I'll redecorate the back wall in brains… Luncheon however…' Terrowin pushed his bottom lip forwards and tried to put on his best mayorly tone. 'Most agreeable.'

'Vivian?' the mayor called down the hallway. 'Would you be able to make up a light lunch and have it brought to my office? No olives.'

'Are you not joining me?' Terrowin waggled his pistol playfully.

'Make enough for two,' the mayor added.

A distant "yes Mr Perrin" was heard in response.

'Now that's all sorted, Walter, would you like to take a seat in my office?' Terrowin gestured to the chair opposite.

The mayor followed his instructions, but seemed to be taking distinctly less enjoyment from the situation.

'It's Mayor Perrin to you, this is my office, and that was my father's desk, so if you would *please*…' The mayor was silenced by another wave of the pistol. He sighed and folded his hands in his lap as he sat down. 'Would you at least tell me why you're here if not to kill me?'

'Did I say you could lower your hands? I want them so high in the air your arms might just pop from their sockets.' Terrowin raised a stern if diminutive eyebrow at the mayor, enjoying the power a flintlock gave him. The man did as instructed. 'What I told you, if you were listening, was that I needed something to do to fill my Tarnsday. So here I am.'

'Unless you're planning on balancing books with me, why come here at all?' The mayor was becoming entirely too comfortable with the presence of the gun, and seemed to be of the opinion that just because Terrowin hadn't shot him at first sight, that he wouldn't do it if pushed. 'If you kill me, you'll not get out of the square before my guilders erase you.'

'Your guilders won't give a fuck when you're gone, *Walter*. To them you're just a convenience, the facilitator of a contract that means they won't be stabbed in the back by their nearest and dearest.' Terrowin picked an errant fleck of dry snot from the rim of his nose. 'They might even be glad you're gone, and elect somebody interesting to run the show; they might even choose *me*! I'd be like a feudal lord, lopping your head off and using the stump as a foothold to propel myself to greatness.'

'What a lovely image,' the mayor grumbled.

Terrowin rolled the snot-flake into a little ball and flicked it onto the desk. The mere sight of it produced a visible twitch from the mayor.

'Don't you just find it all so boring though?' Terrowin thrust himself to his feet. 'This town, for a place that's meant to be lawless, is so dull! Everyone just goes about their business, selling drugs and freshly abducted strumpets as if they were flour and eggs! It takes all the fun out of it!'

He prowled around the desk, gesticulating wildly, shaking a ribbon of lank hair free from its sweep.

'I came to this town to be a killer with my back against the wall, hiding from the imperials, and waiting for any number of knives in my spine. Now, I'm just a glorified cleaner.'

He picked a carafe off the shelf and tossed it at the far wall and mimed shooting it with the flintlock. 'Click, bang! Job's done, better spend half the day getting brains out of the carpet so that the guild doesn't get a bad rap.'

'What's wrong with doing the job right?' the mayor blustered.

'What's wrong with it?' In a sudden burst, Terrowin dashed for the mayor, leaping on him with all his weight.

The chair fell backwards and clattered to the ground. For a moment everything was chaos; Walter tried to escape, roll over, flailed for his captor's gun. It was like trying to catch a squealing pig. But Terrowin was more experienced, both in fighting men and catching pigs. He scrambled atop the mayor, pressed the barrel of the flintlock hard into his cheek, curtailing the fight in an instant.

The mayor screwed his face water tight, cringing away, his head thrust into the scratching carpet. The pistol pressed harder, wrinkling young skin on the man's temple.

'It's boring! Aren't you listening to me? I don't want to tell you again, because that's tedious too. T-E-D-E-U-S. Tedious! Open your ears and shut your flapping mouth for a minute and I might be able to tell you…'

A rifle clapped; the noise thundered around the wood panelled room. Terrowin felt a punch in his side, was knocked off the mayor, and flopped onto his back.

'Do you want me to finish him?' Lord Beechworth reloaded his rifle in the doorway. He was a tall man in a fine-tailored black suit with long tails that hung to the back of his knees. His top hat was off for the virtue of being indoors and his hair was lacquered to his head so tightly it almost looked to be painted on.

Terrowin rolled on the floor, kicking and hooting. He clutched his upper arm; blood pulsed between his fingers. Through gritted teeth, he jabbered, 'now this is exciting, wouldn't you agree, Walter?'

Lord Beechworth readied his rifle with the sleepy superiority that only the nobles could ever truly encapsulate, but followed Terrowin's bobbing head precisely. His finger poised to pull the trigger; a born and bred blue-blooded killer.

'Hang on a minute, Claude.' The mayor staggered upright and tried to catch his breath. 'Let him suffer a little first.'

'I have to admit; that smarts.' Terrowin propped himself up against the side of the desk.

He'd been shot before, and always savoured the thrill of his life-force pumping from a point of burning numbness. In those moments – and he would wager this wound to be one of the worst he'd yet suffered – he felt truly alive. His heart battered his rib cage, his pulse leapt in his throat, every strained muscle gasped for the precious blood congealing on the expensive Suradeshi rug.

Beechworth stood over him, levelling the rifle muzzle at Terrowin's chest. They both knew if he did anything stupid, there would be one more body floating down the Landslide.

'Is there any chance,' Terrowin wet his lips, nodding at the collection of liquor on the bookcase. 'That I could have a snifter off your shelf?'

'I hardly think it appropriate,' the mayor said offhandedly as he stood his guest chair back on its four legs. He set his large rump on it.

'Pity.' Terrowin winced, and clutched his hand more tightly over the wound. 'What time is that luncheon coming? I'll try my best to not bleed out by then.'

'It's not coming.' The mayor slapped his podgy belly; even cased behind tailored grey trousers and waistcoat, it was hard to miss. 'Do you think I've ever eaten a *light* lunch in all my days? It was code for the staff to fetch Claude here. It was quite fortunate you were hungry to be honest. Though we do have numerous "panic" phrases.'

'Oh.' Terrowin slumped forwards and let his hands fall into his lap. Blood ran freely from the hole in his arm, darkening his shirt rapidly. 'But we can't do business on empty stomachs, it's just not the way these things are done.'

'Can I put him out of his misery yet?' Lord Beechworth clenched his jaw, a cord of irritation visible at his temple.

'No, Claude, patience. It's better to know why he's here, don't want anyone else coming uninvited.' The mayor leant forward, intrigued. 'What business?'

'I couldn't possibly tell you.' Terrowin huddled himself tight, trying to feign a more rapid decline than his injury suggested. Perhaps if he faked a quick death, they might leave for the coroner, and he could sidle out the window – of course there was still the threat of a real death looming closely behind. 'Not on an empty stomach.'

'Just let me kill him.' Beechworth eyed down the sights of his rifle needlessly, just to show that he was serious.

'I'll hear what the strange lad has to say.' Exacerbated, the mayor pushed the lord-assassin's rifle aside and paced to the bookcase. He tugged open a drawer, extricated a fancy glass dish, and took a carafe from the shelf.

'Here you go.' The mayor set the containers in Terrowin's lap.

'What are these?' He picked up a small brown nugget from the dish and inspected it.

'Peanuts; from the south.'

'A foreign delicacy?' Terrowin chuckled, and popped the strange thing in his mouth. It tasted pleasant, salty, hopefully that wasn't blood – as far as he could tell, he was only hit in the arm, but shock had a tendency to numb. 'How about some medical attention too?'

'Don't push your luck,' Beechworth sneered.

'Well, we could.' The mayor shrugged a little, his doe-eyed face half-pleading and half-convincing the imperious nay-sayer. 'We can always lock him up should I not like what he has to say.'

'He tried to kill you, Walter.' Lord Beechworth rubbed his forehead. 'You're the leader of The Assassins' Guild, you've got to accept that death is part of the job.'

'Yes, but this lad's a member.' The mayor leaned in to check Terrowin was still conscious. 'You are a member, aren't you?'

Terrowin nodded slowly; a half chewed lump of nut fell from his bottom lip on a trail of drool. The weaker he made himself look, the more the mayor seemed to be warming to him.

'And we have to look after our own, it's the main tenet the guild is based on.' The mayor was more convincing than most lordlings with their nannies. 'And if he'd really wanted me dead, I probably would be. He's just eccentric is all, you know what our guilders are like. You're always saying how I don't understand them, well, this is a perfect opportunity to get to grips with one.'

'Alright.' Lord Beechworth lowered his rifle. 'He doesn't pose much of a threat I suppose. I'll fetch a surgeon.'

'Thanks, old chap,' Terrowin wheezed, unable to resist mimicking the lord's accent.

'Keep a close watch on him, I won't be gone long.' Beechworth picked up the flintlock and handed it to the mayor.

About turning with a military discipline, the lord strode out of the room. Terrowin listened to his footsteps shush across carpet, then get a little louder as he drummed down the wooden steps, eventually fading to nothing. He eyed his pistol in the mayor's grip; loose, uncomfortable, inexperienced. Perhaps now would be a good time to make a daring escape, but his body seemed more reluctant to spring into action than usual. His thoughts were pulled back to the task at hand.

'You mentioned business… that's not a word crosses many lips in our organisation. In fact, if it weren't for me, I dare say the guild would have gone bust by now. There's not many assassins can count higher than a set of fingers, and most are missing more than a few.' The mayor shuffled closer, the legs of the chair scraping against the carpet under his weight. His voice lowered conspiratorially, 'what exactly are you proposing?'

'There'll be gold a-plenty…' Terrowin coughed and wheezed, drawing the mayor closer with ever weakening words. 'Excitement, stakes, a bit of levity for once…'

He trailed off to nothing, dribbling even more mulched peanut. It was a shame to waste them as they were rather nice, but when he got into a role, he played it diligently.

'Go on,' the mayor prompted.

'A competition.' Terrowin pointed lazily at the mayor, his hand was mere inches from the loosely held pistol. Now or never.

He lurched forwards, snatched the flintlock from the mayor's chubby fingers, toppled onto his front, and rolled away like a sausage escaping a pan. He screamed for the duration, having briefly forgotten his injuries in the excitement. Pain and adrenaline thrust him to his feet. He wobbled around to find the window, aiming the gun in the vague direction of the mayor as he did so.

'Stay back!' He floundered about, trying to divide his focus between the two dancing windows. 'No wise man crosses Terrowin the Man-Butcher!'

The two windows drew together with great frowning and effort. He set off at a dash. This whole encounter hadn't gone exactly as expected and it was better to get the hell out while he was still breathing. His thigh collided with the desk and he reeled into the window frame, stopping momentarily before tipping onto the vaulted roof outside.

'Walter!' he bellowed as the world upended.

The slide down the tiles and freefall were pleasant compared to the harsh landing in the street that followed. His body hit the hard earth with a thump, but the pain was shockingly absent. He sprang up, his body ricocheting off the ground like a stick off a drum skin – resilient things, bones. He ran. Somehow, he managed to make it a few paces, his legs swinging under him like the lifeless appendages of a marionette. But it wasn't long before he collapsed onto his back. There was the pain, late and all the more potent for its absence.

He lay in a heap moaning, whimpering, and gasping, but at least he wasn't so bored any more.

'You bloody idiot.' Lord Beechworth's acid-glare swam into view, with a white-coated surgeon at his side. 'I don't think we'll be needing you actually doctor, this one's beyond saving.'

Polished gun-metal glinted in the sunlight as Beechworth readied his rifle. A lazy aim, held at the hip, with the muzzle not six inches from the near-dead intruder. There was no need to overstate his intent for the benefit of anybody watching, his actions would speak loudly enough this time.

'Don't you dare, Claude!' the mayor screeched from the window, but Beechworth pretended not to hear. 'We need boys like that. They've got spunk!'

The rifle swung over Terrowin's head; Beechworth pulled the trigger.

Crows cast to the sky with the thunderous rifle-boom. In such close confines, with houses all around, it was almost deafening. But in a place like Blackbile, there were no screams of horror or people running for shelter when they saw the smoking gun.

'Looks like your firing blanks,' Terrowin spluttered.

Beechworth tossed the rifle to the cobbles in a fit of pique. His bullet had lodged in the barrel and split it like a banana skin. Gun smoke weaved from the rift. It was a testament to the quality of the piece, as many a firearm would have simply exploded from such a jam. Beechworth stalked off.

Without further instruction, and bound by irrefutable oaths, the doctor knelt to treat Terrowin.

1682

Chapel bells announced the morning, and though each peel was more melodic than the last, all they garnered from William was a wince and a groan. It was the first day of the competition, the start only hours away, and he felt a full day short on sleep.

He had been up far too late going over the rules and discussing strategy with Vesta. He had wanted to ensure she was as clear on them as he was, particularly the new rules that related to her specifically as a sponsor. She had fallen quiet for a while upon learning that should she break any rule or attempt to flee, she would be held for execution after the competition was done. She had been almost apoplectic in learning that should William break the rules, he would merely be disqualified, and – even if innocent – she would be executed regardless. The only chance she had to survive was if he kept her safe *and* won the whole competition.

She had scorned at the crooked state of the guild for a while, but her rage quickly turned her back to the feud with her brother. The conversation of her slim chances was put behind them and not mentioned again.

William tried to swallow the dry taste from his mouth, but it just made it worse. It was as if he had been out all night drinking and carousing; his body was sore enough. He had been allocated a small blanket and cold square of floorboards across the room from her modest but comfortable bed. Every splinter and exposed nail had made itself known, waking him periodically, aching his bones and joints. He'd probably be in better shape if he hadn't slept.

He sat up, cracked his neck and back, and took in the bleary dawn-lit space. It was a small room in The Brazen Bull, with a peeling ceiling and stained walls, and the narrowest window it seemed possible to make. He wondered if the mouldering damp had contributed any to his dry mouth and sore head.

Vesta let out a sleepy sigh and rolled over in the covers. Damn her, but it looked comfortable. He could have had his own; his own bed, his own room, his own sliver of light. Once he and Vesta had signed up to compete, he convinced her to part with the rest of her savings, but had opted to be sensible with what little coin they had. A thick new shirt in black – to hide filth – and a hard-wearing pair of brown woollen trousers were his first purchases. The tailor had even hemmed the trousers in oilcloth to protect against the wet and mud, so he was quite pleased with his haul.

His other acquisition was not so impressive. Though he should have invested more money in it, he couldn't compete naked.

He picked up the matchlock and weighed it in his hand; the handle was awkward with a great ball on the end, all carved from wood with flaking lacquer. It was more of an antique than a professional firearm, the sort of thing used by an old pirate with a beard in his name. It did shoot, but not very well. He spent a few of the dozen bullets he could afford trying to hit a bottle from ten paces and had missed each time. He couldn't even use paper cartridges. Each reload he needed to mess about; pour in the powder, tamp it down, and tip the bullet in the muzzle.

Vesta sighed again, mumbled something sleepily. He set down the pistol and supposed it would have to do.

'Morning.' William yawned and stretched the kinks from his spine as if he had only just woken up. He didn't want her to know he had a poor night's sleep; her life was riding on his skill and he didn't want to distress her.

'It's the day.' She propped herself up against the headboard with two large pillows and huddled the covers around her bunched up knees. Damn her, but it looked warm.

She squinted at the little slit of a window. He wondered if she was worrying; he was certainly on edge about the whole thing. If she had doubts, she hid them well.

'Today, we kill my brother,' she proclaimed with purpose, 'avenge my father's death, the loss of everything, put him back in his place… maybe get back to a normal life…'

She trailed off.

William considered mentioning "clause four" again. She was so focussed on her own task, he half thought she might up and abandon him once her brother was dead. He decided to trust her, for better or worse.

'Are you ready?' he asked.

She gestured to her nightclothes as if what he asked was ridiculous.

'No, I mean, are you ready for what's going to happen.' He searched her for any doubt, or fear, or regret. So far, there was nothing, just a whole lot of denial. He was sure that would change once she actually saw the death, saw a few sponsors mercilessly cut down. He just hoped the morbid realisation – understanding exactly what she had embroiled herself in – didn't paralyse her with fear, he didn't want to lose her that way.

It seemed that he was more worried about her death than she was. To him, she was just desperate, lost. There was still chance for her to turn back – or there would have been had she not signed her life to him. He had been there once, could have gone back, but had pressed on. Now he was a killer and there wasn't much else he could be; a thief perhaps, but he expected the pay wasn't so good.

'I'm ready.' She made a fist in the covers.

It looked like storybook resolve to William, a lie she told herself, but maybe he was just projecting. He hoped he was wrong, that she was made of sterner stuff than he expected.

'Good.'

They made themselves ready quickly, dressing in their only clothes and heading down to the tavern. Their breakfast of cured meat, bread, and cheese was gifted free by the landlord, who was pleased to be housing a guilder so soon before the competition. They ate their fill and drank from a selection of light teas. William's back still ached a little, but he was as prepared as he could get, given the circumstances. Making sure that they kept good time, he secured his matchlock and they left for the town hall.

Though Blackbile was buzzing with more energy than it had been all week, getting to the square was relatively painless. A whole road had been closed to the public, allowing entrants and sponsors a direct route to the centre of it all. Even prior to the private road, things hadn't been too difficult; the tourists knew better than to be caught out in the streets once things started, and had collected in the numerous viewing zones. Taverns heaved with spectators, towers thrummed with chanting, great scaffolds swayed under the weight of so many viewers. Little islands of mania that would soon become the most peaceful areas in the town.

He spotted a betting den in a small square, open to the road on one side. Men were stood on a raised platform, swapping betting slips for gold, silver, and even imperial grana. Some were changing odds in real time as the bets came in, swapping panels painted with numbers between hooks, and moving assassin's names up and down a list of most likely winners. William suspected his name wasn't even amongst the few banners that had been discarded on the floor, Goldin's might be, but it wasn't up on the board. Lord Beechworth was top of the rankings, even despite his age, and Ojo was loitering in third place, given the uncertainty of his recent whereabouts. William was surprised to see Genevieve had landed the second spot for odds-on winner; perhaps her smug self-satisfaction was justified after all.

There were a few other names on there that he recognised. Ottilie of Sable, the mad bomber, who he recently learned was the rhinoceros ringleader of the Scolds who mocked him. Hester Turani was another he thought he might know, but only in the vaguest of terms. Dr Barber's name was just being discarded from the list to be replaced at position twenty by Luis Lafitte-Dugas; an unknown.

A group of young boys dashed across the roadway to put a bet on while the streets were still safe. William wondered if they had come with parents or without, either way seemed madness. He found it ludicrous and incredible that anybody would to come to the town for the pleasure of watching all-out war, though he was sure the entrants and sponsors were even more unhinged.

As he and Vesta filtered onto the contestant-only thoroughfare, he eyed his fellows subtly. He didn't want to let them know he was measuring each and every one of them. There were meticulous sharpshooters, poisoners, men and women that fought with blades and maces. He saw two stinking brutes whose frames seemed almost impossible in stature. Then he saw the group of Scolds and their rhinoceros woman, who was even larger still, taller and broader than William had dared imagine a human could be.

She had an iron cylinder across her back for launching firework-projectiles. He had tried to ape her enthusiasm for killing in Fairshore; it didn't suit him as it did her. Perhaps, if she hadn't inspired him to do that, he wouldn't have got himself into such a tangle; he wouldn't be "The Masquerade Killer", and he wouldn't be here. It was silly to blame anybody but himself.

He checked on Vesta; she didn't seem too perturbed by the competition. As far as she was concerned, her brother was their only contender. It was a worry, but merely a drop in the ocean at this point.

When they arrived in the town square, between the stacked bleachers, William took Vesta's hand and led the way. He directed them through the red velvet ropes and into the press. While he was trying to remain confident, there had to be a few hundred assassins here, and each one of them had a sponsor. There were so many strange and familiar faces; wanted-poster-ghouls, guild legends. He began to doubt his chances of success. He could shoot – at least he could with his flintlock – but there were so many here, he couldn't see the winner being decided by anything other than dumb luck. At least that made the veteran champions less terrifying.

Swift movement caught his eye; a waving hand in the closest tier of bleachers. It was the ugly bug child, who stood beside his lanky friend. Strange that they remembered him; he wasn't as distinctive as them, and impressive that they could pick him out of the crowd. The child did have awfully oversized eyes; perhaps that gave him an advantage. William wondered if it was them who had stolen his pack from the cart. Goldin would have surely mentioned it to him otherwise. Thief or not, it was nice to have at least one fan out there. He waved back lightly.

'William, fancy seeing you here!' The red-faced cultist thrust through a group of sponsors, all smiles and friendly hand gestures. It seemed everyone was on the lookout for William today, and he hoped that didn't bode too badly once the shooting started.

'And Vesta, my dear sister,' he continued. His face had been freshly painted, vibrant and dripping. The burned side revealed entirely too many teeth. 'It is *so* good to see you again!'

A clutch of six other cultists pressed tightly around him, armed with a variety of grenades, rods, guns, and spears. The man himself had a particularly impressive silver pistol at his hip; William's flintlock.

'I have to admit, you really have made my competition, William.' Red-Face beamed, gesticulating dramatically, as is a pseudo-preacher's want. 'My superior has come all the way from Vitale to see us win this thing for the Cause, and now I get to prove myself by sacrificing my very own sister.'

He fanned at his eyes with a free hand, welling up from the sheer deific joy of it all.

Vesta was sneering so hard William thought she might actually let out a growl. He didn't blame her for wanting to kill her brother, it seemed like more of a mercy than anything else. The man was quite mad.

'We should be going.' William tugged on Vesta's arm, fearing a premature outbreak of violence. In that moment she was a pit-bull, and he just had to ease her away. 'I arranged to meet a friend, don't want to keep him waiting.'

Friend. That word sounded odd coming from his own mouth; as it would on many an assassin's lips. It was a lonely profession, and he had been on his own for so long. The prize was a strange event for all, but he was getting used to making allies and enemies again. If only the transition back to solitude after the competition would be so easy.

'Don't go. You can stay here can't you?' Red-Face spoke like a welcoming host. 'We don't have to fight, do we? You keep Vesta here, we'll take care of her. You can bow out of the competition. I'm sure I can make it worth your while.'

William mirrored Vesta's sneer; wishing death on the slimy sycophant. He was half tempted to stay and get the fight done as soon as the competition began; get what Vesta wanted, get his pistol back, wipe that unnatural smile away. But there were too many cultists at the zealot's back, too many chances to get shot.

'Don't worry.' He let Vesta take his hand again. 'We'll be coming back for you.'

'I'm glad you managed to find yourself a sponsor.' Goldin drove a path through the clutter of waiting assassins. 'I worried you'd miss out on all the fun.'

Though William had planned to meet with Goldin at a large flag set up in the centre of the square, they had happened upon one another in the crowd while still on route to the landmark. Goldin then insisted they get a better spot, so that he might see the stage, and hadn't reacted with much humour when Vesta had offered to hoist him up.

'Fun?' Vesta scoffed. 'This isn't exactly my definition of fun.'

'Quite talkative, isn't she? Ever considered gagging her, like mine?' Goldin jostled the wriggling cocoon of bandages and ropes across his back, producing a muffled moan. The bound body clattered against his blunderbuss – on a loose strap over his other shoulder. It was a wonder the little man was still so sprightly as he weaved through the crowd, his sponsor must have been almost half his weight, and the blunderbuss nearly as tall.

'It might be a good idea.' William weighed Vesta with his eyes, wondering with a smirk as to how practical it might be to keep her across his back. He certainly wouldn't have to worry about her dashing off to battle her brother. Vesta's baleful glare cut short his flight of fancy.

'I don't think that would work for us,' he added more seriously.

'I'm only pulling your leg anyway, and no offence meant miss.' Goldin offered Vesta a cheeky wink. 'You could do much worse than William here.'

They swerved around the giant twins William had seen on the road; they stank even worse up close.

'I'm hoping to find another pistol fairly quickly.' William laid out his strategy. 'We're better off working together, I think. We'll have a better chance of success if we can both shoot. There's nothing in the rules against it.'

'Aye.' Goldin mused before adding grimly, 'I've heard some sponsors are fully paid-up assassins themselves.'

William didn't like that. An amateur was one thing, but partnering with an experienced murderer seemed a little underhanded. Now that the gate had slammed closed over his own avenue for cheating, he was dead against that sort of thing.

A not-so-distant cry prickled the hairs on the back of William's neck. He slowed to a halt and listened. Vesta and Goldin didn't notice, pushing ahead through the crowd. The sound came again, like a distant moan. He couldn't make out what the words were, but the timbre had an eerie familiarity to it. Something that raised a primal fear in his gut, but also washed him with pleasant nostalgia. He couldn't put his finger on quite what the noise reminded him of.

Assassins balked and blustered as they were heaved aside by a strong figure heading straight towards William. He heard the stumbling footfall first, the laboured breath second. Then, as a refined lady assassin – with vast frills and keenly sharpened rapier – was thrust aside, he saw the half-silhouette.

'Fissss!' the mentally stunted man screamed joyfully at the sight of William, somehow recognising him after nearly ten years. Hot spittle sprayed from his mouth, and he shuffled closer, trying to shudder out the word. 'Fiss- sseee.'

William's mind conjured the slick stench of northern seas, fish guts, and smoke. He didn't know what to do. The shambling horror seemed friendly enough now, even if he had tried to kill him as a child. He wondered exactly how sapient a man with half a head could be. Lamebrain; that's what the other slaves called him.

'Fisss…' The slave leered at him like a long-lost friend. Unnaturally strong hands grasped William by the wrist and pushed up his shirt sleeve. A long, bony finger prodded at the large red blotch of a scar that ran the length of his forearm. Proudly, the slave proclaimed, 'gut and shhh-kale.'

'Yes.' William smiled nervously, tried to gently pull his arm away, momentarily worried that Lamebrain might continue where he'd left off all those years ago. 'Gut and scale; well done?'

'What are you doing?' An assassin with long black ringlets and a chin the size of a ship's bow shoved William away from the slave. 'It's rude to speak to a man's sponsor, don't you know that?'

'Excuse me?' William looked the foppish hitman from head to toe, unable to hide his disgruntled expression. 'He spoke to me first. We're old friends… in a way.'

'Yes well, he belongs to me, and he's not interested in speaking to the likes of you.' The ringleted dandy puffed out his barrel chest and placed bejewelled fists on his hips. William came to recognise the embroidery on his frockcoat; it matched the symbol from the back of the carriage that had clipped his arm and ruined his last shirt.

William wasn't so eager to get into an argument, he wasn't even that pleased about the crooked horror coming back into his life. Though Lamebrain didn't look quite as horrific as William remembered. The man was shorter than him now, deathly pale and thin – though seemed strong from relentless labour. He was assuredly the victim of some dreadful accident, a casualty of the Scold War perhaps, or one of the countless southern conquests. There was a leather belt around his neck, and sore skin beneath it; the privateer-type had been leading him about like a dog on a gilt rope. There was great injustice in it, but William couldn't intervene, not with so little time left before the starting bell.

'Goodbye, Lamebrain.' William clapped the slave on a hunched shoulder. He didn't feel so good about calling him that, but the slave seemed to delight in being remembered. 'And good luck.'

If only there was a way to wish the sponsor luck, without wishing it to the entrant too.

'Yes, and good luck to you.' The privateer chuckled, steering his slave away with the fancy leash. 'An honourable death to us all.'

'Bye fi-sha,' Lamebrain called after him. Words fell out in gasps as he loped away, 'fiss, fish, fishhy.'

William waved farewell. Something about seeing Lamebrain again brought a smile; despite the mad slave's sour circumstances, he seemed happy enough with his lot. It gave him hope; if an emaciated, braindead slave, with chains on his arms and legs, could survive a burning and sinking ship, then he stood a chance at winning. It also sparked the thought that Lamebrain might surmount the odds and survive the competition, of course that would mean the privateer had to win: a terrible thought.

'Everything alright?' Vesta asked as he caught up. She and Goldin had found a place well suited to the little man and stopped.

'Just a bit of a misunderstanding.' He massaged his scar. He could still feel the line Lamebrain had traced down it with his finger.

'William, remember Dr Barber?' Goldin reintroduced the wheelchair-bound scientist and his sponsor. William wasn't sure whether it was coincidence or prior arrangement on Goldin's part, but he was glad to be at the opening ceremony again with such an esteemed committee member. Maybe this time he might not make such a fool of himself.

'Nice to meet you again, William.' The doctor smiled crookedly. 'This is my sponsor, I call him Barbie. He's one of my doppelgangers.'

The cripple's sponsor looked eerily similar, but straightened out, and with full use of his legs. If Dr Barber was punctured offal, his sponsor was a freshly inflated pig's bladder, ready for street urchins to kick. He offered his hand for William to shake; he took it.

'Nice to meet you.' William smiled weakly.

'And you.' The doppelganger nodded like a well-trained servant.

'Good, isn't he?' The crippled doctor smiled. 'He's the brawns to my brain.'

'Are you twins or something?' William looked from one face to the other. Despite the lop-sidedness of one, it was uncanny.

'Something like that, yes.' The cripple stroked the doppelganger's arm with his chicken-foot hand. 'I won't bother explaining it. I tried to make it simple for Goldie and he still couldn't fathom it.'

'Goldie? Are you two friends now?' William chuckled at Goldin's bizarre ability to turn any adversarial encounter into something quite amiable.

'Oh yes.' Barber rubbed his claws together. 'We got drinking together in Melting Moments. I was there to watch Barbie take on some of those big women and...'

'You wouldn't start without me, would you?' Genevieve appeared through the crowd, she was holding two mugs of effervescent liquid. 'Have you sampled the refreshment stands yet? I'm quite certain they're not poisoned; I had my sponsor take a swallow and he seemed alright.'

She navigated her mouth to a reed that bobbed in one of the mugs. Quite unable to stop himself, William fixed on the delicate work of muscles around her mouth as she sucked.

'Are you all as excited as I am? It feels an age since I last killed someone; this week has been hell.' She looked about the group, seeing that Goldin and William had joined Dr Barber. As she spotted Vesta, her eyebrows twitched into a momentary frown. 'Hello, are you a guilder? I don't believe we've met.'

'I'm William's sponsor,' Vesta replied flatly.

'Oh, you found one then? And she's pretty.' Genevieve gave William a look as if he was bringing home his first girlfriend. The way she cocked her eyebrow and gave him the slightest smirk brought a scarlet warmth to his cheeks and the tips of his ears. He glanced away, foolishly choosing to appraise her fighting gear: form fitting panelled leather, white kid gloves and scandalously tight trousers sliding into high boots. She had a sniper's rifle over her shoulder on a strap very similar to Goldin's, but the buckle had been properly adjusted, and sat just right.

She leaned close to Vesta, fixing her with a sly expression, and said in what could only be described as a pantomime whisper, 'lovely to meet you; hope you don't die too gruesomely.'

Vesta was taken aback but hardened quickly, sneering, 'and you.'

Leaving no time for the animosity to simmer, a small boy sidled up to the group. A pickpocket or beggar; perhaps a marketeer's boy here to sell last minute supplies.

'We're not interested.' William shooed the little boy before he could peddle whatever nonsense he was peddling.

'What?' The boy scowled and pouted. He certainly did have an attitude on him. Spoiled from the look of it. He had a thick shirt that put William's to shame; plaid, as was the fashion in Garland. He even had little suspenders and a cravat, as if a rope belt was beneath an urchin such as himself.

'We're not interested in whatever you're selling.' William rolled his eyes. 'And we don't want to be minding our pockets, so take your pilfering little fingers elsewhere.'

'William.' Genevieve cast a withering look his way and set her hand on the little boy's shoulder. 'This is my son.'

He opened his mouth to quickly back pedal, but she hadn't finished yet.

'And,' she drew the tension out a little, clearly enjoying herself, 'my sponsor.'

Any lingering interest William had in the lissom markswoman faltered and died. That she had a child was no deterrent, but the wanton sacrifice of a life she had created, doused his lust as surely as the northern seas had stolen his breath.

'Quite ingenious, don't you think? My motherly instincts will surely give me the edge in battle.' She smiled at the poorly hidden surprise on William's face. 'And weak willed sops who like to call themselves assassins, but don't have the guts to kill a sweet little cherub like mine, will be easy pickings.'

Stunned, unable to find the words to put together just how cruel Genevieve was, all William could do was stare at her. He didn't dare to look at the smug child. Somehow, she had even convinced her own son that this was the best way she might win. The kid really had no clue just how horribly he might die.

The crowd shivered into silence, the absence of excited chatter raising a new chill in William. A short distance away, the mayor took to the stage for the final time, initiating proceedings that would begin the deathly competition.

1667

Terrowin woke to the high whine of his own ears; the sort of bodily phenomena caused by a history of shooting firearms and then the absence of any other sound. The ceiling above him was dreary grey stone and the wall at his side was equally bland. Across the room was a heavy door set in a row of iron bars. A jail cell. Exactly where he didn't want to be. It was far more meticulously kept than any imperial dungeon; there were no torture devices, or rats snuffling around, not even an interesting growth of mould to fixate on.

A cell like this one meant he'd be sentenced to years of hard labour for his intrusion. Bleeding to death would have been preferable. He had only been awake for about twenty seconds and the near insurmountable life of drudgery that lay ahead was already weighing on him like a slab of lead.

He sat up in his cot, swinging his legs to the floor. He could vaguely remember a few interactions with visitors. Until now, he had been too short on blood to gain a full hold on consciousness, so his recollections were only the vaguest smears. They had interrogated him, but he couldn't remember his answers or even the nature of the questions. From the dullness of the pain across his whole body, and the dramatically reduced sting in his arm, he could reasonably guess that he had been recovering for a while. The fuzz on his chin certainly supported that claim.

There was a distant memory of being bathed with a sponge and his mouth lacked dryness – still tasted of gruel. They had been treating him well enough. None of that would matter in five minutes, however; he had a good mind to take his own life. He wasn't bitter about it; they said you only live once, but they – whoever they were – also said the afterlife was a paradise. He didn't see much wrong with arriving there a little early, he would be able to see his mother again, get on her nerves in that way he did as a child. That would be nice.

He refused to live out his life as some chain-gang slave. He had come here for the chance of excitement, and while it had been worth risking his life, it wasn't worth a slave's lot. His mind was made up.

He stood up and studied the roughly cut rocks that made up the far wall, until he found a particularly aggressive brick. Without taking another second to think about it, he ran as fast as his legs would carry him, with his head down and his hands wrapped behind his back.

The pounding thump that echoed through his skull floored him for a good ten minutes of constant screaming and crying. He might have killed himself in one, had his legs not been so atrophied; another good hit might finish him off entirely.

He dragged himself up and tried to find the same spot on the wall. In any other circumstance he could have located it easily, as it was marked with a big red patch of blood, but for some gods' forsaken reason the stain had decided to multiply and dance in figure eights across the wall.

He grabbed a fist of air, fell to one knee, and then eventually slumped onto his arse. Time lost definition. Maybe twenty minutes passed, maybe a few hours. He wondered whether the pain would ease off, and if it did, whether it would set him back to square one. Perhaps his first collision was banked for later, so only one more major head trauma would sort him out.

'Are you alright in there?' The mayor's familiar voice pierced through the haze. 'I told them to get me when you woke, but I didn't expect you'd be halfway to killing yourself by the time I got here.'

Terrowin tried to push himself to his feet to go for another round of head-versus-wall, but his legs were failing to keep him upright.

'I don't want to be a prisoner.' Terrowin tried to make out which of the two fluttering mayors was the real one. 'Freedom's boring enough. Could you do me a favour and just finish me off? I don't really mind how I go if I'm honest, a blaze of glory would be great, fading out here would do, but it's a bit drawn out. So, if you'd just grab something heavy and stove my head in, that'd be grand.'

'You really are quite mad – an exemplary guilder – and I just can't fathom you. Beechworth's right, it's harder to get in the head of a guilder than I thought. He thinks I should get my hands dirty, kill a man, then maybe I'll know what it's like.'

'Kill me then; stove my head in, then maybe you can have a little root around.' Terrowin tried to stand again and flopped against the bars.

'Not my cup of tea. My father's maybe, but not mine,' the mayor chuckled. 'I was interested to hear out your proposal. See, I've inherited the run of this guild, and I don't want to lose it. I need guilders to steer me, tell me what they want, and I'll filter it through some kind of sanity. I need people like Beechworth, but I also need people like you; common, deranged, brilliant in your own way.'

'You're quite a talker,' Terrowin groaned.

'Beechworth had you locked in here for the safety of others, didn't want you hurting anyone in your daze. Since you were feeling better I was actually going to let you go. But now... that'll have to wait until your head's fixed.'

'No! I'm fine, look.' Terrowin slithered up the bars. 'Just let me out, I'm not disposed to prison life. I'm fine, just...'

He let go of the bars and tried to stand. It was like he was balanced on top of two five foot needles; the world spun around him, he staggered, slipped, and fell. His face cracked on the rusted iron bedframe. It took him another quarter of the way towards death, knocked three teeth from him, and plunged him into unconsciousness.

Chains dragged on Terrowin's wrists and ankles. Not exactly ideal, but a brisk march through wintry streets was infinitely preferable to any more time in the cell. Two guilders escorted him, both armed with blunderbusses that could blow open his chest with the pull of a trigger. He presumed they were taking him to meet the mayor, but there was also the possibility they were leading him to the hangman. He found the second prospect far more tantalising; whenever he had seen men hanged before, he would always daydream on the possibility of a daring rescue or escape. The thought of being the man on the gallows, moments from the end, then fighting his way to safety, set him tingling with anticipation and put him in a rather good mood.

Though the sky was overcast and the sun only a hazy white disk, he thought the way the perpetual twilight caught the ash stacked rooves of the buildings was a delight. The air was frigid, but his breath came out in pleasant steamy gusts, and the sting of cold around his temples made him feel alive. In comparison to the hellish solitude of the drab cell, it was all so wonderful. So lovely, in fact, that he thought it worthy of note.

'Lovely day,' he noted.

One of the guards grunted in response and gave him a nudge to quicken his pace; evidently not so awed by the mundane beauty of the world. Since the attention from the mayor's doctor, Terrowin's legs felt sprier than they ever had. He might have been tempted to make a break for it, had he not been chained to a heavy iron ball.

Ash was falling steadily and the crows – that usually plagued the townsfolk for scraps – huddled in eaves to keep clean. Terrowin opened his mouth, caught a falling flake on his tongue and instantly regretted it. He doubled over to choke out the taste.

One of the escorts, a tan-skinned southern guilder – with red and white feathers in her powdered dreadlocks – pushed a trumpet-like musket to his back. She spat to the mud, and drawled, 'appreciate it without dawdling, hm?'

'No need to be miserable about it.' He contorted his face into a parody grin, but started walking as she instructed.

'Turn right up here.' She responded to his petulance by shunting his jail-ball with a well-placed boot, dragging him sharply into the next street.

She was all business and no joy this one; didn't even carry a flint-headed throwing axe, or wear a necklace of scalp flesh and rotting ears like she was supposed to. At least that's what the empire veterans had assured him when they showed him some caricatures. The little etchings had been pinned all around the conscription depot.

At the time, the prospect of fighting "real savages" had been a tempting one, but ultimately he'd refused. Orders and Terrowin went together like Waiting and Terrowin; not very well. He suspected now that he had made the right choice; this assassin was just like any other guilder, no more terrifying or savage as far as he could tell. He doubted she would last that long in Scold, let alone the northern reaches of Scoldland. He had barely come out with all his sensibilities intact, and he was definitely more savage than she.

As the road opened to the town square, Terrowin was more than a little disappointed. There was a distinct lack of gallows, a pyre or even a crowd to see him off, so a death defying escape would have to wait. They were escorting him instead to the town hall. It was a comfort that his idea would at least be heard, and that would bring him one step closer to the all-out madness he craved.

The two guards led him through the main doors; the more conventional route to the mayor's office. The chequerboard foyer, blonde bespectacled receptionist, crisp sign-in sheet and sweeping staircase were distinctly less exciting than the column he had scaled and the roof apex he had balanced along last time. He was kept in his chains, but one of the guards did pick up the heavy iron ball so Terrowin could ascend the stairs easier; very generous.

'There you are!' Walter extricated himself from a desk full of mayorly paperwork and greeted Terrowin as brightly as if he were Lord Beechworth himself. There was a half-finished glass of whiskey in his hand, and the remnants of a distinctly heavy lunch peppering his three pieces of tweed. 'Feeling better?'

'Terrible, thank you.' Terrowin showed his teeth, and the gap behind his canines. The motion on his face pulled at bruises that seemed to be all over his head. It served as a quiet reminder of his failure in killing himself, of which, currently, he was quite pleased about. Not since his last visit to the mayor's office had he felt this level of anticipation.

'Please, sit.' The mayor ushered Terrowin to a side chair. One of the guards doubled over at Terrowin's sudden movement and nearly dropped the iron ball on the expensive parquet floor – the equally lavish rug had been removed, presumably for an attempt at washing out all the blood. Quite generously, Terrowin quickened his pace, causing the guard to fumble the ball and score a line in the expensive lacquer.

'Would you like something? Food, a drink perhaps?' the mayor added, with a wince for the state of his office. 'I've heard you can't do business on an empty stomach.'

'I could murder one of those savoury nuggets.' Terrowin collapsed into the chair. 'A peanut, was it?'

'Yes.' The mayor directed the southerner to the shelf with a click of his fingers, and instructed the other to remove Terrowin's chains.

The two killers reluctantly obeyed their clerical master. The shackle unclipped and Terrowin stretched himself out. He couldn't help but chuckle, the most lawless people in the world obeying a simple bureaucrat for the comfort that a contract provided. He kicked off his worn boots and reclined like he was settling in for the night.

'You wanted to see me Walter?' Lord Beechworth padded into the room. Terrowin didn't turn around, but he could tell the exact moment the man spotted him because his footsteps stopped with a stomp. 'Do you want me to fetch my rifle?'

Terrowin barked a laugh, all this caution over someone as minor as him.

'That shouldn't be necessary.' The mayor took a filled glass from a silver platter offered by a superbly obedient murderer. 'You were a little trigger happy last time, these guild-fellows will provide security for today.'

Beechworth harrumphed. The mayor ignored it.

'So, explain this proposition you had. A business venture, was it?'

'Well, I've been thinking to myself; I miss the good old days. The days before the guild took hold, when every assassin was just out for number one and would kill anyone for the right to a contract. It was exciting not knowing whether you were going to get a bullet in your head; kept you on your toes.' Terrowin wiggled his, agitating a hole in his grimy sock, and sunk further into his seat. 'Now everything goes a lot smoother, I can just pick up a job from a guild drop-off and get on with it, but… where's the danger?'

He shrugged, adding, 'it just gets to the point where the killing becomes tedious. Farm boys and fat country gents are all I get nowadays, and frankly they're beneath me.'

'Do you want more high profile contracts? If you're good, we're always looking to up-skill our assassins.' The mayor tried to proffer a solution, but it seemed that he just couldn't understand.

'They're all beneath me Walter. I don't want to kill an accountant, or a magnate, or even a king. I want to kill an *assassin.*' He let the mayor fully absorb that for a moment before continuing, 'and I'm sure I'm not the only one. Sooner or later this monotony will spread and your whole empire will crumble beneath you.'

He shoved a fistful of peanuts into his mouth. 'Lunatics breaking into your office is only the beginning of it.'

'Well, what do you propose is done?' The mayor was leaning so far forwards his arse was beginning to peel off his chair. Terrowin hadn't the patience for fishing, but he suspected this was what it felt like to be reeling in a big one.

'A competition, of course!' he proclaimed triumphantly. 'A bout open only to guild members. We'll gamble our lives for the prize, and only one can be donned the champion. The rest will be sent home in boxes.'

He thought for a moment.

'Or several small boxes.'

'And what, pray tell, would be a prize worthy enough to tempt my assassins into what is tantamount to suicide?' The mayor still didn't understand, damned bureaucratic fool.

'Winning! Being proclaimed the best assassin that ever was! Going down in history as a hero rather than a crook.' Terrowin spread his grin despite the pain.

'I doubt a little scuffle in our town would be history worthy, we must lose five men a night in tavern brawls.'

'We could promote it as a big event,' Beechworth posited, pacing from behind Terrowin to peer out the window. 'Invite imperial citizens to watch, they love a good hanging – a blood thirsty group the lot of them.'

'You're not taking this seriously are you Claude?' Walter shook his head in disbelief; took a swig of his whiskey.

'We could sell tickets, make this hell-hole *the* destination for people to see some top-tier death and destruction. It would be a boon for our floundering economy, that's for sure.'

'Aye!' Terrowin was getting giddy at the thought of it, the scale could be far grander than even he had envisioned. 'Little kids won't want to grow up imperial knights or Vitulan centurions anymore, they'll want to be killers, and they'll idolise the guild, the competition winner above all.'

'The logistics of it, it doesn't work out.' The mayor pinched the corners of his eyes. Terrowin couldn't help but think that Walter's father might have gone for the idea by now. 'We'd lose too many members, that's if anybody would enter. I can't see any right minded guilder-'

'I would.' Beechworth leant against the wall behind the mayor with one finger pressed to his tightened lips. 'When you become an assassin it's ever so exciting. When you master the craft it becomes as tawdry as anything else. As much as I hate to agree, Terrowin is right. Look where I've ended up: in a town hall of all places, guarding a trumped up quill-shifter. No offence meant.'

'I'll enter,' the southern woman chimed in, caressing the stock of her blunderbuss. 'I fancy my chances. Even if I didn't win, I'm sure I'd come close. I'd still get remembered. One of the toymakers might immortalise me – I always used play with the jousters. Imagine that, children playing with assassin dolls; looking up to us.'

'If Zabal's doing it, I am too. I'm not getting left out.' The last assassin puffed out his chest, his cauliflower ears tinged red against the pasty flesh of his bald head. 'If you can have people remembering you, I want some too.'

'What am I supposed to do when you're all dead?' the mayor interrupted, souring the atmosphere somewhat.

'I'm not going to die.' The southerner scowled. 'I'm going to win.'

'Me neither,' the bald assassin added. 'And if we're not, there's no way Claude will fail, he's the best by far!'

'I don't think you quite understand how this works.' Mayor Perrin pushed his chair back and stood. Normally a move like that would signify the meeting was drawing to a close. But from his subordinates' lack of movement, they didn't seem to agree.

'We don't need to understand it, we're assassins, not mayors!' Terrowin nodded as if he had talked Walter into a corner.

'I've heard enough.' Perrin scowled at his guilders urging them to action with what little presence he had.

'As have I.' Beechworth pursed his lips for a second, then smiled. 'I think it's a brilliant idea. We'll raise the profile of the guild, get some money flowing, and – most importantly – have a little fun for once.'

'Now, hang on a minute Claude-' the mayor blustered, but was pushed aside effortlessly by his noble subordinate. He collapsed into his chair with a grunt, nearly tipping it over.

'Let's make it official, shall we?' Lord Beechworth held out his hand for Terrowin to shake.

'Aye, but I'm in charge of the whole enterprise.' Terrowin reached out, but Beechworth's hand retreated.

'Fifty-fifty.' The lord cocked an eyebrow. 'We'll plan this thing together, can't have you running amok unchecked.'

'I'm not good at sharing.' Terrowin's fingers trembled.

'Neither am I.' Claude offered his hand again.

Chaos and excitement hinged on a see-saw bargain, while tedium loomed dismally behind him. There was a subtle shift in Claude's otherwise collected calm; a slight widening of his mouth, the clench of his white teeth, a flare to his nostrils. The lord was as hungry to escape his sedentary existence as Terrowin himself.

'Deal.'

1682

The mayor had finished his initial speech of the opening ceremony, and rather than launching things into motion, handed off to his fellow committee members for further dawdling oration. Tobias Lietner, the great weaponsmith and inventor, talked relentlessly about the guild's successes over the past two years. Baradus Brindle, famous thug, bored everyone about future prospects. When he was done, and everyone was at their wits end, chief apothecary, Klava Ilyina, took to the stage to recite the key rules.

Dr Barber blew air through pursed lips. 'I always thought this part exciting when I was on the stage doing the rambling. Now I'm here, I see how tedious it is.'

'Quiet down a second.' Goldin craned up to see better, as if it would help his hearing over such a distance from the stage.

'Everyone received a complete copy of the rules at sign-up. For the illiterate, I shall repeat the most important points,' Klava announced.

Goldin tossed a wink William's way; for the little man's many talents, it seemed reading wasn't one.

'First and foremost,' Klava stated blandly. 'You may not kill an assassin that has a living sponsor, or if they withdraw once their sponsor has perished.'

William wondered exactly how a woman so dull might have come to join The Assassins' Guild. She wore a long black smock, had her hair in tight bunches, and though she spoke with a loud authority, her monotone was invasively draining. It seemed that all the anticipation in the square had seeped away like water in a cracked bucket.

'Get on with it!' An assassin ten yards in front of William started protesting.

'Once a sponsor dies, the entrant has one minute to clearly state their intention to withdraw or continue; during this time they must not be detained, injured, or slain. A declaration to continue is binding, and you are free to kill.' Klava paused to let the information sink in. 'If asked by entrant or referee, you are obligated to tell them if your sponsor still lives.'

'We don't care!' the protester shouted again, 'just get on with it; we want some blood!'

The subtle approach of a man amongst the committee members drew William's eye. Through a process of deduction, he assumed it was the spymaster, bent to whisper into the ear of a nearby guilder; bad news for the bored protester.

'Blackbile is an open battleground, excepting the spectator havens forbidden to competitors. Regardless of this space, your sponsor must stay within fifty feet of you while they still live.' Klava's bland speech swept over the protestor without pause.

'When the starting pistol is fired, a single hour of grace will commence. Killing may only start at the toll of the chapel bell. Once we are down to twenty entrants or fewer, by our referee's best approximation, the bell will toll again; you must lay down arms and return to the square.'

'What's a referee?' Goldin asked Barber in a hushed voice.

'Hired arbiters or non-competing volunteer-assassins. They stalk the streets, send messages back to the town hall. It's so the committee can follow the event; we've got a whole town to play in after all. You'll see them; they carry cages of birds.'

'After a brief respite and medical aid, the competition will continue in a more confined battleground until we have a winner.'

A moment of quiet followed as she shuffled a few papers and folded them under her arm. The mayor cleared his throat pointedly.

With a brief huff of exasperation – a large gesture on such a blank canvas – Klava added, 'killing referees is strictly prohibited; any offenders will be disqualified and barred from future contests.'

Without a thank you or a goodbye, she returned to her seat.

In the time it took the mayor to return to the podium, William noticed the protester had fallen suspiciously quiet. It seemed the guilder sent by the spymaster had been expediently deadly and silent under the murmur of the crowd.

'Thank you, Klava.' There was a weak smattering of applause, mostly from committee members, who had a higher risk of ingesting one of her poisons. 'Now, if you'll please welcome to the stage our two returning champions for this year: Lord Beechworth and Ojo Azul!'

While the further extension of proceedings had elicited a groan from the crowd, it quickly turned to a furore of excitement. The two greying legends walked onto the stage: Beechworth with a rifle and imperious bearing, and Ojo – armed with a longbow. It was a surprisingly inconspicuous weapon for a champion, but in the hands of a man so ruthless, it could be as deadly as any firearm or pipe bomb. William knew all too well that the old-hand's old hands had the strength to throttle a man with little effort.

'Welcome, to the eighth bi-annual Man-Butcher Prize!' Ojo's voice was as strong and distinct as William remembered. Even across the distance, and the hordes of rabid fans screaming and cheering, the rich timbre carried. 'Those of you who compete here today will go down in the annals of history; no matter the outcome.'

Lord Beechworth loaded his rifle. The bullet casing glinted in the sun; copper – the new design, available to only those with the right connections and wealth to burn. William had heard they were a vast improvement on hand-folded cartridges of paper, powder, and shot; the new loading devices made him shiver. Hard to believe, but rumour said there were rifles that could shoot ten times before requiring a reload. He just hoped that Beechworth was unique with this advanced weaponry; it hardly seemed fair.

Ojo waved the crowd to a hush and continued his rousing speech.

'What a pleasure to compete with such fine assassins. Without further delay, I, Ojo Azul, prize champion of seventy four, and Lord Beechworth, who needs no more introductions, declare this year's competition has begun. To a good and honourable death!'

Beechworth aimed his rifle for the sky; the single shot echoed over the erupting cheer of the crowd. The mayor clapped both legends on the back, whispered something in Beechworth's ear, and retired to a safe viewing platform.

'Is that it?' Confused, William looked around at the somewhat anticlimactic sight of assassins slowly milling out of the square. Genevieve had already disappeared.

'Well, yes,' Goldin chuckled. 'We can't rightly start shooting here and now can we? The prize would be given out before the hour was done. It'd be a bloodbath, entertaining no doubt, but over far too quickly.'

Goldin licked his finger and raised it skyward to test the wind. It probably wasn't that good of a gauge, as at arm's length it was still lower than the average height of the crowd.

'I'm headed west.' He grabbed William's hand and shook it. 'Go east, and I'll see you when this is all over, lad. Don't want to be shooting each other's sponsors or anything.'

'No,' William agreed. He watched Goldin filter into the crowd.

Vesta shuffled behind him. She had been silent for some time now, weighing the consequences for the first time it seemed. He patted her shoulder, thought about saying something, but nothing he could think of was particularly comforting. Victory was her only chance.

A furious screech diverted William's floundering consolation attempt. Barber was struggling to leave the square. The wheels of his chair had become embroiled in a thick patch of mud, just beyond the periphery of the dirt-stained carpet.

'No, no, no!' He thumped the armrest with a chicken-foot hand. '*Lift* and push; don't just push, you're making it worse.'

Barbie shoved harder, only serving to sink the chair further into the mulch. Smirking, and glad of the distraction, William stepped forward to assist, but someone else beat him to it. A knotty arm hefted the front of the chair, the wheels slurped from the mud and rocked onto semi-solid ground.

'Help-ing-g-g,' Lamebrain proclaimed with a wide smile, spread right to the edge of his half-width face. 'Helping.'

'Get off him!' The foppish privateer, ever close to his enslaved sponsor, slapped one of Lamebrain's hands making him recoil like a child.

'Do as you're told – I am so sorry about him, doctor.' The privateer sounded quite sincere in his apology to Barber; the doctor was a prize committee member after all. 'He's normally so obedient, but this crowd has him over-excited.'

William was caught between action and observation, and only now realised he'd been glaring at the exchange, disgusted. He and Vesta should have been well on their way by now. Yet the sycophancies of the privateer and Lamebrain's plight held him fast.

As if he could sense William's burning glower, the privateer straightened, bristling with lace and buoyant curls.

'If you wanted to watch a show, you should have stayed with the spectators, *Masquerade Killer,*' the privateer hissed, jutting his chin. 'Get away from me, and my sponsor.'

'Fish-ee,' Lamebrain shuddered out playfully, though it was cut short by a tremendous yank on his leash. The privateer's boot sent the slave sprawling, another strike made him wail.

William's matchlock was half-drawn when Vesta snatched his elbow, fixing him with wide eyes. The hour of grace had barely begun, and there were other things to worry about than Lamebrain and his master. His neck prickled, aware that others in the crowd would know who he was too; making more enemies was a bad idea. Settling on a final scowl, William rammed the pistol back in his belt and stalked from the square.

The hour-long amnesty was nearly at a close. William had planned to reach the market to loot a few quality weapons, but he and Vesta had made slow progress. The streets were heavy with the worst mud yet, and as he had feared, the main road was popular with the majority of assassins.

'I'm scared,' Vesta spoke for the first time in – he didn't know how long.

'I know.'

It felt as if a little string had been noosed around his heart and she had given it the lightest tug. The fact that she had volunteered to be his sponsor did little to assuage the guilt of accepting the offer. He swallowed the feeling; something he had excelled at throughout his murderous career. Only now was he beginning to feel full.

'I'm going to keep you alive,' he asserted, though it sounded more like an admission that she would probably die.

He stopped on a corner and leant out from the boardwalk, taking stock of the vicinity. There were possibly twenty other teams within range to start a small war once the bell tolled, and it was all so perfectly positioned under the shadow of a spectator tower. He wondered if the other entrants had flocked to this spot in particular to kick things off with some blood.

Afraid Vesta might crumble under the mounting pressure, William laid a hand on her forearm and presented the facts as softly as he could. 'We won't get to the market in time. Going through the backstreets will take longer, but we might not cross paths with anyone else. It's our best chance.'

They'd be less likely to stumble into any cultists too. Vesta's red faced brother wanted publicity for his cult as much as he wanted to take her head. William had to hope that would keep any Lambs near towers and bleachers; well away from him until he was ready for them.

'I don't like it out here anyway.' She scowled across the score of assassins; some took positions in buildings, others stood out in the open, just waiting for the bell to toll. 'We're too exposed.'

They slipped down a narrow passage.

Outside of the main roads, Blackbile was a stinking maze of crooked buildings, alleyways, and slums. William tried to keep them on a course parallel with the larger thoroughfare, but lost his sense of direction rapidly. He couldn't even tell how far away the main road was. He had hoped to pinpoint the sound of the spectator towers that ran the length of it, but all the cheering added to a melange of sound that hung over the town. Their meandering route would be hard to track, but it didn't stop him imagining Red-face surprising them from every shadow. He kept it to himself, Vesta didn't need that weighing on her too.

Using the weak sunlight, filtered through sulphurous skies, they turned in the direction most likely to be east, where the buildings became a little better kept. Perhaps further removed from the sweeping destruction that came with the prize every two years. There wouldn't be much glory here to salve his reputation, but with a lack of glory came a wealth of safety.

Large wooden buildings – broken up into small apartments for let – bordered narrow roads, and though shanties had sprung up in any gap wide enough, they were no longer the main thrust of the architecture. There was less human waste but more ash, and it seemed most of the people in this particular district had vacated for the prize's duration. There would be a few kitchen knives inside and maybe some owners would have left a gun or two. Blackbile residents likely owned more firearms than could be reasonably carried out of the town on a whim.

No sooner than he had thought about pillaging the apartments, Vesta was on her knees picking a lock. She might have seen his gaze linger a little longer than usual on a doorway, or perhaps had taken the initiative all on her own. The unknown ability surprised him, but he didn't comment on it, too nervous of drawing attention should anyone pass.

He pressed his back to the apartment wall and pulled out his pistol to cover her; just in case. He couldn't shoot anyone just yet, but the bell could toll any time.

The alley remained empty, and Vesta worked quickly. With a click, the door swung inwards. From the collection of mail boxes and scrawled names in the cramped foyer, there were easily twenty apartments in the building. The place would take time to search; but would also make them harder to find.

With a final cursory glance into the alley, William closed the door. The catch remained open. He closed the door again, hoping for some click in the mechanism and for the bolt to slide out. No amount of shaking would budge it.

'A pin jammed,' Vesta mumbled guiltily.

He nodded and tried his best not to show too much disappointment.

A skeletal pot plant did a reasonable job of holding the door shut. It wasn't exactly heavy, a stiff breeze might knock it over, but it was the best thing he could find in the circumstances.

The ground floor consisted predominantly of common rooms, and the remains of a leaflet distribution centre. There was still a selection of prize flyers scattered about every surface advertising "Mayhem and murder" or "Death and destruction". He had seen similar posters in nearly every bar and pasted at most street corners in imperial towns. For more local fans, the competition was celebrated like a summer fête with fliers boasting "a family friendly massacre".

It seemed there had also been a pre-fight variety show at Melting Moments, featuring the voluptuous Delia in tantalising Vitulan dress. He presumed the whole thing to be some saucy mockery of Emperor D'elia, which was probably why such details had been absent on posters sent to the imperial cities.

'Will, there's nothing in there,' Vesta hissed, waving him back to the foyer and stairs. He was inclined to agree; they padded quietly to the first floor.

There had been an attempt to make this particular tenement quite handsome when it was built; the iron railings that girded the stairs had floral insets every third spindle, and the lighter curls of iron might have once been painted. Blackbile degraded things quickly however, and though it was plain maintenance was done on the building, the caretaker was fighting a losing battle. Most of the landing windows had been boarded up, paper was peeling from the walls, and something oozed through a crack in the ceiling.

With a calming breath, William let his pistol precede them upstairs; the hammer was cocked, his finger curled around the trigger. He didn't have much faith in it, but it didn't hurt to look the part. Vesta was close, he could feel the heat of her at his back, and the hitch of her breath every time a floorboard creaked.

As he gained the first floor landing, the chapel bell tolled distantly. Ten chimes that shingled his spine and stood all his hairs on end. The air around them turned stale and tense. The hour was up. Then the first claps of gunpowder started, most distant, but some unnervingly close.

'We should split up to search the apartments; quickly.' Vesta looked frantic.

At first, William was reluctant. Partly because he thought she might run and get herself killed. Then she swallowed nervously, and he spotted her hand tight on a small knife. He wondered if she'd found it while he was distracted downstairs, or if it was another of her little surprises. When she met his gaze, her eyes were steely.

'My thoughts exactly,' he agreed and kicked in the door to the first apartment; there was no time to dawdle now. He left Vesta to search and moved on to the next door. 'Search under beds, in wardrobes-'

'Look for loose floorboards and holes in the walls. I know.' She offered a brief smile as she sloped through the door.

'We need more guns, and any powder and shot you can find.'

The second apartment – a three room abode, deserted by the occupant – wasn't locked. The kitchen yielded a cheese knife and quarter-cut of festive fruit cake; nothing of much use. The living room supplied only an arm chair, a long-cold stove and small table. He took his search to the bedroom.

There was a commotion in the street outside, but before he had time to react, an explosion burst the apartment windows in a shower of sparkling dust. He threw himself to the floor, readying his pistol to shoot at anyone who might surprise him. Shards of glass settled on him like a blanket, covering every surface with sharp beads and glittering fragments. It smelled like sulphur, but that might have been the fresh Blackbile air spilling in.

He heard Vesta shout, heard feet hammering on floor boards. For a moment, he thought the cultists had tracked them down so easily, then she came running into the room. She was fine; had just come to check he was alright, and that he'd not been turned to paste by the explosion.

'Are you alive? Are you ok?' Vesta asked, but he couldn't quite make out the words.

'What?' he yelled, ears whining.

Guns fired in the street outside. There were shouts, a gurgling scream as someone was hit. William's senses faded back to him, leaving only a persistent ring in his ears. He pushed himself up. 'We need to keep looking!'

Motivated by the proximity of the fighting just outside, Vesta tipped the mattress off the bed with a scatter of raunchy postcards. Then she turned out the wardrobe.

William dusted himself down, shook glass from his shirt, and checked his pistol. Through the reducing hum in his ears, he heard what he had been dreading. Downstairs, the front door clattered open; someone had heard them from the street. Perhaps it was the cultists.

He cursed and crept to the apartment door, straining to listen. The echo of a gun being cocked focused his hearing. Heavy boots stamped up the stairs.

'Vesta, you need to hide,' William tried to whisper.

She dashed behind the bedroom door.

The footsteps moved quicker. Only one set, just an assassin. He would need to focus on protecting Vesta before he could think about attacking.

'You, on the stairs!' William called out. 'Is your sponsor still alive?'

'Yes.' The man was just out of view. 'So you can't kill me.'

How the hell was he going to stop this man if he couldn't kill him? Come to think of it, William couldn't be killed either. He emerged into the hallway, just as his assailant crested the stairs. He aimed his matchlock. 'My sponsor is still alive too.'

'*You?*' The privateer rolled his eyes, tossed his curly black hair, and took a step forward. 'Are you stalking me?'

William eyed the privateer's weapons. He had a black-iron flintlock, and a boarding cutlass in his off hand; worse, despite his arrogance, he was experienced in their use.

'Where is your peach of a sponsor?' The privateer advanced slowly. His petulant grimace became a grotesque leer.

William couldn't lose Vesta at this early stage, but to kill the privateer, he'd have to kill Lamebrain, and he didn't want that either. So William took a step back, as if Vesta was hiding in an apartment further down the corridor.

'You'll have to get past me first; I'm not going to let you, so you might as well turn back now.' He retreated further.

'Oh, back there?' The privateer glanced only briefly into the first apartment, and continued to the second door. The cutlass scraped the wall menacingly. He pointed through the door with his flintlock. 'Not in here then?'

William flinched. That was enough to give the privateer the indication he needed. With a triumphant yell, he raised his pistol, and barged into the room. There was a thud and a flintlock fired.

William hurtled after the assassin. He grabbed hold of the doorframe and swung himself inside at full momentum. He collided with Vesta and stumbled over the fallen privateer, their legs stomping around one another in a losing battle to stay upright. They toppled to the floor.

'What are you doing?' William shoved himself up. 'You can't kill him.'

'Hush.' She pointed to the large stone ashtray beside the sprawled privateer, still breathing softly. 'I didn't kill him.'

He looked at her wide eyed; impressed. He hadn't envisioned Vesta doing much, other than hiding and relying on his protection, but there was definitely more to her than had first appeared. Already, she was stripping the privateer of his equipment: the curved sword and his flintlock, along with two handfuls of paper cartridges from his bandolier.

Vesta swished the cutlass in the air, then seemed to disregard it as a nuisance and tossed it out the window. She hitched her skirts over her knee and stowed her knife in a garter sheath. William blinked and looked away; it didn't seem right to watch her close the miniature fastenings. Instead, he focused on the privateer for fear he would wake.

'You can load on the go.' William decided to let Vesta keep the better of the two pistols. His would be far too awkward for her, it was far too awkward for him too, but at least he could make his shots count.

He stepped out of the apartment door, not wanting to linger. Any number of people could have heard the gunshot and be heading this way.

'Fissshhhyy!' Lamebrain screamed joyously. He was creeping up the staircase, his one eye fixed on William. Saliva trailed from his mouth, spread into a manic grin, and sporting only a quarter portion of teeth. He wielded a fat bladed knife aptly designed for taking the heads off fish.

'Gut an' shale!' The slave giggled, appearing to think this competition nothing more than idle fun. He set off at a lumbering dash, cackling and slobbering.

As a reaction, William raised his matchlock and fired. Smoke puffed out, the bullet flew wide; definitely not his fault. The slave surged closer, delighted by the game of life and death. He raised his cleaver. There was no time to reload; there was no time for Vesta to even draw her knife.

'Run!' William grabbed Vesta by the wrist, accidentally knocked a collection of cartridges from her hand, and hurtled for the far end of the corridor.

He had hoped that there would be another way out, tenements like these usually had secondary stairs or a service entrance. Yet, step by step, what he'd hoped to be a doorway, was in fact just a window. Quite a large window, left open to air out a vomit stain on the rug below.

Gripping Vesta's wrist tighter, he forced himself faster. She shrieked when she understood his plan, but didn't stop running. He prayed there was a balcony outside, or a fire escape, or at least a vaulted roof. Even a one storey fall was more conducive to survival than facing a knife-toting-maniac with an unloaded pistol – he would still rather avoid a drop. They reached the end of the corridor and leapt through the opening.

The time in the air was relatively brief, but managed to turn his stomach three revolutions nonetheless. The ground slapped him. Vesta landed better, catching herself like a cat on all fours in the mud. William's face squelched into a pool of muck and his body curled over him like a scorpion's tail. It seemed like the momentum would carry his spine all the way over itself and snap it, but he sprang back before too much damage was done. His body collapsed flat into an oily puddle.

He pulled his head from the mud with a rat-squeal gasp at the immediate, but mercifully fleeting, needle of pain. Gritting his teeth, he rolled onto his back, ready for the half-brained halfwit to follow them out of the window into the street. Desperately he spluttered ashy-sludge from his mouth and tried to catch his breath while reloading. He trained the matchlock for the window. Lamebrain didn't appear.

'William!' Vesta hissed and slapped him quite forcibly on the shoulder. 'William, look!'

He squirmed onto one knee. Apparently, their trek through the back roads had led them in a damned circle. The apartments they had searched bordered the main thoroughfare, and the window spat them out exactly where they didn't want to be.

'I'm going kill your kiddie.' Ottilie, the mad bomber, was stood in the street screaming at a tall slim building on the far side. 'Genevieve! Come out and fight me like a woman!'

William spotted that a window on the top floor was open; perhaps Genevieve had been up there moments before, aiming her rifle into the street. He imagined that if she was, she would be hurriedly vacating the premises via the rear entrance. Having to fight that great rhinoceros of a woman wasn't an appealing prospect.

'We're going to kill your little one,' echoed Ottilie's sponsor; the Scold that had mocked William in the street. Shorter than average, red haired, with crooked glasses that William had stomped into the mud. 'And then we're going to kill you.'

'This'll teach you to enter your own child in the prize!' Ottilie took a projectile proffered by her sponsor and loaded it into her pipe launcher. 'You give all women guilders a bad name. They say we're cold, and I'm not having that. I'm going to put a stop to it, and you, and your wee child. Fire!'

The sponsor raised a linstock primed with a smouldering match cord; William had seen a similar pole used by the Imperial Bombardiers to light their cannons. The man wafted it a little to encourage its flame then poked the lit end through a small hole in the rear of Ottilie's cylinder. A volatile shriek clawed across eardrums as the obnoxious projectile blasted from the launcher. It drew a trail of smoke between Ottilie and her target, then exploded against the wooden frontage in cascades of red and green light. The whole building crumpled inwards at the first floor. The top of the façade tipped forwards and fell, sticking into the mud like a blade in flesh.

'Pretty.' The sponsor took another projectile from a pull-along cart and handed it to Ottilie. 'I like that one; green, I like green.'

'And the fire,' Ottilie muttered.

'Aye, and the fire,' the sponsor agreed. 'That's good too.'

'Are you alive in there?' Ottilie took a step forwards and shouted at the ruinous wood. If Genevieve had been in there, she wouldn't be answering any time soon.

William looked across at Vesta. Her eyes were wide, her arms and legs caked in mud, she had a graze on her arm – must have clipped the window frame. He took her hand to gain her attention, and she peeled her gaze from the menacing Scolds. He sank low into the mud to keep out of sight, gesticulated several times, tried to get his plan across, and pointed in the direction he hoped was north. Even if his hand signals didn't mean much, Vesta got the message. They had to leave, quickly and quietly.

1668

'Right… Welcome all, to the inaugural…' The mayor cleared his throat to gain the attention of the crowd and started again. 'To our first ever Man-Butcher Prize!'

The five hundred rag-tag spectators cheered with brutish gusto. Significant pride swelled in Terrowin's chest; he had built this. It had taken an excruciating six months to properly organise and promote the event. There had been bleachers to build, and posters to paint, and all other manner of things to do. Granted, he hadn't actually lifted a finger to do any of those tasks, but he had come up with the initial idea, so it was all his own doing nonetheless. Now, the day had finally come, and in ten sluggish minutes the competition would be underway.

Forty-three assassins entered the competition in total, all vying for a prize with *his* name on it. Whether he lived or died, one thing was certain; the Man-Butcher Prize would be the most fun he'd ever have, and would be remembered for generations. He tingled with anticipation. The thrill, the rush, and the exquisite sounds of pain – it was all so close! Stood shoulder to shoulder with other guilders, at the brink of almost certain death, he could barely contain his excitement.

Most of his adversaries were armed with blades: bollock knives, daggers, tower hangers, scimitars, a vicious and impractical flamberge, and even more he couldn't name. Some had things a little more exotic; a man in a round helmet carried a crossbow, a frontierswoman coiled her whip with menace, and while not exactly refined, he saw one brute wielding a club spiked with a dozen bloody nails. None of those would be especially effective against the collection of firearms he'd spotted in the crowd, but each to their own, he supposed. Maybe they were crazier than he was, and liable to win. He suspected the explanation for such outmoded weaponry was simpler than that; those with coin to afford pistols and powder would be far less likely to waste their lives than destitute dagger-men.

Terrowin had his own tools of death. As the Man-Butcher, a name he'd earned early in his career, it was only right that he carried a cleaver to justify the handle – held in a custom scabbard under his arm. His weapon of choice however, was also his most prized possession; a silver flintlock engraved with wild flowers. His mother, a retired trick-shooter, had gifted it to him when he set out in search of fortune. He didn't imagine she'd think he'd use it kill well over three scores of men, women, and anyone else who got in his way, but liked to believe his success would make her proud anyway.

'Are you excited?' he asked a huge woman to his side. He was giggling between each word, and almost delirious with anticipation.

'Aye,' she grunted; another Scold. Terrowin had to suppress the urge to ask her exactly what shire she was from. He was almost as excited to meet a fellow countrywoman as he was to compete for his very own prize, but she didn't look in the mood to talk.

She slapped a metal rod in the palm of one of her meaty hands, and added, 'it's been far too long since I've let loose. I'm about to shine like the north stars.'

'Good to hear that.' Terrowin's fingers shivered, anyone watching might have thought him scared, but his smile and childish splutters dismissed that notion. 'I'm Terrowin by the way.'

'Aldreda.' She nodded. 'The Man-Butcher.'

'What? Man-Butcher?'

'Aye, I figured even if I don't win, people will probably think the whole thing was named after me.' She slapped her iron rod into her hand again and Terrowin noticed that it was actually a rolling pin. 'I'll get remembered either way.'

'*I'm* the Man-Butcher!' Terrowin prodded himself hard in the chest, suddenly outraged at this pretender to his title. It had taken him an entire night to earn that name, and she thought she could just take it from him?

'Yeah, of course you are son.' She pointed with her rolling pin to another entrant, who had a bloodied apron tied around his midriff. 'And I'm sure he is too. We're not the only people with the idea.'

'This is ridiculous.' Terrowin scowled. 'Butchers don't even use rolling pins.'

'So… Without further ado.' The mayor pulled a flintlock from a holster that looked absurd on his hip. 'Let's kick this whole thing off.'

As the mayor raised the starting gun to the sky, the crowd of spectators fell to silence. Terrowin readied himself, flexed his fingers over his flintlock, spat to the dirt, and took one long, calming breath.

The shot clapped over the square; the fight for the prize was on.

Terrowin's silver pistol spat a deafening retort and was echoed by twenty more. Every single entrant with a firearm shot at the nearest man. In one fell swoop, over half of the combatants were dead or mortally wounded. The rest dashed for cover in the roads that splintered from the square.

Terrowin cheered, adding his voice to the cacophony, and ran east. He hopped over a tumbled-down body, dove into a front roll to dodge a stray arrow, scrambled up and hastily reloaded.

His sights found an assassin with a wide brimmed hat and narrowly trimmed moustache. The man had yet to reload his own firearm and turned to run. Terrowin pulled the trigger. A hot ball of lead propelled from his pistol and struck the back of the assassin's skull, exploded out of his face, and spread his little moustache across the dirt. His body crumpled into the side of a sugared fennel snack-stand; the vendor was long gone.

Terrowin reached the edge of the square and ducked behind a small bleacher. Some of the spectators were already fleeing for their lives, a few had taken the brunt of the gunfire already; others were blinded by the adrenaline and bloodlust, cheering for their favourite hitmen. Terrowin could hear a few chants of "Man-Butcher", but couldn't be entirely sure that they were for him.

He set himself against the back of the bleacher and delved in his pocket for another paper cartridge. Beneath the screams and cheers and distant shots he became aware of a rattle to his immediate right. In his haste he had forgotten to search about properly for opponents and it seemed that he wasn't the only one reloading behind the bleacher. Terrowin jumped as if he had just seen a particularly hairy-legged spider and dropped his cartridge.

The other assassin – a short blood-stained man, with a pistol – was equally as shocked that Terrowin had stumbled into his little haven. He fumbled a cartridge, aligned it with the barrel cock-eyed and nearly dropped it, fingers fluttering like the legs of the aforementioned spider.

The two assassins locked eyes, both with unarmed pistols. It was like a duel of sorts – Terrowin had always wanted to be in an old-fashioned duel. Whichever of them was the slower to reload and shoot would lose their life. The bloodied assassin gritted his teeth, steadied his hand, and slid the paper cartridge into the barrel.

Terrowin whipped out his butcher's knife from the scabbard under his arm and swung it in a smooth arc, grinning as it slipped a good two thirds of the way into the man's skull with the satisfying *schunk* of a spade in clay. The assassin dropped his gun and was dead well before it hit the ground. Terrowin smirked; a fair duel would have to wait.

A little calmer now that his cover was his own, he reloaded his pistol and retrieved his butcher's knife. As he put his boot on the man's face and set about hefting the blade from the groove in his skull, he noticed his victim had been the man in the bloodied apron. Disgusted, he kicked the body as further punishment for stealing his moniker.

'I'm the *real* Man-Butcher,' he proclaimed triumphantly, tugging the cleaver free of blood and bone. He slipped it into its leather holder, still slick with gore.

It occurred to him then, that such a kill, one that reduced the number of assassins presuming to steal his name, was more than a little satisfying, and something he should take the time to revel in properly. In a fit of spontaneity, he stripped the corpse of its apron and donned it, wondering why he hadn't thought of wearing a costume before. He glanced through the bleachers to the main square, hoping to spy the big woman so that he could add her rolling pin to his collection of trophies before the competition was done.

The sound of shooting had died down a little. It was quite possible the entrants were reduced to single figures already; it had all been rather fast. He crept to the edge of the bleacher to get a clearer view of the battlefield. All he could see was a mess of bloodied corpses and still-writhing soon-to-be corpses. One was ranting about how magnificent her figure would be in the toyshops.

A glint of bright white caught Terrowin's eye; a scope. He ducked into his cover just as the rifle clapped, wooden splinters exploded off the bleacher and showered over the ash-heavy ground.

'Are you dead?' Lord Beechworth's noble drawl echoed over the hubbub.

'You'll have to try better than that!' Terrowin couldn't help but laugh. 'I've still got my head.'

'Not for long!' Beechworth replied, there was a curl of humour in his tone.

A hole blasted through the bleachers just over Terrowin's head, this time showering him with dust, splinters, and the blood of some unfortunately placed spectator. Terrowin cackled, and ran for more substantial cover while the lord reloaded.

'You missed!' He bellowed as he darted across the open road, pausing to throw a rude hand gesture at Beechworth's position. 'I won't!'

He spotted a rather sorry looking shop, with broken windows and a smashed-in door; the perfect place to take cover. He skidded inside on strewn shards of glass, took a quick glance for assassins hiding in the gloom, and slammed the door shut behind him. Spying shutters, he quickly flung them closed over the broken windows.

A bullet pierced the wooden slats, missing him by inches. He leapt over the counter, partly because he'd always wanted to try it, but mostly to provide better protection from Beechworth's onslaught.

He waited as patiently as he could for another shot, or for the lord to follow him inside, but nothing came. Perhaps the posh git wouldn't deign to set foot in such a place; it was rather run-down.

The general store was wrecked, it looked like two combatants had fought their way through it already. Terrowin was reasonably sure that there was nobody still inside, but the possibility that there *was* quite excited him.

He puffed out air, starting to regret retreating into the shop. He wanted to be at the centre of the action, but he knew if he walked out of that door Beechworth would take his head off. He eyed the wares – so easily distracted once boredom set in. Cured meats, string, little tools, news sheets, and confectionary.

He twisted the lid off a tall jar and helped himself to a fistful of hard candies. They were tart, lemon flavoured, not his favourite; he would have certainly preferred peanuts. He sucked noisily for a minute or so, listening to the faint clapping of gunfire and chinking of swords outside, allowing himself to catch his breath before he ran back out into the fray.

The front door burst open with a thump, one half-smashed panel fell free and clattered on the floor. Terrowin jumped and dropped his jar of lemon sweets; barely a foot to the floor, but glass shards and glossy bon-bons skittered everywhere. He peeked over the counter to see who might be coming for him, not even thinking to fear a bullet in his head.

'There you are!' Aldreda, *the Man-Butcher Imposter*, stomped inside, her gelatinous flanks barely missing the edges of the doorframe. In this more hostile light, Terrowin saw her for the beast that she was. Easily three heads taller than him and inhumanly strong, judging by the smooth movement of her vast body.

He pulled out his silver flintlock, she raised her rolling pin, and he pulled the trigger. Not exactly a fair match up, but he would take the easy wins without complaint.

A spume of fire exploded from the barrel, sending a ball of hot lead in Aldreda's direction. It drilled into the thick leather corset around her midriff and knocked her a half-step back. There was a crack of metal on metal and the bullet ricocheted into a shelf of confectionary – spilling fudge pieces, barley sugars and marble-like imperial mints across the floor. The huge woman grunted as if she had been thumped in the gut, but there was no bulging of her eyes or sense of impending doom about her. Terrowin assessed that she had some kind of armour plating under that leather and removed himself from behind the counter.

His eyes trained on the malevolently gleaming rolling pin, sheened with the cranial blood of at least five other men. She could swing that before he had chance to reload, but he had the edge when it came to agility. He turned for the back-room door and fled.

The sole of Terrowin's shoe was leather, buffed to a near frictionless lustre from excessive wear and little maintenance. Normally, he was deft enough on his feet for such concern to be beyond him, but in his mania to escape one misstep was all it took to upend him. One foot kinked on a sweet, the other kicked out to keep his balance, but landed on another slippery lemon pebble and skidded across the wooden boards. There was a moment when his arms whirled where he might have maintained his balance. Unfortunately, both feet slipped in opposite directions. It was possibly his best ever attempt at doing the splits, but little pride came with the fall.

Aldreda's rolling pin missed the top of his skull by inches and smashed into another glass jar, cascading yet more sweets onto the perilously strewn floor. She roared and stomped like a raging bear. Terrowin flopped onto his belly and scrabbled for the back room. He struggled from his elbows and knees to his hands and feet, and grabbed a rack to heft himself fully upright, before tipping it across the doorway behind him.

He delved into his pocket for another cartridge and loaded it. He could hear the big woman fighting with the shelf, pinioned between heavy wood and the unforgivingly narrow counter. He dashed to a set of stairs at the far side of the room, turned and took his aim. This time he was determined to hit her between the eyes, foregoing the possibility of the bullet colliding with any more hidden armour.

'I'm going to gut you like a fish.' She smashed her rolling pin *through* the rack, splintering it like matchwood. 'I'll butcher you like a pig!'

In the dim light of the store, with her eyes in shadow and her hair at all angles, the woman really did look quite terrifying. She definitely looked more of a Man-Butcher than Terrowin, but he wasn't about to give up his title lying down.

He took his aim. She marched closer, her bulky thighs chafing, and raised her rolling pin. Terrowin fired. The second bullet was much like the first, exploding triumphantly from the mouth of the pistol in a wreath of fire, and flying purposefully for its target. Rather amazingly, and likely nothing to do with any skill on the big woman's part, the bullet collided with a fortunately timed sweep of the rolling pin and pinged into the wall.

'What?' Terrowin looked at his pistol as if it had been replaced with a toy.

'I'll mince you like… like…' She gurned at him. 'Mincemeat!'

He dashed up the stairs, narrowly missing another rolling-pin strike that crunched wooden spindles like wheat. He started to reload again, certain that she wouldn't be able to cheat death three times in a row. The stairs turned ninety degrees at the edge of the building and he followed them up to the next floor.

'I'll skin you like…' Aldreda stomped up the stairs after him. He counted the steps, worked out how far behind him she still was. Each wood slat let out a pained creak as she ascended.

'I'll skin you like…' She tried again. 'Like a potato!'

It seemed that her competence with threats was lacking, but it didn't matter much, her presence was intimidating enough.

Terrowin reached the top of the stairs and stopped. The room before him was so filled with boxes and other clutter that the way was almost entirely impassable. Even if he did manage to squeeze through, there didn't appear to be any other way out.

He turned and cocked his pistol. This was it, the last stand, him or her. He would not miss again.

'I'm the real Man-Butcher!' she spat as she rounded the corner, 'and I'm going to kill you to take away any doubt.'

His thoughts exactly.

She slapped her rolling pin into the palm of her hand, bloodshot eyes glinting with menace. She was five sagging, creaking, groaning steps away from Terrowin. Nearly in arms reach. No chance of missing.

He took his aim and squeezed the trigger.

Before the bullet could lurch out, the step beneath Aldreda gave way to her mass, and she slipped through the floor in a mess of dust and fragmented wood. Her shriek of surprise and fear was cut short by a foundation-rattling impact on the lower floor. Terrowin's bullet struck the wall.

Disappointed that he had missed yet again, Terrowin was still happy enough with the result; and they said history was written by the victors anyway, he could just make something up.

He took a step towards the edge and peered down the hole Aldreda had driven for herself. It went all the way down to the cellar, where she lay in a heap of splinters and blood.

'That'll do.' He nodded to himself and hopped over the hole to the lower steps. 'That'll do nicely.'

1682

Wriggling backwards on hands and knees through heavy sludge, William and Vesta scuttled away from Ottilie and her pipe launcher. Another rocket screeched down the road and folded the front of a grocer's shop; wattle and daub tumbled away with half of the internal floors in a clatter of furniture and glass. The rhinoceros woman cackled with her sponsor, both of them caught up in the glee of destruction. The force hit William like a kick in the ribs, rolled him onto his back and left him winded. He blinked up at the glaring sunlight like a displaced turtle. Vesta squeaked beside him.

'*Pathetic.*' Genevieve leered down, her pretty face twisted with disgust, shiny rifle barrel aimed for his chest.

Under her scrutiny William felt less like a turtle and much more like a woodlouse. He realised it was not Ottilie's explosion that overturned him, but a well-placed boot from the riflewoman; a bruise he was already starting to feel.

'Don't shoot,' he gulped, palms up in surrender.

'I wouldn't waste the powder,' Genevieve scoffed at him, but her attention followed Ottilie.

Cheers echoed around them from the spectator tower looming over the battleground, grinding his pride to dust. She wouldn't sully her reputation with such a meagre kill as William the Woodlouse; a coward lower than a civilian.

Genevieve dropped to a crouch with a stifled gasp, sharing their meagre cover behind a stone horse trough. It seemed the proximity of the pipe launcher and the mad bomber's ire had more influence on her mercy.

'Did she kill your son?' William whispered, fingers curling around his muddy matchlock. Genevieve's sponsor was nowhere in sight; he could shoot her and make a run for it. Surely he and Vesta were faster than the hulking rhinoceros woman.

'He's fine, so don't even think about it.' She didn't even glance at him, but lowered her rifle, appearing to think better of tackling Ottilie. 'Another time.'

The markswoman shouldered her rifle and sprinted across the street. In a moment, she had barged open a rickety gate and disappeared into a passage through the buildings.

William exhaled, his body limp in defeat; hardly the heroic exchange he had anticipated when signing up. He definitely should have shot her. Grinding his teeth against his shameful performance, he refused to wait around to become target practice for either of the female assassins.

'Come on.' He hauled Vesta up, and bolted for a side street.

In a short distance, they were spat onto another road lined with hotels, inns, and brothels. William thought Melting Moments might be nearby, but his geographical knowledge of the town was limited.

Most of the establishments were locked and shuttered against damage, but through a handful of darkened windows, people moved. A few heavies, hired to protect valuable assets, or locked-in spectators, drinking and watching the carnage away from the crowds in the official zones. There was always the chance assassins could be lurking, but there was no avoiding that risk. William's skin prickled, feeling eyes from every direction.

'How many do you think are left?' Vesta asked in a hushed voice.

'I don't even know how many entered.' He stepped onto the boardwalk at the edge of the road, keeping his distance from the hotel doors and windows. 'There must have been over two hundred. I doubt we're down to double digits yet. Right now, we need to focus on getting better weapons.'

They paused to peer into another alley bisecting their route. Empty, with the exception of a mangy dog rooting in a stack of overfull bins. With a flick of his wrist, William led the way to the next boardwalk, dashing across the open space. They pressed against the wall of a garishly painted saloon to catch their breath.

'Can't we just hide until nearly everyone's dead?' Vesta suggested.

'What?' William rounded on her. 'I entered this competition to… I'm not going to skulk in the shadows.'

'Don't beat yourself up for following basic human instinct,' Vesta snapped, but softly added, 'you're doing your best to keep us alive.'

'We won't find your brother if we're hiding.' William cocked an eyebrow; his sentiment seemed to resonate with her somewhat.

The inn door burst open and a young man staggered out, filthy and bruised, and a gag flapping around his neck. He discarded a short length of rope and ran. An unwilling sponsor, escaping. He might have made it, had he not insisted on looking back for his pursuers. The motion took his shaky legs off balance and he sprawled into the road.

William pressed Vesta tightly against the flaking paintwork, just as two brutes thumped out of the door. They weren't quite as enormous as Ottilie, but there were two of them, which made them all the more menacing. One had a knife stuck in his back, pushed to the hilt in his thick flesh. Though the wound bled freely, it did nothing to hamper his meat-footed progress as he charged after the errant sponsor. The other weighed a lump hammer in his hand, then tossed it with frightening accuracy. The head smashed into the escapee's leg, raising a blood curdling shriek and halting his shambling progress.

William readied his pistol, eyes darting up and down. That scream could have been heard from some distance, and any minute now other assassins would arrive looking for a fight. It was best to get away, find a vantage while the brutes were distracted with maiming their unruly sponsor, and prepare for whoever else came.

'Mercy! Please!' the sponsor snivelled and dragged himself away, ruined leg trailing blood behind him.

A perfectly placed bullet blasted through the escapee's head, splattering bright gore over the grey street. William glared in mute horror at Vesta; the privateer's pistol was tightly clasped in her hands, barrel smouldering.

Instinctively, William readied his matchlock and stepped to the fore, shielding his wayward sponsor. In that moment, he had never felt so brave or so foolish, but Vesta was his responsibility. The brutes lurched around, fixing him with flinty eyes; they looked like they wanted to tear him apart with their bare hands, and they probably could.

'Would you mind telling me whose sponsor that was?' he tried. It had sounded far more menacing in his head, but he lacked the gravitas back it up. So he squared his shoulders and swung his pistol between the two titans, trying out his best impression of a fearsome guilder.

'No,' they replied in flat unison. One of them moved into the road, circling behind to cut off any escape.

'You *have* to tell me.' William's demand came out in a petulant squawk. 'If you don't you'll get disqualified.'

'There's no referees here.' The stabbed-brute grunted as he pulled the dagger from his back. 'Who'll know?'

A quick glance side to side proved them right; rules didn't count for much when there was no chance of punishment.

William fired at the circling-brute; the matchlock clapped and burst out smoke. It was still painfully inaccurate, and while he had aimed for the man's torso as the easiest target, the bullet flew wide and struck a fat-swaddled kneecap. It seemed Luck could give as well as take. The man's bloodied leg collapsed into the wet filth of the street.

'Brother!' the stabbed-brute roared and lunged with the knife.

William dodged at the last moment, and the blade impaled the wooden siding at his back. It stuck fast. He smashed his gun in the brute's face, then leapt from the boardwalk to gain enough space to reload – he would need more than usual, thanks to his matchlock's archaic design. Vesta was one step ahead, cocking her stolen pistol in trembling hands and skittering aside.

The brute followed William with unexpected dexterity, took a lump hammer from his belt and started swinging. His hammer struck the wall, crunching wood, then passed a hair's breadth from William's head.

Vesta fired, taking a graze of flesh from the stabbed brute's shoulder. The brief distraction was all William needed to put himself out of arm's reach and frantically reload.

With a dull slap, a small glass orb landed in the muck between them.

William looked down at it, even the brute stopped in his confusion. The orb had a thin trailing wick that was being eroded by a sizzling ember. It was familiar, but William's thoughts were slow as cold molasses. Just as realisation dawned, the orb exploded with crackling phosphorus, throwing the pair to the ground in torrents of blinding tears.

William muffled his screams under his hands, thrashing in the road until the worst of the eye-searing pain had passed. Then, mole-blind, he scrambled for his pistol and powder. Most spilled into the dirt, but he managed to get just enough into the barrel before the pouch was empty.

Colours and shapes began to coalesce, enough that he could make out ten figures decked in sheep-hide, marching down the street. They floated across one another, awful parallels of men. He was seeing double.

Four of the cultists pulled rifles from their backs and aimed at the boardwalk, the last place William had seen Vesta. He fisted each eye to clear the haze, kept his pistol high and waited for his split vision to focus. Though as moments passed and ten figures still advanced, he understood the sheer number of them was true.

'Which of you are sponsors?' he called, awkwardly scraping his damp cheek on his shoulder.

'I am!' The cultist, who had bought William an ale in Melting Moments and so fondly called him brother, held up his hand with an amiable wave. His smile was short lived, as regrettably William had to blast it off his face. Somehow, the disorientation from the explosion counteracted the pistol's blanket inaccuracy; the cultist fell backwards to the street, dumping grey matter into a brown puddle.

'Nobody else tell him.' Red-face elbowed his way to the front of the group, scowling. 'William, where is *your* sponsor?'

'I'm not telling you,' he replied, trying to pinch enough wasted powder from the muck to reload.

'Well, there aren't many places she could have gone.' Red-face swung his rifle at the tavern door. 'Let's try here, shall we?'

Five rifles unloaded at the inn, punching holes through shutters and worm-bitten wood. Hinges creaked and dust fell. Red-face gave the order to fire again.

William was overwhelmed by another cluster of cultists. The matchlock was kicked from his grip, his arms dragged behind and wrestled into the firm hands of a large Lamb. He was hauled to his feet, his shoulders threatening to pop from their sockets. There was little he could do against so many, especially disarmed and still disoriented. He stayed still, let them think he was complicit, and prayed a plan would come to him.

Red-face ordered another volley of shots into the façade, puncturing wood, glass, and furnishings. Shot-by-shot, a growing sense of unease crept over William; perhaps Vesta *had* gone inside the inn after all. He couldn't see anywhere else to hide.

'Are you still alive in there sister?' Red-face called jovially.

There was no reply.

'Someone bring her body out.' He waved two cultists nonchalantly inside, and handed his rifle to another for reloading. He turned to William. 'I'm rather disappointed; I thought we had a deal. Yet you've chosen death.'

'You can't kill me.' William strained against his captors. 'We don't know if Vesta's dead.'

Gods, he prayed that she wasn't.

Red-face repeated William's words in an almost unintelligible whine, the infantile mockery delighting his lackeys. Guffawing, he swept aside his long fur-trimmed robe, revealing the etched silver flintlock tucked under his belt; William's treasured pistol.

'There's a referee around the corner,' William lied through gritted teeth. 'Rules are rules.'

'*Of course* there is,' Red-face scoffed, but glanced at the alley doubtfully. Recovering his bravado, he drew the flintlock and aimed at William's leg. 'But I can blow your kneecaps out like you did to that mewling ox over there. Injured isn't dead, after all.'

The brutish brothers were no longer a threat, but they still lived. One wheezed, long glass shards in his chest, and the other was crawling away as his sponsor had, a wasted leg holding him back.

Wind whistled in William's ear; a crossbow bolt skewered Red-face's arm. With a howl, he jerked and fired, accidentally striking the large Lamb with hot lead. The pistol was discarded, empty, as he clutched his injured arm and retreated into a circle of cultists.

'Who in the seven hells was that?' Red-face shrieked, furious and bleeding. 'You can't just shoot a man while he's distracted!'

Wheels rumbled down the boardwalk. It was Doctor Barber, reloading another sharp bolt into a crossbow with chicken-foot hands. His robust assistant Barbie pushed as fast as he could, stomping in the wake of the chair, whooping victoriously.

'Kill the cripple!' Red-face screeched as another well placed bolt embedded itself in a cultist's throat. His eyes bulged with fear and the small huddle of devotees drew tighter around him, readying weapons. 'Kill him now!'

One tossed a grenade for the boardwalk, another launched a spear; bullets clipped buildings. Barbie veered into the street to avoid the explosion, completely ignoring his master's protests. The small wheels of the chair dropped off the boards and sank; they somersaulted through a wooden railing, took a yelping cultist with them, and slapped face down in the mud.

'And kill William!' Red-face retreated into an alley, sleeve dark with blood.

William had already snatched his beloved silver pistol from the mud, smeared it as clean as he could on his filthy shirt, and relieved a dead Lamb of his ammunition. He was halfway to his own cover by the time the cultists thought to look for him, and well-hidden before any could fire.

William heard a bullet fly over his head; another smashed the corner off the tipped-up cart where he sheltered from the carnage. It worked well enough for now, but a building would be better. He peered out, took a shot at a cultist; knocked the top of his head off. Damn, he was pleased to have his flintlock back.

The Lambs were settling behind cover of their own; triggers pulled, grenades popped, spears flew. Barbie's heart was pierced by a well-trained shot while Barber floundered in the dirt.

Footsteps stamped up the road towards William. Aghast, there was no time to reload as a man leapt atop him, screaming and brandishing a glimmer of steel. William collapsed against the cart side as they wrestled, slapped, and strained against each other. A serrated cheese-knife sank into William's forearm, drawing an agonised shriek.

'Where's my pistol, you thieving bastard?' the privateer spat, ripe breath cutting through the sulphurous malaise of the town. He thrust the knife deeper and twisted it, grinding his tobacco-stained teeth. 'I'm going to kill you with it.'

William writhed under the weight of his attacker, struggling in such close quarters. He bucked and elbowed, then bit the man's hand, catching the thumb between his teeth. That caused a flinch. He shoved his head forwards and snapped down again, even harder. He could feel the bone, hard between his molars. Fingernail scratched the roof of his mouth, coppery blood smeared over his chin. The privateer screamed. William thought the thumb might just come off in his mouth. He spat and his attacker recoiled, leaving the knife in situ as he scrambled away.

William's eyes span in his head, rolling over the sky and mud – past his wound, not daring to focus. Without thinking, he clambered up, spurred only by the will to survive. He heaved on the cart, hand sticky with his own blood, and found his footing. The sound of a bullet whipping past his ear made him flinch, bunching all his muscles and shooting lances of pain from his arm. It pushed a beastly growl from him.

'Lamebrain!' He heard the privateer shout. 'Gut the fish!'

Feet dragged on the boardwalk and the hollow childish laugh followed.

William cast about, frantically searching for an escape. He staggered on, still unsure of where to go, or what direction he was heading. Everything was a blur, and the sounds of shooting and laughing and screaming were closing in all around him. Then he spotted a ladder, abandoned against the side of a low building. Two buckets of grimy water at its base suggested it had been a window cleaner's. A more pointless job in the ash-rained town of Blackbile William couldn't think of right then, but he was grateful for it.

'Fisssshhh…' Lamebrain breathed out. 'Fishy, fishhhy.'

The slave was close, but exactly where William couldn't say. Buoyed by his terror, he slipped his gun under his belt and collapsed against the ladder. One foot followed the other, trembling muscles made strong by fear. One hand grasping rung after rung in a desperate attempt to maintain balance, the other hanging loose like a leaden weight, trailing blood, and throbbing. He made it to the top, tumbled over the high façade, and crumpled onto the flat roof behind.

A woman cried out and thumped his nose; the least of his worries right then. Momentarily dazed, his nose dripping red, he tried to clamber up to push the ladder away from the building.

'William,' the woman hissed viciously, 'stay down.'

'Vesta,' he spat her name out.

'Shut up and stay down.' She peeked over the edge, dipped back down for a second, then peeked again. 'It's a mess down there, more and more keep coming, I can't believe you got out. That half-headed monster nearly got you. I should pull the ladder up-'

'No.' William swallowed a lump. He was still in a daze, but at least the world had stopped spinning. 'Like you said, we don't want anyone to see we're up here.'

He looked about the rooftops. 'We can get away across these. Then you can pull this knife out.'

1668

Terrowin burst into the mayor's office, flintlock ready to despatch any that might be waiting there. There was nobody; good.

Fighting in the prize was equal parts exhausting and exhilarating, and as only the most cautious combatants remained, it seemed the contest would stretch well into the night. If he hoped to win, he would need food and rest to give him the edge. So the mayor's office was an ideal spot; no-one else had thought to come here, or dared to. It was also the nearest place to the square with a reliable stash of refreshments. He smacked his lips, hungry for the taste of those salted peanuts he had tried last time.

Something rustled under the desk, and Terrowin levelled his pistol. The mayor peeked around the drawers, his lip purpled by nervous nibbling and eyes glassy with fear.

'What are you doing down there?' Terrowin chuckled, spun his gun on his trigger finger and slipped it into the holster.

'Hiding, *obviously*.' The mayor's frown meshed his lustrous brows together. 'You shouldn't be here, what if you've been followed? I don't want to end up like those spectators. Did you see? More than half of them are dead!'

He started to mumble about the mess, body count, and cost of the whole enterprise; figures seemed to comfort the chubby mayor.

'I'll re-join the fray soon.' Terrowin strode directly to the bookcase and helped himself to the heavy dish of nuts. 'Just need a quick breather – *umph*, these are delicious.'

Shovelling a generous handful of nuts into his mouth and chewing loudly, he wiped his salty fingers on his shirt, then lifted the stopper from the mayor's finest decanter. A deep sniff told him it was good whiskey; very expensive. In three hearty gulps he'd drained nearly half the contents. He exhaled loudly, relishing the liquor-burn that suffused his chest and insides. Even wasted in big swigs, the taste was far superior to the usual swill he drank.

'Are you not enjoying the competition, Walter?' He let out a particularly hot, wet, and satisfying belch.

'Not in the least.' The mayor flinched at a gunshot outside, then crept back under his desk and out of sight. 'Far too much death involved for my taste.'

'Ah, Walter, all us mortals are headed to the other side eventually.' Terrowin tipped the dish, sliding the last few nuts into his open mouth, and chewing with gusto. 'Today, tomorrow, or next week; it hardly matters.'

He rounded the desk and lolled in the mayor's plush chair. It was roomy and padded, and had a delightful mechanism that allowed him to tip back just enough to rest his feet comfortably on the desk.

'Live fast, die young, eh?' He sucked salt dust and grease from his fingers. 'It's much better than the drawn out ache of old age, I'd say.'

'I can't say I agree with that.' The mayor receded further into the hollow of his desk like a turtle into its shell, covering his ears against a gurgling death-scream in the distance.

'Mayhem is my favourite, for sure.' Terrowin sighed wistfully and leant back in the chair, observing the square through the window. Two assassins were fighting with swords, blood-flecked, ash-smeared, their long coats and wild hair ruffled in an artistic breeze. He was surprised to see them still alive in such a prominent position; but it was a wonderful sight. A good marksman, should any be watching, would wait until one bested the other to save on ammunition and keep their vantage a secret.

Aldreda, the *Man-Butcher*, had survived her tumble through the guts of the shop, and marched into view. Terrowin sneered and spat on the mayor's lush carpet. The two swordsmen saw her approach, but they were too engrossed in their feud to stop her. Together, they might have stood a chance against such an ominous foe, but they clearly couldn't put aside their differences. One was knocked to the ground with a meaty fist and lost grip of his sword. The other was blasted with a blunderbuss the big woman must have scavenged. There was a bit of excitement as the floored man scrabbled to regain his blade, but too slow; his head was crushed under her monstrous boot.

Terrowin jeered quietly.

A stray shot missed Aldreda by inches. She ducked and barrelled after the shooter. Terrowin couldn't believe she had dodged death again.

'She's going to win this fucking thing if this carries on,' he muttered, worrying that her unprecedented good fortune was the result of Saint Barnham's blessing or even the god of luck herself. That chafed; it was definitely cheating. He shook the foolish thought from his head. Saints didn't ordain the winners of competitions like this, and gods didn't often favour killers.

'She can't win, Walter!' Arcane influence or not, he could *not* let her succeed. 'Anyone but her.'

Absorbed with his scheming, Terrowin failed to hear the approach of another assassin until the office door swung open.

'Good gods, Walter; it's wild out there.' Beechworth swept in with his rifle slung over his back. He dusted the ash from his overcoat, slow to realise the man sat behind the desk was not the mayor at all. He cocked an eyebrow at Terrowin. 'Why am I not surprised?'

'Claude!' Terrowin beamed, unmoved from his recline, save for the mouth of his pistol which was now aimed directly at the lord's heart. 'Having fun out there?'

'I was.' He smiled shallowly.

Terrowin could sense Beechworth's indecision, weighing up the pros and cons of trying for his rifle. There was no chance he'd ready it before Terrowin shot him, but surviving wasn't one of his options now. It was just a matter of whether he wanted to go down fighting.

'Glad you had fun, old chap.' Terrowin pulled back the hammer on his flintlock. 'See you on the other side. That Man-Butcher-imposter will probably send me after you in a few minutes.'

'Wait.' Beechworth raised a palm for peace. 'It's hardly sporting to deny a man a last drink, is it?'

'Your tricks won't work on me.' Terrowin smirked, then jerked his chin at the cabinet. 'One glass; but no funny business, understand?'

'I am a gentleman-'

'And I'm a saint. Just leave the rifle by the door.'

Obediently, Beechworth slipped the rifle strap from his shoulder and let the weapon clatter to the floor. Even with the man disarmed, Terrowin wasn't about to lower his own gun. He used the muzzle to track the lord's progress to the bookcase loaded with drink.

'I think I'll have a spot of this Smelter's Whiskey as the mayor's not here.' Beechworth selected a diminutive bottle from amidst the decanters. The cork was sealed over with blue wax and green ribbon. He pulled a short dagger from a concealed pocket and peeled it off, sending a playful wink Terrowin's way. 'It's his most expensive stuff.'

'I'm here, Claude.' The mayor's voice was muffled underneath his desk. 'And I'd prefer it if you didn't open that, I was saving it for my birthday.'

'Then let me wish you a happy birthday now, as I'm unlikely to see your next. Cheers.' Beechworth popped the cork out and took a swallow straight from the bottle. 'Would you like some?'

Terrowin politely declined, trying to focus on the dagger and wondering if Beechworth was any good at throwing. It was hard to stay alert and affect nonchalance at the same time, but he would be damned if he'd take his feet off the desk. Any sudden movement could see the blade lodged in his guts, and even if a knife toss missed, there was a chance the blade would fly out the window and alert Aldreda to his location.

Beechworth moved closer, slipped the knife back home and peered out of the open window. He used two fingers to hold aside the wafting curtain and took a slow sip of the liquor.

'The gall of it; the effrontery.' Beechworth tutted in mock-sympathy. 'Someone stealing your name, then killing you. I wouldn't be able to die happy, knowing I had left a score unsettled.'

Terrowin didn't reply, still intent on keeping alert.

'On your deathbed, one missed opportunity is worse than a hundred misadventures; the sparing of such an *imposter* would be quite simply the worst of missed opportunities.' Beechworth rounded abruptly. 'Well done, however; you have me cornered. I know I'm as much as dead already, and you my killer. I won't get the chance to make you pay what you owe, but we could make things a little fairer.'

'I'd take more enjoyment watching you beg for your life, *milord.* You've only yourself to blame, marching in here without a second look.'

'Ah, yes.' Beechworth paused for a moment in thought, then laid out his proposal, 'What say we make an alliance, of a sort? Spare me now, then we'll depose that charlatan Aldreda together. You keep your name and-'

'And what? You get to shoot me in the back?' Terrowin blew noisily through pursed lips; an ungainly sound that made Beechworth grimace and tut.

'And then do me the honour of a duel, as payment for my assistance. Imagine the enraptured crowds gathered to watch our final showdown; the two greatest assassins, gun to gun.'

For a moment, Terrowin's vision blurred as he let his mind picture the scene. A chill crept up his spine, raised gooseflesh on his skin and thrilled to the tips of every hair. He'd always wanted to be in a duel. There was something so very tempting about such pre-meditated madness.

'Is there anything in the rules forbidding alliances, Walter?' Terrowin set his boots on the floor, blood rushing pins and needles through his legs.

'In all honesty, I was so busy with the flyers that I didn't get around to the rules, other than "last person standing wins",' the mayor replied from his refuge.

Beechworth smiled over his now empty bottle, any sign of nervousness evaporated. They both knew it made sense to join forces. 'My word is my bond; I shan't attack you until that fraud is dead and we've walked ten paces in the square.'

It would be a rather dull ending to their relationship to shoot him now. Tonguing peanut from between teeth, Terrowin knew he wouldn't be satisfied if he fought Beechworth any other way than in a duel; the perfect concoction of skill and luck. Besides, with Aldreda dead, he would keep his moniker regardless of the outcome. Tucking his flintlock under his belt, he shook the lord's hand.

1682

William tried to keep the knife still in the fleshy sheath of his forearm, holding the limb close to his body. Blood darkened his hand, warm and sticky at the edges, but the battleground below made it impossible to administer aid. Other assassins had joined the fray, drawn like ravening wolves to the scent of death, and it was only a matter of time before he and Vesta were spotted.

They crossed three roofs quickly, two flat and one with a shallow incline, before reaching a more steeply pitched roof. Arms wide to balance, Vesta gracefully crossed the central ridge of clay tiles, while he wobbled and shuffled after her.

Reaching the end, William realised the next building was too high to climb onto; though it had looked surmountable from their starting point, his injuries made it impossible. Going back down the ladder would put them in the heart of the current shoot-out, and any attempt to hold the rooftop would be tantamount to suicide.

He looked down. There was an alleyway to one side – narrow and damp with only two gated exits – which they could have vaulted with a sprint-start if they weren't shot out of the air beforehand. Acrobatics were out of the question.

On the other side, two storeys down, was a small cobbled courtyard. It was surrounded by a network of cheaply made outbuildings, warehouses and squats; a criminal complex that acted as a base of illicit trading operations and housing for its members. William had infiltrated enough such establishments in the imperial cities to know how they worked.

Gang signs had been stencilled on the grey plaster walls and a half-rotted corpse swung in a cage, horrors undermined by strings of frilly knickers and colourful stockings strung across a wooden veranda on the first floor balcony. Such garments meant a staff only flop-house lay within, and hopefully that would also include an onsite doctor to patch up his bleeding arm. Though it looked temporarily vacant, the complex held innumerable hiding places for competitors and thugs alike.

'That's probably our best option,' he pointed the way with his chin. The veranda was below them, strung with coloured silks and linens to shelter the bawds on their breaks. It looked awfully precarious and rotten in places, but it was the easiest way down.

Carefully, Vesta sat down and helped him do the same. Then, sliding gingerly over the ash-dusted roof tiles, she slithered from the apex to the gutter and dangled her legs over the edge. Her eyes bulged as she tried to find the veranda beams with free swinging feet.

'I can't reach.' She gulped. Her fingers were white and trembled as she clung to the tiles.

'Hang on.' William slid himself towards her, his descent hastened by his mud slickened clothes and the worn soles of his leather boots. Before he slipped over the edge, he rolled onto his stomach and braced his feet on the gutter; the fixtures squealed in protest.

'Ready?' His smile was pinched as he offered his good hand to lower her the last few inches.

'I don't have much choice, do I?'

She wasn't heavy, but William's position was awkward and his body was drained. He ground his teeth and his back curled uncomfortably as she reached blindly with her legs. They lurched as one of her feet collided with a beam.

'Just a little lower!'

William grunted and bent as far as he could. Instinctively, he braced with his free arm and barked in agony, almost dropping her as his muscles gripped around the embedded cheese-knife. Then Vesta found her footing, just as an explosion shook the building to its foundations. A row of tiles plinked and scraped over the edge, one after the other, to shatter on the cobbles below.

'Your turn.' Vesta offered up her hands, almost frantic.

The gutter bent and scored his stomach while his boots scraped over the plaster, his arms trembled, certain he had over-shot. Vesta's hands clutched his midriff. She took some of his weight and steadied him. His toes reached for a beam, but he wasn't as tall as she.

'I've got you,' she gasped, adjusting her grip about him.

Exhaling, he trusted his weight to her, and let go of the roof. She guided him to a beam expertly, but he nearly toppled off and had to brace himself against the wall. Tears squeezed from the corners of his eyes.

'That wasn't so bad.' She patted him on the back. 'One more, then we're down.'

With assistance, William sat down on the beam, and slipped from it to the veranda in a controlled drop. The landing sent a jolt of pain through him and his knees quivered, but he was happy to be down nonetheless.

Vesta handed him a small collection of paper cartridges, half of what they had left from the privateer's pilfered supply, and he loaded his silver flintlock. It snapped shut and sheared off the back of the cartridge, exposing the powder within to sparks of the flint when fired.

Confident now he had his own pistol back in hand, he stalked ahead and kept his back flush to the wall as he approached the first large window. A quick peek revealed the gaudy room inside was empty. He waved Vesta on, and hurried past more windows until he reached the flop-house doors.

The double entrance was carved with cherubs cajoling in bunches of grapes and had obviously come from a far grander building; it was a recent addition and yet to be plastered-in properly from the exposed brickwork at its edges. Keeping his gun ready, he nudged the door and was surprised to find it unlocked.

Perfumes and pipe smoke hung on the air; stale yet distinct. There had been people in here, perhaps as early as this morning, but it was empty now. Unlike the ill-used saloon interior of Melting Moments, this one aped the grandeur of the private clubs in Fairshore. Expensive fabrics covered chaises, velvet drapes and silk cushions were abundant, crystal shades glittered over oil lamps. Yet nothing matched, and the flagrant disregard of tasteful colour combinations was making William feel dizzy. He scowled, focusing his attention on the shadows and the wider room with substantial effort.

A brothel of this size should have the medical supplies they required. After all, without the requisite elixirs and tinctures to keep various rots at bay, a courtesan wouldn't last long in a place like

Blackbile. At the very least there would be a supply of opiates and the ever-popular ether to numb William's pain.

On quiet feet, eyes watching for any sign of movement, they gained the next floor and padded across the landing. Only the echoing retorts of the fight outside reached them; perhaps this was a brief respite in their run of bad luck.

William didn't want to tempt Fate, so approached the final door with caution. It was painted in a shade of smart forest green, while the frame had been striped in alternating red and white; a notice that the doctor was both a barber and a surgeon. William nudged the door open.

Inside, a man lay on a well-used bed, quite naked save for his lab coat and an ether-mask hung loosely around his neck. He had a soft gut and grey at his temples; most likely the flop-house doctor. A similarly attired woman and younger man draped either side of him in a contented fugue.

Vesta pinched the back of William's arm, and glowered. He realised he'd been staring longer than was necessary. With a savage prod in his good shoulder, she indicated the medical supply cupboards. Then, quiet as any cat-burglar worth her salt, she rummaged in drawers and shelves while William aimed his pistol between the comatose staff and the door.

At her silent nod, they escaped the pungent medical office and returned to the relative safety of the main room. To William's surprise, Vesta shoved him into a chaise, glaring as he tried to protest against her ministrations. In no time at all, she had dashed the knife wound with a burning tonic and wiped it clean with a fresh linen swab. He took a quick huff from an ether bottle – the odour rising sour memories – then bit hard on the wooden dowel shoved into his mouth.

Vesta counted quickly from three to one and yanked out the fat blade. Every bitter serration added to his guttural growl, despite the tonics. Squirming, he tried to free himself from her grasp and was slapped like a misbehaving child.

She worked quickly. Four neat stitches closed the wound, and once it was dressed and hidden under his ragged sleeve, he could almost forget it was there – that might have been the lagging effect of the tonics. It pulsed hotly, and the sensation of fine gut-thread passing through the flesh of his arm had made him queasy, but all in all, Vesta had done well.

'You've a knack with a needle.' William tried to make hushed conversation, hoping he could turn it to something less gruesome.

'I've a knack for fixing up idiots that get stabbed, you mean?' Vesta pushed the small bottle of tonic, now half full, into his hands and stowed a few rolls of bandage in her pockets. 'You learn a few things when you have to look after yourself.'

William bit his cheek, holding back a scorching retort. She didn't have the first idea about what he'd been through. Softly, he touched his arm, remembering that humid, fishy hold where he'd first met Lamebrain and the scrape of the scaling knife over his flesh. Every scar was a lesson, every bad memory a distant nightmare that kept his senses sharp.

His musings were interrupted by a square of damp cloth being rubbed on his face. He jerked backwards and snatched it from Vesta. Stitching him up was one thing, but he was perfectly capable of washing his own damned face.

'Just remember, you're the sponsor and I'm the assassin.' He shoved to his feet and tossed the soiled cloth to the floor, a black scowl over his split nose.

'What the hell's that supposed to mean?' She huffed after him, trotting across the flop-house to the fancy door.

'Exactly what I said; I'm in charge.'

They eased cautiously onto the veranda; at the far end was a flight of wooden steps leading into the courtyard. Seeing no-one else, William hastened down the stairway towards the back door of the hotel, skirting the empty stables and stone edged well. He could hear Vesta following closely behind, and ignored her hissed protests for an explanation.

She was trouble, though he'd known that when she'd first pointed out the Church of the Sacrificial Lambs. He'd hoped she at least had the sense not to run around shooting other people's sponsors, or disappearing in the middle of a fight. Her position needed to be made clear. She was gun-fodder as far as every other assassin was concerned, and she had to be careful.

'Just lay low, stay quiet, and do as you're told,' William snarled as they reached the back door of a small hotel. Vesta wrenched it open, slamming it against the crumbling render as she followed him into the tap room.

He turned a cold shoulder to her fury; there was far more at stake than her feelings.

Rapidly scouting the room, he was glad to find it as empty as the flop-house. The bar staff had even abandoned half-eaten breakfast plates and glasses on otherwise uniform tables and chairs. There were posters fixed on several purpose-built notice boards advertising the Man-Butcher Prize, amongst smaller internal memos and one enterprising request for human teeth; good money paid.

The far wall was dominated by a gilt-framed painting. The Blackbile town hall was instantly recognisable, officious against a volcanic backdrop, with the main square stuffed with spectators, mangled corpses, and a winner's podium. William took a closer look at the proud figure holding a golden trophy, noting the tan skin, piercing blue eyes, and ruffled locks of lustrous black hair. It was heavily romanticised – almost good enough to be an original DuVale – but there was no mistaking Ojo Azul.

If William ever wanted to be immortalised on canvas, and copied in the hundreds by counterfeit criminals, then hiding in the hotel bar was not an option. He'd taken at least one of the cultists out of the running, and hopefully the brutish brothers were dead, but a few potential kills were not enough to get himself whitelisted. He was a good assassin, but depressingly inferior to the likes of Genevieve and way out of his depth in this competition.

Flinching against a stray shot outside, he forced his gaze to Ojo's eyes, depicted in the most vibrant blots of blue oil paint he had ever seen. William had been trained by a winner. More importantly, this competition was a contract now. There was no room for error and no more time for self-pity.

He strode away from the painting, passing between neat rows of tables until he could peer through blue velvet drapes to the carnage beyond. He could see at least eight bodies sprawled in the road, both twins and three cultists among them. Two men were engaged hand to hand, one whirling barbed rice-flails, the other meeting the onslaught with a stave that moved so quickly William could barely see it. A man screamed as he was thrown through a window. The sun winked from a rooftop, half a dozen shots rang out, and another body tumbled into the street.

William swallowed. One wrong move would see them dead.

They needed a distraction, or a lull in the fighting. He and Vesta could burst out, guns blazing, and run for it. The problem: there were only two of them, and a whole host of assassins outside. Even as he watched, the stave-wielder's jaw was smashed out with the rice-flail, a cart of barrels were unloaded onto a middle-aged woman, and the frontage of an artisan bakery was engulfed in flame.

'Help!' a rasping screech could be heard across the road. 'A hundred gold pieces to whoever pulls me out of this pit!'

Still upturned in the sludge, with Barbie twitching in rigor just beside him, was Doctor Barber and his wheelchair. The withered cripple struggled and grunted as he tried to rock the chair, his chicken-foot hand twitching ineffectually.

A shop advertising piano tuning and top quality garrotting wares, exploded outwards with a hail of ivory keys and tuneless twangs. Ottilie was nearby, and from the cavalier way she loaded and loosed a volley of blazing explosives, they didn't seem to be in particularly short supply.

'Damnit, someone help me!' Barber shuffled more dramatically, but only succeeded in sinking further into the mud.

William threw himself sideways as a trio of bullets peppered his window. Glass smashed and the velvet drapes were pocked with holes.

Vesta grabbed his shoulder. In a flash, his pistol was drawn and pressed under her bosom. He felt her still, recognising his raw anger; with one squeeze of the trigger, hot lead would tear through her heart, and her plans for vengeance would die with her.

'If you hadn't shot that sponsor, we wouldn't even be in this mess!' he bellowed. 'We're trapped in a warzone *you* created!'

Her dark eyes glistened, moist with unshed tears. She was afraid, but even as William glared at her, that fear became hurt. For a moment, he wasn't looking at a woman with a shady past, but the girl she used to be.

'I couldn't watch him suffer.' She sniffed. 'He was a sponsor, like me. He deserved a quick death, not that beating those thugs were metering out.'

William dropped his aim, and dragged her into a tight embrace. He shouldn't have made her his sponsor; he shouldn't have accepted her contract. She had been on the tipping point between the last chance for a normal life and... *this*.

'I'm sorry for...' He couldn't quite bring himself to divulge it all. 'I'm sorry.'

'We're a team.' Vesta's throat was tight. 'We can get through this.'

'How touching.' The privateer's oily drawl broke them apart. He had a gun trained on them – William's matchlock – the hexagonal barrel perhaps accurate enough at such close quarters. Smouldering match cord glowed ominously in the shadows, wisps of sulphurous smoke curling around him in a sinister haze. 'Put your gun down. My sponsor – who you seem to like so much – is still alive, so you can't kill me.'

William fired. He'd had all he could countenance of the infuriating man. In retrospect, it was an ill-advised move, a gamble that could have seen either one of them dead, but it bought them a modicum of time. The bullet clipped the privateer's shoulder and sent him scuttling into the back room.

'Wait!' He grabbed Vesta's wrist to halt her following shot. 'He's got no powder, we took it all, remember?'

'Lamebrain, get in here!' the privateer yelled from his cover; they could hear him fumbling around crates and barrels.

Prompting Vesta, they ducked behind a table, out of sight. He reloaded quickly, eyes darting between all the entry points; he would be ready for when the mad slave revealed himself.

'*Gods above!*' Vesta breathed a warning, and pointed.

A pall of eerie silence smothered the street; expectant and fearful. Then Doctor Barber resumed his pleas, "help" echoing from every building. The hotel drapes were stirred by the breeze, revealing the colossal beast beyond. In the centre of the road, broad legs braced while she loaded her next rocket, was Ottilie.

'You can't hide!' The huge woman cackled, yellowed eyes bulging from their sockets; the projectile locked into position. 'I'll drag your body from the rubble!'

Vesta made ready, but William shook his head and whispered, 'She's hunting someone else.'

He wasn't sure if Ottilie's sponsor still lived, and asking politely would only draw her attention to their combustible position. Luckily for them, the big woman sneered at something – or someone – out of view, and set off at a march.

People shouted in the street, guns joined the commotion, and boots pounded on the boardwalk. There was another explosion. In the aftermath William could still hear the doctor vehemently pleading for rescue.

'Your brother and his Lambs probably fled into the buildings like we did.' William crawled behind a table closer to the window, trying to make more sense of the fighting outside. 'We need to get as far as we can from here.'

He adjusted his footing and stood up, back against the wall, pistol close to his chest. He trained his senses away from the privateer – who was still rustling around in the back room – and the unfolding events outside. Gradually, Ottilie was herding the fight up the street, though was only a short distance from the hotel herself.

'We should make a run for it, head into the alley behind.' William touched Vesta's shoulder, urging her to stand.

'Not with her still out there.'

'We could make it…' William stopped mid-sentence, startled by a loping figure gambolling across the street towards the stranded wheelchair. There was no mistaking the half-headed man. Lamebrain grinned wide as a spaniel, his tongue darting about gurning lips.

'Helping. Help-p. Hel-ping,' Lamebrain sang as he wrestled Doctor Barber from the muck. 'Hell-ping Dodder Barrr.'

'Lamebrain!' the privateer screeched from the back room, equal parts horror and frustration that his slave was misbehaving.

Not only did Lamebrain hear the command to heel – cradling the frail and sludgy form of the doctor in sinewy arms – but so did the rest of the street. Like a well-trained hunting dog, the slave raised his head, grinned and loped straight back to his master with his prize.

Ottilie grunted as she stamped around to face her new target; William and Vesta had no chance to stop him before he bounded through the hotel door.

'Run!' William dragged Vesta back the way they had come; Lamebrain followed, giggling. They kicked aside chairs, toppled tables, made temporary allies by their common enemy as they escaped the hotel for the courtyard behind.

The moment was shattered in vibrant purple glitter, blackened wood, and roof slates. William and Vesta were thrown by the explosion. Barber and Lamebrain tumbled with them. The whole building burst outwards then plummeted, burying the privateer under a weight of rubble. Smoke billowed out. Fires caught and spread. Ears rang and eyes wept and throats choked.

William groaned. He wanted nothing more than to lay in his heap on the ground, conscious of every bruised and jangled nerve in his body, but the proximity of death was a good motivator. He flopped onto his hands and knees, covered in dry plaster dust, which was grittier and even more irritating to the skin than the constant coating of filth and ash. He snatched his flintlock up, finding its gleaming barrel easily in the debris. Forced into a dead-end, he knew surrender was not an option.

He stood, showering grey dust and glass shards, and glared across the smouldering ruins. Ottilie cackled on the other side, her mad eyes finding his through the haze of destruction.

'Another.' She held out her hand for a rocket. Her sponsor was behind, obscured by her girth.

The rules were clear; the sponsor had to die first. Beside the well, Vesta was just stirring from the blast, still alive and hopefully unhurt. A single rocket from the mad-bomber in such close confines however, would see them both as dead as the privateer. An idea occurred to him; it was a long shot.

'You can't kill us,' he yelled. 'There's an assassin under this rubble, killed by your bomb before his sponsor; you're disqualified.'

Ottilie sneered, asserting again to her sponsor, 'rocket.'

William cursed, was there nobody except him playing by the rules? The sponsor poked around Ottilie's broad thigh for a heartbeat, depositing a fresh charge in her huge hand. William held his breath and fired, aiming not for the sponsor, but for the rocket itself.

A burst of orange and yellow engulfed the pair of bombers entirely. The flames spread out and licked at the sponsor's cart of explosives. A glorious rainbow of light erupted. Deafening screeches added to the cacophony. Every projectile Ottilie had was spent. She was knocked away by the second blast, charred and made less by the loss of her arm. It seemed her girthy frame was enough to save her from being split into a thousand little nuggets like her sponsor, but she was defeated nonetheless. Still breathing, but unconscious, blood seeped from her stump. Death was inevitable.

'You did it.' Vesta clapped William on the back. 'Now kill *him*.'

She grabbed him by the shoulder and turned him around. A cartridge was pushed into his hand and she pointed at Lamebrain. 'Then we can get away, find somewhere safe. Can't have him hunting us.'

William loaded his flintlock, advanced across the yard with Vesta behind him. She was right. The sooner the privateer's sponsor was dead, the safer they would be.

Lamebrain was near the flop-house steps, huddled beside Doctor Barber, his single eye looking up; dumb and trusting as a faithful hound. The half-wit had ever been a thing of terror, a nightmare that plagued William's sleep as a youth. As he levelled the pistol and took aim, he knew there was little room for compassion – and if there was, it was surely a mercy to send the half-headed slave to the next world. William had to be the cold killer that this competition required if he hoped to win. He took his pistol in both hands to steady it.

'Wait!' Doctor Barber slumped across Lamebrain's chest. 'I need him. He's one of mine. Look at that head stitching! You don't think anyone other than the great Doctor Barber could do that, do you?'

William shrugged.

'I've already lost Barbie, I can't lose another. Not so meaninglessly.' He raised one finger on his chicken's foot. 'And I've bowed out of the competition, I need someone to take me back to the square.'

'He does make a fair point.' William lowered his pistol with a subdued sigh. Pity moved him, for the plight of the slave and all he had endured. 'We can't take away the doctor's only chance at survival.'

If anyone challenged his decision, William would simply say that Doctor Barber was on the prize committee. Surely aiding such a valuable member of The Assassins' Guild would entitle an automatic reinstatement to the whitelist, at the very least a good mention.

'Yes we can.' Vesta grabbed William's arm, pressing her fingers into his knife wound to try and direct his unwilling limb.

'No!' He discharged the pistol into the ground.

Fresh blood seeped through his bandage, hot and wet. Vesta looked at her fingers, spotted red, and humbly met William's gaze. He knew she didn't understand exactly why he couldn't kill Lamebrain, but at least she was sorry about trying.

'This way!' a man shouted in the street. 'They must be here somewhere.'

Any pent up resentment William and Vesta shared was washed away with the realisation that they were still pursued by her brother and his cult. He nodded at her, confirming their silent agreement to escape without further bloodshed, at least in the immediate.

'Good luck, doctor.' William set his sights on a distant clock tower; that was as good a thing to head towards as any. He wouldn't let himself get turned around in the back roads again, that was for sure. He grabbed Vesta's hand and set off running.

1668

'Is that it?' Aldreda bellowed from the centre of the courtyard, her arms spread wide. Clamped in one fist was a woman's scrawny throat; purple faced, body dangling lifeless below. In her other hand was an old pistol, dull and caked in filth. 'Have I won already?'

Terrowin could hear Aldreda as clearly as if she were next to them, even through the thick hardwood of the town hall doors. He knelt at the keyhole, watching the Man-Butcher-imposter flail her grim prize around like a rag-doll. The rolling pin was secured tightly in her belt, bloody and unmistakeable.

'Well?' Beechworth hissed from the cover of the brick door frame. 'What's happening?'

'Get your own keyhole,' Terrowin growled, knowing full well the lord would claim that gentleman didn't do anything as sordid as peek through keyholes. Though, it was more likely he didn't want to get his face blown off with a stray shot. 'She's in the centre.'

Terrowin scrambled up, and they braced their backs on each side of the door frame, waiting to burst outside with a hail of fire.

'Ready?' Beechworth swung his rifle from his shoulder, pressing the stock against his body.

Terrowin broke open his flintlock to check that the loaded cartridge hadn't absconded while he wasn't looking. He let go a long, soft breath to steady his nerves.

'Mayor Perrin!' Aldreda screamed. 'Get your arse out here and declare me the winner!'

The crowd cheered and whooped for her, assuming that she had won. Terrowin's grip tightened on his pistol; their adulation needed to stop, and quickly. He spat out a single word, 'ready.'

'On three then.' Beechworth inhaled steadily. 'One…'

'I am the Man-Butcher!' Aldreda's bellow echoed from every bleacher and building still standing. 'The best assassin there ever was!'

Terrowin couldn't take it anymore and thrust the door wide open with a well-placed boot. Aldreda whirled exuberantly; no doubt she was disappointed Terrowin wasn't the mayor. Recognition drained her mood into a sour sneer of disdain.

She raised her pistol, but he was faster. Two bullets fired in gusts of smoke and an echoing clap that silenced the crowd. All that Terrowin could be sure of in the immediate was that her bullet hadn't found him.

Beechworth was a heartbeat behind him, firing from his hip at the brutish woman as he hurried to keep pace with Terrowin. The two men collided with their respective pillars and sank to their haunches to reload at roughly the same time. Terrowin rapidly searched in his pockets for another cartridge, entirely unaware of Beechworth's furious eyes focused on him.

'I said "on three". Not *two* or *four*. You'll get us both killed if you carry on like that!' Beechworth packed his next shot into his rifle and armed it. 'What say you?'

The pointed tone startled Terrowin; the provocation that had caused the lord's face to redden and his pencil moustache to twitch, entirely unknown. In this sort of situation, it was always better to apologise, even if he didn't know what for. 'Sorry?'

Now loaded, Terrowin leant out to take another shot, but Aldreda was nowhere in sight. He furrowed his brow and leant out a little further. The square was strewn with corpses, body parts and indeterminate human sludge, though no sign of the imposter. It was as if she had vanished into thin air. He sidled out of his cover completely and readied his pistol, hoping to lure her out with his vulnerability; she didn't appear. Maybe she had been killed by his shot and now blended perfectly with the sprawl of corpses for the virtue of being one.

'Sorry? You're *sorry*? I could be dead right now. If you can't work as part of a team then…' Beechworth trailed off as he became aware of exactly how long Terrowin had been squatting outside of cover. 'Is she dead?'

'Missing.' Terrowin scoured the array of dead assassins and spectators.

Like a bubble popping in a cauldron, Aldreda thrust up from a heap of bodies, a pistol in each hand. She let off a shot for Terrowin, grazing the inner side of his arm, which sent him scuttling back into cover like an exposed cockroach.

'There she is.' He winced and clamped his hand over the wound.

Beechworth allowed himself a moment, snapped his rifle ready, and peeked out. A bullet collided with the pillar, showering them in chips of brick and dust; the second of her two shots wasted so carelessly. Then he stepped out, emerging from the fading gun-smoke with such dramatic emphasis that even Terrowin's mother might have applauded it.

Unwilling to be left behind, Terrowin followed, gritting his teeth through the pain. He was just as good as the noble where killing was concerned.

Aldreda tossed her half-loaded pistol to the muck and roared. Teeth bared and hands outstretched like claws, she charged at Beechworth. She was like a bear made human, a Scold giant with the favour of the gods. Despite her size she made good pace and it seemed she would be upon them – tearing them limb from limb with her immense strength – before they had a chance to fight back.

Beechworth's rifle thumped a shot into her midriff, colliding with the armour but knocking the wind from her. She balked and choked, and quickly recovered her footing. The lord staggered back, reloading, but there was no outpacing the barbaric assassin.

Terrowin had been calmly preparing to fire, breathing slowly as he aimed, not entirely bothered about the immediate threat to Beechworth. His arm was steady and his aim was true; as she passed by him, he pulled the trigger. Aldreda was too focused on the lord to notice the flintlock aimed for her, and didn't even realize the danger she was in until the bullet skewered the flesh under her arm.

The pain didn't hit immediately, but the shock did. She tumbled from her great stampede, and swept Beechworth down with her. The pair staggered through the double doors, slid together on the polished floor and crumpled in a heap within.

Terrowin reloaded quickly and followed them inside. He had to finish her now, before she had the chance to retaliate; but when he got to her side, she was already dead. His bullet must have hit something vital and took away the life she had been so lucky to keep this far.

Pints and pints of dark blood pumped over the hall floor, hot and coppery against the cold tiles. Terrowin wasn't too familiar with anatomy, never having had the patience to read about it, or even learn how to read, but something important had definitely been ruptured.

Beechworth wriggled beneath her dead weight, sputtering and clawing to free himself. There were only two entrants left, and one of them was pinned weapon-less beneath the bulk of a dead assassin.

Terrowin aimed his pistol between Beechworth's eyes, victory a hairsbreadth from his finger.

'Wait.' Beechworth stilled and drew his hands up in the most pitiful plea for his life. 'We made a deal, I help you take her out, and you give me a fair shot at the prize.'

'Yes…' Terrowin readied to shoot. 'But *I* was the one that killed her, you just happened to be here.'

'You wouldn't have killed her without me, as well you know!' Beechworth's spite surprised Terrowin, but he supposed that the man was in quite the stressful situation given his penchant for breathing. 'Moreover, you gave your word. A gentleman's agreement is sacrosanct.'

'I never did consider myself much of a gentleman.' Terrowin scratched the side of his nose with the flintlock as he mused. One trigger pull; the lord would be dead and he would be crowned champion, but everything would go straight back to the mundanity of normal life. 'Why not?'

He lowered the hammer on his flintlock softly and slid it into his holster, then crouched down to heft the great weight from Beechworth. The duel would be one last treat, Terrowin decided. One last thrill before he took the prize.

1682

Ottilie's bombardment made getting onto the rooftops far easier than it had been getting down, but conquering the ruinous slopes of three purpose-built warehouses made William sweat and shiver in ways he rarely felt. Blood loss and fatigue made him feel leaden; as he crested the rubble a wave of dizziness threatened to topple him off the edge.

Forcing his heavy limbs onward, William focused instead on the clock tower. It was a huge structure of grey stone, prominent even against the ashen backdrop; an excellent landmark to stop them staggering in circles again. It was imperative to increase their distance from the threats left behind. More cultists had entered the competition than he first thought and he could still hear them shouting from the street. In truth, it was a blessing they hadn't been spotted ascending to the roofs, though Ottilie's explosive downfall doubtless gave the Lambs pause.

Only a fool would get too close to the clock tower; the building was too obvious. Certainly other assassins would be lurking nearby or fighting over the vantage point. He could imagine Genevieve at the top with her rifle, calmly increasing her kill-count in relative safety. He didn't like the thought of Vesta being cut down from such an impersonal distance. He didn't like the thought of her being cut down at all, but there was no protection against an assassin with a scope. So, he reasoned, he would choose a different landmark soon enough, and shift course.

'Lambs!' Vesta's shrill cry made him stumble to a halt.

She pointed; a rifle-toting Lamb guarded a balcony on the other side of the road, aiming right at them. William yanked Vesta's arm, pulling her over, just as a bullet pinged off the tin roof. He cursed through gritted teeth, his plans dashed.

Leaping up, they ran the length of the warehouse roof and dropped onto a flat-topped administration building. They tripped over garden furniture and pots of canvas dahlias; a half finished glass of sherry shattered as they toppled an occasional table. Whoever had indulged in the sour beverage was long gone – a still-open trapdoor yawned darkly in the centre.

Behind, the balcony sharpshooter fired, and a terracotta pot exploded beside them. William cursed; Vesta was already wriggling through the trapdoor.

'There!' the Lamb cried, alerting unseen comrades in the lanes below.

'Faster!' William urged Vesta on, practically throwing himself in the hole.

The office within was still, but muted shouts of pursuit still reached them. They careened around a desk and sprinted into the clear walkway, papers ruffling at their passage. Double-doors swung wildly as he barged through, and they hurtled down three flights of stairs. Together they skidded on the highly polished stone floor in the reception area and stopped.

Outside the wide doors – inlaid with frosted glass – were the blurry figures of four or five men in wool trimmed robes. William cursed a third time; naming Fate as the wretched being that must have doomed him so.

'How many cartridges have you got left?' he hissed.

Vesta dug in her pockets and pulled out a small handful from each.

'Maybe eight?' She shared them out and surreptitiously checked her stolen pistol was loaded.

'We need more.' He paced to the back of the room.

'We don't need to kill them all.' She took her position at his shoulder. 'Just shoot my brother and be done with it.'

'If only it was that easy.'

On the other side of the glass, the cultists were ready. One of them began a count down from five, holding the handle, ready to charge in. It seemed the Lambs couldn't see the dark interior through the translucent glass and didn't realise their targets were waiting inside with the advantage. William decided to take the fight to them.

By the time the cultist counted to one, William burst out of the door. The man who had been poised to rush inwards had his eye socket cracked by the corner of the wood. Another was knocked down a trio of steps, collapsing in the mud. Two of them took a bullet; one each from William and Vesta as they charged into the street. One died instantly, the other was shot in the gut and crumpled to the floor for a long and excruciating end. William smashed the butt of his pistol into the jaw of the last Lamb, but didn't stick around to finish the job; there were more approaching. It seemed the entire cult had rallied against them, flagrantly disregarding the rules in their zealous mission.

Shoulder to shoulder they made the sanctuary of an alleyway and plunged into the confusion of backstreets. They ran, panting, sweating, and swearing, turning right and left until they skirted the back yard of Melting Moments – painted the same lurid pink as the front. As soon as he was able to, William dragged Vesta onto a main street, located the clock tower, and ducked into another alleyway. His plan of evading the Lambs entirely might have been dashed, but getting away from them now required similar tactics.

Echoing cries followed, bouncing from every direction. Vesta pulled ahead of William, her legs were longer than his, and she was far fitter given his blood loss. He tried to catch up in case she came face-to-face with another assassin, but the threat of the Lamb-hunt leant her matchless speed.

As they rounded onto another small street, the clock tower loomed overhead. Too close, too late, they were headed straight for it. There was a glint above; perhaps just the sun on a damp gargoyle, but more likely a waiting sniper.

'Turn right,' he shouted. Vesta had to get out of the imagined-rifleman's line of sight.

Gunpowder clapped behind and a pawnbroker's sign was knocked off its hinges. William dared a glimpse back as he followed Vesta into the next street. He only got the briefest look, but he could have sworn there were at least ten cultists.

When six more emerged at the far end of the narrow road, Vesta veered into another alley, barely avoiding a hail of gunfire. The firing squad reloaded rapidly as William wheeled after Vesta; a shop siding was turned to woodchips in his wake.

It seemed all the rules were out as far as the Lambs were concerned. William prayed for a referee; the town was supposed to be flooded with them, but somehow he had managed to avoid every single one. Another curse was sent Fate's way.

The clock tower was dead ahead; a huge stone edifice – clustered with demonic statues and flowery finials – that loomed higher than any other building except the Lambs' own chapel. Aggressive iron spikes adorned ledges to dissuade climbers and slick stains of ash trailed from the mouths of vomiting gargoyles. Vesta turned and skirted the graffiti-covered outer wall.

William sprang after her, finger curled around the trigger of his flintlock. He weaved around barrels, stinking waste, and a fly-covered body. Footsteps thumped behind him; he was sure if the roads hadn't been so relentlessly winding, both of them would have been dead by now. Perhaps Fate gave as well as took.

After a dozen steps or so, the clock tower wall turned ninety degrees, and from their new vantage it was clear it made a sizable walled courtyard; the tower itself dominating one side. Dashing down the narrow alley between the wall and adjacent buildings, they did their best to avoid damp sluices of ash, indeterminate remains and a pool of congealed blood – its former owner had been delightfully skewered on one of the vicious iron spikes.

Yet more Lambs – who had circled around the other side of the clock tower – headed them off at the next junction. There were no more roads to take.

'Hurry up!' Vesta slipped in a pool of muck as she changed direction, disappearing through a wide archway into the tower courtyard.

The heavy iron gates were open, the securing chains discarded in the street; someone had picked the padlock. Vesta didn't pause to look into the small cluster of buildings crouched inside, and didn't stop until she had climbed the steps to the tower door opposite. William was only a beat behind her. They were heading straight into a dead end, but there was no other choice. He sent a bullet flying for the herd of Lambs and followed inside. Vesta slammed the door and dropped a locking bar, securing it.

'Get back.' He thrust her aside as holes were punched through the wood; shafts of light floated with dust and splinters. 'The door won't keep them long'

'Any sign of my brother?' She gasped, bent double.

'This isn't the time,' he grumbled, reloading. 'We need to get away from this door, get upstairs; somewhere we have the advantage.'

A wooden staircase clambered around the square sided tower, coiling upwards at least seven times before reaching an obscuring floor. The small anteroom, and the tower proper, were illuminated by slatted windows and ash-hazed air. It would not be a short climb, but with luck, it would be a solitary one. Unless they had stumbled into another assassin's hide-out.

Vesta began her ascent as the Lambs drummed on the door. The wood was weakened by the bullet pocks, and it only took a few strikes before that tell-tale sound of splintering sent a shiver up William's spine. It could only be minutes before they got inside. He wasted no time and followed her up the stairs.

The tower was austere by design and far more impressive to look at from the outside. At intervals an unlit torch had been set in a wall bracket, and with the exception of a few masons' marks, it was drab. But this wasn't a leisure trip. William sweated and panted; the previous exertion weighed on him heavier than ever. Aching, dizzy, and sick with exhaustion, he struggled after Vesta almost on his hands and knees.

The Lambs pounded the door; the wood creaked and groaned in complaint. William prayed for five more minutes, but just as he sent his hopes skyward, the door ruptured and the Lambs poured in.

He leaned out from the stairs and looked down; they were gathering on the ground floor, starting to spiral the stairs in single file. He shot one near the front, briefly hampering their progress. The body was tipped over the handrail, slapping to the flagstones as he bled out.

Vesta neared the doorway to the next floor. If they could get inside and bar it, they would be able to distance themselves from the Lambs. Beyond his pounding head and burning lungs, William struggled to think of a way out; a skilful climb down the sheer stone perhaps, but nothing realistic. They were doomed; Vesta's brother had rallied all his brainwashed masses to hunt them down and hadn't even bothered to show his scarred face for the victory. A better assassin would have handed Vesta to the Lambs to save himself; there was no point in them both dying. William fixed his sights on her, feeling his chest tighten, and knew he wouldn't do it.

The top door thrust open and Vesta staggered backwards. William caught her in his arms, lost balance himself, and slumped back onto the stairs. He nearly fell off in his efforts to keep her and his pistol from being lost. They sprawled upside-down, legs and arms floundering.

'Don't shoot.' An assassin emerged from the doorway, rifle in one hand, some sparking device in the other. He fixed his dark eyes on Vesta and William, then took another step forwards and peered down at the advancing Lambs.

The weapon he held looked similar to the orbs used by the cultists, but was larger and made from studded iron instead of glass. The flaring string was perilously short, on the verge of setting the thing off. Before the man threw it into their midst, he fired three shots into the crowd of Lambs without pausing to reload. Then, as they looked up to see who was bombarding them with gunfire, the assassin let the orb roll off his palm with a half-hitched smile.

A deafening explosion shook the whole tower, rattled chunks of mortar free and kicked up dust. William closed his eyes to the flash, felt the heat of it at his back and pressure against his head and ears.

Lambs screamed as they were taken apart in mere moments; easily a third of them were killed, most were burned and left writhing. A few that had been outside, or lucky enough to avoid the worst of the blast, retreated in terror.

'There's more where that came from,' shouted the rifleman.

William's head throbbed. His eyes struggled to focus and when they did, the assassin had his rifle aimed directly at Vesta. Slim and well presented, wearing a shirt – somehow crisp and white in the filth of Blackbile – and black suit trousers; the man was unmistakable.

'I should have killed the pair of you when I had the chance.' Lord Beechworth sighed, massaging his temple. 'I knew you'd lead that rabble here somehow…'

William knew he hadn't imagined that winking scope atop the clock tower. Vesta had been as close to death then as she was now, but at least he could do something about it at this range. His pistol was firmly in hand, underneath Vesta, hidden from the old champion.

'I had to listen to that damned doctor…' Beechworth cursed to himself, and added, 'I should finish you off here and now.'

William shifted his grip, trying to think of any way to get his gun in a position to fire before Beechworth could pull his own trigger.

'This tower's compromised, and those Lambs don't give up; it's only a matter of time before they come back.' His hand slid from his temple to his jaw. He stroked his slender moustache with a finger, worried his lip with a canine as he mused. Though his rifle was held in one hand, it was steady as a rock. 'There's no way I'll get them both out…'

William scowled, twisted his hand, and slid his flintlock from under Vesta's leg.

'You brought those damned Lambs here.' Beechworth lowered his rifle, his lips making a thin line below his thin moustache. If William was going to shoot him, now was his chance. 'And you'll help me keep them out.'

Beechworth offered his hand; William's scowl deepened.

'Teamwork is the only way to keep the tower. If those zealots can join forces, why can't we?' There was a look of desperation in the old champion's eyes, but a hint of something sinister made William distrust him. 'What do you say, allies?'

There was no telling exactly how many shots Beechworth's rifle could hold. Perhaps it was empty and this whole thing was an elaborate bluff. William could just shoot him and be done with it. He and Vesta could flee before the Lambs rallied again; all they had to do was stay unseen.

'We'll do it.' Vesta made the decision for him. She took Beechworth's hand and made it official with a sturdy shake.

1668

Mayor Perrin sweated profusely and mopped his hairline with a spotted handkerchief. He wore a large pantomime grin for the benefit of the bloodthirsty audience. Over the short distance his efforts were enough to trick the crowd, but Terrowin could tell the man had no stomach for the swathes of viscera running through the square.

It had taken the afternoon for volunteers to clear the majority of the carnage. They were methodical in their work, battlefield professionals as it were, able to strip a body of anything worth salvaging and direct the loot through the necessary dealers in record time. Every trinket, weapon, bead and button was accounted for by three clip-board-toting invigilators with hawkish eyes; any coin recouped bolstered guild coffers.

Once all of the remains were carted away, the mayor took his cue, and led the last two assassins from the shade of the town hall. Blood pooled between the cobbles like glistening puddles after a spring shower, punctuated with spatters of minced flesh; a perfect setting for a duel that would never be forgotten.

'This is about the middle.' The mayor nodded, dabbing his brow for a final time.

Terrowin grinned at Beechworth, who imparted only a brief and anxious glance in return. It did seem like an oddly organised way to bring an end to the chaos, but all the same, it was exciting. Terrifying. He would have expected the noble assassin to be more relaxed; the blue-bloods were renowned for duelling, though it took an iron will to stand firm and shoot true in such circumstances.

'I'm glad to be bringing proceedings to a close personally!' The mayor looked more uncomfortable than Beechworth, as if he might vomit if he looked at the wrong crevice in the cobbles. He watched the spectators gathered in the bleachers instead – any corpses amongst them diligently removed.

'We will follow traditional Garlish procedures,' the mayor declared. 'Ten paces each. Once a duellist's foot touches the ground on the tenth step they may turn and take their shot.'

The victor would be determined as the last man standing, or the least wounded if they both happened to strike true. Usually, at such close quarters, it all depended on who fired first.

'How are you feeling?' Beechworth's usually acerbic drawl was muted.

'Ecstatic.' Terrowin rubbed his hands together, trying to dispel some of his surplus energy. 'I've never duelled before.'

The heady mix of tonics and quick-fix salves on Terrowin's wound, combined with the crowd and the imminence of his death, was going straight to his head. He waved at the bleachers, threw a few kisses their way, inciting uproar and cheers. Even Beechworth raised his hand, refined compared to Terrowin's mania.

'Gentlemen! Back to back, if you please?' The mayor directed them to their positions. 'Make ready your weapons, then march with my count, understood?'

'Yes sir!' Terrowin stamped to attention with his back just brushing Beechworth's shoulder and held his pistol tightly to his chest. He clicked the hammer into place 'Ready.'

'Man-butcher…' Beechworth spoke quietly as he cocked his rifle. 'This courtyard is rather big, wouldn't you say? Why don't we make this a little more interesting?'

'I'm all ears.' Terrowin angled his chin to better hear over the crowd's encouragement.

'Why don't we throw caution to the wind and walk fifteen paces instead of the conventional ten? We're both good shots; this whole thing will be over all too quickly if we only take ten.' Beechworth's nerves had been supplanted with the exhilaration that shivered down their spines in mutual glee. 'What do you say?'

Terrowin considered that the assassin was simply trying to give himself an advantage; his rifle would be far better over thirty paces than a pistol. But he had never shied away from a challenge, and the underdog always won in the end.

'Deal.' Terrowin nodded eagerly, already imagining the scene as two crack-shots were let loose on each other.

'One.' The mayor started counting.

Terrowin leapt a full yard, bounding like a greyhound released from its trap. His heart was thumping in his neck and ears, every nerve tingling. It was impossible to be more excited without rupturing something. Sombrely, Beechworth took a single measured pace.

'Two.'

Terrowin crunched a bloodied mulch of ash and sawdust with his next step, straining to match the noble assassin's slow pace.

'Three... Four...'

It occurred to Terrowin that Walter wasn't aware he was now supposed to be counting to fifteen, but imagined that he and Beechworth could continue the count themselves. It would be a tremendous surprise for the audience, and would drum up the tension to unknown levels.

'Five...'

An eager spectator thumped his boots on the bleachers, a noise rapidly emulated like an ill-timed marching band, as people rapped and banged on any surface they could find. Terrowin felt a wave of fanatic adoration. The crowd cheered his name, they cheered for Beechworth too, and they screamed for the barbaric joy of it.

'Six.' The mayor's voice was almost lost in the din. 'Seven.'

Nearly halfway. Terrowin jammed his lips together, puffing his cheeks and grinding his teeth in an effort to restrain his maniacal laughter. There was nothing like the thrill of gambling with life and death.

'Eight.'

The drumming and cheering trailed off, the anticipation becoming too great. There was nothing anyone could do but wait and watch.

'Nine... Ten.'

Terrowin took another eager step forward, only five more to go.

He heard Beechworth's foot strike the ground, and then a loud scrape as it was twisted in the dirt. That exact sound had been part of Terrowin's life since before he could walk, when his mother had dazzled crowds with circus trick-shots. It was the same noise made at the very moment she would pivot on her heel, and sight-unseen blast an apple off an unwilling participant's head.

It seemed Beechworth had tricked him, and Terrowin would soon meet the same fate as those delicate apples; blasted to a hundred pieces and dashed on the dirt.

He whirled around to face the lord, only a fraction of a second behind. Beechworth's rifle came up. Terrowin took his aim. Gunpowder clapped, and before Terrowin could squeeze his trigger, hot lead punctured his eye and exploded through the back of his skull.

1682

William and Vesta entered the tower chamber. In the low light, dust hung thick in the air and clumped around well-defined footprints on gnarled wooden boards.

Columns shadowed the room further, blocking most of the meagre light that bled through the narrow, slit windows. They held up a maze of walkways overhead, weaving around vast cogs and coils that made up the clock mechanism. A low whir and ratcheting click were a constant, occasionally accompanied by the clunk of a large gear or twang of a spring.

Lord Beechworth was visible through the door, studying the smouldering wreckage his bomb had caused. When he seemed satisfied the tower hadn't caught fire – and the minced Lambs below were no threat – he followed them inside. He slung his rifle on a strap over his shoulder and rolled his shirt sleeves up as he walked, positively nonchalant in the company of a rival assassin. A confidence only afforded to a man with a living sponsor.

'The pair of you look…' Beechworth wet a dry crack in his lip, searching for something more polite to say than he was no doubt thinking. 'Tired. Have you been running about since we started?'

'More or less.' William shrugged.

'Better come with me; we've plenty of food, and wine – helps still the old trigger finger – or perhaps an elderflower cordial instead?' Beechworth strode ahead into the gloom. 'Just here, behind this stack of parts.'

William scowled; only a lord would be having a damned picnic up here while others died in the streets. The wealthy toad would never understand the struggle of entering the prize wielding an antique pistol and an empty purse. Still, he wouldn't refuse food and drink on principle; that sort of nonsense would only invite death.

Navigating a dozen wooden crates, spilling over with brass trinkets and clock spares, they entered a meagre pool of candle light and joined a rather cosy gathering.

'William!' Dr Barber exclaimed. He sat on a red and black chequered rug, withered legs stretched out beneath him, body propped against a wicker hamper. It was strange that he was on the floor, as a wooden-framed wheelchair with little iron-spoked wheels had been pushed to the back of the crate heap and abandoned there, empty.

'It's so good to see you well,' the doctor added, 'and Vesta too!'

Confusion and a modicum of delight lifted William's dour mood; he couldn't help but respond, 'how did you get here?'

'It's a long story.' Barber picked up a heel of bread with the larger of his withered hands. He bit off a piece of crust and crunched it between misshapen teeth. 'My friend over there is not too reliable when it comes to directions.'

He indicated with the crust to the pooling shadows beyond the candle light. William could just pick out the hunched slave, his one bulging eye and bony frame. Lamebrain appeared more subdued than he had been in the chaos outside and picked slowly at the carcass of a cooked chicken; grease dribbled down his chin. It was just possible to hear him muttering about fish, presumably a result of William's arrival, but he seemed contented to stay in his corner and eat.

'I saw the pair staggering about.' Beechworth set his rifle against the stack of crates. He sat cross-legged beside an old woman opposite Barber on the rug.

William hadn't noticed her at first, dismissing her as a pile of blankets, but now he spotted her sagging face amongst the wools. She was pale and wheezed softly. He recognised her as a matter of fact. It was the old woman he had met at the opening ceremony who had been so proud to sponsor her grandson. He reasoned that the abandoned wheelchair must have been her own. Beechworth set a hand to her forehead, brushed a sweat-lank strand of hair from her face; he tutted and shook his head before returning to his tale.

'I couldn't likely leave the good doctor out there to get shot, could I? I went out, collected the pair of them; which was a task in itself –

that half-headed chap is too skittish by half.' Beechworth picked up a small brown vial and fed the contents to his grandmother. 'So I brought them back here; I'd say it's the safest place in town, outside of the havens of course.'

Beechworth corked the little bottle and set it back on the rug, then took up a small plate, decorated with painted holly and golden berries. 'Please, sit, you must be starved! Do help yourselves.'

'What if the Lambs come back?' William looked across at Vesta, but she was already settling herself down beside Barber.

'Those stairs creak like you wouldn't believe, and the first flight is completely destroyed now.' Beechworth used a small prong to collect a trio of cured meats from a platter and added them to his plate with a small bunch of grapes and heel of bread. 'The spymaster himself couldn't get in here unheard; we might as well relax.'

'Please join us, William,' Barber encouraged him, patting a space on the blanket.

William saw no reason not to, other than this whole situation seeming completely incongruous. He shrugged, sat down, and filled a plate for himself. Barber offered wine, but he declined in favour of a glass flute of cordial; the calming effect of alcohol on his trigger finger would prove dangerous given his diminished supply of blood.

'What are these?' He held up a bowl of deep green grape-looking things, glossed with golden oil.

'Olives,' Vesta rolled her eyes.

'Finest Vitulan olives.' Beechworth skewered one with a steel cocktail stick. '*Franccino,* I believe.'

William added half a dozen to his plate and popped one in his mouth, instantly regretting his decision to commit to so many. It was salty and not at all *normal* tasting, and he almost broke a tooth on the pit.

'My young Barbie used to love olives.' Barber sighed. 'It was a shame I had to lose him. Still, his brothers await me at the workshop. The sooner I get back there the better, I shouldn't have left my work for so long.'

The doctor cast a wistful gaze around the shadowy chamber and added, 'this little foray was… ill advised.'

'Events have not unfolded according to any of our plans.' Beechworth looked down at his grandmother; she had started to shiver. William was unsure if that was an improvement on her previous pallid rigor, but he suspected not. 'The old girl wanted to go out with a bang…hardly likely now; she can't even hold her head up, let alone a rifle. Nothing short of nightmarish getting here, and I had to haul that damned chair up.'

William glanced at the cumbersome wheeled chair; thinking of all those tower steps made him dizzy.

'What about you, William?' Beechworth asked, catching him off guard.

'I guess you know who I am; that I've been blacklisted? I hoped to clear my name, get back to business again. Earn a fair wage doing what I'm good at…'

William realised he was sat eating a light supper with two of the most powerful guilders; two men who could reverse his fate and get him on the whitelist. Though he wasn't so sure that contract-killing was the right career path anymore.

'We're going to kill my brother,' Vesta added darkly. She crunched a fig-topped cracker as she said it; so matter of fact in her delivery. 'I can't imagine how many people he's killed, or convinced to sacrifice themselves. He leads the Lambs here – that's why they're after us – and we won't rest until he's dead.'

William winced; he didn't possess the same bloody resolve as Vesta in the matter, but he didn't discourage her.

'Once he's dead, and this folly of a competition is done, I can start a fresh life.'

There was a marked moment of silence where everyone present elected not to mention that she was likely to die. Then Beechworth set down his plate, wiped his hands on a monogrammed napkin, and stood up.

'I'll keep vigil for a while. If I spot any Lambs coming, I'll let you know.' He shifted his gaze to the doctor. 'Watch over my grandmother would you?'

'Certainly.' Barber nodded.

Beechworth pulled on a thick grey overcoat, shouldered his rifle, and slipped into the gloom. His footsteps echoed upwards to the clock balcony, a door opened and shut, and he was gone.

After that, Barber tried to lift the mood by telling tales of previous prize winners. He focused mainly on triumphs against the villainous dead, and in the end managed to engage William and Vesta in the good-hearted thrill of it. Lamebrain inched closer until he finally slumped beside the old woman and took more than his share of remaining food. It was unclear if he understood exactly what was happening, but his eye gleamed in a way William had not seen before.

Some hours and glasses of Beechworth's wine later, Vesta fell asleep. She pulled a corner of the rug over for warmth and curled up beside William. He wanted to stay awake and alert to protect her as his sponsor, but even without the wine he was exhausted. As another of Barber's tales drew to a close – of Man-Butcher Karin and how he had preserved her from death with a very particular and entirely secret cocktail of tonics – William followed Vesta to sleep.

It was some time before he woke, but when he did he felt surprisingly well rested; he had expected the effects of his injury to linger much longer. Perhaps he had lost less blood than he thought, what with Vesta insisting he keep the blade in place for so long to stem the flow.

Looking up to the light shafting through the high window slits, he could assess it was morning. He felt a pang of shame for succumbing to his exhaustion, but now at least he knew Beechworth could be trusted. By accident he had given the man ample opportunity to kill his sponsor. Vesta was still sleeping but more importantly, still alive.

With care he untangled himself from Vesta, who had opted to use him as a pillow, and sat up to stretch the kinks from his back. Barber was snoring and Beechworth was still nowhere to be seen. The old woman and Lamebrain, neither of whom were particularly good prospects for conversation, were both sleeping too. The former was wheezing harder than ever; the latter had returned to his corner and curled up with an empty bottle.

William stood, and as he stretched again, he noticed his pistol was not at his hip. It didn't take him long to find; the flintlock had been discarded on the floorboards just beyond the old woman. It appeared that nobody had tampered with it, but the fact remained that somebody had lifted it from his sleeping body. That put him on edge, made him suspicious of everyone in the room, no matter how enfeebled. As a precaution, he broke open the pistol, took out the cartridge and replaced it with another from his pocket. All in all, he only had four left, and that was if he trusted the one in the pistol when it was taken.

'I should have a few of those,' Beechworth spoke from behind William, making him jump. 'Mine only takes copper, but nanny's old-fashioned; she wanted to use my father's rifle. That pistol looks like a large bore; it'll probably take what cartridges she has left.'

'Thank you.' William stuffed his cartridges into a deep pocket, making sure to keep the one he didn't trust separate. He wondered if the old marksman had been in here long, he certainly hadn't heard him approach. Perhaps it was Beechworth that had lifted his pistol, and had abandoned it when he stirred. It didn't make any sense, if the lord wanted him dead, he would have done it by now.

'Here we are.' Beechworth pulled a handful of cartridges from a small satchel that had been deposited by the crates. 'I've seen movement in the streets; more Lambs are coming and they're being incredibly cautious not to get in my line of sight. Prepare yourself as best you can.'

William woke Vesta and ensured she had enough ammunition; by then the doctor and Lamebrain had risen. Barber looked worried when he heard the news, but couldn't do much about it, and the hunched slave was more concerned with breakfast. Reluctantly, Vesta stayed in the chamber, on the proviso that William would fetch her the minute her brother showed up. William agreed, but he didn't think the zealot would show his red face unless forced to.

'What's the plan?' William found Beechworth in the tower stairway; he had taken position at the top and was ready with his rifle.

'Shower them with lead.' The lord scratched his nose with the back of his hand, marking his cheek with gun oil. 'They'll have to set up a ladder to surmount the bottom staircase. Their numbers are great, but if we can kill them faster than they advance, we won't even work up a sweat.'

'What about powder-bombs? You said you have more.' William looked at the mess of dead bodies and smashed carpentry in the square courtyard below, blackened by the explosion.

'It was a bluff. I wanted time to get you on side; but not this much time.' Beechworth clicked the loading mechanism on his rifle and eyed the backs of three copper coloured cartridges, ensuring the thing was loaded. 'They've given us the whole night; I fear they've planned something bigger than a simple assault.'

Beechworth's worry spread to William. He wanted to add something to the plan or reassure the old assassin, but the man was a damned prize winner. If he was unsure of their success, what could William do?

There was a boom outside, somewhere between a gunshot and cannon fire. The pair tensed, ready for the foundation of the tower to shake. It didn't. Instead, they heard a clanking of metal overhead, somewhere up on the clock tower balcony.

'What the devil was that?' Beechworth balked.

William knew exactly what it was. He recognised the empty clang of wrought iron; the way it chimed when a curved prong struck stone. The things were never as quiet as one hoped, always a last resort when it came to infiltration, and this one had been fired all the way up to the clock tower by some siege device or pipe launcher.

'It's a grappling hook,' William confirmed as he heard the scrape of a metal thorn. 'They'll be coming from both sides.'

William headed back through the door into the chamber. There was another boom, and a second hook clanged onto the balcony.

'Wait,' Beechworth snapped, 'they seek to divide our efforts. We can't let them play us.'

'And I can't just let them come up behind. I'll cut the ropes; they can only have so many.' William steeled his resolve and slipped from view. 'Just hold them off until I can get back to you!'

'Damn.' Beechworth started shooting. It was plain that this attack was more coordinated than the last, and the Lambs were pressing in as William retreated.

'Knife!' William insisted at Vesta; she understood quickly and pulled the small blade from beneath her skirts, handing it to him hilt-first. He took it and raced ahead.

'Can I-' Vesta stood.

'No, stay there,' he called back. 'Guard Barber and the old woman.'

He located the narrow steps up to the mechanism walkways quickly and hoped the task would keep her from doing anything foolish. She was going to get herself killed if she wasn't more careful, and her obsession with her brother wouldn't be doing her chances any favours.

Surmounting the steps, he thumped across the walkways, which were little more than long planks laid between the steelwork of the clock-parts. Every board shifted and sprained under his weight. He used the flex of one to spring him onto a sideways cog and scrambled over, cutting out a significant detour. If he got to the balcony before any Lambs it would make his job a lot easier.

Lamebrain groaned in the dark below. It was impossible to tell if it was fear or excitement, but the sound of another hook slamming into the stonework just overhead drowned it out.

A rickety set of steps led up to a door and burst out onto the balcony. Though the sky was overcast and the day was only just beginning, it was almost blinding compared to the gloom of inside. He shielded his eyes and moved to the closest hook, setting about the rope with the blade.

Each hook had thumped into the clock; two had cracked the expensive marble face and another had bent the vast minute-hand. The lines were tangled around iron spikes – whose job it had been to prevent any maintenance men falling, and also discourage any climbers. William reckoned there might have been some irony in there somewhere, but was too busy frantically sawing with the knife to focus on much else.

Beechworth's gun made a rhythm in the background. Bang, bang, bang, pause. Bang, bang, bang, pause. If he was hitting a different man every time he was surely piling up a ridiculous quantity of dead. William couldn't be sure, the entrance was on the far side, and he could only see the group dedicated to climbing. About ten of them were still on the ground and the three ropes held five each.

He made eye contact with an ascending Lamb. She had climber's tools in each hand that did the majority of the work for her. She slid one hand up after the other, and they gripped hard into the rope, making her progress far quicker than William could have expected.

The Lambs were as fanatic about seeing Vesta dead as she was about them and their leader, and William had gotten himself square in the middle of it all.

There was an explosion from inside the tower and Beechworth's gun stopped firing. William cursed, realising his mistake. In his hurry to take part in the lord's fine food and drink he had failed to plan sufficiently. He hadn't even told the old assassin about the spark-powder grenades the Lambs used.

'Fuck!' He bellowed in frustration, thrusting the knife, and severing the last threads in one cut. The rope flicked at him as the load was released and five Lambs fell to their deaths. Only three reached the floor. One was impaled on the spikes set into the wall, and the other was merely raked and left hanging to bleed out. William looked away, but found a Lamb was already clambering over the fence at the next rope.

He lunged, and before the Lamb had chance to hop over the fence, sank the little blade into her throat. Fingers grasped for William's shirt, hoping to bring him over the balcony but he shoved her away. The knife was lost, falling in the woman's neck to the muddy streets far below.

'Shit!' William screamed, feeling the pressure mounting.

He whipped his pistol from his belt and fired at the rope. It snapped in an instant, sending four more cultists to their end. It was so infuriatingly easy, and he kicked himself for not thinking of it sooner. He reloaded and shot through the final rope before the next climber got anywhere near. At that, the Lambs in the street seemed to consider their climb a fool's errand, and rounded the building to assist the front door bombardment. Once William saw them abandon their grapple launcher, he left the balcony.

When he returned to the clock-chamber, Beechworth was knelt massaging his eyes; the lingering effect of the flash was harder to shake for the shaded confines. When he realised someone was still shooting in the stairway, and cast about for his sponsor.

'Where's Vesta?'

'Keeping the Lambs at bay,' Beechworth grunted and pinched his closed eyes with his finger and thumb.

'We're supposed to be protecting our sponsors...' William abandoned his anger at the lord and dashed for the door to the stairs. He worried that Vesta's naivety had given the Lambs exactly what they wanted.

He barrelled through the door and found her quickly; she was leaning over the wooden railing, shooting down at the advancing Lambs. They had managed to make it onto the stairs and their boots were thundering up. A shot from below smashed part of the railing as Vesta retreated to reload; the bullet barely missed her.

'Get back to Doctor Barber, you're going to get yourself killed.' William lurched forwards, sent a shot down the spiralling stairs for an approaching Lamb, and grabbed Vesta by the rucks of her dress.

As he looked down, he saw just how bad it was. Tens of robed men scrambled over the bodies of their fallen brothers, each filled to the brim with righteous fervour. It was as if Vesta's brother had made *her* a test of their faith. Each fanatic amongst them was eager to prove himself to the gang-come-cult and whatever damned god gave them purpose.

William dragged Vesta away from the railing, and though she screamed like a petulant child for vengeance and let off a stray shot for the ceiling, he thrust her through the doorway. She tripped and fell onto her back, then pushed herself even further away, digging into the boards with her heels. She shouted at him and spat venom, but the detail of it was lost in the building chant of the cult. William spared one more glance for the Lambs and slipped back into the darkened room, closing the door behind him.

'We'll never keep them back; there's too many.' He swallowed a lump and dashed away from the door to find himself even the slightest cover. He could see Vesta taking position behind a pillar and readying her pistol. There was no point arguing with her now; they were all going to die anyway.

'I'll hold them; I have the best rate of fire.' Beechworth looked to have recovered. He stood, though his eyes still streamed, and started to quickly reload his rifle. 'But I'll need ammunition; would you get me some? With the clock spares.'

William hesitated a moment, unsure of whether to go, or stay and shoot.

'Go!' Beechworth shouted. 'I'm the first Man-Butcher - the best assassin there is!'

'Just keep them back,' William replied. He didn't know why he was still bothering, it all seemed so futile now. He might even be better fleeing to the clock balcony and throwing himself off, at least then he would be the master of his own fate.

He knelt at the stack of crates and quickly pulled the top off one. The lid had been nailed down, but had recently been levered open and placed back on top. Inside were the lord's medical supplies for his sponsor: little brown bottles, branded elixirs, unknown tinctures, a large flask of ether, and sterile cloths.

'What's all that commotion?' Beechworth's sponsor spluttered out the words in a fit of choking. 'Where's Claude?'

'We're being attacked. He's keeping us safe.' Barber tried to reassure the old woman, but it seemed she needed no reassuring.

She tried to stand and collapsed back to the floor with a grunt.

'We can't let him die,' she whimpered, 'he's too young.'

William thought it was rich that she was so worried about her grandson's untimely death, given that he had as many years as William and Vesta put together, but he didn't say anything and moved to the next crate.

The Lambs were funnelled through the door, falling in groups as Beechworth and Vesta fired into the melee. Every time they reloaded the Lambs crept closer, their wounded tumbling into a heap, only to be climbed by yet more cultists.

Standing, William peeled the lid off another box. Rusty nails squealed, his fingers whitened at the knuckles, but then the thing came off in a great wrench and he flung it involuntarily across the room. Inside was the most ridiculous quantity of bullets he had ever seen. Pack after pack of red and black card containers were stacked inside. Only two had been opened, one was empty and the other spilled shimmering copper bullets. William couldn't help but wonder exactly how much wealth lay before him in the crate; more money than had ever passed through his hands before most likely.

'Get off,' the old woman barked.

She and Barber were having a pathetic tussle over the wheelchair. Limbs slapped and pulled at each other, glasses and food were kicked and smashed.

'It's my send-off!' The old woman shook off the cripple with a well-placed fist, but collapsed in her attempt to get into the wheelchair. 'Unhand me! I need to protect Claude.'

'There's too many.' Barber rolled over, pulled the bottle of ether out of the low crate and poured its contents onto a sterile rag. 'I'm supposed to be keeping you well, if you have a death wish, I'll have to put you under with this.'

William recoiled as Barber flailed for the old woman with the ether soaked rag, coming ever so close to igniting the volatile fluid on a candle. For a second William thought he would die; a single flare of ether would set the bullets off in a storm that would tear him to shreds.

Across the room, Beechworth shrieked as Lamebrain leapt upon him from the darkness. The half-headed slave pummelled him with fists and elbows, sank teeth into his neck. The old assassin dropped his rifle and tumbled to the ground, punching and kicking at the surprise assailant. The pair rolled across the floor screaming, grunting, and growling.

Vesta's shots were far slower than Beechworth's and the Lambs out-paced her quickly. In no time, a group had amassed in the doorway and started to spread out in the gloom.

'Vesta; Beechworth! Get down!' William screamed and thrust forward.

The old woman glided out of the darkness on her chair, doused in ether, clutching the crate of ammunition tight to her withered body. She spat out a burning candle and shrieked with all the air in her weakened lungs, 'die, you bastards!'

Flames caught across her, and like kernels of corn popping in a pan, the bullets began to fire. William ducked behind the crates with Barber, covered his ears against the torrent of sound that followed. Bullets ripped Lambs limb from limb, shattered wood, pocked holes in masonry. The old woman became a rolling bomb, spreading fire in all directions, spitting balls of lead from copper casings. She rolled through the door raining death all around her, then tipped over the edge and fell down the centre of the spiralling stairs.

Tens of Lambs fulfilled their destiny and became sacrifices to their profane god, but were also denied their goal. Not one of them would kill Vesta that day, but William wasn't entirely sure that he hadn't just done their job for them.

The cacophony died down, bullets still popped, echoing from the bottom of the tower. The room fell still. Barber rolled over, looked at William and nodded. The two of them still lived.

'Vesta?' William called, pushing himself to his feet. He picked up his flintlock and shuffled out into the open, fearing what he might see.

Dust had kicked up thick in the air and made it hard to breathe. The wooden partition between the room and the stairwell had been obliterated by the shower of lead. Hazy shafts of light bled in. One Lamb staggered inside, somehow spared by the blaze of gunfire. William put him down without much thought. The body slumped onto a heap of its fellows.

'Vesta?' he called again, hearing a rustle of clothes from the darkness.

Beechworth's silhouette limped into the light at the far end of the room. He had his rifle aimed at William.

'You killed my grandmother,' the older assassin sounded aghast, like he couldn't even believe it was true.

'She was going to die anyway.' William sneered at the gun toting legend, expecting him to come to his senses any time. 'It was what she wanted.'

'That's not your place to say.' Beechworth jutted his jaw and sniffed the air; listened for any movement in the shaded corners of the room. 'But, as it seems you sponsor is dead, it doesn't really matter what your say is.'

William fiddled with his gun, feeling it light in his grip. He had wasted the bullet so carelessly on a half dead Lamb.

'Goodbye William.' Beechworth raised his rifle to fire. 'At least you were bested by a Man-Butcher, not many can say that. You might be famous in hell.'

He chuckled at his own sour humour.

'You… no Ma-an-Butcher,' Lamebrain panted as he dragged himself out of the darkness. His half-jaw was even more crooked than usual, blood trailed from his lip, and his one eye was purpling and fat. 'Beet-worth a liar and chee-eat.'

The old assassin's rifle faltered.

'I see you now,' Beechworth's smile closed, but it remained in a smug line. He was still the only man left with a loaded weapon. 'Barber always had a penchant for bringing back Man-Butchers. I thought Karin was the first, but I'm not always right. Perhaps he'll bring me back when I'm gone, but that won't be for many a year yet.'

Beechworth shifted his rifle.

'It pains me to do this again, it really does.' He pulled the trigger and a bullet punctured the crooked slave's guts.

Instead of crumpling, Lamebrain roared from the pain and charged forwards. He was a windmill of ropey muscle and bleeding flesh. He took another bullet before he reached Beechworth, but nothing would stop him. His fists pummelled the old assassin, pushed him back, wrenched the gun from his hands and tossed it away.

'Wait-' Beechworth cried weakly but any more words were cut off by a solid fist to the side of his face. The slave wrapped his arms around him and charged, more certain of this than anything since William had known him. The pair staggered together, then with one final thrust of Lamebrain's legs, they toppled over the edge of the stairway and were gone.

After a muted thump of two bodies landing far below, the room fell to an airy silence punctuated only by the ticking of clockwork and distant gunfire.

William fell to one knee, exhausted again, and tried one last time to call for his sponsor, 'Vesta?'

'I'm here,' she replied softly, somewhere in the dark. 'A beam has me pinned, but I think I'm alright.'

'Good,' William sighed, feeling more relief than he had expected.

'I'm still alive too, just in case you were worried,' Barber added, bringing a chuckle from Vesta. A chapel bell started to chime in the distance. 'Sounds like you made it to the final twenty; give or take a few. Would you mind carrying me to the square?'

PART 4

1674

'How would you like it sent?' The teller picked up the small padded envelope and inspected the destination address through small, round-rimmed glasses.

'Courier.' William relayed Ojo's instructions precisely. 'One of the guarded transports.'

The teller cocked an eyebrow, assessing the young boy who had come alone into his office. It wasn't an unusual sight, other lads and apprentices from local businesses had come and gone all afternoon, but William was a stranger and that always meant the price was adjusted accordingly. Subtly, the postmaster fingered at the contents of the envelope: a letter in Conejan and small glass vial filled with what William assumed was blood. Ojo had tried to keep the details of his deliveries a secret, but William had spied on him while pretending to sleep.

'Something like that doesn't come cheap.' The teller was sat behind a thick sheet of glass, on a stool so high that he would have been able to look down on Ojo had he been there; to William, he was positively towering.

He gave a thin-lipped smile, used to the scrutiny of self-important postmasters. It seemed the life of an assassin was more in the correspondence than it was in the killing. If he and Ojo were outside of a city, away from a guild outpost, Ojo would send off for his contracts, post details of completed jobs, and collect payments. That wasn't even accounting for the mysterious side-line: sending away bearer bonds, collecting strange vials, and sending them on to someone Ojo called "his patron".

'Our top service comes in at…' The postmaster set the package onto a brass scale, counterbalancing it with iron blocks to assess the weight. The sour twang to his voice had dampened through his natural reverence for anybody who might be willing to pay an exorbitant amount. 'Seventeen grana.'

'That's fair.' William didn't bother to complain or barter.

He fished his hand into his pocket, retrieved a small pouch and tipped a handful of tiny silver coins into his palm. Grana, minted by The Vitulan Empire, were about the size of his smallest fingernail and worth ten times the value of the metal from which they were forged. It was an effort to make the task of transporting one's wealth all the easier for the imperial gentry; William could think of worse problems to have. He set the money on the counter.

'Thank you very much.' The postmaster gathered up the payment, his greedy green eyes lingering for a moment on the pouch that was still heavy with the little coins.

'Excuse me… sir?' William tried his best to look as innocent and simple as possible. 'My master asked me to find Samuel Morris… he had a job for him – I think.'

Usually it was a mistake to ask a man for the whereabouts of an assassination target, but the contract that Ojo had taken was for both Samuel Morris and the Postmaster Daniel Burgess. The latter had been easy enough to find; Ojo had even tailed him to his meagre accommodation the night prior. Morris had proven a little harder to locate, and Ojo was keen to leave the town as soon as possible.

A shame, William thought. Henningley was a pleasant town with old Garlish charm, of a kind that made him nostalgic for the years in Fairshore he couldn't quite recall. There was a farmers' market and cider press, neat rows of cottage traders and townhouse residences, and none of the Vitulan-inspired white block monoliths that blighted the cities. But no matter how quaint or pleasant an imperial city might appear, it would never knowingly welcome an assassin. Men hanging from gibbets in the town square were a testament to that.

'Do you know where I could find him?' William pressed.

The teller pursed his lips a moment. William watched the man's expression flicker with suspicion until it softened and took pity on the thin and grubby young boy with the large pouch of coin. As intended, the man's greed had supplanted his good sense.

'It's a postmaster's job to know how to find any man, woman or child in his district. How else would I be able to direct each and every letter to the right location?'

William thought about mentioning postal addresses, but didn't bother, instead letting the glorified cashier finish his spiel.

'Such information is both vital to my position and worth a great deal, I cannot simply give such things up for free. The gift of information is as much a service as the transportation of a package or…'

The postmaster trailed off as William poured a few more coins into his palm and handed them over. 'He lives on Hallows Place; at the end of the street, conifers, large red door, can't miss it.'

'Thank you, sir.' William beamed, pulled the laces of his coin pouch tight and thrust it into his pocket.

'Have a pleasant day.' The teller followed him to the exit, flipped a small wooden sign from open to closed, and locked the door behind William.

The last pink and orange hues were disappearing from the sky and William hurried across the road for his mentor and waiting cart. There were men out in the streets with long shafts used to light the high streetlamps. Ojo had already lit the cart lantern and was using its glow to peruse the lies of a news-sheet while he waited.

'Did you find him?' He glanced over wilting paper.

'A house at the end of Hallows Place.' William had only just hopped onto the back of the cart when Ojo urged the horse to a brisk trot. He sat down on the flatbed, amongst the supplies collected for the next few weeks.

'Good.'

Ojo was very sparing with his praise and could have a temper on him should William fail in any task he was assigned, but had looked after him well for the most part. Between jobs they would relax, camp in the wild, and hunt with Ojo's bow and arrows. The man could be kind and was a good teacher, but it seemed that he was a perfectionist when it came to his contracts and that shortened his fuse somewhat.

'I remember seeing a Hallows Street to the east.' Ojo commented. 'Hallows Place shouldn't be too far from there, we'll see if we can find it before asking anyone for directions, shall we?'

He directed the cart through the streets towards the Hallows district, an area of the town built on the old estate of a once prominent family. He had to direct the lamp to check each road sign in the fading light, so progress was slow.

As he steered around a bend, an uneven cobble jolted the cart and William's satchel tipped onto its side. A boule of stale bread rolled out and dropped to the road, the silver flintlock slid after it with a skittering quantity of emergency-only cartridges. With breathless horror, William slumped forwards and landed with both palms over the pistol and the majority of the ammunition. The loss of three or four couldn't be helped now; Ojo was driving too quickly for William to retrieve them unnoticed and asking to stop was unthinkable.

As he sat back, the pistol winked in the lantern light; he followed the etched curves on the silver barrel to the ivory handle. Beautiful; terrible. It felt right in his hands, and he thought himself much safer with it close by.

'What did I tell you?' Ojo spoke over the rumbling cartwheels.

Alarmed, William shoved the pistol back into his satchel. Ojo thought guns were not sportsman-like and deemed them far too impersonal for any assassin worth his salt. But Ojo wasn't referring to the pistol, he was pointing to a road sign illuminated with a glass lamp; Hallows Place.

'We'll pay our *friend* a visit.'

The cart turned onto the street. William kept a hand on his satchel to stop it falling over again. There would be no room for such carelessness, not if he wanted to follow in his master's footsteps and make a name for himself.

At the far end of the road was an imposing three storey residence flanked by meticulously trimmed conifers and a black wrought iron fence. It was quite distinctive, just as the teller had described. Their cart came to a halt.

Ojo alighted and tied the reins loosely around the railing. In a moment, William was by his side, satchel on his shoulder. Other than smoothing his dirty hair away from his face, and trying to dust himself down, there was little William could do to improve his appearance without soap and water. They had been on the road for a while, and because of the contract, the visit to this town was a fleeting one. They wouldn't stay in a tavern again until this job had paid.

The latch and hinges on the gate were well oiled, and it swung inwards without a creak. Their shoes tapped on the smooth stone path and up a small flight of stairs.

'Stay silent, watch and learn.' Ojo rapped the knocker on the large red door, echoing in the hallway beyond.

After a moment, the brass doorknob turned and the door opened just enough to reveal a thin sliver of the well-lit indoors. A man eyed the pair suspiciously through the gap; a small gilt chain prevented the door from being opened any further. 'Can I help you?'

'Samuel Morris, is it?' Ojo inquired placidly.

'Yes… Can I help you?' Morris eyed the strange pair that stood outside his house.

William had seen Ojo gain entry to many a house and establishment. There were plenty of ways to do it: disguise, stealth, a lock pick, and – more often than not – a well prepared story. Ojo had a gift for weaving a lie, perhaps pretending he had found William injured in the street or making up some credible alias for himself. Amongst others, he had been a guard, an investor, and an executor of a distant relative's will. There was no end to the assassin's creativity when it came to intelligent infiltration. Today however, he employed a different tactic.

Ojo thrust forwards and shunted the door with his shoulder. The small chain was no match for the force, splitting into several sprained links that scattered across the floor. The door cracked into Samuel Morris' face and sent him reeling. Ojo was less than a second behind, one hand wrapped deftly over Samuel's mouth, the other crimped onto his windpipe. The pair staggered inside, Ojo wrapped his foot behind the target's leg and they toppled to the floor.

William followed instinctively, cast a glance back to the street – nobody in sight – and shut the door behind him.

Ojo writhed with his target on the floor. His hand slipped from the neck and his arm wrapped tightly around it, not allowing a moment for a scream to escape. His other hand gripped his wrist and he pulled on his arm like a lever, bulging Samuel's eyes and forcing his mouth agape. Fingers clawed weakly but there was no fighting with Ojo's practiced technique.

Only when Samuel's bloodshot eyes rolled back into his head did Ojo relax his grip.

'Is he dead?' William asked timidly.

'Not yet.' Ojo rolled the body onto the floor and swept a hand through his hair, neatening the usual pristine coiffeur. 'He's lost consciousness, but he might wake up in a minute; the sooner you finish him off the better.'

William swallowed spittle. Though he had been with Ojo for over a year now, and seen more than his fair share of death, he hadn't actually taken a life himself since he shot the pawnbroker.

'What do you want me to do?' He swallowed.

'Kill him.' Ojo dusted himself down and peered through a doorway to a study with a warm hearth and liquor cabinet. 'Strangling's best, it's the quietest way – and the most honourable. You actually feel their soul pass from their body. If not that, you could stove his head in, but that can get messy.'

William felt panic rise in him. If he'd known earlier that Ojo had intended to pass the job over, he could have prepared.

'I'll wait in here.' Ojo stepped into the study. 'I think it's important that your first kill is alone, just shout if he starts to stir and you feel that he might overpower you.'

The assassin tossed a reassuring smile William's way, then softly closed the door.

Feeling a tremor in his hands, William wrung them tightly together. Of course, being an assassin's apprentice, he had known it would come to this eventually, but perhaps not quite so soon. Anxiously, he approached the target, far from eager for the kill.

The face looked dead; sagging flesh, open mouth and drooping tongue. The body was twisted a quarter turn from feet to head in a way that looked extremely uncomfortable. The only sign of life was the shallow rise and fall of the man's chest under his dressing gown.

William picked up a small marble figurine from a side table topped with final notices and unpaid bills. He knelt beside the man and took the statue in both hands; a naked woman, headless and armless, atop a small but hefty plinth. One of the corners would easily crack a skull. Tightening his fingers around the woman's cold stony body, he raised her high over Samuel's temple.

He wanted to smash the man's head in, make it quick, but couldn't quite muster the courage. He gritted his teeth and tried to concoct a fiction about the man; that he was bad, as bad as the pawnbroker or the man on the ship, but seeing how helpless Samuel was made him falter.

The figurine refused to come down, held still by William's reluctance. Then it slipped effortlessly to his lap, comforting against his shame. Almost overwhelmed, he fretted his bottom lip; afraid he wasn't cut out to be an assassin after all. Samuel was just unlucky enough to have made an affluent enemy; murder would be better employed against those who truly deserved it.

A floorboard creaked from inside the study. William swallowed again, but his mouth was arid. Ojo would disown him if he couldn't kill this man, and then he would fall back to his life of abuse and servitude. Granted, he was still beholden to the assassin, but at least he could hope to become as free, rich and independent as Ojo.

He set down the statue. One hand delved inside his satchel and found the smooth ivory handle of the pistol. He pulled it out and set it in his lap, the etched silver winking in the warm light, more like a work of art than a sordid instrument of death. Something about it comforted him.

A solitary cartridge was pushed into the hungry firearm.

William's instinct prickled at him, and suddenly he was staring into the eyes of the man he was tasked to kill. Samuel's breathing was audible now, rasping and laboured. He saw the gun and the boy, and seemed to recognise something was wrong when the pistol was armed and readied. Caught in a state of half consciousness, he probably thought himself dreaming, or in a nightmare.

William knew he had to kill him; he wouldn't go back to silent slavery, and though he knew shooting the man was far from Ojo's preferred method, it was still better than failing in his task. He pulled back the hammer; felt it click into position. He held the gun in two fists and wrapped both index fingers around the trigger. Screwing his eyes shut, he squeezed.

The gun clapped and he winced away. He saw only the briefest glimpse of a blood spatter, but as he closed his eyes again the image remained, seared into him. Dark red pooling across the boards, lifeless eyes unfocussed. He nearly vomited from the sudden rush of it.

Ojo burst from the study, eyes wide with panic and rage.

'*William*,' came the furious hiss. His mouth tried to wrap itself around all the condemnations he had, but as his ire built, not one coherent thought was vocalised. Abandoning his tirade, he grabbed William and heaved him through the front door.

Nearby windows were illuminated by candles and lanterns. Curtains parted and people peered into the gloom. There was no doubt that some would see the man and boy running from the house, a few might have even caught a glimpse of the shimmering pistol.

William was tossed into the back of the cart in a sprawl; Ojo sliced the reins from the gate post and slapped the horse into motion. By now, residents and manservants had come to their doors to watch. Runners were shouted from their beds to inform the town guard. There was no way to stop them all. It was too late to avoid being seen, but if they made haste it was still possible to escape.

Ojo's silence was more awful than the beatings from the broker. This life had been William's choice, a chance at a brighter future, and it sickened him to disappoint his mentor so. He watched Ojo snap the reins, pushing the horse hard, funnelling his rage into positive action. The cart rattled through the cobbled streets as fast as any messenger's stallion. With any hope, they would be long gone before the town guard caught wind of them, and maybe then he could put things right. Even as William thought they might escape, Ojo dragged on the reins and the cart rocked to a halt. The horse tossed its head and snorted in agitation.

Alarmed, William looked around, fearing a guard regiment or violent mob had cut off their path; the road was clear. A single street lamp burned at the far corner, and nearly every window on the tidy terraced street was shuttered against the night. It was quiet here, far removed from the sound of his gunshot.

'Out.' Ojo glowered.

'Why have we stopped?' William asked quietly, petrified he was being left behind. 'We need to get out of here.'

'We still have work.' Ojo was matter of fact. 'There will be no coming back here after tonight, we need to finish this now. Get out.'

Ojo approached the nearest house and thumped the door several times before William had scrambled down to the cobbles. Stilted silence followed, filled only with the muffled creaking of movement from inside. A dog barked a few houses away.

William shrivelled in the moment of silent contemplation, the vision of the man he killed coming back to him. He swallowed something acrid that tried to force up from his gut. His chest ached and he started to breathe heavily. The lock clicked loudly, startling William from his spiralling thoughts.

A sleepy-looking man peered from inside as the door opened, confused as he recognised William. He didn't have time to speak before Ojo barged the door wide open. What followed was a similar skirmish to the last, but the assassin was even more vicious, venting his rage on the target. He kicked and elbowed and might have even bitten the man in his animal fury. It was certainly a less economical take-down, but garnered the same result in the end.

'William, come here.' Ojo dragged the man to the floor, throttling him. 'Forget the door, just come here. Now.'

William scurried closer, just as the target's limbs stopped jerking. Ojo released the man and rolled him aside, limp and cumbersome as a sack of onions. The face trailed blood, a few teeth were absent in his mouth, but the postmaster was easily recognisable.

'Right, finish him.' Ojo sat on the floor, a deep frown making peaks of his brow. 'And do it properly this time.'

'How should I do it?' William swallowed; his mouth deathly dry.

'Throttle him.'

'I- I can't,' William admitted. It was too close, too real.

'Can't?' Ojo interlaced his fingers and bent them backwards producing a flurry of little clicks. He eyed William for a moment, then lunged. He wrestled him effortlessly to the cold boards, clamped a strong arm around his neck and crushed his windpipe.

William kicked out, clawed at the assassin's arm, gasped and panicked. He could feel the pressure building in his skull and behind his eyes. His mouth was biting for air that wouldn't reach his chest, and his body filled with the overwhelming sense of impending doom.

'Do you want to die, William?' Ojo whispered into his ear. 'Do you not remember what I said? Life feeds on death; it's kill or be killed.'

William's head was pushed up by the force of his mentor's arm. His eyes stared towards the open doorway. For three hellishly long seconds everything faded to grey. Then the world came rushing back with a single gasp of air. The hall swam into focus with a wave of nausea. Ojo was talking, but he couldn't make sense of the words. He tried to kick but his legs seemed a world away. Pressure was released again, allowing him a second breath.

'William? Do you want to die?' Ojo's words came through softer than before. William's head shook vigorously against the assassin's grip. 'Good. Then reach out, wrap your arms around this man's neck; take his life and save your own.'

William hadn't the capacity for reason, only the will to remain alive, and for that he would do anything. Ojo shuffled to the postmaster's side, his arm still pressuring William's neck. He spat out a command, 'kill him, William.'

As Ojo did with his victims, William looped one skinny arm under the postmaster's chin. His other hand held on to his wrist, pulling his forearm tightly across the man's warm throat. He pressed hard on the windpipe, struggling to maintain pressure after being throttled himself. He grit his teeth and snarled from the effort of it until Ojo let go, allowing him to fully refill his lungs and pull tighter on his target's throat.

As the assassin had said, William felt the postmaster's soul slip away as his body fell limp and heavy. He stayed still, breathing slowly, gorging his lungs, heart beating wildly.

'He's dead,' Ojo commented calmly.

William stood up and looked down at the postmaster. The haze had nearly passed, leaving behind only a sickness in his gut and an emptiness in his chest. He had killed another, his third in total, but it was too much to think about right then. He felt numb.

'Time to go.' Ojo pulled his clothes straight. 'The imperials will be here soon.'

William trudged for the door, but just before the threshold, Ojo set a hand on his shoulder.

'The first few are always hardest, but you get used to it.' The assassin smiled warmly.

William took another step forward, away from his master's praise, feeling like he had left a part of himself behind.

'William.'

He paused at the soft command.

'I'm proud of you.'

1682

'This is looking good.' Dr Barber slathered a purple-tinged salve over William's arm. It was abhorrently fragranced but immediately soothing; even when Dr Barber's clawed chicken-digit skirted the edge of the knife wound there was barely even a tickle. 'Vesta is a good field medic.'

'She's good at a lot of things.' William flicked a glance to his sponsor, but she was far off in a daydream, staring out into the crowd.

At a tug, William turned his attention back to the doctor's work. Barber was stitching his flesh back together; he had reopened the wound to thoroughly clean and treat it with secret elixirs. There was no pain, but the friction of the thread through his skin made him feel queasy. With a pair of scissors tailored specifically for his chicken-foot, Dr Barber snipped the trailing strand and wrapped the arm in clean bandage.

'How's that?'

William flexed his hand, he could barely even tell that he had been stabbed. The potency of the doctor's elixirs were akin to the fantasies of village shamans. He wondered if the stories Barber espoused about curing death could really be true.

'Why are you helping *her*?' William nodded to a hulking mass wrapped up in clean linens and pocked with needles.

A group of referees and Barber's underlings had been helping the remaining entrants back to the square for the last few hours and treating their wounds. Some were better than others, and a few were not far from death; Barber's men had saved them all.

'Anyone who survives until the chapel bell sounds is healed, no matter how wounded. Ottilie is no different.' Barber regarded her mountainous form. 'It appeared most of her wounds were cauterised, I imagine that's how she lasted so long. Still, most in her situation would have bled out; she's as strong as an ox that one. Despite the loss of her arm and *minor* damage to the brain, she'll live.'

Another glass of blood was hung on an iron stand and connected via a pipe and needle to the huge Scold's vein. She groaned in pain as the doctors wrenched her another few feet from death; one of Barber's workers squeezed on a pig's bladder hung on a similar stand, forcing more tonic into her body.

'What if she dies now?' William probed.

'Then she dies.' Barber shrugged.

'You wouldn't bring her back?'

'William,' the doctor chuckled, 'you are naïve.'

It was a kind of relief to hear Barber finally relent. William didn't like the doctor casting doubt upon what should be the undeniable truth of death.

'The ingredients required are far too expensive to waste on the likes of her.' Barber handed off his scissors to his new assistant, who shared an uncanny resemblance to his deceased sponsor. 'I used to have a supplier, but he disappeared. Now, the components I require are well guarded and too remote. I financed several expeditions, but they all failed.'

'So you *can* bring people back?' William pressed a hand to his forehead, wondering what to do with such information.

'No, William. You're not listening to me. It would take the wealth of a small nation. Don't get yourself killed, because there's nothing I can do for you.' The assistant took the handles of Barber's chair and angled him away. 'I have more patients to attend. Good luck, truly.'

'Right.' William nodded. 'Thank you.'

He turned to Vesta, eager to demonstrate how he could clench his fist without the slightest pain, but her attention was fixed on an entrant at the far side of the enclosure. Her brother was hunched in a chair, eyes hate-filled and trained on the pair of them. Half of his face paint had trailed to his neck in streams of sweat and one of Dr Barber's assistants was stitching closed a gaping hole where his ear had been. Despite his attempts to stay out of Harm's way, Harm had found him anyway.

A small huddle of his remaining devouts were gathered at the far side of the rope, proffering ceremonial blood vials and their own elixirs. A broad man in a grey suit was among them, and though he wore none of the cult garb, William could tell he was the superior from the way the others fawned about him. He had sparse, dark hair, a wide, pock-marked face, and the sourest expression William had ever seen. He liked to think the man's exasperation was down to the vast losses suffered by the cult, but knew that if their red-faced champion won the competition, scores more would flock to their cause – whatever that happened to be.

Vesta breathed heavily, her features stern and still; William could feel the bench they sat on shift as all her muscles tensed. One of the doctor's assistants passed between them, breaking line of sight.

'William! Vesta! See you made it through in one piece.' Goldin tramped onto the wooden platform between two referees who had parted the velvet rope for him. He dropped his little bound sponsor with a thump, collapsed onto a bench opposite, and promptly kicked his mud-caked boots off, releasing a pungent aroma. He didn't seem to mind the grimaces of his fellows, sparing no time in peeling off socks sodden with sweat.

'William.' Vesta had not offered Goldin more than a cursory glance. 'I'm going to have a quiet word with my brother; this might be the last chance before we kill him.'

'I'll come with you.' William was already halfway to his feet. It was against the rules for the Lambs to harm her before the competition resumed, but he didn't like giving them the opportunity. There was something about their doctrine that quashed their urge for self-preservation, and he could easily imagine a Lamb sacrificing himself to a guild execution just to be the one that had killed Vesta for "the Cause".

'I'll be perfectly alright,' she insisted, then stood with a wicked gleam in her eye.

Watching her stroll across the roped-off square, William felt a twist of anxiety. His palm itched for his flintlock.

'Bloody hard work, killing trained killers.' Goldin pulled one foot up over his knee and started massaging a blister on the side of his big toe. 'I'll be glad when it's all over and I'm back to knocking off rich old women for inheritances.'

William forced his gaze away from Vesta and tried to concentrate on the little man.

'It *is* good fun,' Goldin continued with a wince as he popped the cherry-swirled aspic from the blister. 'Though I do wish the excitement was as brief as it is exhausting. I'm craving a hot bath, a generously proportioned woman, and a bed so vast I could get lost in it.'

The referees welcomed another assassin. Genevieve and her son, both impeccably clean and unharmed, stepped onto the raised platform. She greeted Goldin with a distant respect as she crossed the corral, but paused when she saw William, theatrical surprise describing her amazement that he should have survived to this point. She might have said something, but Ottilie growled and snapped her teeth, aides crying out as they wrangled with the injured bomber. It seemed she hated the markswoman with a fiery passion, even after the extensive damage she had endured. William fingered his pistol and ground his teeth, united in his hatred, determined to wipe that self-satisfied smile off Genevieve's face. Fortunately, the markswoman strode to a vacant bench some distance away.

To distract himself, William counted the number of collected assassins; twenty-two in all, with sixteen sponsors amongst them. It was amazing how the referees had managed to keep tally given the vast battlefield of the town, assuming no more stragglers were still making their way for the square. He could feel victory in his grasp, whether that be the prize or simply coming close enough to earn his way back onto the whitelist. Still, to keep Vesta alive he would need to win, and that meant any contestant here would have to submit or be killed.

The two referees guarding the corral parted, permitting a final assassin. Panting from the battle and the long walk back to the square through tacky mud, was Man-Butcher Azul. William swallowed a lump. In the mania of battle he had forgotten the man had entered, but there he was, as plain as day.

'Ojo!' Goldin waved his hand, a brown stained sock trailing in his grip.

'What are you doing?' William hissed.

'He's your mentor, isn't he? Thought he'd want to sit with us.'

'Yes, he is but...' William scowled and fidgeted. 'It's a bit more complicated than that.'

Ojo strolled over. There was a look of mild confusion on his face, but there was free space on the bench and it seemed he would gladly put up with the likes of Goldin to have somewhere to rest. He nodded in greeting, throwing them a false smile, and sat down.

'Tough competition out there this year, last time I...' He made his best attempt at idle conversation, but trailed off as he came to fully appraise William. 'I... Is it? William, is that you? What are you doing here?'

The man's face contorted. To William it looked like equal parts embarrassment and shame, but he could just have been seeing what he wanted to see.

'Well, it's been a pleasure to meet a man-butcher in the flesh.' Goldin was hastily donning his socks, accurately predicting an uncomfortable conversation. 'I think one of the weaponsmith's apprentices wants to speak with me over there.'

He pulled on one boot and started hopping away as he tugged on the second, adding, 'truly, a pleasure.'

'It's me.' William tried to keep his features impassive. 'And I'm sure you know why I'm here. Our time apart hasn't been too kind. I managed a few years alright, but ran into a spot of bad luck. You seem well though... the last I heard you were dead. Feeling better?'

'Yes... I did plan to come back for you.' Ojo pursed his lips. 'It's hard to explain, so much happened. I won the prize; came into a large sum of money. It was brilliant for my patron, damn near saved him, but it wasn't enough. It's still not enough.'

'So you faked your death and abandoned me?' William glowered. 'I wasn't ready. I could have died, I nearly did a few times, and if you'd trained me properly, I might not be sat here now: blacklisted.'

'I could say I was sorry, but I don't like to lie.' Ojo sighed and shook his head. 'I did what was best for everyone.'

'I find it hard to believe. You never cared about much other than yourself.' William stood, considering the conversation done. It would have been better if his old mentor had stayed dead.

'Perhaps it's best that we leave things on this bitter note.' Ojo turned away from William to greet one of Barber's underlings. As he rolled up a sleeve to reveal a long but shallow cut, he added with some finality, 'if we both survive to meet again, odds are I'll be choking the life from you.'

William scoffed, felt his hand flex for his pistol, but stopped himself. He watched his old mentor for one last moment, seething. He wanted nothing more than to give Ojo a hard time, to make him know what suffering he had caused, but he also knew it would be wasted on the old fool.

As he watched, the student physician retrieved a handful of elixirs and a roll of bandage from a leather bag. He quickly set about cleaning and dressing the minor wound, but as he did so, he passed one of the bottles to Ojo. It was a small vial that had drawn William's attention as soon as it emerged. It looked as though it was filled with blood, but William recognised the dark syrupy tincture. As an apprentice, they had posted many such vials to Ojo's patron; a cure for a mysterious ailment. Ojo drank from it promptly, unaware that he was still observed.

William turned away and headed to where Goldin had sequestered himself. He had seen all he needed to see of his mentor, and understood more than the assassin might think. Though he still begrudged the old bastard for his callousness, he pitied him also.

The next few hours passed mercifully quickly, eating and dozing around the corral. The mayor announced the location of the finale – a small area around the Landslide and southern bridge – and an apprentice of the weaponsmith took orders from each entrant. Taking advantage of the free equipment, William had opted for a new pistol for Vesta and two dozen cartridges each. Considering how many entrants were left it was quite extravagant, but it was better to be safe. Vesta returned from taunting her brother and had suggested explosives, but William didn't like the thought of a grenade on his belt catching a bullet; he didn't want to end up like the groaning mass of anguish Ottilie had become.

Before long, the assassins began their trudge through the streets for the steaming Landslide River. Not one of them seemed particularly excited. The rest and treatment over the last day had invited lethargy and each wished that the fighting was done already.

A gloomy sky and persistent fall of ash doused the mood further, while mud-choked roads sucked at boots.

The mayor and a huddle of referees led the parade with a purposeful march. William took a position with Vesta towards the rear of the ragged column, Goldin and his bundle of a sponsor beside them. Behind, was a second and third rank of referees, and beyond that was the crowd following with an encouraging roar of approval and excitement.

The roads that bordered the Landslide had been cobbled, and though cluttered with hastily abandoned market stalls, they were free of the cloying mud that saturated the rest of the town. Already, the myriad roads that finished at the riverside were filling with spectators; it seemed their new arena was far smaller than the mayor had suggested. The competition might even be done before the hour was out – both a worry and a relief.

The roadside ended abruptly with a sheer drop to the swirling river of earth, black slurry, and spuming steam. Vast chunks of warped rock that had recently oozed from the mountain rumbled past in the torrid current. They cracked into one another and split to expose glowing magma with sulphurous belches.

The referees parted to allow the mayor to address the assassins. Unfurling an officious scroll from an embossed message tube, he began to read aloud, his voice drowning the growl of the river.

'This fight will resume in two parts. Ojo Azul, Alfred Voss, Adelia Burnham, Ottilie of Sable, Hester Turani, Nathanial Wraith, Jillian Dunn, and Violet Reeve; the fight for you and your sponsors will resume on this side of the river.' The mayor rolled up the parchment. 'Anyone else please follow the head referee to the starting point on the far bank.'

The group split in two and William followed the referee across the sturdy bridge to the far side of the river. The air was stifling, filled with a sour stench and thick with steam. Very few words were exchanged as the assassins prepared themselves to kill one another.

There were a few William didn't recognise amongst the combatants on his side of the river, but he had come across some already. He didn't much like being on the same side of the river as Goldin, he had come to think of the abrasive little man as the closest thing he'd got a friend after Vesta, and didn't want to fight him. Genevieve and Vesta's brother would be fighting on this side of the river too, and he didn't much like that either. With Genevieve odds-on to win and the cultist actively hunting them, it narrowed William and Vesta's chances significantly.

'How are you doing?' He asked Vesta, who had been almost mute since she'd returned from exchanging final words with her brother. William suspected it was her solemn way of coming to terms with her likely fate, but hoped that she remained as optimistic as he wished he could be.

'I'm fine.' She wiped sweat from her forehead with the back of her hand. 'My brother's on this side of the river with his sponsor, and this place is crawling with referees. He can't cheat us again, and we'll kill him in a fair fight, easy.'

'Just… don't get carried away.' William tried to temper her ire. 'He'll die if we win, let's not get ourselves killed sending him to hell.'

She nodded, but William got the impression that she wasn't listening.

'What did you say to him? Did you threaten him?'

'No.' She smirked. 'I reminded him of old times, before he tore our lives apart, before he gave himself up for his life as a crook and fell for his own made-up doctrine. I don't just want him to die, I want him to regret having lived so long.'

William nodded, but didn't press any further. It was plain that it wasn't possible to keep Vesta level-headed through talk, and if it was, he wasn't silver tongued enough to do it. He simply had to hope they would kill her brother quickly so she could focus on something he valued higher than she did – keeping her life.

The far side of the river was rough even by Blackbile's standards. While the town side had well-kept market stalls for cover, this side had a large gallows and stacks of tainted produce sold as fermented delicacies. A collection of hands and tongues had been nailed to a board near the gallows, and the bodies of drawn men had been left to rot. More conveniently, a selection of public toilet stalls hung out over the river so one could defecate straight into the water. William almost missed the pervading odour of sulphur present on the bridge.

There were less spectators here too, all crowded in alleyways and adjoining roads. Whereas the other side boasted erected bleachers and the awaiting winner's podium. William wondered if he and the others selected for this side were chosen specifically because they were less likely to win. Then he remembered Genevieve had been chosen to start at this side of the river, and he reconsidered. To him it seemed she had been placed here with the lesser assassins so that she might more certainly survive until the final showdown. It was a move that ensured a few bets would come good on the part of the committee and a few other higher-up assassins.

The referees started to spread everyone out, placing each assassin at twenty yard intervals along the cobbled riverbank. William and Vesta followed directions up the roadway to stop beside the gallows. Red-face passed by, taking position forty yards further down the road.

'We need to kill him,' Vesta muttered.

Genevieve sashayed into the adjacent starting position between William and Red-face, shooting a sly wink and a casual smile. William nodded a greeting back to her, swallowing his trepidation. She would not go easy on him again, and she only had done so before to avoid a barrage from the mad bomber. With Ottilie on the far side of the river, Genevieve would have no qualms in shooting both him and Vesta. The only way to fight back was to kill her sponsor. He wondered if he had what it took to kill her son; he was just a young boy.

'Five minute warning.' A referee with a small wooden wheelbarrow stopped in front of William and fished a bag from a pile of similar hessian sacks. 'This is for you.'

William took the sack as it was bundled into his hands.

'Sign here.' The referee thrust a board and parchment at him, nearly forcing the sack from his hands, then slapped a glass dip-pen on top. William scrawled his name on the dotted line and the referee was off towards Genevieve without another word.

He delved his hand into the sack, retrieving the flintlock and ammunition along with a bottle of salve and roll of bandage he hadn't actually asked for. He wondered if Barber had slipped them in personally.

'This is for you.' He passed the pistol to Vesta. 'It won't match mine, but it should do better than the one you stole off the privateer.'

'Thank you.' She smiled and fumbled open the flintlock, loading it as he charged his own. She affixed it to her belt then quickly checked the knife under the folds of her dress.

He tossed the sack into the space under the gallows and stood up straight. As he pocketed his share of ammunition a little confidence washed over him. They were well prepared and motivated. Vesta's luck and his skill just had to withstand the next few hours.

1675

Valiance, the second imperial city, had been the Garlish capital before the country had joined the empire, and it was even more sprawling than Vitale. Ruled by both a lord mayor and high cardinal, the city boasted some of the finest residences and the largest cathedral north of Baignon. The first shells of impressive warehouses, mills and factories were under construction, dwarfing their timber ancestors and promising prosperity for all.

As they had entered the city, William was awed by the vast blocks and iron sheets hauled high on ropes thicker than legs. He spotted men clambering around high beams without ropes or harnesses, like ants round twigs. Though the sight of them made his stomach flip, the workers seemed completely at ease, even resting to eat their midday tiffin at such a height.

Ojo left the industrial district behind, and took a detour through a vast estate of parks and extravagant townhouses, the cathedral dominating the skyline all the while. Though William wished they would, they never passed close by it. Instead, their horse and cart blended into a steady stream of similar delivery vehicles as they passed an impressive statue of the new gods – Luck and Fate.

In William, the thought of Valiance conjured childhood legends. The place was a vista of what a united empire could achieve; a skyline of high vaulted roofs and glinting spires of supplementary chapels in every district. Robed and sandaled monks bustled through the streets and all manner of business people darted in between. There was a promise made here, that anyone could make their fortune; shops for artists, poets, potters, and masons stood testament to the fact.

Ojo insisted the opposite, rather hampering William's wonder. According to his master, this was where the religiously brainwashed made pilgrimage, only to be trapped in sweatshops or mines to afford living in the outskirt slums. William doubted his assessment. From what he could glean, Ojo followed some old Conejan doctrine that not even the Conejans believed anymore. It was a widely accepted truth that The New Gods had killed the old, and it was pointless to believe in anything else; certainly Ojo's bitterness about this coloured his opinion of the marvellous city.

'How are you feeling?' Ojo tossed a glance at William, but couldn't deviate his attention too much from the busy thoroughfares.

William had done the lion's share of the killing over the past six months. No longer finishing half-dead targets, he had progressed to completing the job from start to finish, all under the assassin's careful supervision. He had become rather good at wrangling men to the floor and throttling the life from them. Although he stood at only three quarters the height of most, the work and time on the road had strengthened him.

'I feel well.' He nodded. 'Better.'

Ojo had been wrong in saying that killing got easier. William felt the same pang of regret each time he took a life, but he was getting better at swallowing that feeling and putting it behind him. The death and the dead no longer plagued him.

'I'm glad.' Ojo slowed the cart to a stop outside an unmarked building in a procession of uninteresting businesses and more unkempt homes. They had arrived in a poorer end of the city, though it was no worse than some of the villages they had passed through. 'We have a big week ahead of us; you especially.'

The assassin's mysterious demeanour was more worrying than it was exciting. William slid off the back of the cart, grabbing his satchel as he did so. While Ojo had confiscated his pistol after the incident in Henningley, he had managed to earn it back and had been training with it at any given opportunity. It seemed that Ojo didn't mind the added protection of the firearm now that he was on an imperial list of wanted men. It was obvious to the pair of them – no matter how much Ojo tried to convert him – that once William was ready to set out on his own he would shoot men instead of using his bare hands.

As Ojo clambered down to the street, a man strolled from a narrow passageway between two of the grey buildings. William grabbed for his pistol, paused for Ojo's instruction to shoot; he didn't want to cause another scene that saw them run out of town, not unless it was his master's decision. Yet Ojo was not surprised. The two men exchanged quiet words and the cart was passed into the newcomer's care; William secured the pistol in his satchel.

Then, rushing after his master up a short flight of steps, he quickly neatened his dirty clothes and caught up just as the front door was pulled open from inside. The assassin entered without a word.

Muted light spilled through three storeys of windows, visible only for the absence of floors. Every wall, strut and staircase had been smashed out, leaving a dusty room near thirty feet in height. In the centre, two thick beams bore the load of the roof.

'Good morning.' Ojo was almost jovial in his address.

William's attention snapped away from the rafters to three heavily armed men, and a trio of battered leather armchairs. A short way behind them was a stairwell, leading into the bowels of the building. The men nodded and murmured a similarly cordial greeting, a gesture that felt out of place from such mean-looking folk.

These people knew Ojo, and his business, and seemed as unperturbed by this knowledge as a baker might be with a flour trader. William trotted after his master, intrigued by the new aspect of the assassin's life.

The stairway was narrow and steep, and the treads were cluttered with rubble and splinters of broken wood. William braced himself against each side, drawing runnels in the damp-salted walls and determined not to stumble. Perhaps if he had not been in the shadow of his master, the way would have been easier.

Soon enough they entered a cramped room, dimly lit by a single tallow lantern set on a scuffed console table. He supposed this was meant to be welcoming, after the heavies upstairs and the treacherous route down, but the wilted pot plant beside it made the whole thing feel much more sinister. The iron-banded door opposite, however, was a fairly standard security arrangement, at least for anyone with something important to hide. Just below Ojo's eye line was a small hatch, latticed with bars. It was closed.

Impatiently, Ojo rapped his signet ring on the metal frame, two dull thumps that went unanswered. The assassin exhaled nasally.

'Ojo Azul,' he announced himself loudly, 'I'm expected.'

The little room darkened and William realised they had been followed by one of the guards from above. A hulking brute with a prominent chin and steely glint in his eye barred the way back. His meaty fist curled around an ornate club, a claw clutching a sphere of dark stone, pitted with use. There was no doubt that if their entry was denied, William's little head would be cracked wide open with it.

The hatch on the door slid open and a single cursory eye cast up and down the assassin. The face that accompanied the eye was deeply rutted with wrinkles and scars, and the sore wound where a second eye had once been was sorely lacking an eye patch. Not wishing to draw any attention, William focussed on the plant, queasy at the sight of such malady.

'Who's the boy?' the voice gurgled like a spluttering drain.

'My apprentice.' Ojo proudly shunted William to the fore. The firm grip on his shoulder gave him confidence to meet the judgemental eye peering down at him.

William fixed that eye with his best stern look, his jaw tipped upwards and his back stretched just a little straighter. Bravado was important in situations like this; he was a killer now and refused to be underestimated.

The man grumbled something unintelligible and the hatch slid shut. Bolts clattered on the other side and with the squeak of poorly oiled hinges the door swung open.

A narrow landing gave way to a spiral set of wide brick steps, well-lit and girded by a sturdy polished hand rail of dark wood. William didn't give the one-eyed man a second look as Ojo lead the way, keeping his attention on the route ahead.

At the bottom, through a set of heavy velvet curtains, the cellar opened into an extensive catacomb with vaulted red-brick ceilings and warmly glowing lanterns. Mismatched tables and chairs crowded any space that wasn't occupied by gargantuan casks. The containers of foreign liquors loomed up to the ceiling and served as dividers between ill-disposed patrons. A few men sat and drank in isolation, each glaring or grimacing at the new arrivals.

Ojo approached a highly glossed bar that seemed to have been ripped out of another tavern by the rough edges at each end and scuffs across its front. He stopped at a pair of stools opposite a barmaid. Before greeting her, he turned, slipped his hands beneath William's arms and hefted him onto one of the high barstools. William sneered at him, feeling belittled, he was a damned killer after all and Ojo should respect him as an equal.

'Good day Mr Azul,' the woman offered a brusque greeting as she procured three glasses and a pair of brown envelopes from beneath the bar.

'And you,' Ojo grunted offhandedly. He took the envelopes and opened one immediately, more interested in his correspondence than any idle talk.

Two glasses were filled with vinegary smelling liquor and one of them was slid under William's nose. He had always wanted to try an adult drink, but didn't want to risk angering his master by not asking permission first.

'Here.' Ojo tossed the letter over. 'Read that and drink up.'

William took the letter off the bar and flattened it where it had levered itself closed on well-worn folds. He started to read, realising quickly that it was the detail of a new job. One of the magnates in the city had died, and his two eldest sons had been passed over for their inheritance. An entire empire of industry, gold, and property had fallen to the third in line: their target.

'What do you think?' Ojo was reading the second of the letters, but paused to take a sip of his drink. 'It's not a job many could take, but it pays very highly. Though the target might seem young to me and many other assassins; maybe he does not to you.'

'I'm not sure.' William looked back to his own letter, noticing that the target was only one year senior to himself. The thought of killing someone so young made him feel ill, compounded with the fact the boy was completely innocent. He just had to think of a way to reject Ojo without provoking one of his tirades.

'I need to tell you something William.' Ojo set down the second letter. 'I'm sure you know by now I've been funnelling our pay into medicine, but not quite for why. My patron, he's not well. I got into this damned business to save him, but the elixir just keeps going up in price. I'd hoped you might help increase our profitability, and you have, but it's not enough.'

William pursed his lips, feeling his opportunity to reject the contract slipping away.

'I've made a deal with the supplier of my patron's elixirs. He will supply my patron with free doses until the day he dies if I pay for one expedition to the east for him. It won't be cheap and I need the money now.' Ojo drained the last of his liquor and pushed the empty glass out for the woman behind the bar to refill. 'This job will set us free from my financial obligations. We won't need to kill as much, and we can live far easier lives.'

William considered a moment. He really didn't want to do it, but in doing so he might save many more. Though he knew Ojo might simply be appealing to his distaste for death. It was too much to think about all at once, and Ojo was desperate for not only an answer, but *the right* answer.

'I'm sorry to bother you with this Mr Azul.' The barmaid returned, a square of good paper in her hand. 'A few of the guilders from Blackbile came by yesterday. They've been going to all the hideouts and spreading the word about this year's prize; I just wondered if you might be interested.'

William was impressed that she did not falter under Ojo's withering stare. Instead, she set the small painted flyer on the bar and cocked an eyebrow. 'This year the winner gets gold.'

Ojo picked up the leaflet and looked it up and down. He sneered, and much to the barmaid's distress, screwed it up and dropped it into his empty glass.

'They say it's the best thing to do if you're backed into a corner,' she tried.

'Fortunately for us, we aren't in such dire straits. Fetch a bottle of grade-four ether, then we'll settle up and be on our way. We have a job to be getting on with.'

'Certainly, Mr Azul.' The woman bobbed her head and strode to a steel door, fitted with complicated locks. Keys rattled, but the mechanisms were well oiled. Only when she had slipped through into the store room and locked herself in did Ojo continue.

'You'll do it then?'

It was as much a command as a question, and William felt he had no other option than to say, 'yes.'

The woman returned from the back room and set a small glass bottle on the table. The clear liquid glugged sluggishly from side to side. It was slower than water, more like thin syrup that left an oily sheen on the glass. Ojo tipped a fist of imperial grana from a pouch and passed them to her with a quiet thank you.

'This is ether.' Ojo slid the bottle over to William.

'What's it for?' He tilted the swaying contents to better examine it.

'The barber surgeons use a similar variant as an anaesthetic. *This* version is far more volatile, concocted by one of the guild's doctors. It puts a person to sleep very quickly, and shortly after, brings the inner workings of their body to a halt.' Ojo shunted the empty glasses aside and leant on the bar, looking at the ether with malicious glee. 'It's painless, hard to trace, and the tool you'll be using in your upcoming job.'

William pressed his thumb on the cork to ensure that the bottle was firmly sealed, then set it on the bar, too afraid to toy with it. He watched the oily liquid settle and thought about his contract. All he had to do was sneak into a boy's house and drape an ether soaked cloth over his mouth. A painless death for enough money to see him and Ojo right.

'I can do it,' he affirmed, 'I won't let you down.'

'You'll make an assassin yet.' Ojo clapped him on the shoulder. 'Let's find somewhere to sleep tonight; a hotel. I think I can stretch our money to that.'

William wanted to thank Ojo, but he wasn't sure exactly why. Maybe it was because the assassin seemed less disappointed in him, or because he was maturing into the killer he feared he might never become. He didn't voice his gratitude, but deep inside he felt as though things were starting to smooth out between them, and that was cause enough to be happy.

'Mr Azul,' the barmaid called them to a halt. She was wiping down the bar with a cloth and held their empty glasses in one hand. 'Good luck.'

1682

William looked up and down the line of his adversaries. He couldn't see much on the other side of the gallows; the supports were thick and seemed to be placed almost precisely between him and each assassin. He wished now that he had paid more attention to the remaining competitors, even basic information such as the weapons each favoured would have proven invaluable.

Taking stock of all that wasn't obscured by great steam clouds belching from the river, he noted the positions of all the entrants he could see. Each assassin had been marked with a referee, who would follow them until death or victory. It was an effort to ensure whoever ended up on the podium won without any underhanded tactics or rule breaking – a mild reassurance after the chaos so far.

William's referee introduced himself as Abelino, and had quickly reviewed a few pertinent rules, stressing on one in particular: once the bell rang there would be a minute with no combat, to allow all assassins to take up strategic positions. William had read all the rules at the competition sign up, but for Vesta's sake he was pleased to be reminded. Now she was fully aware that killing her brother before the grace period was up would result in her execution as a rule breaking sponsor.

She was becoming increasingly irascible, and though he could only imagine the stress upon her, he knew that if they could just win this damned competition, all of their problems would be washed away. Liberty was within reach; the gold afforded by winning the prize would ensure he never needed to kill again, and with Vesta free of her oppressive past she might join him in a less shadowy future. He stopped his thoughts, pushed them away; he had to stay focused on the competition or that future might never come to pass.

As the referee bid his goodbyes and took his position five paces behind, Vesta checked her pistol was loaded for the third time.

'Not long now,' she muttered.

'It can't be more than five minutes before the bell,' William added, seizing the opportunity to continue their conversation. He couldn't help but feel that things had been getting on top of them since the competition had started, and though they were supposed to be a team, they hadn't been communicating as perhaps they should have.

'No,' Vesta replied in a hushed tone, for a moment William thought she was shutting him out, but then she continued, 'Not long until this whole thing is over. Then we can put this horrible town behind us.'

William lingered on the word "we". He wondered if she had been thinking along the same lines as himself, that they might move on from this together. She could also mean that they would both move on, albeit separately. He wanted to ask, but for the moment, living with the doubt was better than being rejected entirely.

He continued his study of the battleground. To his right, Genevieve and her son stood with rod straight backs waiting for the bell. She had a standard issue pistol strapped at her hip and an unusual black iron rifle clutched in her hands. Silently, she pulled mechanical catches and slid a small cage of what William could only assume were cartridges into a slot. He squinted to try and make it out better, worried that such an unusual contraption might be even better than the marvel that had been Beechworth's rifle. He wondered if he had made a mistake in asking for only a simple flintlock when the weaponsmith's workshop had been opened to him.

The bell in the chapel on the hill rang out over the river. Its peal skewered William and set his heart aflutter. He stood there for a moment, unsure of how long it would be until the next bell, and completely uncertain of where to go. The other assassins were already on the move; Genevieve dashed by in the direction of the bridge. It seemed she intended to fight on the other side of the river, where there were bleachers of VIP spectators to impress.

'William!' Vesta shook his shoulder. 'Why are you just standing there? We need to do something. We can't just stand out in the open.'

'Yes. Yes.' He spun around slowly on the spot in his search for cover, but there wasn't much except for the gallows and they were already sheltered well enough by that. There were carts of refuse downstream near the bridge, but he didn't want to follow Genevieve too closely.

Red-face ran by, skirting the river's edge, following a similar path to Genevieve. He would want to fight by the bleachers too, to raise the profile of his cult under the watchful eye of his superiors.

'For Luck's sake!' Vesta cursed and sprinted ahead. By the time William realised, she was yards away, tailing her brother for the bridge.

'Vesta!' William growled and set off after her, his marked referee following in his wake.

She didn't listen to him, doubling her efforts to catch her brother. He couldn't keep up.

'Vesta, stop!' he shouted again, but all it served to do was rob air from his lungs and make the chase all the harder.

As his path curved to the edge of the riverside and he dashed along it, he could see down into the churning waters some ten feet below. The river ran in a walled channel through this section of the town and looked to be certain death should anybody slip into the waters.

Red-face rounded onto the stone bridge. If Vesta followed, she would be trapped with the cultist. William called her back, but a blur in the corner of his eye and a thump to his chest stopped him.

He staggered, winded. One foot tangled behind the other and he slipped over the edge of the channel. He clawed out, narrowly missing a grip of somebody's shirt that might have prevented his fall. His fist struck the stone bricks, scratching knuckles and beading blood. The heat and humidity from the river covered him like a blanket as he passed over the lip of the road, certain he would be washed in the searing tumult.

He slapped to the ground, enveloped in warm silty earth. His body throbbed with the force of the landing and he rolled onto his back. A gout of steam erupted nearby and he breathed in sharply as he was splashed with scalding water. He sat up and recoiled from the edge, quickly taking stock of his surroundings. He had landed on a little island of muck that fringed one of the stone pilings of the bridge, the construct itself reaching ten or so feet above in a series of arches to the other bank.

Echoing through the murk, the second bell sounded. William's stomach knotted and before the chime finished it was drowned out by the sound of gunfire.

'Shit,' he hissed, scrabbling to his feet. The wall stretched above him, barely a hand hold in sight on the smooth, cut stone. He had no idea how he would get back to Vesta. At the top, his referee was peering down at him. 'Abelino, help me up. Get a rope or something.'

'You're not dead then?' The referee wiped his nose with the back of his hand and reached for something tucked into his belt. 'Shame.'

A pistol glinted over the bridge, snatched up in the referee's hands, an ugly grin splitting his features. 'You will not hamper the Cause any-'

William shot Abelino in the gut. The damned referee had tried to knock him in the river. He stepped aside as the man crumpled off the wall and landed beside him. A kinked neck cut off any cry of pain or further cult patter. With a well placed boot he rolled the body into the water, not wanting to be caught murdering a referee, even if that referee had been placed illicitly by the Lambs.

Mercifully, it seemed he was hidden from all spectators and invigilators in his current position. Whatever stewed in the volcano, thrusting ash into the air and turning the river to a black slurry, had angered over the past ten minutes. The waters bubbled with an intense heat, shot out great gouts of sulphurous steam that hung in the air like a thick fog. Even now, tendrils of the fetid smog were curling up over the bridge and spilling over the riverside walls. He pulled his shirt up over his mouth and nose to breathe easier and reloaded, feeling the pressure of Vesta left unguarded, and set about finding a way back to street level.

Though the small island petered away as it weaved around the bridge pilings, it was still wide enough for him to skirt around. Scalding spray flecked his boots in black and brown. The river roared like a beast, echoing under the stone bridge, the wind howled by. His feet slipped on the soft silt a few times, and one boot dipped into the steaming water. A rugged lump of volcanic rock that rumbled along in the current clipped his foot and nearly dragged him in, but he spun around and dug his nails into a groove in the mortar.

He sidled around the remainder of the bridge support to another small deposit of dirt and waste, scattered with little cages from some ill-advised fishing attempt. There was a steep muddy path that he could clamber up to the paved riverside. He could make it back to Vesta, and if he could do so quickly, there was still a hope that she lived.

Mud clumped under his smooth leather soles and his hands gripped ineffectual fists in the muck. He slid back down three times over before backing away and taking the slope as fast as he could. His feet pounded into the slippery mulch, but his momentum carried him far enough to get a hand hold on the edge of the stonework.

He hefted himself up the ledge, his feet running in frictionless channels. With a stunted leap, he got both arms over the lip of the road, squirming until he could heave one leg onto the edge. Huffing and snorting through ground teeth, he gripped with his hands, toes, elbows and chin to roll his whole body over the side. He greeted the road with the flat of his back, breathing hard.

'Wha-?' came the startled yelp, and the distinct sound of a person priming a gun to fire. William pulled his pistol from his waistband and rolled onto his side. The mouth of his flintlock found the open maw of a blunderbuss.

'William?' Goldin squinted to recognise him through his fresh coating of filth.

'Goldin.' William took a breath as a chill washed over him; now that the competition was underway, he realised the little man might actually shoot him. It seemed his friend had reached the same conclusion. So the pair remained with their guns towards each other, neither daring to move an inch.

'What are you doing, sneaking up behind me like that?'

'I didn't realise I was sneaking up on anyone,' William wheezed, but kept his aim true. 'You're not going to shoot me, are you?'

'Depends.' Goldin flicked his tongue to the corner of his mouth, somewhat reluctant in his manner. 'Are you going to shoot me?'

'I'd rather not.' William let out a sharp gust of breath through clenched teeth that might have been a chuckle had he not been staring down the barrel of a blunderbuss. Slowly, he lowered his pistol, but kept his finger on the trigger for what good it would do him.

'Likewise.' Goldin sighed and lowered the muzzle. 'How did you get from down there anyway? You're not even wet; filthy, but not wet.'

'I fell, but landed on a– I don't know.' William thought of the toilets suspended over the river some way up and wondered whether a vast accumulation of human waste could form an island like that. 'Mud, I guess.'

'You're lucky,' Goldin commented. 'My referee fell in the water and he didn't seem to enjoy it that much.'

'So did mine.' William wondered whether the fate of Goldin's referee had been more similar to his own than either of them would admit.

'Awfully clumsy these referees.' Goldin had a wry smile that all but confirmed William's suspicions.

With a dismissive snort, he leant his blunderbuss beside a rifle in the crux of the bridge siding and an upturned handcart he had been using for cover. He rolled his shoulders, shaking his bound sponsor off and dropped him to the floor. There were other things more important than the misadventures of the referees. 'Where's Vesta? Is she…'

'Dead? I don't know.' William toyed with his pistol. 'We got separated.'

'I'm glad, I thought she'd died and you'd chosen to keep fighting.' Goldin took a tin out from his pocket and opened it. 'You're no fool though, are you?'

'What do you mean?' William watched as Goldin's sponsor wriggled onto his side and tried to shuffle away.

'No prize is worth staking your life on.' He gathered a pinch of dried root from the tin and pushed it into the side of his cheek. There was a polite inclination that William could help himself, but it was declined with a wave of his hand. 'When my sponsor dies, I'm done.

I'll try again next time. No point getting myself killed over a pipe-dream.'

'I suppose you're right.' William crawled to the upturned cart and peered through a crack. An assassin was knelt maybe forty feet away beside a sugared fennel stand, hidden from another assassin, but perfectly in view from Goldin's vantage. 'I'd better be getting back to Vesta, if she's still alive. Keep myself in the running. Would you kill that assassin? He's too far for a pistol.'

'I don't see why not.' Goldin stashed his tin back in his pocket and picked up his rifle. Standing on his tip toes he rested it on the edge of the handcart and took his aim. A shot echoed over the roadway and the assassin collapsed. Moments later a hole was punched in Goldin's cover, showering him with splinters and making him fall onto his arse.

'Damn that bloody woman!' Goldin growled, tossing the rifle down in frustration. 'She knows my sponsor's not dead. It's like she's toying with me, I can't even see where she's shooting from. Think she's trying to keep me pinned down.'

'I need to get to Vesta.' William tried to stand, but was forced down by one of Goldin's strong hands.

'No.' He was stern. 'You don't know if Vesta's still alive, but Genevieve probably does from her vantage. If you stand up now, with her eyes on us, and your sponsor happens to be dead already, you won't be far behind.'

'If I don't go now she will be dead.' William tried again, but Goldin gripped his shoulder tightly. 'What are you doing? Let me go.'

Goldin's sponsor scrunched up like a worm and thrust forwards, edging ever-so-slightly further away from his captor. No sooner than his head left cover, it was blown from his shoulders. Blood fanned out across the stone slabs and his body fell limp and lifeless.

'For Pity's sake,' Goldin harrumphed, galled at the inconvenience of his sponsors' death. 'I'm out. I'll put up my hands and retire to the crowd. With any luck, that Genevieve'll watch me go and you can slip out. Go save Vesta.'

The little assassin jumped to his feet, his arms held high in the air.

'My sponsor is dead!' he bellowed, 'I'm stepping out of the competition.'

There were no shots and he didn't immediately lose his head. Goldin breathed a sigh of relief and turned to go, offering William a final goodbye, 'good luck, Will.'

He set off walking then stopped, adding, 'oh, and if Vesta is, you know, gone... just bow out. The gamble's not worth it. We'll have a drink when this is all done.'

'I'd like that.' William smiled, but as Goldin tramped away and became obscured by the swirling fog, so too did his smile fade.

1675

The young target's townhouse was located with instructions written in the letter of engagement. The building was as white as most others, but as it was situated in one of the more affluent areas of the city, it bore a few distinguishing features. The windows were larger than the majority of the neighbours, crisscrossed with lead, and each of the upper panes bore a stained glass depiction of industry. A brilliant red front door boasted a polished brass knocker and handle, and beside, a black and gold plaque still bore the name and business accolades of the target's deceased father.

'I'll go through the cellar window-' William was dragged to a halt, his shirt caught in Ojo's iron grip.

'You can't just walk in there,' Ojo chided him with rare levity. He shook his head. 'We wait. We observe.'

William raised his eyes to the house and the distant shadows of servants moving inside. He supposed the middle of the day was not the best time to commit murder; Ojo was right about that.

Anxious knots turned his gut; he had wanted to get the wretched task done with as quickly as possible, so that he and Ojo might move on. A delay meant more time to think on the task ahead; he had lost enough sleep already, and knew it wasn't the result of the cold or lack of a bed.

They had slept in a hotel on the first night, but Ojo had quickly returned to his miserly ways and the following two were spent rough. It was all in aid of the task at hand, even if Ojo had saved extra funds to spend on his patron's medicine. They had taken it in turns to rest, sleeping like vagrants in a small park near the target's house, and observing the servant's schedules.

The closer William came to assassinating the young boy in the house, the more certain Ojo became that things would go wrong. He seemed to regret spending so much money on the night in the hotel and tried to recoup funds wherever he could. One evening they had scavenged scraps of stale bread and pastry from a nearby kitchen waste, the second they ate a rat that Ojo had caught scampering from a roadside drain. To reduce the chances of being seen with a small fire they waited until gone midnight to eat. The meat was soft inside and had a crunchy exterior, baked to near black to rid it of any lingering plague. William ate it for strength, but would have preferred to go without.

Despite his discomfort, he had to admit that the meticulous observation was worth every moment. From only three days and two nights they had managed to piece together a regular routine in the building. Most of the servants would leave for home after dusk, leaving a skeleton staff to bank fires and lock doors. Around three hours later the lanterns on the top floor would be extinguished. Ojo surmised that this was the young master being put to bed by a minder or relative. Then, just before midnight, the front lanterns would be snuffed, and house cast in darkness.

On the third evening Ojo disappeared leaving no other instruction than to wait. William wasn't frightened that someone might see him alone on the bench, he could handle himself, and he had his pistol for emergencies; but he did fear that the assassin might never return.

After almost an hour he saw his mentor emerge from the leafy pathway that led behind the target's house. Perhaps Ojo had gotten bored of waiting and had completed the job for him. The thought was surprisingly calming.

'I found a way in.' Ojo sat back down. 'Are you ready?'

The assassin asked casually as if he were enquiring about supper, but the words set the boy on edge. Despite three days of mental preparation, William felt as though the job had been suddenly thrust upon him.

'Be ready when the lamps go out.'

Night crept in, and before long the top floor lighting was extinguished in the target's house. Ojo pushed himself to his feet, startling William with his sudden movement. The feeling of unpreparedness swelled like a sickness in his stomach.

William took the glass bottle of potent ether safely in both hands and stood. As soon as he was on his feet, Ojo whirled around and was away, striding out of the small park and across the wide slabbed street with all the confidence of one of its affluent inhabitants. He didn't wait for William, or even pause a second, before taking the dark path through the buildings.

William followed as quickly as he dared with the volatile liquid clamped between his fingers, only catching up to his mentor in the somehow brighter moonlight that bathed the rear garden of the townhouse.

'Up there.' Ojo pointed to a trellis that spanned the side of the building. William's eyes followed the ivy and bramble that snaked up the wall until he found an open window, just in reach of the trellis for a confident climber – not something he would have ever considered himself. His fall into the ocean had dampened his enthusiasm for heights somewhat, but he couldn't afford to let Ojo down, not when the assassin had pinned both their futures on the success of this one contract. Once this was done Ojo was a free man. His patron's elixirs would be paid for, and they wouldn't be beholden to the costs or the deadlines for murder they created.

His mentor's adage had been right; this boy had to die so that they might live. Even asserting it to himself in the moment, William did not feel entirely convinced without Ojo's worldly timbre to bolster the sentiment. Without a word, he knotted the bottle neck to his belt and readied himself for the climb.

'I'll be right here,' Ojo assured quietly as he unfurled a surprisingly clean handkerchief from his jacket. 'Douse this and hold it over his mouth until the pulse stops. Shout if you need me, I'll make my way in and get you.'

The assassin didn't need to continue, William understood there could be no mistakes. If the assassin did follow through with a rescue, every person in between would have the life choked from them.

William balled the handkerchief and shoved it in his pocket, then set his hand on the trellis. His first foot left solid earth, then his second, making him feel too high, though he had not yet reached his mentor's eye level. He turned his head upwards and started to climb.

One hand after the next grasped the diagonal battens, bringing the open window closer. Terror leant him speed, and before it could set into his knees and make them tremor, he reached the sanctuary of the windowsill.

Inside was dark. It seemed that the boy's carers had retired to bed early. William was less likely to be seen, but people lying in bed awaiting sleep tended to have the sharpest hearing. He leaned across and opened the window to its fullest extent, pleased the gap between trellis and sill was closer than it had appeared from the ground. The recent oiling of the hinges was noted by their silence.

He took a leap of faith and slipped cat-like into the building. He sank to his haunches in the gloom and allowed his eyes to adjust to the grey haze of the elegant hallway. After a moment he could see the darker outlines of the many doors ahead; at least one served as a bedroom from the faint snoring from within.

Confident he had not been heard, he scuttled from under the window. At the far end of the corridor was a short landing serving two sets of stairs; one heading up, the other down. With a quick glance over the rail he could see right down to the ground floor, illuminated by a single lamp. Fearing the light was held by a night-owl butler, he pressed himself against the wall, heart thundering in his ears as he strained to listen. Thankfully, there was only the distant snore, and a gentle puff of wind through the eaves. As he peered over the rail again he saw the light had remained stationary, perhaps from a table lamp a maid had forgotten to extinguish.

William crept from the scratchy carpet runner on the landing onto the highly-sheened hardwood of the first step. He expected it to creak, but it didn't. According to Ojo's observations, the target was on the next floor up.

Every step was silent and though there were three doors that opened onto the top floor landing, the first one he chose was into the bedroom of his target. A single taper flickered on the bedside table. Wan light made him pause, blinking against the unexpected brightness; it had looked so dark from street level.

The boy was a little portly, and even in sleep his cheeks were blushing with large red blotches. His brown-haired bowl-cut was tousled from half an hour turning in bed before sleep. A slight whistle ebbed from his nose with each breath, and as much as William wouldn't have liked to have noticed, his lips bore the faintest of smiles signifying a pleasant and peaceful dream.

William's arrival had been so unexpectedly effortless. Yet now he was here, watching the steady rise and fall of the boy's chest, he found himself wishing that he was still downstairs, confronted with a late night maid or impassable stretch of creaky floorboards.

Steady fingers unfastened the ether from its ties and placed it gently on the side table. The handkerchief was unfurled from his pocket and the creases flattened; he set it beside the bottle. He just needed to get the job done.

Not knowing exactly how to go about dousing the pocket square, William uncorked the bottle and poured an oily stream of spirits onto the fabric. Excess liquid spilled down the front of the bedside table and patterned the floor. Over low breathing, the drips on the floorboards were positively deafening, but as fortunate as ever, the boy didn't wake. Everything was ready.

William didn't want to touch the cloth. He worried his lip as he looked at the boy again, willing him to wake and fight him off, and perhaps even win. Panic fluttered in his chest. In this moment he realised one painful truth; he wasn't meant to be an assassin, he wasn't meant to kill indiscriminately. He hadn't the stomach or the heart for it, but even as his mind was made up, his arm reached out and took the handkerchief.

He felt like the driver of a carriage pulled by a crazed horse, unable to stop, charging towards the inevitable. His hand lowered over the boy's mouth and nose, draping the cloth over his face, and then clamped hard.

Maybe Ojo was right and one more kill was all it would take for this kind of life to click. Maybe he would change, become better at ignoring the heartlessness of his actions.

His fingers tightened, squeezing the sour smelling solution in beads down the target's face. The boy beneath the cloth awoke with a start, disturbed from his slumber and still not feeling the effects of the serum. All William had to do was hold on tight and wait, but he couldn't. As soon as his fingers felt that visceral jerk of life, they retracted in fear and regret to his chest.

The boy screamed and reeled out of his bed, coughing and retching. He tore the cloth from his face and tossed it away with his thin summer blankets, toppling the candle and snuffing the room to darkness. His arms flailed for the intruder, but William had already backed a few paces away in stunted shock. A dull thump preceded the ether smashing on the floor, filling the room with its foul stench in an instant. William prayed that it wasn't potent enough to rend him unconscious from this distance.

People clattered from downstairs. Feet stomped along the hallway on the floor beneath them, moving from one end of the building to the other at a frightening pace. William wanted to run to Ojo and the safety he had come to feel in the assassin's presence, but couldn't face becoming such a disappointment.

The dark in the room brightened to a warm glow. The light didn't peel across the room as it would if the boy's carer had entered with a lantern, but instead welled from the top of the bedside table. A small flame built on the peak of the handkerchief where it draped over the candle and started to spread. Fire spilled across the cloth and wood like a liquid, glowing as fiercely as the gods' nectar, and fell to the already sodden floorboards in incendiary droplets.

William had only the briefest of moments to lock eyes with the boy, who in the warm light looked maybe two years his junior. His pyjamas were soaked in the flammable liquid, his pupils dilated and his face slackened as the suffocating fumes took hold. The moment the blaze began to lick around his toes, he toppled forwards with a wet slap, kicking out a fan of ever-advancing flame.

When the door opened and the first adult found the fire and unconscious boy half-consumed, they had no time nor care to confront William, who barrelled past them through the doorway and down the stairs. A second servant failed to recognise he was out of place before he was beyond reach, and left him to run in favour of fighting the fire and the hopeless task of saving his master.

The last stretch through the corridor and down the vines to the garden passed in less than a blur. When William's foot touched solid ground he expected a tirade from Ojo, but as he turned around and scoured the small moonlit courtyard, his mentor was nowhere to be seen. His heart sank into his stomach and was tied in knots as he was presented with abandonment. Perhaps this failure had been one too many and he had been left at the mercy of the guard.

William turned and ran for the side gate they had entered by, stomping along the flagstone pathway, hidden by tall foliage on one side and the shadow of the adjacent building. The pool of lamplight in the street made the shadows well darkly behind bushes, obscuring the path. His leg struck something large and he sprawled forwards, carried by his own momentum into a scuffed heap on the stones. He thrust himself up, terrified he'd found some sleeping guard dog, but faltered as the figure became clearer in the gloom.

'Ojo, are you alright?' William shook his mentor.

The assassin was collapsed against rough brickwork, his legs stretched across the pathway. He wasn't asleep or unconscious. Light glinted from open eyes, staring up to the bright moon.

'Ojo?' William shook him again, but there was no response. 'Ojo!'

He punched the assassin in the chest, fear quickly washing over him and compelling him to act. He didn't even think of the consequences should he hurt the insensitive killer.

'Ojo.' He thumped again, took the man by his dusty lapels and shook him. He might have even struck the man's head against the bricks in his worry and desperation, but the wide azure eyes shifted from the sky to William.

'I feel drowned.' Though Ojo's words were clear, they seemed to come from far away. 'What's happening William?'

'I don't know, you fell, I guess.' William pulled him up by the lapels to prop him upright again after the feeble beating. 'You don't look well, you were… gone; distant somewhere.'

Ojo came around at that, his confusion steeling to rage.

'Damn it boy, don't tell such lies.' Ojo slapped him across the face. Stinging the cold cheek and snapping his head around, a burning sensation swelled in pulled muscles. 'I can't abide liars. Have you been reading my letters?'

'No. Get off.' William struggled as the assassin attempted to grapple him, but the man's grip was practiced and strong. Just as an arm slipped around William's neck, cries from the house above seemed to startle Ojo again and his rage all but evaporated. He released William and looked about with a fresh fear.

'What happened?' He asked, his head tilted skyward, picking out the first trails of black smoke from the windows.

'Fire,' William uttered, 'the boy's dead. Two witnesses, not sure about them.'

Ojo's hands clamped tightly around William's shoulders and he flinched ready for a beating. Then the assassin pulled him into a tight embrace.

'I'm proud of you, William,' the words came out softly; kind. 'Things didn't quite go according to plan, but you got the job done and that's what matters. We'll wait in the park and if anyone comes out *I'll* despatch them. You get your rest; this was a big step for you.'

William was confused and scared, but the praise seemed genuine and it was so rare that he ever got any. He buried his face deep into the soft fabric of his mentor's jacket; the warmth and care of his guardian alleviated the sting of the night's events.

The assassin struggled to his feet, still clutching William tightly, lifting him in his arms and cradling him like a father might do a son.

'Thank you,' William whispered between sniffs and gasps. *Thank you.*

1682

William crouched in the hidden corner between the bridge and the upturned cart, wearing his misery as heavily as the sludge he was covered in. There was no feeling quite like being cold, wet, and unbearably close to the fetid stink of the Landslide swell. Of course, there was also the crippling anxiety that Vesta had already perished while he struggled out of the riverside muck.

He waited, listening and shivering, until he could no longer hear Goldin, hoping that the riflewoman's gaze had drifted from his hiding spot. He wasn't afraid, he kept telling himself he wasn't, so he couldn't have been. Several more moments passed as he sat there, biding his time for as long as he dared.

He peered over the handcart. There wasn't much to see. There were no visible entrants except for those gunned down by Genevieve. The whole place seemed desolate, too quiet, like the lull before an ambush; but William was confident there weren't any other entrants remaining. The crowds – that had huddled in alleyways to watch the fight – had used another bridge to get back to the town-side of the river to catch a glimpse of the final kill.

It was now or never.

Prompted by a distant explosion, he took up Goldin's blunderbuss, pressed the stock to his shoulder and moved out from behind the handcart. Heavy steam curled over the bridge obscuring the other side, hiding him from any entrants beyond, the riflewoman included. He dashed ahead.

His feet thumped on the stone slabs and he quickly lost his breath. Slightly too late, he realised that running wasn't the easiest of tasks in clothes weighted with soaked-in water and mud. He kept running despite his building fatigue, more willing to chafe his throat with heavy breaths than catch a stray bullet.

The smell in the fog was horrendous, sulphurous and burnt. His vision was obscured by the steam, making his eyes run; he choked down every swallow of air. Though the warm breeze at least helped to alleviate the cold from his sodden clothes.

Hearing a rifle clap some way ahead, he ducked behind a market stall and peered out. He could only have been halfway across the bridge, trapped on both sides by the scalding waters and funnelled directly towards Genevieve – somewhere unseen in a dark window.

As a thick choking cloud gusted out of the river, he dashed for the next market stall and hid. He waited a moment for the rotten fog to clear, breathing through his shirt, then peered out again. The buildings at the far edge of the riverside road were beginning to pick themselves out faintly, and closer, he could see Red-face crouched similarly behind another stall. The man was injured, blood slick down one arm, coating it almost entirely, save for the streaks cleared by a generous splash of some elixir. He was almost finished bandaging the wound, and appeared to have not heard William's spluttering approach over the torrent of the river.

A lance of fear pierced William as he realised that Red-face had preceded Vesta. Barely drawing breath, he looked more closely at the scattered corpses on the bridge, and only exhaled when he saw she was not amongst them. A relief, but it didn't make him any less nervous; his target, albeit injured, was so very close.

Quietly, he set down the blunderbuss; it would be no use over the range between him and the cultist, and he didn't much feel like running over there. The man had been shot, perhaps by Vesta, but more likely by Genevieve. It wasn't worth getting a quick shot off if it meant he would be picked off at a distance by another.

He pulled his pistol from under his belt. With a well-placed shot, he could complete his contract without any risk to himself. He sighted the cultist through a crack between two boards and measured the distance. Taking a breath he thrust himself up, both hands on the pistol to steady his aim.

In that moment, the cloud that had emanated from the river dissipated, allowing a better view of the bridge and road ahead. Vesta was hunkered down behind a stone bollard at the very end, hiding – as Red-face was – from the overlooking riflewoman. She had a pistol ready and pointed towards where her brother had hidden himself to administer aid, but couldn't get to him to finish the job. William wondered exactly how long they had been stuck in this stalemate, but was glad that he could put an end to it all.

A flare of white light scorched through the sky. It was too bright against the fog hanging overhead. Buildings at the far end of the bridge burst in a torrent of fire and scattering bricks. William's finger jerked against his trigger, wasting a bullet inches from the cultist's head.

'Vesta!' William bawled her name at the top of his lungs. He prayed she would hear him despite her proximity to the deafening blast. 'Vesta, run!'

One of the buildings had been levelled, perhaps killing Genevieve. The oppressive force of a watching markswoman was immediately alleviated, and like greyhounds out of traps, everyone on the bridge began to move. William hurtled for Red-face, praying he could reach him before he took his aim at Vesta.

Red-face had gained his feet, rounded on William and was ready to fight. The pair collided in a flurry of fists. William struck the cultist's wounded arm prompting a scream, and tackled him to the floor. They skidded across the flagstones, Red-face wailing as his ruined arm was mangled further. It seemed Barber only spared his best numbing agents for those that he favoured.

'Vesta!' William cried, searching for her in the tussle. 'Vesta, you need to hide!'

Red face took the opportunity to tip the scales; he thumped William in the eye and again in the stomach as he reeled.

'Vest-uh!' William struggled out as the cultist grabbed his open jaw and wrenched him to the ground. Stabbing nails drew blood under the crook of his tongue, needling pain that saw his advantage quickly reversed as Red-face pressed his bulkier body on top of him.

An elbow crushed William's throat. The pressure slowly crimped his windpipe closed. Mortal terror filled him and he lashed out with both fists. A few good hits slammed into unprotected ribs, but the mad cultist could not be unseated. Red-face's knees cinched tight around William's waist, even as he bucked and scratched and slapped at his attacker.

A hissing ball with white fiery tails flew directly over Red-face's head. Instinct pressed William's open palms to his ears and screwed his eyes tight. He wouldn't fall victim to another debilitating blast. A market stall eight yards back on the bridge exploded in a plume of purple smoke and green fire. The force threw them across the flagstones like toppled skittles.

The hard stone side of the bridge slapped William, knocking the air from his chest and a tooth from his mouth. Ears ringing, dazed; noise filtered through the high-whine in his head and he spat out his tooth in a fan of blood. A laboured breath whooped in, then still dizzy, he pushed up with his hands, but couldn't gain his footing.

'Vezda!' he wheezed ineffectually and rolled himself over.

Red-face had nearly been blown clean off the bridge; he was sprawled across the low wall at its edge, his head and one arm dangling into the mist. He scrambled for purchase, afraid as he realised how close he was to falling into the scalding waters. When he saw Vesta had her pistol trained on him, he steeled himself, his hatred washing away any trace of fear.

Vesta uncurled from her hiding spot, her aim never wavering as a slow and feral smile lit her face. Behind her, hobbling through the smoke, was another entrant of unmistakeable proportions. William tried to shout for Vesta's attention, but his voice was still too weak.

'Vest- Vesta…'

Ottilie loomed out of the sulphurous murk, burned and scarred but all the more petrifying for it. She had a glass jar strapped across her back, filled with oily liquid, and connected to her veins with gut-pipes and strapped down needles. Attached to her blackened stump – that looked more like the end of a discarded root-cigar than any living appendage – was a custom-built bomb launcher. It was another wonder of the weaponsmith's armoury William had denied himself through a lack of imagination. Iron rods, bolts, and belts held it in place, and she supported it with her good hand.

The foul device was levelled at Vesta and Red-face. She leered as the mechanism huffed steam; a pipe shaped bomb slithered into the barrel.

'Vesta!' roared William, 'behind you!'

Those few awful moments slowed around them, thoughts moving like treacle, instincts bubbling to the surface. As a wisp of river steam curled aside, something caught Red-face's eye over the side of the bridge – the sludgy island surrounding the pillars, William knew. The cultist slipped over the edge. Vesta didn't see, she was staring doom in its trollish face, pistol limp at her side.

Ottilie cackled as she pulled the trigger on her launcher. The mechanism clicked, a shower of sparks burst out.

William sprinted towards Vesta, the pains in his body temporarily numbed by the thrill of near-death. His body moved of its own accord, his mind completely departed from the idiocy of his actions; they would both be blasted to naught but sinew and slurry in the same moment. There would be no miraculous cures or mechanical limbs at such close proximity to those rockets. Somewhere in the back of his mind he knew this, but still he ran faster.

As William enveloped Vesta in the protective shield of his arms, pressing her tightly to him and setting her head to his shoulder, the bomb launcher exploded.

The blast hit his back as a hot wind. Blood, metal and flesh plopped and clinked in a gory fan around them, drenching William. An animal howled in agony, worse than a bear in a dog-pit. Guttural, blood curdling; the sort of sound that would haunt a man for the rest of his days. It was only then that William realised both he and Vesta were still alive, and for the most part, unharmed.

Ottilie was on her back, her new limb jagged and broken and her once good arm pulped out of recognition. Somehow she lived, keening with her rage and pain to the ash-filled sky above. Her suffering perhaps protracted by a foul cocktail of medicines denying her the release of death.

William's thoughts caught up with time, though his arms would not let go of Vesta, paralysed with shock. He scoured the terrain and buildings around them. Had he imagined the wink of a scope, or the memory of a rifle clap?

'What happened?' Vesta shivered. 'And where's my brother?'

'I think someone… saved us?' He couldn't contemplate why or who, but had far more immediate worries, like re-arming himself and being stranded in such an open space. He dragged Vesta to an abandoned fruit stand and they huddled behind it, taking the moment to quickly reload. 'And your brother, he went over the edge.'

'He's dead?' Her face lit up, mouth twitching with shock and giddy excitement. William had expected that when the time came and her brother had been killed, that she might have instantly started to regret her decision to contract his death; it appeared that wasn't the case.

'Oh William!' She clutched her pistol to her chest like any high society girl might grip a bouquet of flowers. She was overwhelmed with emotion, tears pricked at the corners of her eyes, happy and satisfied. 'We did it. That whole sordid chapter is done. I'm done.'

For a moment William thought she might just get up and leave. She thought her brother was dead and her task was complete, and would have little reason to stay other than the threat of execution for desertion. He didn't imagine she would fear that threat too much; she had entered the competition readily enough.

'Now we just need to win this thing and we'll both be free.' She nodded, resolute. It was the only true way out of the competition alive and it was a relief that she understood that.

'There are…' William stopped himself. While his initial instinct had been to tell her about the islands in the river, and her brother's sudden readiness to throw himself down, he reconsidered. Vesta had become increasingly reckless, desperate to kill her brother, and if she believed he was dead then maybe she might be easier to control; easier to keep safe.

'Are you still alive, William?' Genevieve's distant shout could be heard faintly over the roaring current. 'Just step out, my son could use the target practice!'

'Damn.' William peered out of cover. The smoke from Ottilie's crater was enough to obscure his view and he couldn't make out anything beyond. 'We need to get out of here.'

'What if she's the one that saved us?' Vesta's nerve appeared to be steadying.

'I'm sure it was entirely by accident.' William looked around for a way to get off the bridge that didn't involve walking directly towards Genevieve. Fire crackled at their backs, still burning from

Ottilie's rocket; on either side was the torrential river. 'Stay here and hide, I'll go out, tell her you're dead and that I've backed out of the competition.'

'You can't.' Vesta shook her head. 'It's against the rules. There are referees all over the place, all it would take was for one to hear you; you'd get disqualified.'

'Right.' William thought about exactly what would happen to Vesta should he be disqualified. Death by execution was something very few ever deserved. 'I'll go out there, tell her you're still alive so she can't shoot me, and you can get away while she's distracted.'

'If that's the best you can come up with...' Vesta grumbled.

'It's a good plan.' William squeezed her shoulder to reassure her, glad that they were back together, even if it was proving to be quite the challenge to keep them both alive. He raised his voice for the riflewoman in her high window. 'I'm coming out, don't shoot!'

He heard no response.

'My sponsor is still alive and there's a referee here.' He didn't think a little lie like that would hurt his position too much, and if there was a referee in earshot he technically wouldn't be lying. He made his way slowly through the choking smoke. The smell was more akin to roasted pork than sulphur, and there was a wet sheen of innards underfoot.

As he emerged from the smoke, the first thing he saw was Ottilie's body. Four yards in front of him, a wreck only clinging onto life by the finest strand.

'What are you going to do?' William called. 'You can't shoot me, Vesta's still alive, and she's not going to come out. We might have been dead already if it hadn't been for you. Did you want all three of our deaths on your hands? Couldn't bear the thought of Ottilie killing more than you?'

He didn't know where Genevieve was, so directed his question at the terrace row as a whole. There were multiple windows open and she could be in any one of them, and in all likelihood had been changing location in the building regularly to prevent anyone shooting back at her. Her son would be in there too, though whether they were sticking together or watching from separate vantages he couldn't tell. She didn't reply.

Ottilie groaned as William drew alongside her. Her face was crisp at the edges and moist with blood and pustules of blistered skin around her cheeks and eyes. She had tried twice to kill him, yet he felt only pity for her. She was only playing by the rules of the competition after all; they were supposed to kill each other. Even now, one of her only remaining fingers curled weakly on the trigger of her bomb launcher, flexing the crooked loading-arm back and forth as it repeatedly grasped for, and missed, a fresh bomb. He was surprised to see the ammunition that remained in the device was still unexploded, but saw it as a testament to the skill of the guild weaponsmith.

'When the smoke clears, I'll take your sponsors pretty head off her shoulders,' Genevieve shouted, 'so you might as well save us the wait.'

William listened carefully for the direction of her voice and narrowed her location to between one of two windows.

'You could never win this, William,' Genevieve was still shouting, but she affected a more friendly if unconvincing tone. 'Just let me kill your sponsor and you can go and relax in the stands. Goldin's there, I'm sure he'll have a drink waiting for you. I'd rather not waste the shot, Ojo Azul and that undying cultist are enough of a handful.'

William tensed, but didn't say anything, not wanting to encourage further talk of Red-face. He knew how blinded Vesta was when it came to her brother.

'I saw him scrabbling up from the riverbank, he was injured but I let him go.' Genevieve's tone was unnervingly pleasant now. 'I heard you have a vendetta against him.'

William could hear Vesta moving in the smoke, tempted to run by the threat of her still living brother. Any second now, she would bolt from her cover and be killed just like Goldin's sponsor. A single bullet was all it would take.

William made a choice. He turned his head downwards to Ottilie. The dying brute grunted under his scrutiny. He wasn't sure what it meant, or even if she still had the capacity of thought in her state of agony and protracted death, but he did know that she hated the markswoman with a passion and would thrill in her downfall.

Vesta's shoe scraped on stone as she broke into a run. William caught sight of two scopes glinting as they flicked to the smoke in anticipation. He stomped on Ottilie's new pipe launcher, bending the loading arm so that it rocked closer to the next charge, gripped it, and slid it into the barrel. A wheel – rimmed with oleaginous bristles – rotated, painting the back of the rocket. Chemicals fizzed to life and sparks hissed out.

William dove to the floor, grasping the launcher and angling it to where the rifle scopes winked. The rear of the pipe blasted off in a shower of fire, thrusting it skyward. It screeched like a banshee, yellow smoke pluming as it arced through the air, ending in an almighty boom that erupted from the building where the gunners were hiding. A rainbow detonation of flame and fury curled outwards.

Ottilie stilled, a jagged grin across her ruined face. She exhaled one last time.

The building was still falling when Vesta helped William to stand. His ears rang, his head pulsed, but his daze cleared quickly. Their lives were still in peril, and nothing was more sobering. Thankfully, the tell-tale glint of the rifle-sight was gone, Genevieve and her son likely crushed under rubble.

Vesta patted him down, prodding at every cut and bruise she could find.

'Nothing's broken,' he assured her.

'Stop jumping in front of bombs.' She scowled. 'Anyone would think you had a death wish. Now, come on, we need to find my brother before it's too late.'

She took his hand and tried to lead him away from the bridge and burning wreckage.

'We don't even know if he's still alive. He probably drowned in the river, or boiled to death.' William drew up short, halting her progress and pulling her round to look at him. The focus on this vendetta was in danger of hampering their chances of victory.

'My brother, he's resilient… and canny.'

'Genevieve was lying to draw you out.'

'No! He's still alive, I know it.' Vesta scowled into the middle distance before affirming to herself, 'I know he is.'

1675

A shot punctured the simple wooden target; the second of three to land in the crudely drawn bullseye.

'I win again!' Cathal, the Giant of Gael kicked out one leg and looked as though he might have burst into dance, but a swift coughing fit hampered his celebrations. This far into the old tunnels the mildew seemed to addle him.

'God's blood!' He spluttered, collapsing into a worn armchair and swaddling himself in his vast fur lined coat. He hadn't bothered to take off any of his outer wear when he had arrived in the guild outpost and even refused to remove his hat during the shooting competition. Not that the wide brim had hampered him in any way, he had won after all.

William set down his silver pistol and eyed the two targets sullenly. A collection of lanterns flickered over rubble and rotting crates, casting strange shadows over the painted rings. His first shot had shattered a glass lantern and a damp breeze had quickly snuffed it. The last two bullets had barely clipped the wooden target on opposing sides of the widest red circle.

'Would you prefer them on or off?' Cathal propped his boots up on a small table. He had bet a gold piece in the unlikely occurrence William won their competition, and as the boy had little in return, allowed him to stake a shoeshine should he lose. 'It might be easier with my feet in them, else they're a bit limp, and you might not get that sheen I'm looking for.'

He tossed William the coin he had offered as his stake.

'Give that to Marilyn; ask for some brown polish and a cloth.' Cathal was still wheezing from his fit of coughing.

He was a large man and a well-respected assassin, and though he had been retired for some time, was still allowed to frequent the guild's establishments. He claimed the early retirement was due to a gunshot that had collapsed one of his lungs, but William found the tale a little tall given the vastness of his barrel chest. Surely if an organ had perished it would have drawn him in; made him look hollow.

'Leave them on.' William scowled, noting the thick road dust on the tattered boot, annoyed to have lost.

He had been practising every day since the botched assassination – mostly to avoid Ojo who had been in a foul mood – and though he had improved dramatically, he still couldn't compare to any of the life-long killers. His shot was consistent when he was alone, but in competitions with stakes his nerves got the better of him. It was precisely why he had accepted Cathal's challenge, to steel his resolve, but it seemed he still needed practice.

'I'll be back in a minute.' He picked up a lantern and sloped off.

The shooting range was far beneath the ground, even lower than the guild outpost itself, and located at the far end of a collapsed catacomb. Rumour and speculation varied; some said the passages had been part of an ancient tomb, while others claimed they were long abandoned mine shafts. William suspected from the vaulted block ceilings that it was the former. Either way, he was glad for the shooting range and its secret location; it meant he could practice without leaving the city or drawing the attention of any guards.

He dawdled through the passages, reluctant to return to the tavern where he might cross paths with Ojo. Nor was he in a rush to get back and polish Cathal's boots. He tramped up slick steps, holding on to a wooden rail that had been secured to the wall with heavy bolts. Slow as he was, it wasn't long before he reached the outpost proper.

Suspiciously, he eyed a clutch of newcomers in much the same way the regulars had regarded himself and Ojo when they first arrived. He understood why now; there were those amongst the guild who liked to cause trouble, and since William and Ojo had been staying here, he had seen two good assassins killed by callous madmen. The newcomers seemed well intentioned enough, a pair of bright eyed Gierans who dipped their heads at his appraisal. He nodded back.

Ojo nursed a glass of dark spirit in a shadowy corner. His blank eyes followed William's progress through the tables, but he didn't call out. William hurried by without a word, grateful to be spared his master's ire a little longer.

He had taken to reading all of Ojo's correspondence since the assassin had accused him of doing just that, but what he had discovered was disappointingly mundane. It turned out that the man Ojo referred to as his patron was merely his father, not some overbearing crime lord as William imagined, and the story of his illness rang true. He had read a few letters between Ojo and the supplier of his father's medicine, so knew the costs and the cause of the assassin's woes.

There had been no mention of Ojo's strange turn at the assassination, so William had to assume that it was unrelated, perhaps owing to stress at the failure of the job, or maybe he had tripped and hit his head. Either way, he didn't want to mention it and risk angering Ojo again. Besides, Ojo didn't trouble himself with the matter; it was as if nothing had even happened. He could have such a level head when he wanted to, he just never did with William.

'Did you win?' Marilyn greeted William with a wide smile. She liked him, and though he secretly liked her mothering him he often pretended that he didn't, which seemed to endear him to her all the more.

'No.' He pursed his lips.

While Marilyn acted and spoke as any other barmaid, carefree and bright, there was a lot more to her than William had first suspected. She ran the outpost, dealing in all the guild's affairs, managing contracts and distributing funds. She had even liaised with tenured killers when a few of the city guardsmen began to suspect their location for a guild-owned outpost. William admired that in one breath she could talk death and dealings, and in another she would be joking with a drunken patron. One day, he hoped to be as content with guild life as she was.

'Never mind, eh?' She smirked. 'What's the forfeit this time? Need to borrow my washboard again?'

'No.' William shuddered at the memory of washing his last challenger's dirty linens. 'Polishing boots.'

Marilyn cackled as she opened a cabinet under the bar and started fingering through the items inside. 'Well at least you're picking up a few skills along the way – brown or black?'

'It doesn't matter.' Ojo's voice cut through the joviality like a knife. 'He won't be polishing anyone's boots – William, where have you been? I've been looking for you.'

'I'm sorry, I'm here now.' William made himself look even more abashed than he was, hopeful that the question would just go away. The last thing he wanted was for Ojo to forbid him from target practice. 'What did you want me for?'

Ojo held his gaze for a moment causing him to wonder if the man knew his letters had been read.

'Come,' Ojo said softly. 'We need to talk.'

The assassin led him away from the bar. The gentle meandering pace weighed dreadfully on William's shoulders. This was it, the gloom that had been circling his mentor was about to come to the fore.

'Sit.' Ojo gestured to a wing-backed armchair beside the fireplace.

William did as he was told. He felt lost in the vast chair, too hot at this proximity to the fire, and afraid of what the assassin might do to him if his rage bubbled over again.

'I'm sorry this has to happen...' Ojo spoke then paused a moment before starting again. 'I'm sorry I took you for an apprentice.'

The assassin leant one arm on the mantel, staring down into the undulating flames.

'I shouldn't have. It was wrong of me to take a boy so young without the ability to dedicate myself fully to your teachings.' Ojo waved his hand, stopping William from interjecting, then pulled a fire poker from the stand and started to encourage the flame. 'I had enough of a responsibility to my patron. I made a promise that I don't intend to break, but I cannot afford to support him if I am to tutor you as well.'

From the letters, William knew that the payment from their botched job would not be forthcoming and Ojo could not afford the doctor's expedition any time soon. As such, there would be no ready supply of medicine for his father. He had suspected this might lead to a frantic string of killings to accrue the expedition funds in a desperately short amount of time.

'I'm left with a choice: him or you.' Ojo plunged the poker between two smouldering logs and twisted it. 'And though I wish it were different, that promise I made… maybe fifteen years ago now, has me bound to side against you.'

Ojo pulled the poker from the fire and turned to face William. It was hard to tell if his eyes were glassy from the sting of the smoke or from regret, but he held the poker with menace and squared his shoulders in determination. He might have said a quiet sorry in the brief moment between leaving the fireside and thrusting the searing iron into William's arm, but the ensuing pain was enough to make William forget.

Iron scorched flesh; Ojo's knee pressed into William's chest to hold back his writhing. The wings on the sides of the chair stopped him from rolling out, and all he could do was kick and scream. He could smell his own skin burning like meat in a pan, an odour that stirred up a natural revulsion and rolled his stomach inside his writhing belly.

Then the pressure was released and the pain died to a white-hot throb in his arm. William curled himself up, panting. He looked at Ojo, eyes bright with terror, then braved a glance at his arm. Tacky, blotchy and crooked; William recognised the shape of his wound. He had been marked with the crest of the Assassins' Guild.

'I'm going to have to leave you.' Ojo slipped the branding iron back into the stand with the fire-keeping tools. 'I've spoken with Marilyn; she'll keep you in the bar if you'd like, or you can take contracts if you'd prefer. Only the easy ones at first, you're still a beginner, but I can tell you have potential.'

'Where are you going?' William choked; he teased at his arm a few inches away from the sore welt, wanting nothing more than to bathe it and bind it, but knew any contact would be far too painful. 'Why?'

'Do you believe in the afterlife?' Ojo turned from the fire to face William. 'Because you should; life as a killer is all the harder without it.'

Ojo pulled his jacket straight and smoothed his black hair thoughtfully.

'Everyone we kill, their essence isn't extinguished. They just pass before the time nature had intended.' Ojo swilled down the last of his liquor. 'Even the non-believers' thoughts and memories, their personalities, they all go to the other side. But... those who succumb to the fugue, their minds are lost in life, their very selves gone. They are the only ones who cannot go.'

Ojo paced to William's side and knelt to inspect the wound.

'If I'd been stronger willed as a child, as you are, I could have killed my father and saved him from his fate.' Ojo took the branded arm in his hands. William noted that he hadn't bothered to say "his patron", but didn't let it show on his face. 'Instead, I just watched everything that made him who he was sift away, until there was nought but a shell. Now, only the elixirs return his clarity, and it becomes more costly by the day – that doesn't look too bad, it will heal well.'

He stood and dipped his head.

'I'm going to do something foolish. If I succeed, I'll have enough money for that damned expedition. I won't have to pay for my father's elixirs anymore, and I'll be able to come back to finish your training. If I fail, you'll both be on your own.'

'Can't I come with you?' William could feel a potent unease in his chest, a longing more fierce than homesickness.

'You're better off here.' Ojo dug through his pockets and set all of his possessions on the little table between the armchairs. A few coins, a small vial of what looked like blood, and a folded piece of paper with an address written on it. 'If word of my death reaches you, seek out my father and give him this treatment. When he seems most lucid, kill him.'

Ojo turned away.

'I'm leaving you everything except the horse. Good luck William.'

1682

'You might be right.' William relented. There was no point insisting to Vesta that her brother was dead when they already suspected the contrary. 'But we need to keep calm, we're nearly done. There must be less than ten entrants now.'

'And you think my brother's still alive?' She nodded to herself and worried her lip with a canine. The difference from moments ago when she thought her brother dead was stark. She needed him dead, she had pinned her entire future on it.

'Yes, I think he might be.'

'We should find him then. Kill him.' She paused for a moment. 'He'll be hunting us too, we're better off with him out of the picture.'

Across the street, slates and rubble crashed to the cobbles reminding William of their latest conquest. A small boy and his mother had been crushed under that pile. It was a sorry situation, but for William, it was also a hopeful one. With Genevieve out of the contest his chances of success increased dramatically. As Red-face was likely one of the few surviving entrants, Vesta's goal was not so distant from his own. They would kill her brother and whatever stragglers remained, then leave Blackbile victorious.

'Alright.' He nodded sombrely, and was about to add "don't get reckless" when Vesta's brother dashed from behind a riverside shack.

His skin wasn't any redder than usual, and though he limped and cradled his arm against his chest, Red-face didn't appear to be in very bad shape at all. He certainly hadn't fallen into the steaming river. The bridge footings had saved him as they had William, though he did appear to have lost his weapons in his mad dash to survive. He would have been put down easily if he was closer.

Vesta had barely the time to finish an excited, revenge-fuelled cry before her pistol had been raised and fired. The bullet dropped from the air well before it had covered the distance. She set off in pursuit and fumbled cartridges as she ran, failing again and again to reload and take another shot in her desperate tremor.

'No!' William cried, 'Vesta don't!'

He swore to himself and seethed. Hissing spitefully through gritted teeth, he set off running after his unruly sponsor.

Red-face wasn't as fast as his sister, and though Vesta gained ground, he leapt through the front door of a drab terrace and disappeared inside. Vesta drew away from William, and didn't listen to any of his protests. She disappeared inside while he was still twenty yards behind.

William was panting and exhausted. Though his limbs still functioned well enough through the lingering effect of Barber's elixirs, he felt tremendously drained, as if the medicines were drawing from his own well of energy to keep him mobile. By the time he reached the door of the building, both his sponsor and Red-face were long gone.

He almost fell inside, tripped by a displaced set of dusty floorboards. Despite the appearance on the outside, the whole row was derelict. The internal stud walls were cratered and plaster mouldered away in brackish swags. He could see through at least two more houses before remnants of walls obscured his view. Even the levels above were pot-holed and growing colourful lichen.

Not knowing which way they had fled, he paused and closed his eyes to better tune his hearing. He rubbed his calves and pushed himself straight, though his back protested. He could feel his sponsor drawing further away with every laboured breath he took. Then, far down the terrace, he heard a gun blast.

With a single throat-grating sigh, he set off. He clipped plaster and thin slats of wood as he progressed sloppily through partially demolished walls; they crumbled easily enough to his momentum. As he progressed through the houses they became more decrepit, holes appeared in the outer walls and the roofs were rimmed with black mould. A cold wind blew perpendicular through glassless windows and stirred ash in whirlpools at his feet.

He stumbled on, clambering through a wall and over a broken hearth into the next house. The building after was just as empty, but there was far more debris and deeper shadows to hide in. Surreptitiously he checked his pistol. Yet before he could blunder into the next property, something stood out to him. There were splinters on the floor; fresh ones.

The next gust of wind rattled a door in its frame; the lock clinked with a metallic retort. He peered through the intermittent gap at the street beyond, and swallowed. This door had been kicked *inwards*. Red-face and Vesta hadn't gone this way; someone else had come in.

He turned and pressed his back to the wall beside the doorway, half expecting an assassin to have been standing directly to his rear. There was nobody behind him.

He could feel a pressure building. The longer he was separated from Vesta the more likely she was to die; that couldn't happen.

He took a moment to think. The front door could have been kicked-in at any point in the competition, even before it. Everywhere had its homeless folk and drug-abusers looking for somewhere quiet. There were so many possibilities that could have come through that particular door, that the chances of another assassin entering unseen in the last five minutes were incredibly slim. On the other hand, if it was an old break-in Vesta could have gone that way. He committed himself to a decision, praying he was making the right call to any saint that would listen.

He set off through the remainder of the rotten houses. Splinters of light began to peek through walls as he drew towards the end of the terrace. The last house in the row had been destroyed entirely, perhaps by one of Ottilie's stray bombs. He quickened his pace, squeezing out every last jot of energy from his legs, certain this was where Vesta would have followed her brother.

Bricks, wood and shards of glass from the last house spilled into the one preceding it, forcing William to slow down. The floorboards bowed under the weight of the masonry and threatened to cave into the cellars. He took his time, but was bulled on by another gunshot, this one closer and crisper.

When he reached the mass of rubble he dropped to all fours and clambered over the shifting detritus. The smell of sulphur, burnt hair, and dust was almost overwhelming. As he reached the crest, the same riverside roadway came into view, but he was further along and much closer to the VIP bleachers and winner's podium. William scoured the scatter of purposefully placed carts and obstacles in the street, a frustrating technique of set-dressing that ensured the VIPs saw a more exciting shootout.

William couldn't see Vesta from his vantage, but he could see Red-face. He was crouched behind a divan that had been hauled from one of the still-occupied houses. It looked as if he was trying to get as close as possible to the VIP bleacher. Only an attention-seeking despot would want an audience at his sister's death.

Perhaps that was it! The zealot wanted to slaughter Vesta under the watchful eye of his superior. Red-face hadn't been on the run at all; he had led Vesta here with a sick purpose. Desperately then, William searched the crowds for more Lambs.

Vesta leapt from behind a pallet of spices and took a shot for her brother, puncturing the fabric of the divan, but missing her target. Her brother loosed an equally poor shot into a sack of turmeric, the garish colour clouding the drab air.

William cursed; he didn't know where Red-face found the gun. It was probably part of the elaborate ploy to get Vesta here. Holding his breath, he steadied his aim; he was still a little too far away, but certainly the best shot out of the three of them. The sight of his pistol lined up with the small and distant cultist, and his finger flexed on the trigger.

At the same moment, the air whispered behind him and agony erupted in his calf. It was as bad as a bullet wound, but there had been no other gunshot except his. He tumbled over from the searing pain in his leg; whatever had struck him was protruding from the wound and dragging in the rubble and grit. An arrow. He swore; no-one used a bow and arrow these days. Gods damn it the pain was excruciating. He gritted his teeth and tried desperately to cram a fresh cartridge into his flintlock.

As he lay on his back looking up into the ruptured house, William spotted his attacker in the gloom. Crouched on the edge of the first floor, on splintered boards, was his old mentor. There was no warmth or familiarity in Ojo's face. William wondered if there ever had been.

Stony-eyed, Ojo hopped down to the mass of rubble, spry despite his years. Though he looped his arm through the empty bow and slung it over his shoulder, there was no denying the murderous intent of the former champion. William pushed the cartridge into his pistol with a panicked thumb, tearing it and spilling the powder across his shirt. The fastening mechanism caught on the stray paper and refused to close.

Ojo sneered at the feeble attempt to fight back and snatched at the arrow skewered through his leg. One twist of the shaft was all it took to send William writhing in agony. His pistol flew free from grasping fingers.

Keeping one fist on the arrow, and the other around William's foot, Ojo dragged him screaming from his discarded weapon and into the dilapidated terrace. Words spilled from William's mouth amidst the shrieks, but everything came out overlapped and incomprehensible.

'Ojo please…' he managed to splutter in the brief moment between his leg being released and his throat being clamped tight in the assassin's hands.

Despite his age, Ojo's grip still had all the strength it ever had. The fingers clamped tight and William's windpipe crimped closed. For the second time, he was at his mentor's mercy, and this time he was certain Ojo would not relent. There was no lesson to be taught and nothing but animosity between them now. The assassin hadn't even bothered to exchange pleasantries before killing him.

William's eyes rolled into his skull and his arms and legs flailed aimlessly, feebly, under the mass of the determined assassin. Sleep beckoned him, and beyond that, death. He could feel the energy seeping from him, more serenely than before.

Memories flickered through his mind, even things he thought had been long forgotten. His mother's face. His father's strong grip and one milky eye that, as a child, William had never realised was out of place. He could feel the satisfaction in killing the callous pawnbroker, the shame in burning the young boy, regret and humiliation from killing the mayor of Fairshore in a spectacular blunder. His initial distaste for Goldin and his early fondness for Genevieve. He had been wrong about so much in his life, some things little, some too big to even comprehend. There was a lot he would change, but it seemed his lot had been had.

Just as all hope had been abandoned, air plunged down his throat as William was released from his mentor's grip. His pulse throbbed in his ears and his eyes rolled in near unconsciousness. He gasped and clawed in the dirt and choked on his own spittle. Incapable of protecting himself should the onslaught begin again, he hadn't the wits to scramble for safety. All he could do was lay still and wait for clarity to return.

The splintered ceiling gradually came into focus as he blinked the excess liquid from his eyes. He hadn't a clue what had happened.

'I'm so sorry William.'

The words bled faintly through his haze and he struggled to tell exactly who was saying them. He swallowed rising bile and forced himself up. Ojo was at the far side of the room, crumpled against a rotten wall, staring at his twitching fingers.

'I'm sorry… for not coming back,' he muttered again, making fists of his trembling hands. 'When I won the prize I was so happy, all our problems were solved. I paid for the expedition and my doctor friend agreed to treat my father indefinitely. I knew I'd be able to take my time with you, rather than rushing you as I had initially.'

Ojo's eyes trailed down to William's bleeding leg and the snapped arrow shaft that protruded from each side. 'Did I shoot you?'

William nodded nervously, spurring Ojo to search his inside pockets until he produced a small roll of bandage and a vial of salve.

'I'll fix it.' Ojo shuffled across the floor to William and knelt, before retrieving a small knife. 'It's going to hurt for a little while, but once I've done, the salve should see you right. It's one of the doctor's concoctions.'

'He used it on my arm.' William nodded and rolled his leg onto its side so that the arrow shaft ran parallel to the floor. Ojo took it firmly and started to whittle the splinters from the end as delicately as he could; the pain was palpable.

'I meant to come back for you. I really did.' Ojo flicked a curl of wood to the heap of rubble. His lip quivered. 'After I won the prize I started losing days, getting angry at others and myself, everything

just seemed harder than it used to. It wasn't long after that I realised
– grit your teeth.'

Ojo tightened one fist on the arrow shaft and swiftly pulled it free
of William's leg. It was like nothing he had ever experienced. The
pain was overwhelming, but at the same time he could feel the coarse
wood being drawn through his closing flesh in explicit detail. As
soon as the shaft was extracted it was tossed aside. The wound was
daubed generously with salve and wrapped in bandage before blood
could wash it away.

'You'll live, but I expect your chances of winning have ebbed
away.' Ojo smiled softly. 'Is your sponsor still alive?'

'I don't know,' William hissed through gritted teeth.

'I think it's best if you just slip away. I'm winning, I need to, and
if I lose myself again, I won't hesitate.' Ojo tied a knot in the bandage
and ran his hand softly over the tight fibres. 'Once I have enough
money for more medicine, maybe we can travel the road together?
Would you like that?'

William's stomach knotted. There was nothing he would like
more than a companion again, even one as cruel as Ojo. He tried to
reason that the man's callousness could have been a side effect of his
illness, but couldn't be sure that was true. He also knew there was no
way it could come to pass without resigning Vesta to her fate. He
swallowed a lump, too weak to make the decision.

'Just think about it.' Ojo stood. 'But if I were you, I'd take myself
to the bleachers with the rest of the eliminated entrants. The last
thing I want is to kill you.'

The assassin crossed the room to a flight of shaky stairs that led
only halfway to the next floor and reached up to retrieve his quiver
of arrows. Silently, he counted how many remained then nodded to
himself; he had enough to finish the last few assassins. As he
returned across the rubble-laden floor, one of the worm-bitten
boards snapped underfoot. His leg fell through the hole, and his knee
crunched loudly as it hit the wood.

Ojo's mouth opened and his eyes screwed up, but only a gurgle
sputtered out. His breathing elevated and his arms skittered about to
rescue himself from the hole; a second break in the boards would
plummet him into the cellars.

William dragged himself towards the assassin to assist, but was too afraid to put any weight onto his leg. He wrapped his arms around Ojo's torso and pushed with his good leg against an upright length of broken board. Together they heaved and Ojo slid away from the hole, pulling his leg from the gloom below.

He gasped as the extent of his injury was revealed and the pain began to wash up his leg. Blood oozed through fabric and his shin bone protruded through both his flesh and his torn trousers. For a moment, his eyes flitted in jealousy and hatred towards William's leg and the valuable salve and bandage that had been used there. He sneered at his once apprentice and pushed himself away, his lips quivering words under his breath.

'I have an elixir.' William delved his hand into his pocket, feeling the wet and knowing the worst before he produced the cracked bottle. It was empty.

Ojo closed his eyes and swallowed audibly before taking a long, calming breath.

'It seems my chances of victory are as slim as yours.' He hissed out a faint chortle then returned to his deep musing. 'I don't begrudge you the salve, it would do little for me with a broken bone, I'm sure.'

'I'll get help.' William tried to reassure his mentor. 'I'll get you back to the stands, the doctor will be there; he'll fix it.'

'I'm beyond that.' Ojo sneered again, but this time it wasn't directed at William. 'When my sponsor died, I carried on in the competition. There's nothing for me now except victory or death, and one of those is...'

William moved closer to Ojo. He pushed himself on his injured leg, and despite feeling weak, it only ached dully as a result of the powerful salve.

'At least I'll be killed in this moment of lucidity. My essence might still pass on.' Ojo bit his lip, then looked up at William with a sad hope in his eyes. 'Will you do something for me, one last thing?'

'Anything.'

'Don't leave me to the others.' Ojo gripped William's shirt. 'Finish me now, while I'm still coherent, before I lose myself again. Do it how I like.'

Ojo fixed William with his wide brilliant-blue but somehow pathetic eyes. Tears welled in the corners and he pursed his lips determinedly.

William felt sick, and that oh-so terrible feeling of dread returned to his chest. He wouldn't make the old man beg. Penitently, he rolled up onto his knees and shuffled to the rear of the crippled assassin, softly slipping one arm around the wrinkled swags of his neck. He gripped his wrist with the other hand.

'Thank you, William.' Ojo's voice broke, and he sniffed his last breath.

William pulled his arm tightly towards him, sealing the assassin's throat and slowly asphyxiating the life from his body. Ojo didn't struggle at first, he was resigned to his fate, and knew it was better to go now than at the hands of an unknown assassin. But as the life drained from him and his instinctive mind overpowered the dying embers of his consciousness, his legs began to kick and his hands reached of their own volition to release his throat. Soon after, William felt what Ojo had told him he would: the life force passing from the body, leaving nothing but a dead weight.

He laid his former mentor across the dusty boards that had claimed his life, and took a moment to choke out a few tears. Even when he lost his parents, William had the merchant, and when he lost the merchant he had the broker. After the broker was Ojo, and after that, Marilyn. Then, when the time came, he left her behind to pursue his career as an assassin. There was always something there to keep him from grief, but in losing Ojo again, it felt as though he lost everything he ever had. He was left with nothing and nobody – yet if he could save Vesta that might not be true.

He pushed himself purposely to his feet, wobbling slightly on his stinging half-numb leg, and hobbled across the broken boards. His foot dragged through splinters, then dirt as he moved onto the heap of rubble. As he leant to pick up his pistol he almost fell, barely managing to stay upright, despite a needling pain shooting up his thigh. He reloaded quickly, forced himself up and over the mound of rubble and out to the roadway beyond.

The roar from the VIP bleachers hit him like a wave of furious wind; triumphant, angry. Their wordless swell of excitement battered the senses, but William cast them from his mind. There was no time for showmanship now.

Vesta and her brother had emerged from their respective covers and were circling each other in the wide expanse. Red-face's paralysed arm was coated in blood and he looked to have been clipped by the bullet William fired before Ojo's interruption. The pair were still too far away from one another to fire with any kind of reliable accuracy, neither dared to be the first to expend their only loaded round, but with each side step they spiralled towards each other.

Red-face was at the far side of the road from William, but glanced at him as soon as he emerged from the houses. Vesta was closer, but her back was towards him. He wanted to let her know he was there, but didn't want to disturb her until he was able to assist. Slowly, he shuffled closer, knowing that the nearer to Vesta he got, the itchier her brother's trigger finger would get.

'It was your fault.' Red-face sneered. 'You were the one who cost us everything we ever had. I was trying to reclaim it, but you couldn't leave well enough alone.'

'Shut up.' Vesta spat and flailed her pistol hysterically. William cursed; her brother was inside her head. If he taunted her to fire first she would surely miss at such a range and be as good as dead. 'You were only trying to help yourself!'

'Thanks to you, *myself* is all I have left.' Red-face jeered, his eyes now solely fixed on the slowly approaching William, just over Vesta's shoulder. 'You were the reason the house burned down. You were the reason father turned to drink. And ultimately, it's your fault that he had to die.'

Vesta shrieked and fired. Blood spattered from her brother's side; a lucky shot, but not lucky enough. He staggered backwards a few paces and gritted his teeth, hissing breath.

'Bad luck, sister.' He lurched forwards and trained his pistol on Vesta. William took his aim and prayed his shot would land before Red-face had the chance to pull the trigger.

The sound of four gunshots clapped in such quick succession that they couldn't possibly have been from a single gun, but none of the pistols in the standoff had yet been fired. Blood erupted from

Vesta's midriff; four gouts, each thumping powerfully in turn. She stumbled forwards and her pistol tipped from outstretched fingers. A whimper slithered out on a trail of drool and she crumpled to the floor. Her hands grasped at the pocked fabric over her gushing stomach, trying to bunch it together and stem the torrent. As she fell, Red-face's eyes found William's and they looked at one another for a moment in abject horror, unsure of whether to move.

'Vesta!' Red-face cried out, tossed his gun to the side and dashed for his sister. William kept his pistol trained on the cultist and tried to match his pace, hoping to protect his sponsor. His leg buckled under the strain, agony lancing to his hip and halfway up his back. He collapsed to the floor with a crack to his cheek that split the skin, but his pistol stayed firmly in hand.

'Not like this.' Red-face crumpled to his knees and took Vesta in his arms. 'This wasn't supposed to happen.'

William looked up from his prostrate position, unsure if he had knocked the sense from himself in the fall. As he trained his pistol on Red-face he could almost swear that he was crying.

'You're ok, you're ok.' As Red-face stroked the side of his gurgling sister's face, his tears fell in red droplets to disappear on her already sodden shirt. 'We're going to get you help. You've been shot, but it's not bad. You're going to be ok.'

William couldn't understand what was happening; it was as if he had awoken from a bad dream and found himself completely out of place in the world.

'What happened?' Vesta's hands fumbled around mindlessly. One reached out to grab her brother by his collar and weakly pull him closer, the other rolled around at her waistline ineffectually. 'What's going on?'

'Somebody shot you, but I'm going to make sure you get better.' Red-face gagged on his tears. 'Then we'll set things straight. I'll kill you like I was supposed to. A proper sacrifice, how it should be, it's what you deserve.'

Red-face balked and gasped, suddenly stilled as he held himself over Vesta. From his mouth, a long trail of spittle was caught in a sulphurous breeze. A short shriek burst from him and a dark torrent of blood gushed from his gut; Vesta's arm fell limp, a knife still safe in her hand. She smiled gently while Red-face puckered for air like a fish out of water, then finally he slumped over her.

William scrambled forwards, somehow believing there might still be something he could do for Vesta; scrape the excess salve from his leg to heal her wounds or drag her to Doctor Barber. There had to be something, some way to save her. Yet he knew he was as useless as the fear-muted child he had once been; small, unseen and ineffectual. The world was dark and unfair, and there was nothing to be done as The Wheels of Fate turned and pulped his last glimmer of hope.

He heaved himself upright, hopping every half step on his bandaged leg. Blood was dribbling from his soaked bandage. He dropped to his knees and tipped the cultist's limp body from atop his sponsor.

'Wi…' Vesta grunted with a weak exhalation.

'It's going to be alright,' he lied.

'We did it.' She smiled as wide as she could muster.

Her eyes were closed from exhaustion and her teeth were swirled red with blood, but at least she looked content. Her face held in that expression for what seemed like far too long, then softly returned to neutrality as her last breath faded.

William's hand shivered down the side of her face, neatening her hair and brushing his own tear from her cheek.

'We did it.' He agreed with the faintest veneer of excitement for the chance that she might still be able to hear it.

He felt hollow, sick, like someone had reached into his chest and not only wrenched out his heart but half of his organs too. There was a pit of despair inside him, ragged around the edges, and left wanting. The grief was keen and made sharp by confusion. He longed for this to not be real, that it was all some sour dream, or trick of his dying brain. He half hoped that he was still in Ojo's iron grip, and this was some hellish hallucination before the end. He still couldn't understand what had happened. Nobody had fired, but somehow four bullets had drilled through Vesta in quick succession.

'How does it feel?' a voice called out over the silence of the roadway. 'To have your sponsor taken from you like that? Has your heart has been crushed inside your chest? Has the sun been blotted out? I've seen the way you look at her; maybe you'll understand an ounce of what it is to lose a child.'

Genevieve descended a rubble heap as gracefully as it was possible to, her rifle in hand and her face streaked with charcoal lines from her eyes.

'So what are you going to do Will?' Genevieve sneered. 'Are you going to back down like a coward and go to the bleachers with the rest of the spineless herd? Or are you staying in, in your feeble hope for revenge? I would much prefer the latter; because it means I can kill you now, rather than hunting you down *after* I've been awarded the prize.'

She pulled the trigger on her rifle, but all it produced was a pathetic click. Annoyed, she pulled it again five more times, each click ratcheting along the little cage that had once housed up to seven rounds. It slid to the end of its range and fell out of the rifle. She cursed and spat, tucking the gun under her arm as she rummaged for a replacement clip.

'At least you had the chance to say goodbye; I afforded you that much. Let you see her take her dying breath.' She plucked out a clip and began to wrestle it into the gun. Tears were pouring from her bloodshot eyes and she struggled to align the cage so precisely with the slot. She tried to knock it into the mechanism with her palm, but all that served to do was twist the cage and send the copper-clad cartridges tinkling to the cobbles. 'When you killed my son, I hadn't the luxury you had, so he died alone, in a ball of flame or a heap of bricks. Whichever way it was, I'm certain it wasn't pleasant. *I couldn't even find his body.*'

William shook, white hot, dazzled by an all-consuming fury at the injustices of the world. Both hands, grazed and dirty, clenched his pistol; the silver gleamed red with Vesta's blood.

'I'll ensure your death is as equally uncomfortable. Perhaps even agonising.' Frustrated, Genevieve tossed her rifle to the floor and pulled a small flintlock from the folds of her pinned up skirts. The hammer cocked. 'So what's it going to be? Delay the inevitable, or shall we settle this like assassins, right now?'

William swallowed a clot of phlegm and straightened up to meet the grief-stricken gaze of his assailant. He squared his stance, balancing his weight, though his injuries protested. For a moment, a shaft of light broke the ash-grey sky, glinting on engraved silver flowers.

1676

Cathal spluttered as he pulled the trigger, sending his shot wide of the target. It was the first time William had ever seen the man miss, and hope swelled in him; he might actually stand a chance of winning.

The old Gael grumbled something and slumped back into his chair. It squelched under his weight and creaked as he found a comfortable position. The chair had been an expensive item once, but no sooner than it had been dragged into the dank depths of the under-sewer catacombs, it was ruined.

Heavy breaths whistled through Cathal's grey-sprouting nostrils, his breath caught in the back of his gullet; he was pale and flushed all at once. He blasphemed under his breath, annoyed at himself, but never towards William. All in all, this had been his worst round yet. His first shot had landed in the outer ring, and though his second had been a bullseye, the third had cost him greatly.

William, on the other hand, had put up his best effort to date and had yet to take his third shot. He had hit the inner circle with both bullets and would have won already if one of those had been a bullseye. All he had to do to win was hit the target, but it was respectful to finish the round trying one's best, and he was eager to score his first perfect round – a feat Cathal had achieved many times in their competitions.

'Take it steady now lad,' the retired assassin wheezed out between chokes of phlegm, 'steady your breath, don't rush it.'

William held out his flintlock and measured his aim. The pistol felt right in his hand; he had grown into it, and its grip sat comfortably in his palm. He took note of where his previous two shots had punctured the painted board, just inches apart, and set his sights between them. Cathal started to cough and subdued himself with a thick woollen scarf over his mouth. Water dripped into a bucket from some salty stalactite that trailed from the arching brickwork. It fell right in William's vision, made a constant plip-plip as it landed. He focused his mind, let all the distractions fall away.

His finger tensed on the trigger.

As to not so thoroughly best the old assassin, he had briefly considered shooting wide, but Cathal seemed as intent on his progress as he was. He supposed it was nice for the old man to pass on his craft, especially given his circumstances. William didn't like to think about it, but the man had grown sickly, lost weight, and the white in his hair had spread. Even despite all this, he remained a consummate marksman, and an assassin to be respected. He deserved to be bested by nothing less than a perfect round.

The bullet thumped a hole though the board, not quite in the dead centre, but almost perfectly between the last two of William's shots, exactly where he had wanted it. A smile brightened his face; he had won, and though he was fairly certain he wouldn't be able to replicate his success so easily, this was proof of his improvement.

'Good shot.' Cathal stood with great effort. 'I dare say you would have beaten any killer here with a shot like that.'

'I didn't just beat any killer.' William smirked. 'I beat you.'

'That you did, but you'd better not go bragging about beating some wheezing old man. Most don't know I can still shoot, and I'd like to keep it that way. Retirement's not really *retirement* if there's folks out for your blood.' Cathal picked up his crutch from against the wall and propped it under his armpit. 'What say we head upstairs and get ourselves a drink? I'll buy. It's only fair, I don't think I'm in much state to be polishing your boots, do you?'

'No.' William smiled, but faltered. He could hear distant footsteps hurrying down the passageway. Even so quiet, the sound of leather soles scuffing against dusty stone was unmistakable. 'What's that?'

Cathal stopped his shambling and craned his ear to the sound, before concluding, 'it'll just be someone coming to test themselves at target practice.'

He was about to resume his slow clamber back to the outpost, but William waved a hand for him to stop.

'No, listen.' William reloaded his flintlock. 'They're running.'

Cathal cocked his head again then nodded in silent agreement.

The pair readied themselves, fearing the worst – that the imperial guard had found the outpost and opted to raid it rather than extort it. Cathal leaned against the wall and readied his pistol. William ducked behind a barrel and aimed over the top, to where the passage curled out of sight at the top of a small flight of stairs. He held his pistol in both hands and let the firm wood sure his aim. Should he need to fire on whoever appeared around the corner, he would not let himself miss.

The footsteps came clearer as they approached down the distant corridors and stairways. William steadied his breath.

A figure emerged around the corner and barrelled down the steps. William's finger tensed, degrees from releasing a bullet.

'What in the hells are you doing?' Marilyn staggered, almost falling over in her effort to stop. She had her skirts bunched in one fist and an envelope clutched tightly in the other.

William's trigger finger relaxed.

'What are *you* doing?' Cathal smirked. 'You could have gotten yourself killed, running up on us like that.'

'I didn't think you'd be so skittish in outpost grounds.' She cocked an eyebrow and produced the letter, still panting from her dash. 'William, it's for you. It's from that doctor; about Ojo.'

William stood, leaving his pistol on the barrel, and took the envelope. He had received one such letter already, detailing Ojo's performance in the competition; how he had sustained great injuries, including a badly fractured hand, but had ultimately come out on top. He had been informed that Ojo would be staying in Blackbile until he had mended, after which he would be returning home. He assumed this letter would be confirmation that his mentor had begun his journey and hurriedly opened it.

His eyes flitted over the page, taking in the information relayed by the Blackbile doctor. As the smile faded and his eyes glazed over, the joviality between Cathal and Marilyn turned to concern.

'What does it say?' Cathal asked, his words catching phlegm in the back of his throat.

'He got better, set off here with a guarded transport,' William summarised the doctor's letter, 'but it sounds like bandits or highwaymen came looking for him; for his winnings. Or maybe an assassin was after the prestige… He's dead.'

Uttering the words made it all the more real than just reading the news on paper. William started to cry. His mentor was gone, the money and their easy life, lost; taken away by callous assassins or thieves.

It was selfish but William pictured himself back out on the street, or in the clutches of another slaver. He had stayed in the outpost so long with these people, but never once had he considered fully what would happen should Ojo never return for him. Cathal didn't mind teaching him to shoot, but he was well beyond taking him out of the outpost to kill, and Marilyn was simply a guild clerk.

He slumped against the wall and slid down, curled himself into a ball on the floor, and wept.

'What's that?' Marilyn approached William with a soft smile; her bun was loose and lopsided, with sprays of hair escaping in a messy halo. Her breath was a little heavier than usual and there was the faintest smell of sweat beneath her perfumes, exhausted from a day of aggressive cleaning.

William looked up at her blankly. He hadn't spoken to anyone much since he had received news of Ojo's death. He had confided in Cathal, but the old assassin succumbed to his ailments a few weeks after the letter arrived. After that he had kept to himself, and for the most part he had been left alone. He had been in that state where grief longed to release as anger, and nobody had wanted to instigate him, not when he kept his flintlock so close. Now that rage had all ebbed away, leaving only a sour taste and longing for something more.

'That paper,' she asserted again, pressing one hand to the base of her spine and stretching the kinks free. 'What is it?'

'This?' William brushed his thumb over the writing to straighten out the creases. The letters were neat and well formed, but dotted with over-zealous blotches of ink from pressing too hard with the pen. Ojo's hand was rather distinctive; it was the address of his father. William had been asked to kill him should Ojo die.

'It's… nothing.' He suppressed a shudder and turned over the note, making sure to conceal Ojo's writing on the back. 'Just one of the flyers from last year.'

She scowled at it for a second, but decided against further questioning. She started taking glasses from a sink at the other side of the bar and drying them before lining them up on the back wall. 'Would you be able to help out in the bar today? There's a large band of guilders passing through tonight.'

'I'd rather not.' William crumpled the paper into his pocket. 'I don't want to hear about Ojo anymore. Everyone's talking about him, laughing…'

'Will.' She leant forwards on the bar and fixed him with her best approximation of an assertive yet motherly glare. 'This place isn't exactly flush with grana; if you don't help out at least a little I won't be able to justify keeping you here. I know it's hard for you-'

'I know.' He cut her short. 'I can't stay.'

He scrunched the piece of paper in his pocket into an even tighter ball. He had made a promise to his mentor. Killing Ojo's father was saving him, in a way. Provided what Ojo had told him was true, and not some fiction to make his next kill pass with a little less guilt. It was just too hard for him to comprehend right now, he wasn't ready to set out on his own and kill the only link he still had to his mentor.

'I want a contract.' He pursed his lips. 'Somebody bad, someone that deserves it. I need to get back out there… before I lose what I've learned.'

'Are you sure?' Marilyn looked surprised, but instinctively she moved from the sink and reached for a ledger under the bar. After all, assigning assassins their contracts was what the guild employed her to do.

'I'm sure.' He ran one hand through his hair and tapped his other nervously on the bar. He didn't want to end up a beggar.

Marilyn set the ledger on the ale-ringed oak and opened it to a page marked with a thin red ribbon. Slowly she traced down the list with her finger, skipping over the jobs that were crossed out, but reading each and every contract that hadn't yet been fulfilled. She was almost to the end of the list before she found something suitable. She tapped the paper with her fingernail as she read the contract details over.

'I think I've found one you might be interested in. I'll get the full contract from the back.' She slapped the ledger closed and stowed it under the bar. 'Just promise me that you'll try to keep safe, I don't want you getting yourself killed.'

'I'll do my best.' He shrugged, trying not to linger on it.

1682

William pictured Genevieve holding her prize aloft. Something twisted in his stomach, he felt ill. The notion of Vesta's killer being lorded made him spit. He shored up his footing; gave in to his anger and venom.

'I'm staying in.' He sneered at the markswoman.

The words had barely finished tripping off his tongue when Genevieve's arm snapped up and pulled the trigger. The sound of the shot tensed him, and for a moment he thought he was as good as dead, but the bullet flew wide. Genevieve's hands moved quickly, and a second cartridge was already halfway loaded by the time he had his wits about him to move.

Shooting to kill would have been the best decision to make at that moment, but William had been spooked by the markswoman's readiness to take his head off; he dashed for cover. His leg pulsed with pain and he was certain to be leaking blood.

Locating a thick sided refreshments cart, he raised his hands to shield his head and diverted his course towards it. Genevieve's gun clapped a second shot, but yet again the bullet passed him by.

He skidded behind the cart and took a frantic moment to collect himself. He had his gun, and a fair few cartridges left – perhaps six – but his fingers were quivering too much to count the contents of his pocket. He was still alive, but the markswoman might be his most difficult kill yet. She could have any number of cartridges, and was tipped to win the prize. His eyes began to dart about in panic, from the steaming river to the stand of VIP's.

All the brightest and best in the criminal underworld were sat watching him quiver behind a fruit stand. He could see referees gathered with the mayor and committee members to watch the final kill. He scoured the crowd for a friendly face or even a stranger that wasn't party to the growing chant for Genevieve.

His gaze passed over the assassins whose sponsors had been killed, the ones who hadn't been so foolish as to continue, those who could be certain they would see a new day. He dreaded the chance of catching Goldin's eye, and the disapproval that would surely linger there. The little man had told him not to waste his life, but he hadn't heeded him.

Then he found the dwarf in the crowd, nestled between two bandaged hitmen, cupping his hands and bellowing. His mouth moved, but the words were completely hidden behind the chant for Genevieve. Even so, William could tell it was encouragement. A slight smile pushed to his lips. He had to at least try to win this thing. He *had* to win, he was so close.

Tentatively, he shuffled to the edge of the cart and peered around the side to relocate the markswoman. There was another clap and an urn of exotic pink juice smashed, spilling its sickly liquid down the cart siding. William flinched at the sound, but managed to keep his head out of cover long enough to spy Genevieve behind a heap of flour sacks. She was reloading again and keeping her position to fire, despite being far too distant to make an effective shot.

It was then that it dawned on William; she wasn't nearly as proficient with her sidearm as she had been with her rifle. They were fighting on his terms now. A giddy excitement fought to blossom and force a grin to his lips, but a calmer head prevailed. He couldn't let her inexperience with flintlocks allow him to get sloppy.

He took a moment to double check that his pistol was loaded and stuck his hand just outside of cover. Genevieve let off another shot; this one didn't even strike the cart. She was as blinded by rage as he was nervous. He pushed himself to his feet, wobbling on his seeping leg, and made a move for the nearest cover. By the time she shot again, he was already out of sight.

He skidded to his arse behind a broken barrel and stifled a yelp. A thick splinter had pierced the flesh between his finger and thumb as he thumped against the wood. He recoiled instinctively, but his skin snagged and was ripped into two flaps. His pistol clattered to the ground. He clenched his teeth, screwed up his eyes, and swallowed the pain. If Genevieve detected any weakness, she would come hunting.

He sank low behind the barrel and took stock of the damage. Blood was flowing readily, covering his palm; his fingers were trembling. He pulled the bandages from around his leg to untie them; there was plenty of linen to share with a second wound. Blood oozed from his leg, but pressure wasn't alleviated for long. He had soon unravelled a length of bandage, wrapped it around his hand, and retied what remained around his leg.

His palm stung fiercely and the bulky linen stopped him from holding his pistol right, but with his lack of fresh salve that would have to do. There were more pressing matters at hand, primarily the worry of how far Genevieve might have advanced while he administered aid on himself.

Though his off-hand was still a little numb, he gripped the pistol tightly, and was glad the limb seemed mostly functional. Doctor Barber had done a much better job patching it than Ojo had on his leg. He could barely even feel that his arm had been so recently stabbed.

He peered between two planks, spying Genevieve just as she hid behind a crate. She was in range now; he just needed a moment to aim without being shot at. If she had to reload he would have time, but for that he needed to tempt her to shoot again. Though, at this more realistic range, there was a better chance she would actually hit him. He just hoped her grief and anger were keeping her reckless.

He raised his gun into the air and twisted it against the setting sun so that it glinted towards Genevieve. She shot and missed again. He rounded the barrel, thrust to his feet and moved towards her. Blood spurted from his leg like bile from a bursting boil, and though the serum's effect slowed any heavy flow, dread rippled through him. He raised his pistol, ready to shoot Genevieve right between the eyes, but his fingers lost their grip and the flintlock tumbled to the flagstones.

Blood trickled from his bandaged wrist. A freshly made bullet wound became apparent in the serum-numbed flesh. When he taunted her, Genevieve *had* hit him. He fell to his knees and clutched for his pistol with both his near-useless hands.

The flintlock was scooped up with his numb hand and wedged into the agonising grip of the other. He rolled onto his back with the pistol facing limply towards the crates.

Genevieve emerged, her own weapon trained on him. She realised her advantage quickly; smirked as he scrambled in a pitiful pile on the floor, fumbling to pull his trigger – covered in blood, Barber's serums and wet with tacky fruit juice. In her arrogance she waited a moment too long. The mouth of her flintlock found him as he sighted her; they pulled their triggers in unison.

A hot ball of lead skewered under William's ribs. Genevieve was caught in her neck or shoulder and knocked backwards off her feet. The pair shrieked in gruesome harmony, concealed behind the joyous roar of the morbid crowd.

William clutched his side; he could think about little other than the fact he was certain to die. His best hope for survival was to lay still and hope that he didn't bleed out too quickly, but he couldn't go without knowing Genevieve's fate. Vesta wasted her life to get vengeance on her brother; it would all be in vain should her killer go unpunished.

He pushed himself upright. His cries of pain had turned to a low guttural moan that built with each nausea-inducing motion. He picked up his pistol, tucked it under his armpit, and rolled over to push himself upright. Everything hurt so much that it was almost as if he hadn't been injured at all. The pain was at the other side of a thin veil, and though he was pretty sure that meant he was a dead man walking, the calm of it was surprisingly comforting.

He shuffled sluggishly around the crates, and reloaded his pistol as precisely as he could with the few fingers that still moved.

Genevieve was sprawled on the floor, her hand clamped over her neck. The other was grasping for her pistol, but gave up once she caught sight of William looming over her.

'Looks like you've won.' She hissed blood between her pink stained teeth. 'Unless you bleed to death before you can pull that trigger of yours.'

William closed the pistol with great effort, sheering off the back of the cartridge and exposing the powder within to the strike of the flint. He aimed between her eyes.

'You need to cock it.' Blood pulsed between her fingers. 'Don't drop it now, or you'll definitely die first.'

William slid the pistol onto his forearm and clamped it to his belly to cock it with his other hand. He fumbled it back between two palms and rested his ring-finger on the trigger.

'Go on then,' she wheezed, 'you might as well do it.'

William hesitated and his eyes flitted to her pistol, a hair's breadth from the tip of her finger.

'You want me to go for it, don't you?' She sneered. 'It's not even loaded, but you want me to reach for it, so when you kill me it feels as though you have to. I knew you weren't fit to be an assassin, and now you've lucked your way to the prize. It makes a mockery of the whole thing.'

She withdrew from the pistol.

'I'm not doing it.' She struggled against a coughing fit to set her mouth in a grim line. 'If you want to win, you'll have to kill me in cold blood. If you can't, I'll just wait you out.'

William looked into her eyes. She was so filled with hatred; he had killed her son, but she had no remorse for entering the boy as her sponsor in the first place. She didn't deserve to be reunited with him in the afterlife, but she didn't deserve to live either.

William squeezed the trigger. The bullet hit Genevieve's forehead and killed her in an instant. There was no more screaming, no more blood; just a callous mother dead in the street.

The last of William's energy was spent tucking his pistol under his belt, then he succumbed to his exhaustion. As he toppled over backwards, the ground came up to meet him faster and softer than expected. People had huddled around him, four or five of them.

'You, slather him with serum, and you, bind his limbs.' Barber was lowered onto William's chest by another of the gathered men. The doctor peered into his eyes and mouth and ripped open his shirt. 'Pass me that syringe, get a bottle of blood. Don't let him slip away.'

A large needle was passed into Barber's deformed grip and he spared no time in puncturing William's chest. In an instant, all of his pains came rushing back to him, so crisp and pure that he would swear he had never before felt real pain. He bucked upright, tipping the doctor onto the road. His heart began to race so ferociously that he thought his ribcage might burst. He could feel the blood surging through his veins and the tingling pain at the end of every extremity.

'Bind his arms, I said. Get the damned blood!'

William was wrestled back to the floor and mounted again by the mad doctor, brandishing what could only be described as a pigs-bladder-come-syringe filled with some foul elixir. William's head rolled and he spent the next few minutes dipping in and out of consciousness, vomiting, choking, and being wrangled away from death.

After a time, he stopped fighting and fell into a more wholesome slumber, only drifting back to consciousness once the corral of assistants had retreated, the doctor with them. He lay still for – he didn't know how long – drifting back as if from a dream. He looked up at the grey swirling sky and listened to music and cheers. It all seemed so distant at first, like he lay in the next meadow from a fête, but then he realised that the jubilation was all around and that the celebrations were all for him.

Noting that he was ready, two of the doctor's assistants drifted back to help him. William was hoisted to his feet, and when they released his weight to him, he was surprised that he still had the strength to stand. He was weak, nearly his whole body was dressed in bandage like some southern corpse, but he was certainly a few paces further from death than he had been moments prior. He staggered forwards.

Surrounded by referees and garishly coloured bunting was the winner's podium, topped by the mayor in a silk sash and a fabulously tall hat. The bleachers trembled as the crowds roared and cheered the new Man-Butcher. Dazed by the chaos, his head swam from the elixirs, but this was real.

Two event volunteers trundled past with Genevieve in their arms and hefted her into the swell of the Landslide. Other volunteers were swarming the streets, clearing them of detritus and bodies. More were ushering the spectators closer to get a better view of William's winning ceremony. He didn't have chance to call out as Vesta and her brother's bodies were taken up and carried away. The crowd circled around, enveloping him. He hadn't a moment to say goodbye to her, or thank you, or any number of unfinished notions in his head. Any ridiculous future he had imagined with her was gone; any thread of happiness snipped off and discarded.

'Presenting our glorious champion!' the mayor bellowed through a brass cone. 'The winner of the sixteen eighty-two Man-Butcher Prize.'

William moved slowly towards the podium, his limp far less pronounced. The thought of Vesta was pushed from his mind, postponed until a later date, when her death could join his myriad regrets.

He stepped onto the podium with the mayor; the referees made a half-circle behind them.

'You've done it boy.' The mayor slipped his arm around him. 'You should be proud. You're one of the best, better even than Ojo Azul and my old pal Beechworth. It takes a lot to come out on top with assassins of that calibre competing, but you did it, and you're going to go down in history for it. What's the name, by the way?'

'William.' He broke out into a smile. Somewhere out there, he knew that Ojo would be proud of him. 'William of Fairshore.'

'Bring out the prize!' The mayor accepted a golden flintlock from a velvet cushion presented by a referee. 'I hope that it sees you right in your new found prominence amongst our community!'

The mayor proffered the flintlock to William. It had wild flowers etched down the sides of the barrel and looked eerily familiar.

'It's a golden replica of the Man-Butcher's very own pistol.' The mayor smiled as William took it wordlessly in both hands. 'I hope that you treasure it always.'

William turned the pistol over in his hands. The resemblance to his own flintlock was uncanny, so much so that it reinforced his irrational fear that this all was some dying fantasy. How could it be that his own flintlock and this one were identical, down to the last leaf on the etching?

'And now for one final treat!' the mayor thundered to the crowd before digging his elbow into William's ribs and lowering his voice. 'You're going to like this Will, the bloodthirsty Butchers always do – ladies, gentlemen, elses and otherwises! As you know, we in the prize committee like to change things up here and there to keep it fresh. This year has seen the biggest shakeup since the competition began, what with the introduction of sponsors. As such this has created opportunity for one final deathly revel.'

The mayor was brimming over with excitement, gesticulating wildly with the arm that was free of the brass-cone amplifier. 'Bring out the deserters!'

The referees parted and a line of men and women were led onto the stage, each shackled at the ankles and wrists, linked together with a thick chain.

'These prisoners, ladies and gentlemen, are the sponsors my referees found fleeing from the competition. They have earned themselves a most untimely death. This could have been undertaken in private of course, but we in the committee are not ones to be outdone by the imperials when it comes to the spectacle of public killing.' The mayor pumped his fist. 'And we have the new Man-Butcher himself for executioner!'

The mayor delved his hand into his pocket and retrieved a handful paper cartridges. He counted out ten in his palm and thrust them towards William.

'Use the prize pistol.' The mayor winked. 'They'll go wild for it.'

William looked from the line of defeated sponsors, to the gunpowder parcels in his cupped hand, then the rabidly cheering crowd. It didn't feel right; killing was a necessity of his life, the way he got by, but nothing to be celebrated or cheered for. He actually hoped this was a death-dream, and this living hell would soon fade to nothing. But the world stayed as vivid as ever.

'Left to right,' the mayor instructed quietly, 'the first one might leave a sour taste, but it should be forgotten once the tenth man drops.'

William made his way down the line of kneeling deserters, wondering exactly why the mayor found the killing of one man any more unpalatable than the other nine. It all seemed equally sickening to William.

He shuffled like a spoiled child forced into his first chore, slowly and sullenly loading the first cartridge into the spectacular golden pistol. He felt like an imposter, an outsider who had stumbled his way to the very top of the guild, and somehow more out of place than when he had been an obscure laughing stock. He stopped at the end of the line and forced his gaze upwards. If he was the new Man-Butcher, he had to be able to kill these innocents without flinching, but as he found the first he was meant to despatch, his breath stopped in his chest.

'You want me to kill *him*?' he spluttered.

The clothes were singed; his eyes were deathly and bloodshot. One leg was broken at an uncomfortable angle and the heavy chains dragged him down into a spiteful stoop, but Genevieve's son was still very much alive.

'He's a guilder isn't he? He knows what he signed up for. Do it quickly, I'd rather not linger on the child. Kill four or five, then you can draw out *that one's* death; the big bastard.' The mayor pointed to a large muscle-bound sponsor halfway down the line, who looked no less afraid than the small woman next to him. 'The crowd loves to see a big one go down.'

'Right...' William took a step forwards and aimed his gun at the young boy. His finger massaged the trigger, felt its smoothly buffed curve, but refused to inch it back. The crowd cheered, buoyed on by the spectacle, urging him to do his duty for the guild.

The referees waited in pensive silence, blank faced and impartial to the task at hand. William swallowed phlegm, he couldn't bring himself to do it. His mind started racing for any excuse.

'These are deserters?' he asked as he watched tears make tracks in the young boy's soot marred face.

'Yes.' The mayor scowled at William as if he had gone simple.

'And that's why I have to kill them?'

'Yes.' The mayor was getting annoyed. 'Just hurry it along, it's what the crowd wants.'

'This boy didn't desert,' William reasoned, seeing his way out of the foul deed. 'He was trapped under rubble; look at him. He doesn't have to die, he's not a deserter. I know, I was there; he was Genevieve's sponsor.'

'Genevieve's sponsor?' one of the referees piped up, his tone needlessly aggressive.

'Yes?' William half turned to look at the referees, worried that he might have said something wrong. 'A house he was in fell, he must have got trapped. He's no deserter.'

'You killed Genevieve,' the stern referee asserted, exchanging glances with his fellows.

'No, no, no.' The mayor waved his hands. 'You can't just disqualify my winner.'

William realised what he had said. His finger went lax on the trigger, his jaw fell slack. Only moments earlier, he had been praying for anything to come between him and having to slaughter a line of innocent people, child included. Now, he realised, that he hadn't quite meant *anything*.

'William plainly killed Genevieve before her sponsor had perished. We all saw it,' the referee reiterated. 'This boy was her sponsor, she did come second after all. We can still have our Man-Butcher.'

'Wait…' William tried to think of something else to say, but his mind and mouth had become arid. He croaked out something indecipherable.

'We have to be seen to be upholding our rules,' one of the committee members chimed in, with an accompanying grumble of agreement from the others.

'But- well…' The mayor shook his head. 'You're right.'

A signal was flashed to someone behind William and he was grabbed about the shoulders by two large men. The golden pistol was snatched from his grip and passed to the mayor, then he was dragged from the podium. His natural instinct made him fight to stay, but he was thumped in the side. The strike hit his numbed wound and made him retch. He still struggled, but his efforts were less.

'Somebody get this boy up, get those chains off him,' the mayor was frantically instructing his referees and assassins. 'Barber can heal him after we've presented the prize; I'm not accepting any more delays.'

William was bundled into the crowd by the two brutes, left without recourse to watch his stripped prize presented to Genevieve's sponsor.

'Due to unforeseen circumstances, William of Fairshore is no longer our Man-Butcher.' The mayor resumed his presentation, booming through his brass cone. 'What's your name boy?'

'William,' Genevieve's son replied quietly, 'William Cholmondeley.'

'Please everyone give it up for this... *new* William! William Cholmondeley, the new Man-Butcher of eighty-two. The youngest ever Butcher!'

William was ejected from the grip of the two heavies. He staggered back, barely keeping his footing. Now the elation of the win had worn away, his limbs were hanging heavy, and a great hunger had built in him despite the sickness stirred by the elixirs. He sneered away into the crowd, and though they had cheered for him only moments before, hardly anyone paid him any heed. All were too distracted by the new winner and the prize presentation.

Those that did see him, averted their gaze in embarrassment or mocked and laughed when they thought he wasn't looking. This far back, they couldn't be sure of the reasons he had been so unceremoniously stripped of his prize, but ambiguity only flared their imaginations. To them he was a liar, and a cheat, and the perpetrator of any number of offences that invited disqualification. Shame hung over him like a cloud.

He emerged from the rear of the throng without a bronze bit or bullet to his name. No longer an obscure laughing stock, he would be the most publicly derided man in the whole empire. His boots slapped through the heavy mud as he made his way down the street and away from the celebrations. He would be at the edge of town soon, away from the stink and death and bitter memories. Ash fell from the sky in thick flakes, colouring the pristine bandages dark as his mood.

'Excuse me?' A large thin man in a suit and cloak grabbed William by the shoulder and spun him around. 'I wondered, might I bend your ear for a moment?'

'What is it?' William huffed and eyed the little pig-nosed boy at the man's rear. He'd seen these two before, in the farmer's cart on route to Blackbile.

'My employer asked me to come here and beseech the prize winner to take on a very important contract. As the new Man-Butcher is a little on the *inexperienced* side, and taking into account your performance over the past few days, I elected to offer the job to you instead.' The spindly man offered a hand to shake. William could see now that the white ring he spied on the journey to Blackbile seemed to be made out of porcelain. 'I would love to give you further details, should you accept.'

'I'm not sure.' William tried to walk away, but the slender man skirted around him to block his path. The man's insistence made William all the more certain. 'No thank you. I don't want another contract.'

'Just come with us back to our hotel, we can discuss it all there. We pay *very* handsomely.' The man offered his hand to shake again. 'I really must insist. My employer needs a certain calibre of assassin, and though the commoners don't see it, we have an eye for these things.'

The pig-nosed boy's wall-eyes blinked separately, one fixed on William.

'No,' William asserted. He moved to leave, but the tall man stopped him with a firm hand. 'I'm not interested.'

A chunk of brick arced through the air and cracked the pig-faced boy right between the eyes, toppling him over in the mud with a squeal.

'Did you not hear him the first time? Piss off.' Goldin casually waved a blunderbuss in the direction of the tall man. 'Is the greatest assassin in the land not deserving of a damned rest? Leave him be.'

'No offence meant.' The tall man raised his hands and backed off with a bow. He knelt down and pulled his little friend gasping from the slurry. 'Not now then, I'll leave you to rest. Come find me should you need work. Life can be ever so hard for a disgraced man; you might need what I offer.'

'I said piss off. I'm not averse to killing a man, so you'd be wise to go now.' Goldin ushered them away with another wave of his blunderbuss, then turned to face William with a quivering smile. 'Are you alright, Mr Man-Butcher?'

A giggle burst through the little man's pursed lips.

'You can piss off as well if you're just going to laugh.' William tramped away.

'It is quite funny.' Goldin hopped through the muck to keep up. 'You should have seen your face when you realised you'd lost the prize to that little brat, priceless! *Prize-less!*'

'Please, just, stop.' William kept marching until he reached the promenade.

'Alright.' Goldin stifled another giggle. 'Where are we going then? I was thinking the Silken Coast might be nice, it's quite clement there.'

'We?' William tried his best to maintain a grimace, but the little man's good mood was catching.

'I was thinking I might tag along, now you're all famous. I might be able to ride your coat tails to a small fortune. I think it's only fair, you wouldn't have made it to the town without me.' The little man raised his eyebrows.

'You should have just left me on the roadside.' William was trying his best to be downbeat about the whole thing, but the thought of having the little man's cheer at his side made his outlook less dire. He had been so long on his own, five years without anyone, and was warming to the idea like a pan in a fire.

'Don't be like that.' Goldin threw his arm around William's hip, unable to reach his shoulders. 'Our Gertrude, well, her name's Goldie now too. Y'know, the gorgeous one at Melting Moments? She baked a cake for my travels; red velvet, the type you like. I've a slice of it here in my satchel.'

The little man patted the bag at his hip.

'But it's only for travelling companions and the like.' His tooth poked out of his split lip as he smiled. 'What say you then, Mr Man-Butcher? Will you lead me to the coast for a well-earned rest?'

'Just give me the cake and shut up, my head's thumping.' He pressed a hand to his forehead. 'Have you got any liquor in that bag?'

Goldin grinned. 'That's more like it.'

Thank you very much for reading, I hope you enjoyed *Crooked Empires: Vol 1 The Man-Butcher Prize*.

It can be very hard for self-published authors to find their audience, as such I would greatly appreciate it if you could leave a review online and share with friends and family.

William's story will continue in

CROOKED EMPIRES: VOL 2

If you would like to hear more from Charles' world of Crooked Empires you can find fantasy serials and audiobook podcasts on his website

www.charlesxcross.com

and on popular podcast providers.